THE TIGER GENERAL

THE TIGER GENERAL

The Memoirs of a
Vietnamese Intelligence Chief

JOHN HAVAN

Orchid Press

John Havan
THE TIGER GENERAL:
The Memoirs of a Vietnamese Intelligence Chief

ORCHID PRESS
PO Box 1046,
Silom Post Office,
Bangkok 10504, Thailand
www.orchidbooks.com

ISBN: 978-974-524-135-0

CONTENTS

Acknowledgments

Although the events described in this book are as they appeared to me at the time, when I heard about them, or saw them, or actually lived them, they are also the collected views and recollections of some twenty individuals who played a part in this story.

Some were men and women who either actively supported or opposed the government of the day, whether democratic or communist; they acted because they had strong beliefs in what was right and what was wrong. Many paid an unspeakable price for their beliefs.

The rest, the majority, were people who had no preference but didn't have any choice either. They did what they did simply to survive. Many of these also paid a similar, unspeakable price for not supporting one side or the other. I am indebted to all of them and to the families who spoke to me; without them and their assistance this book would not have been possible.

My thanks extend to my publisher, whose support and faith was particularly important; to a relative who played a major part in influencing my decision to write and, last but not least, to my wife whose unstinting love and support during both the writing of this book and the time spent waiting for it to see the light of day made my life easier to live.

JOHN HAVAN
Manila 2011

PART ONE

GROWING PAINS

Author's Foreword

After six years as a senior political consultant to the U.S. State Department, the slim, dapper, white-haired gentleman known as the Tiger General was persuaded by the three people closest to him to allow me to write the story of his life—in English.

These three people, namely Jonathan Winthrop, once the CIA deputy Chief of Station in Viet Nam during the eventful years of the '60s and '70s, his distinguished-looking wife Lan Lan, once a Viet Cong courier, and the Tiger's beauteous soul mate Hélène, once a teenage prostitute, make up the family he never had.

As expected, the general had had some reservations. I am not formally educated, he said, and even now my written English is not good. I'll help edit the results, said Jonathan. I know your story like I know my own.

My story is a very personal story, he said. Who would be interested? One hundred years from now and even beyond that, said Jonathan, the political debacle that was Vietnam will remain a turning point in America's history and the military defeat that was Vietnam will be case-studied in every modern armed forces academy around the world. You had a panoramic front-seat view of that crucial period in Vietnamese history. Everybody is going to be interested.

*I have never been a president or even a cabinet minister, he said. I have never had an insight into key decisions, a top-down view of events. That is for self-aggrandizing politicians and failed generals looking to justify their policies, said Lan Lan. We are the common people, the be mieng thap co people, whose voice is never heard. Your story is **our** story and it must be told.*

My story is also very much the story of my mother, Cinnamon, whose spirit reincarnated in me at the time of her death, he said, weakening in front of the combined onslaught. Let's consult her, said Hélène, driving home the final blow.

And so on the following day, with Hélène and me sitting on a sofa in the spacious bedroom of his Georgetown apartment, a steaming pot of mint tea surrounded by tiny little cups before us, the general lit three joss sticks in front of a lacquered altar which he had brought over from Viet Nam. In a semi-transparent greenish porcelain saucer in front of him, on a small square piece of muslin cloth, lay a stout steel needle embedded in a little green wooden knob carved into a frog. The general explained that he had never had a photograph of his mother, but that the sturdy hatpin immediately brought her image back before his eyes. "When I look at it, I see her in my mind's eye as she was when we lived under the bridge: young and brave, with the pin keeping in place the bun of hair piled up on top of her head." Later, he told me she hadn't looked directly at him as he prayed to her, and her lips had never moved, but he could clearly hear her girlish voice saying she wanted him to tell their story. "Yes, tell the world about your father," she said, "and about the curse we brought upon your head."

With that, the die was cast, and the next day I dusted off my old typewriter and began working on the story of the general's life.

1

Phu My Village

As a boy, things only began to make sense in 1924, when he and his mother were living as vagrants under a railway bridge near the main train station in Ha Noi. Peasants like them didn't bother much with the French calendar but the boy knew he had been born in the Year of the Tiger, so he must have been ten, more or less. Blessed with a good memory, which he could have inherited from his father, his recollections from the bridge days were quite clear. Everything before that time, however, had come in dribs and drabs from what his mother had told him as they lay in each other's arms under a patched up mosquito net, their stomachs growling with hunger, unable to sleep.

Her given name was Que, which means cinnamon, and in the village she was known as Little Cinnamon, not only because she was young but also because she was small in size. His birth name was Meo, which means cat. Later in life, his mother had picked Hai, meaning ocean, as his given name. During the American war in Viet Nam, north of the 17th parallel, he was known as the Grey Tiger. South of the same parallel, a DMZ that truncated the country, he was known as the Tiger General. If Cinnamon had stayed in Phu My village, Meo would have grown up there to become Carpenter Hai, or Well Digger Hai, or even perhaps Farmer Hai. If he had had some peculiar trait or deformity, he would have been known as Limping Hai, or Pockmark Hai, because graphic nicknames are common in the countryside. Or again, if Meo had been recognized by his real father, the Diamond Son from the manor, he would have grown up carrying the Trinh family name, becoming someone of social importance in the province. But he was cursed by the unlucky alignment of the prevailing stars on the day

Cinnamon met the Diamond Son and spent the first thirty six years of his life hiding behind a host of throwaway names that Fate casually handed out.

Cinnamon had become pregnant at sixteen and her immediate reaction was shame. At first, she bound her stomach with a sash so the neighbors wouldn't notice. Her mother, who had arranged everything with Miss Fatty from the manor, had taken to drinking and making scenes in public ever since her husband had left them two years before. She was known in the village as the Drunken Lady. Her many uncles and aunties, some actually related to her by blood and others only by social convention, had stopped being supportive and Cinnamon didn't dare approach them. One morning, in the middle of the dry heaves, she finally got up enough courage to ask her mother how to stop her pregnancy, and, as expected, the older woman flew into a fit of rage. Her face contorted with anger and her voice carried both contempt for her daughter's stupidity and self-pity for herself as she re-hashed in her mind all the bad luck that had started with Cinnamon's arrival in the world. She had been a breech baby and her mother had become barren after giving birth. Her husband, like all the men in the village, had wanted many boys, but she couldn't get pregnant again. Things had soured between them and maybe that was why he had taken the two boys and left her. Ironically, Cinnamon even became her father's favorite and, because she was small, hadn't been required to help in the fields, unlike her mother. It's surprising he didn't take her along with him. But a man needs sons to help him in the fields. Hope it broke your heart, you useless man. And now that your useless daughter can repay her debt, she refuses to do what women are born to do anyway, have babies! "An abortion would ruin everything," she screamed. "The baby is a connection with the manor that will solve all our problems," she shouted in her daughter's face. "Don't you understand anything?" She raved and ranted all evening long, tossing small cups of rice wine down her throat before running out to the market place to let everyone know what an ingrate she had given birth to. Alternately shrieking and weeping, she rolled on the ground, tore at her waist-long hair and beat her breast. Homegrown entertainment was rare during the harvest season and the neighbors all came out to watch her performance

Eventually, as always, they would pick her up and carry her to her bamboo hut, where they would lay her down on the *cai phan*, slip a hard rectangular bamboo pillow under the nape of her neck and cover her with a locally woven multi-colored blanket. In those days, every hut had a *cai phan*, a thick, heavy teak platform that stood on four short, wooden blocks. It was the heart and soul of any thatch-roofed hut. Over the years, through the invisible pores in the density of its hard, polished surface, it had slowly absorbed the bodily fluids of every family member who had ever used it. Generations had been conceived on it, drawing their first breath and exhaling their last when the time came. It was often the unique piece of furniture in the hut, serving as a bed, a dining table, a living room and more.

After helping her home, the neighbors would sit cross-legged around her on the teak board, fanning themselves and gossiping, helping themselves to the Drunken Lady's rice wine every now and again, shaking their heads and looking up at Heaven every time she mumbled something.

Cinnamon's immediate neighbor, the Skinny Lady, one of her many aunties, sold vegetables in the village market and doubled as a midwife when necessary. Although she didn't get on with the Drunken Lady, she liked Little Cinnamon and agreed to help deliver the baby when the time came. From observing the shape of Cinnamon's stomach, the Skinny Lady had predicted a boy, and out came one, normal in size, well formed and light skinned. After sponging up the *cai phan*, washing out the blood soaked reed mats and hanging them out to dry in the sun, the Skinny Lady said that he looked like a boy from a rich family. Cinnamon's mother, sober for the occasion, swelled with pride, her face a mirror of conflicting emotions as thoughts of living at the manor on the one hand and of revenge on the other ran through her head. Revenge finally won over manor life, and her face would turn ugly when she thought no one was looking. Things are certainly going to change from now on. She had long ago made a list of who would have to pay for calling her names and for looking down on her and this list had grown from day to day. They'll all get their comeuppance, you'll see, she mumbled to herself in between forcing herself to smile and thank the neighbors and friends who had come to get a look at the new addition to the village.

The old midwife suggested that the boy be called Meo, until he was five. He's like a little kitten but his eyes are already open, and they are very large, she said. And yellow. Cinnamon, who was barely seventeen at the time, nodded in silence while jumbled thoughts ran riot through her head. Many years later, under the bridge in Ha Noi, she told her son what she had been thinking of at his birth. Half convinced by her mother that a life of leisure and luxury awaited them at the manor, she had decided to call him Bach, after his father's name, to prepare him for a life after she had been installed as the Diamond Son's latest concubine. But as she lay exhausted after childbirth, the family essences that exuded from deep inside the *cai phan* rose like miasma from some of the invisible cracks in the teakwood board and enveloped her, gently vaporizing her dreams and slowly returning her to reality. She opened her eyes drowsily and saw the familiar reed mat, dry but still stained with blood and smelling strongly of herbal medicines and ointments. She briefly remembered the silk sheets and satin coverlets on the Young Master's bed. It all seemed so far away. This is what you have. All you'll ever have. You were born here and you'll die here. And so will he. Craning her neck, she looked at the baby in her arms. Dreamily, she traced her index along the old reed mat to the thick edge of the teak board, her resignation laced with bitterness at the thought that her little son would lead the same sort of life she had led. Then suddenly, like a kite that unexpectedly appears in the sky when one looks up, the preposterousness of naming him Bach appeared in all its clarity. The writing on the kite, in large characters, said that Lord Bach had not recognized his son. That meant there would be no manor life for her. She half-heard the Skinny Lady's last few words and half-rose in shock. You don't have a birth name for him. Oh Lord in Heaven how could you have forgotten! She opened her eyes wide and looked up. Village customs required that a new born child be given a really ugly name to ward off evil spirits, souls of men and women who, not having received a proper burial, floated in limbo between heaven and earth. Unwanted, increasingly desperate for a permanent home, they roamed the countryside in their pain and agony, ruining good crops, bringing bad luck, spreading fatal diseases among newborn babies, especially the ones that had beautiful names which showed how precious they were to their parents. Almost immediately, she made up her mind that Meo sounded all right. Cats were like dogs and chickens. Everyday animals nobody looked after. Her brothers had been named Wart Face and Frog at birth, and she herself had been called Little Ugly till she was six. Looking at the Skinny Lady and her mother, Cinnamon nodded numbly, and little Meo received a birth name that would protect him from harm for the first few years.

The truth was that Cinnamon hadn't really ever thought of a birth name for her son. In fact, busy with the household chores since eight years old, she hadn't thought much about anything in her young life. Helped by her mother and brothers, her father worked all day on the family plot the manor had earlier granted him. In the mornings, the boys attended the village school for two hours and then joined their father in the fields until sundown. Her mother, after Cinnamon's difficult birth, began spending more and more time gossiping with the neighbors, smoking dark cheroots, chewing betel nut with lime and drinking rice wine, gradually neglecting the fieldwork, the housework and the crop planting, and sometimes forgetting to feed the family. Long before her first menstruation, Cinnamon was doing all the cooking, washing and the cleaning in the one-room hut. Girls did not have to attend primary school; they were raised to do the housework at home, then help their future husbands in the field, have babies, cook, wash, mend, grow old and look after the grandchildren.

Like any good husband, her father had tried to beat some sense into her mother, but to no avail. Her mother, in startling contrast to the other village wives, fought back, screaming, throwing things at him and accusing him of not bringing in enough money to feed five people. When the boys were old enough to work, things had become worse and her father had taken them away one day and never come back. This was when Cinnamon had just turned fourteen. Mother and daughter managed to hold on for one year by sub-leasing a portion of their lot, by eating less, and then by bartering household items for their daily rice, but the inevitable time came when they had to call on the village council for help.

The village elders negotiated with the manor staff for Cinnamon to be hired as a helper to the seamstresses working in the manor. Seated cross-legged on a king-sized *cai phan* which stood on curved teak wood legs painted bright red and occupied half of the communal hall, they impressed on the Drunken Lady that she would have to stop drinking now that she was alone in the hut while young Cinnamon worked at the manor. They feared she might get drunk and start a fire, especially during the summer months when the thatched roofs of the village were tinder dry. Kneeling on a reed mat at the foot of the *cai phan,* her mother obsequiously bowed and scraped in front of the councilors, pleading abandonment by a worthless husband, crying and sniffling and wiping her red eyes, swearing she would turn over a new leaf. The old men, the collective soul of the village, knew better but looked on impassively, drawing on their bubbly water pipes, occasionally scratching themselves slowly, importantly, as they gazed far into space, like kings surveying their kingdoms. When the woman had left, they told each other her husband had been a good man, nodding gravely. But he had been a weak man, they added, shaking their heads in dismay, and hadn't beaten her enough. They remembered with silent satisfaction how they had successfully dealt with the same sort of wife problems at home.

For Cinnamon, the moment she could leave her hut for the walk through the fields to the manor at the top of a hill was heavenly. Barefooted, she planted her feet carefully along the top of the raised earthen dikes that separated the rice paddies. She avoided stinging nettles, mud holes and large patties of cow dung, carrying her clean wooden sandals with one hand for later use at the manor, holding her conical hat up to shade her face from the sun with the other, her body a slip of white in the azure green rice fields, her mind already at the manor. Everyone is so fair-skinned there. You must avoid getting darker. Everything is so clean and beautiful inside. People are always well dressed. No one ever speaks in a loud voice, she thought as she tripped along to a world that was as different from hers as day was from night, her heart pit-a-patting a little faster, her mouth dry with anticipation as she approached the manor gates.

A month or so later, her mother told her that Miss Fatty would take her in to meet the Diamond Son. Miss Fatty was a senior housekeeper at the manor and ran the household staff in the east wing, where Lord Giap, the Old Mandarin, lived with the Young Master, known as the Diamond Son.

Cinnamon had asked what for.

"To be his concubine, what else?" her mother had answered in an irritated voice as she looked directly at this slip of a girl, never forgetting that her husband had favored her over the two boys—and even his wife. "You're not bringing home enough money, and you're a big girl now," she said, pointedly looking at her daughter's budding breasts, which were tightly bound flat with a cotton sash to keep them from showing beneath her peasant's blouse.

"You're really lucky I was able to arrange this. There are dozens of village girls who would give anything for an opportunity to open their legs in the manor," she added, laughing coarsely. Cinnamon burst into tears and ran out of the hut.

For a week or so afterwards, she later told her son under the bridge, she went about her work in a daze. I was like a body without a soul, she said. Betrayed by my mother, given away like an object after all the work I did in the house for years. She had always had weak lungs, and when bitter resentment tingled through her veins her chest became tight and she found it difficult to breathe. And because she knew her mother's decision was final, she often felt her chest constricting whenever she thought about it. Everyone knows parents are always right, even when they are wrong. A good child is filial, owes the parents everything and obeys them unquestioningly. Life is like that, she told him.

2

The Manor

Later that week, Miss Fatty led the new girl upstairs to service the Diamond Son. This event was duly recorded by the Chamberlain, the Venerable Huyen, in a large, red, leather-bound ledger reserved for women procured for their Lordships' pleasure. It was important that each sexual liaison, whether by Lord Giap, the Old Mandarin, or the Young Master, his Diamond Son, be duly noted in case children resulted from the union and their mothers later laid claims to the Trinh name or property. On that first occasion, Miss Fatty had taken Cinnamon to a large bathroom and scrubbed her thoroughly, especially under the armpits and the crotch, after which she had rinsed her body with warm water, finally washing her hair with diluted lemon juice. There were many different kinds of scented soaps and lotions in the bathroom, as well as clean towels and face cloths, all neatly folded on shelves. Everything smelt clean and fragrant, except for the squat toilet in the corner. Miss Fatty asked the young girl to open her mouth and smelt her breath.

"Baby's breath," she said, and pulled her lips apart to look at the teeth. They were small, even and white, unlike hers, which had been lacquered and were shiny black.

"Your teeth are white, like his," she said in a voice tinged with envy. "He's a Vietnamese like us but he has many French habits," she said, glancing quickly around her, in a voice that showed disapproval tempered with fear of being overheard talking about a lord of the manor. Cinnamon looked at her, blankly.

Miss Fatty then asked if she had ever been with a man before. Cinnamon, not yet sixteen, shook her head, numb with apprehension.

Miss Fatty then explained what happened when a man and a woman became locked together, a term that made the young girl almost want to giggle. Living in the countryside, she had seen farm animals coupling, but she had never seen how men and women did it. Miss Fatty then demonstrated the sex act graphically, poking her index into a cupped fist and singing out *tap-ep-tap-ep* while laughing with delight as Cinnamon felt her stomach churn.

Miss Fatty then told her to relax and not resist the Diamond Son. She then grabbed Cinnamon, hugging her tightly, pumping her bulging lower stomach against the young girl's groin and breathing heavily into her ear. Seeing her discomfiture, she burst out laughing, her eyes becoming mere slits in her fat face.

"Close your eyes tight and open your legs as wide as possible, even if it hurts," she added when the young girl had recovered her composure. "Don't push him away, don't yell and don't scream. But you can cry if you feel like it. Men like that."

Cinnamon then felt the older woman's hard, stubby fingers kneading the lips of her vulva, and winced with pain when Miss Fatty singled out her clitoris and gave it a tweak. The fat woman then anointed the new girl's inner private parts with an oily balm that smelt of clove.

"That'll make it easier for you, and also keep you clean," the older woman said cryptically.

Cinnamon looked at Miss Fatty, feeling weak at the knees. It felt queasy down there when she moved. When the washing was finished, the fat woman laid Cinnamon's brown vest and black pantaloons on the back of a chair, along with the white cotton sash she used to bind her small breasts. In the countryside, no one wore underwear in those days. Fatty then handed her a loose, diaphanous gown that covered her from neck to toe. It was thin, almost transparent, and smelt of a faint, musky perfume.

The fat woman took one final look at her, liked what she saw, and asked her if she had understood everything.

"Yes, auntie," Cinnamon answered, her lips trembling.

3

The Diamond Son

Young Master Bach, the diamond son of Lord Giap, the Old Mandarin, had a pleasant face and was handsome in a foreign way. He often wore western clothes, like the French visitors Cinnamon had seen a few times at the manor. He was always very clean, she noted, and his hair, which was cut short and parted on the left, smelt of some nice lotion. There were no hairs on his upper lip or chin. Unlike all the adults in the village, his teeth had not been lacquered black. He spoke kindly to her, always looking deeply into her eyes when she answered, as if he was really interested in what she was saying. It was this trait that had first won her over to him because, in the village, no one ever cared what she had to say, least of all her mother.

On that first night, he had been very gentle with her. Not knowing what to expect, she had been frozen with shame at first. In the middle of an immense bedroom that was twice the size of her hut, he had unwrapped the gown slowly and turned her around with practiced hands, his eyes examining all the details that her young body offered. He was very deliberate in his movements, and she sensed he knew he could keep her there for as long as he wanted to.

"Cinnamon, right?" he asked. He had a warm voice, but one that carried authority. She nodded, standing there naked, looking at the floor. He then took her hand and led her to the large bed standing in the center of the room. It was so high he had to carry her onto it. From behind, he placed one large hand across her budding breasts and carefully slipped another between her buttocks, comfortably enveloping her crotch, lifted her up effortlessly and placed her face down on the bed. Many years later, under the railway bridge, she recalled her thoughts at the time when talking to her son, who by then had gone through two names already and was known as Minh. I was like a frog being placed in a frying pan. He was so strong. So big. The pillows and mattress were so soft and nice smelling and my knees had turned to water. He then took off his clothes and slipped in beside me. I was afraid, but also curious. I turned onto my back and looked down there, you know, quickly. The size, the dark red color, took my breath away. Suddenly, I was afraid of what was going to happen. I closed my eyes and froze.

Slowly, gently, he had stroked her head, her face, her arms and legs, talking to her all the time. This had a calming effect on her body although her heart continued to flutter frantically. The cotton blanket was warm, his voice gentle and hypnotic, and his large, soft hands began to massage her pubic mound and breasts gently. Her tense body began to thaw and she realized that she wasn't afraid any more. He took her small hand and gently guided it to his organ. It was knotty and throbbing hot. She held it, not knowing what to do, although by now she had understood what was about to happen, having seen the male and female organs of farm animals and how they fitted into one another. She now understood why Miss Fatty had put that greasy balm in between her legs. Finally, when she was all warm and soft everywhere, he eased himself on top of her, resting his considerable weight on his elbows and knees so as not to crush her. She thought briefly of pushing him off her, but Miss Fatty's instructions came back to her and instead she wrapped her arms around his neck. By this time, she felt herself melting and soon welcomed the unbearably sweet ticklish feeling that ran through her when he rubbed his organ lightly against hers. She clung harder to him, all her nerves tingling, her legs now wrapped around his thighs, her eyes closed, partly apprehensive and partly curious, eager to find out what was going to happen next. Her fear at what would be done to her returned briefly at the moment of penetration, but the pain was gone in a flash, and when his arms enveloping her tightened their grip and his thrusts became deeper she thought for a moment that they were no longer on the bed but flying through space as her senses were violently aroused. Soon, the world stopped turning as their bodies became one, undulating and heaving madly, both reaching for that explosion that was always only inches away.

Cinnamon was of peasant stock and she saw nothing wrong with sex or the pleasures of sex, as long as it was done privately. She recounted all the details to her son to show him how his father had respected her. It was important to her that her son know how their love began. His father had been kind and gentle, and she had surrendered willingly, again and again, once her fear had been overcome.

After the first few times, she said, her weekly nights with the Diamond Son became pleasurable experiences that she looked forward to and relived all week long. He was an experienced and patient man, and he toyed with her body, slowly drawing out an inner sexuality she never knew existed. He made me so happy, more than I can describe, sometimes three times a night, she told her son. But although it was obvious the Young Master shared her joy from start to finish, he very seldom allowed himself to climax. At the end of the sex act, he was the same at as the beginning, extended full-length and still thick with desire. How or why he did this she never asked. He was her first man, and she thought this was how men made love.

In her simple and naïve way, because he made love to her with such consideration and kindness, she came to believe he really cared for her, maybe that he even loved her. I know I loved him, she would say under the bridge. I spent hours thinking about the things I would say to him that night to impress him. I wasn't educated like my brothers but I could think clearly. Using logic, I often beat them in arguments at home, she would tell her son, to show that she wasn't just an ignorant village girl.

Time and again she rehearsed what she would talk about so that the Young Master would not look down on her. Because of his attentive stare, she told herself he was such a kind man there wasn't any need to be afraid of talking to him, even if she often couldn't find the right words to say what she meant.

4

Bitter Reality

Two months after Miss Fatty had brought her in to the Diamond Son Cinnamon became pregnant. She continued servicing the Young Master until her sixth month of pregnancy, but after her son was born, her mother was advised by Miss Fatty to begin looking around for a farmer husband for her while she was still young and could work in the fields. Obviously, Miss Fatty, being a part of the manor's grapevine, had heard something about the Diamond Son and Cinnamon, but, being from the manor and not the village, she would have died before revealing it. Cinnamon was given three months' paid leave from her work as a seamstress to suckle her child. In the meantime, the Venerable Chamberlain at the manor kept her on the Young Master's list of casual concubines and she continued to receive an allowance in addition to her monthly salary as a seamstress. This allowance could continue indefinitely if the Young Master recognized the out-of-wedlock child and this act was duly inscribed into the family records by the Chamberlain, in which case she would be elevated to the rank of concubine, or even higher, to minor wife status. She could be allocated a room, or even a small house within the manor, even if she was never invited back into the Young Master's bedchamber again. The allowance would stop, however, if the child died before five years old, or the mother married another man, or left the province permanently.

As time went by and Cinnamon watched her son suckling at her breast, strong, conflicting thoughts and emotions raced across the deep recesses of her mind, like cross-currents clashing endlessly on the sea bed. She felt possessive and proud and resentful all at the same time.

Meo was the first thing that was hers and hers alone. You're mine, I made you, you belong to me and only to me, she repeated to herself every time she picked him up. You're so beautiful, so white, you look like a baby from a rich family, which you are. The village women were hoping I'd have an ugly baby but I didn't and now they're all green with envy. I may not ever become an official concubine but you're much better looking than their babies and there's nothing they can do about it, she would say to him, drinking in his wide open eyes, his tiny little nostrils and sweet pink little mouth.

Such thoughts would bring her some momentary comfort and cheer her up at a time when the future looked bleak, a situation made worse by her mother, who had begun to drink even more after receiving Miss Fatty's advice. However, though very disappointed, both mother and daughter had decided to wait things out. There was always a slim thread of hope that the Young Master might change his mind when he returned from another of his frequent trips abroad. Nothing was final, either way, until the Venerable Chamberlain had actually announced it.

One night, in a dream, Cinnamon saw the Diamond Son standing on a hill, not far from her. He was facing north, his face the color of mottled liver and he was gnashing his teeth loudly. One hand held a tattered book, the other a bloody sword. In a tree nearby, a raven squawked raucously. She cried out to him, but he couldn't hear her. She ran towards him, holding her son out in front of her, though she was afraid of what he might do. Her feet thumped the ground, crushing the tangled brambles and wild grass, her legs pumping powerfully and she could feel the wind against her face but she was rooted to the spot. Finally, he walked up the hill without walking, growing smaller and smaller. She heard the sound of his teeth grinding until the last moment, when he disappeared altogether. She told Meo later during those long nights under the bridge that she knew with absolute conviction she could see into the future, with precision and clarity. She knew what this dream meant. His father would go north, to talk politics and to fight, but he wouldn't succeed. The raven meant bad luck. In any case, he was lost to them. Her year with the Young Master had been just a dream and now reality had returned. When she had first been brought to him, she said, he had just returned from a few years in China. He already had an official wife, the Lady Nhan, with whom he had had a three-year old son, and a village wife named Phuong, by whom he had had three children. They live in a different world, she told her son, a world where I don't even exist. Even when I stand in front of them they don't really see me as a person, just a nameless servant with a vaguely familiar face. Or an object they own, like a piece of furniture. How could I have been so stupid as to believe otherwise, she asked the boy again and again in a form of mental flagellation until she fell asleep from sheer exhaustion.

Gradually, her love for the Young Master turned into bitter resentment at having been shabbily treated. She told Meo she had thought about smuggling him into the manor and running into his father's bedroom and creating a scene, to shame him into recognizing his child, but she knew the guards would never let her get past the vermilion doors that separated the family's quarters from the rest of the manor. She had thought of bringing him up to the manor gate and slashing her throat there, to die on the floor in a pool of blood, to plead her case, but she knew the guards would probably just clean up the mess and throw them both out into the surrounding fields.

They don't care about people like us, she said repeatedly. It was my mistake that you were born, she repeated many times. I should've cut my throat after sleeping with him but instead I enjoyed it, even wanted to live in the manor. Now I have to live with my shame and do my best to bring you up, she would repeat every time they returned to the subject of his father.

At home, her mother had become impossible to live with. She was drunk every day and sometimes accosted villagers passing by the hut to tell them what a useless man her husband had been and that she hoped he was dead. This led Cinnamon to having another of her dreams. One night, she saw her father digging two small holes in the jungle and she knew that her brothers had died. He was crying as he patted down the earth with his rough hands. Each pat made a rough hollow sound, like a wooden hammer beating on an empty cask. At times, he looked in her direction and smiled. He couldn't see her but she knew he could sense she was there, because she had always been his favorite at home. His kindly face was still the same, but the skin was like goat meat that had been sun dried too long. As she looked, he grew transparent, in patches, until he was invisible, although she knew he was still squatting there by the twin graves because she could still hear him tamping the earth down with his large hands. The picture faded from her mind gradually but the hollow, cupping sounds continued, morphing into the rhythmic bark of a village dog as she awoke. She didn't bother to tell her mother about the dream, but went to the pagoda by herself, lit three joss sticks and prayed Lord Buddha to send the three souls to Heaven and ensure their reincarnation into a better life. She knew from his fading visibility that her father would die soon after burying his two sons.

On one occasion, Miss Fatty came to the village to see the Egg Seller, who supplied the village with duck eggs. This woman had a fifteen-year old girl and it was Fatty's habit to call on the mothers of potential concubines. Many of the village women had crammed into the Egg Seller's hut. As an official from the manor, Miss Fatty was an important person. She could order local handicrafts, she could hire servants, she could intercede on their behalf to right a wrong, and, finally, she could arrange for their daughters to become concubines at the manor. Outside the windows other women were pushing and shoving each other to get nearer to this representative of the Trinh clan in the manor.

"Good afternoon, auntie," Cinnamon said when Miss Fatty came out. She wanted to ask her why it was taking so long for the Young Master to recognize her little Meo. The women swarming around Miss Fatty resented her presence. Good fortune had already smiled on Little Cinnamon, even if it hadn't worked out, and it was now their turn.

"Oh, it's you," said Fatty, her face cold. "Where's your mother?"

"She's working, auntie," Cinnamon lied. "May I ask you something, auntie?" She followed the fat woman, pushing away some of the older women who were trying to crowd her out.

"Tell your mother to talk to me in private. We don't discuss manor business publicly in the village," Miss Fatty answered curtly over her shoulder, turning away.

After that episode, Cinnamon knew there was only one option left. Like all the village women who had problems at home, she went to the village pagoda to consult the Head Nun.

The old lady, who wore a hood over her shaven skull, sat like a stone statue as she prepared to listen to the young woman. Around them many younger nuns went about their daily chores, cleaning and sweeping the pagoda grounds, cooking rice and cutting up vegetables for the evening meal. When Cinnamon had finished speaking, the Head Nun reached behind her for some scrolls containing cosmic charts and horoscopes. Slowly, with upturned palm, counting on the joints of her left hand with her thumb, she made calculation after calculation as her face set into grim, foreboding lines. Finally, she spoke in an even voice, trying to soften the portent of the horoscope as she looked with gentle compassion at this slip of a girl in front of her.

"The day of your union was an inauspicious one. The reigning star in his Marriage House, *Co Than,* connotes sexual proclivity: he will have many women. Yours, *Bach Ho,* connotes loneliness: you will have only one man. Because of this unlucky pairing, three bad stars positioned themselves in your son's Main House. *Thien La,* a cruel star: troubles ahead. *Co Than*: a lonely star: no help from his co-workers. This is the same star as his father's on the day of your union but in the Main House it means different things. Finally, *Dia Khong,* disappointment: success will always be out of reach. These are life cycle stars, each with a twelve-year span, so it will take thirty-six years before they move on. In the meantime, they block out his lucky star, *Liem Trinh,* which predicts a brilliant career in the military or in politics or in government service. From age thirty-six, *Liem Trinh* in his Main House will preside over his destiny for the next four life cycles, until he is eighty-four years of age. During this time, happiness, power and health will reign in every House and he will succeed in everything he undertakes."

Cinnamon sat silent for a long time. Thirty-six years. She was only twenty and her son not yet three. She would have to live thirty three more years before she could see him emerge from under his curse, a curse she was convinced she had unwittingly brought down on his head. You should have killed yourself, or at least you should have aborted him. She felt crushed.

"Venerable Mother," she finally asked in a small voice, "is there any way we can avoid this bad luck? By making merit? By joining the nunnery?"

"Not if you continue to live here, my daughter," the Head Nun answered in a kindly voice. "Buddhists believe that our Fate is written in the stars. But if you go and live among people who don't believe in Fate like we do, it is possible you can shield your son from the bad luck that is written in his stars."

5

The Final Straw

When Meo reached three years old, the situation became untenable. The Young Master had gone abroad again, this time to Siam. Cinnamon had not been called back to his bed and Meo had not been formally recognized. The allowance was still being paid and she continued working as a seamstress within the manor. But the Fat One, perhaps because she felt she owed the Drunken Lady something, was becoming more insistent about an arranged marriage to a farmer who worked on manor land. The man's wife had died of tuberculosis, leaving four children behind and he needed a young woman to look after the children and help him in the fields. The Drunken Lady was naturally all in agreement with Miss Fatty, as she could see herself living off her new son-in-law. She now resented her grandson's presence, a constant reminder of her failure to secure a position at the manor. Every time she saw him, it made her think of all that effort wasted on the Diamond Son for nothing, and now an extra mouth to feed. A worthless daughter and now a worthless grandson. Everything went wrong after her birth. You should have strangled her at the time, she repeated to herself angrily, shaking her head and sighing with self-pity at the bad luck that had befallen her.

During the day, Meo made himself as small as possible so as to avoid attracting his grandmother's attention. She often threw things at him or chased him out of the hut for no reason. Sometimes she would sneak up on him and whip his legs with a fly swatter. He would squat and clutch his legs to protect them, while begging for mercy at the top of his head, hoping the neighbors would come in and stop his grandmother. He often felt he was being punished for having done something wrong but he couldn't think what it was. As soon as the beating was over, he would run outside the hut and hide until his mother returned from work at the manor. He remembered some little figurines of soldiers and horses his mother had molded out of clay and put in the sun to harden them. She had ground henna and other herbs to make a dye with which she painted these toys, making them lifelike. Every time he finished playing with them, he would hide them because the first time grandmother had caught him with them she had crushed all of them under her wooden sandal. If it was raining, Meo would sit in the corner behind the woodpile, or squeeze himself under the teakwood board, where he would fall asleep until his mother came home. Grandma would move around the hut, doing household chores until she felt the need for a drink. Their hut had no furniture except for the *cai phan*, which took up most of the center of the room. Once drunk she would stumble around, trip over the brass spittoon and inevitably fall face first onto the teakwood board, injuring herself in the process. She would then call out for her daughter or grandson to help her. Her cries would get louder and she would thrash around, knocking things over and throwing whatever came to her hand. Once, when the screaming and shouting became unbearable, the Skinny Lady had come in and thrown a pail of dirty water at her to calm her down.

In later years, when they were living under a bridge, Cinnamon would tell Meo he had been a quiet but alert little boy. Unlike other children, who were noisy and always underfoot, he seldom cried, she said, and he had developed a sixth sense for avoiding trouble. She also often said he reminded her of the kittens she had had, friendly but cautious, before her mother threw them away. She said he even had the eyes of a cat, very bright and protruding, with flecks of yellow in them.

"Auntie Skinny was right to call you Meo," she would say, laughing. "All you lacked were the claws."

One day, Cinnamon returned from the manor to see bruises on her son's arms and legs. Her mother was asleep, sodden with rice wine, but Auntie Skinny said the old lady had been seen beating Meo with a wooden stick. In the three years since giving birth, Cinnamon had changed considerably. She had begun to think for herself, because her mother was no longer able to think for them. She had also become rebellious at the unfairness of life. She felt that she had been betrayed by everybody she trusted, and after meeting with the Head Nun she had begun thinking the unthinkable. With each incident, each shouting match, the desire to leave the village and go far away became stronger. Looking at Meo's bruises on that day, she came to a decision. Just like that. She would leave Phu My and go away. She knew the time had come. Where she would go she didn't know, but anywhere away from her mother and her village would be all right. She packed a small wicker basket, picked Meo up and they spent the night at Auntie Skinny's.

Next morning, she stood by the dusty, lonely highway, waiting for the daily bus service that ran all the way into Ha Noi, a city she had heard about but never imagined she would ever see. She had no idea what time the bus would come along. As she told her son again and again later, years later, before she died in his arms, her mind was completely empty that morning. There was no regret for the past, no fear of the future, no hatred for anyone. The Head Nun had said that little Meo would not find peace in the village, and she had seen in one of her dreams that they would find help somewhere, in a very large house with a high domed roof, and that he would grow up to become an important person, even more important than his father. Later, when he was old enough to understand what his mother was saying, he noticed that she often said she had seen this or that in her dreams, and he became convinced that his mother could see into the past as well as predict the future, like those blind women seers in Buddhist pagodas.

Finally, after many hours, the bus arrived in a rolling thunder of noise and dust. It was full, with people perched up on the roof, clinging by their fingernails to the baggage racks, but an old woman yelled out, "There's room here for one more" and reached out for his mother. With a heave of her large hips, the old woman made a small space into which Cinnamon squeezed her thin body, with Meo and her wicker basket on her lap.

6

The Chicken Lady

The old lady had a bunch of chickens all trussed up in a large bamboo basket at her feet. They lay one on top of the other, their beaks wide open, their feet tied in bunches, their wings pinned back behind them to stop them from flapping around. The musty smell of wet chicken feathers and crushed chicken dung was suffocating. The old woman had been chewing betel nut, and her shiny, black lacquered teeth gleamed in a bright red gash of a mouth as she smiled at Cinnamon.

"Running away, are you?" she said in a loud, peasant voice, and spat a red stream of betel juice onto the floor of the bus, spattering the hapless chickens. Before the young girl could answer, the old lady said, "I'm from Phu Hoang village, also on manor land. I've heard about the Drunken Lady. I've heard about you and about little mouse here," pointing at Meo.

After a while, she continued, "What are you going to do in Ha Noi?"

Cinnamon shook her head, her eyes looking at the floor, awed by her first ride on a motorized vehicle and the tightly packed passengers, all talking at the top of their voices. "I know how to sew," she finally mumbled.

The old woman looked at her heavily. Finally, she shook her head. "Sew? That fat witch got you in, right?"

She continued before Cinnamon could answer, "I know from looking at your face and this little mouse here that your story is the same as my grand-daughter's, so don't bother to answer."

They rode on in silence, with Cinnamon staring woodenly at the scenery flashing by. He's not a little mouse. She smiled inwardly. He's a little cat.

After an hour of suffocating heat and dust, the energy drained away from her and she fell asleep, leaning against the chicken seller, while little Meo stayed wide awake, taking in everything but especially the chickens. One of them was a large rooster with a large red comb and fierce, expressionless round eyes which stared straight back at him. Hard. It was as curious about Meo as Meo was about it, and when the boy's bare right foot dangled a little too closely to the bamboo cage, the rooster would shoot his snake-like head through the slats to peck at it, getting his huge comb all entangled when he tried to withdraw his head back into the basket. This led to a kicking-pecking game between Meo and the rooster before the heat exhausted them both.

When they reached the central bus terminal in the city the next morning, the old lady told Cinnamon about a Catholic convent which helped people like her, and advised her to head straight there, giving her detailed directions. Seeing her standing rooted to the spot, looking blankly at the maze of streets in front of her, the old lady turned to a young man, probably her grandson, and told him to get some water and spray the chickens before they all died. Then he was to join them. She nodded to them and walked off, followed by Cinnamon with Meo in one arm and the wicker basket in the other. Everyone around was walking fast, unlike in the village, and the city streets were clean and smooth, with sidewalks on both sides packed with people. Meo had never seen so many people before, and neither had his mother. After turning right and left many times, they came to a square where there was a quiet, green park, with large trees and flower beds. A low, wide building, painted ochre yellow with green slatted wooden windows, stood on the other side of the park. A large sign said *Les Soeurs du Petit Jésus,* but Cinnamon could not read. However, she could see a large cross, a Christian cross, so she knew it was French. On the wall a huge mural depicted the lanky body of a white man with long golden hair, laying on a bed, above which was a shining circle. His heart hung outside his chest, bleeding. Thin trickles of blood also ran out from holes in his hands and feet. A crown of thorns sloped on his forehead, with blood dribbling all around his face. Anxious about what was going to happen, Cinnamon barely glanced at the mural, but Meo thought he recognized something. It is like grandma's blood when she falls and cuts herself. It was horrible and he remembered how his mother or the neighbors would wash the blood away from his grandmother's face.

The old chicken seller walked right up to the massive wooden door and pulled on a thick cord, ringing a heavy bell inside. She seemed very much at home, as if she had done this before. A small metallic aperture in the door opened and the head of a young nun appeared. She looked about the same age as Cinnamon. "Oh, Mrs Tam, it's you again. Wait a minute, I'll call *Ma Soeur* Hue."

That was the first time that Cinnamon knew the chicken seller was called Mrs Tam.

The little door within the door shut, and Mrs Tam turned to Cinnamon and said, "That's Sister Tuyet. You'll be alright here until they find work for you. This city's full of pimps and brothels because there's a French army camp inside the city. Country girls aren't safe here."

At that moment the sound of large keys clanking on a metallic key ring was heard. Whispered phrases were heard as the nuns wrestled with the huge padlock and chain that bolted a little side door built into the massive front gate. It wouldn't open at first. A swearword was distinctly heard.

"That's *Ma Soeur* Hue," nodded Mrs Tam knowingly, smiling.

Finally, heavy iron bolts were slipped, screeching all the way before the side door opened to reveal a stout, severe nun with a manly face. Behind her was the sweet little nun they had first seen.

"My, you're early. Just got off the bus, have you?" said Sister Hue in a low, raspy voice. Meo noticed a thin, dark moustache on her upper lip.

"Yes, and Bich's got some chickens. Will you be wanting any today?"

Sister Hue thought for a moment. "Yes, half a dozen would be fine. Let's see which ones are fat. Oh Lord! I thought I'd told you before not to tie them up so tightly. You are hurting them, and they all look half dead with thirst." Her face was concerned as she bent over, rummaging through the basket, feeling the chickens up.

"Well, they're going to die anyway, so what does it matter how they are tied up?" answered the chicken lady.

Sister Hue jerked up, looked sharply at the old peasant woman, took a deep breath and sighed, very slowly. She shook her head sadly. You can't have everything. At least she has a Christian heart. She goes out of her way to help unfortunate people. Then she caught sight of the mother and child.

"What have we got here?" she asked, perking up.

"Aah, it's the usual story. This poor girl needs help and she doesn't know her way about the city so I brought her here."

"You did right, Mrs Tam, you did right and may the Lord reward you. All right, let's take care of this young thing. That's a sweet-looking little boy you have there," said Sister Hue, turning to Cinnamon. "Come on in, come on in, I'll take you to the Mother Superior. She's French, you know."

Cinnamon did not know how to thank the old lady who had done so much for them and there was an awkward moment which was broken when the chicken lady spat out a stream of betel-red liquid onto the ground, much to Sister Hue's disgust, laughed aloud and pushed them through the convent door.

"You'll be safe here," she repeated, "and the little mouse here can learn to speak like a *tay* †," she said loudly, tweaking Meo's ear. He could see the little flecks of betel-stained spittle around her large mouth and smell the warm, acidic concoction of lime and areca nut on her breath. She then walked off with her grandson and his chicken basket. Sister Tuyet took her chickens to the kitchen while they followed Sister Hue down spacious hallways and staircases until they reached a small office where everyone sat down on cool, brown rattan chairs.

Many years later, when he was living with his adoptive *papa* in a French army camp, he was able to reconstitute his years at the convent.

His second father was a policeman, naturally curious by nature, who always wanted to know what happened—exactly as it happened. Through their long talks at night in a little kitchen that smelt of sausage and cabbage soup, he helped Meo remember the past years so that he could learn more about his adopted son. As Meo dredged up bits and pieces, his *papa* would comment on them, filling out his son's understanding of what had happened to his mother and him in those early days.

† *tay*: a Frenchman

7

Ma Mère Supérieure

When they arrived at the convent in 1918, the Great War had just ended. France, with British, Italian and American help, had won. Germany and the Austro-Hungarians had lost, and the victors were dividing up the spoils at Versailles. At the same time, an epidemic of Spanish 'flu was ravaging Europe, killing millions. In the Far East, however, all these cataclysmic events sailed completely over the magnificent roofs of the Good Samaritan Order of the Sisters of the Little Jesus, over which the Mother Superior Marie presided with grace, style and a will of steel.

A small, dumpy French woman who smelled of mothballs, she had thick, dark eyebrows, a large nose and thin, prim lips. Born in the Loire valley, she had taken her vows thirty-five years before, prior to being sent to the Niger for ten long years. Her next posting was in Morocco, North Africa, for another ten years. Now she was well into her fifth year in Indochina. She had learned the language in one year, speaking, reading and writing Vietnamese so as to be able to deal directly with those that needed her help. Quiet, efficient, totally dedicated to God and the Pope, she dealt with everyone else in the same direct, no nonsense manner that she used in her dealings with the nuns in her convent and the flotsam and jetsam that ended up at her convent's gates. In the Mother Superior's eyes, there were two sorts of people on earth, Christians and non-Christians and her God-given duty was to serve the first lot and convert the second. She intended to see to it that God's will be done, come what may, and there was nothing soft or mushy about the Mother Superior. The new French Governor General of Indochina, His Excellency the Honorable Pierre Hubert de

Pasquier-Joncelle, who sat in Sai Gon but often visited Ha Noi, held the Mother Superior in the highest esteem and had proposed her for the *Légion d'Honneur*. She was a frequent guest at the table of the new French Governor of Tonkin, the Honorable Charles Pichet. The rest of the French community had duly taken note of all this, and it was an accepted fact that what Mother Superior Marie wanted, Mother Superior Marie got.

Over the next few years, this formidable but saintly woman became the anchor to which their lives were tied, but on that first day, Cinnamon didn't know what to expect. Sister Hue stood by, prepared to translate when necessary. As it turned out, the Mother Superior's Vietnamese was good enough for Cinnamon to understand, although at first she thought it was a foreign language and looked helplessly at the two Vietnamese nuns when the Mother Superior spoke to her. Conversely, the Mother Superior, who had learnt her Vietnamese in Ha Noi from educated Catholic scholars, had a hard time understanding Cinnamon's thick provincial accent and country vocabulary, and that was where Sister Hue came in useful. Cinnamon gave her full Vietnamese name, Ho Thi Que, her age, twenty-one, her profession, seamstress, from Thanh Hoa province. Her son's baby name was Meo, four years old. She had no money, no husband, no family she could call on for help. All her belongings were in the basket she had arrived with. She had been brought up as a Buddhist. No, she did not know where the man who fathered her child was. She had trusted him, he had deceived her and disappeared before the child was born. Eventually, she had lost her job. The people she had lived with had thrown her out of the house. The Mother Superior wrote all this down in a large ledger, using a pen made of some sort of animal horn, with a squeaky metallic nib which she dipped into a large inkpot every now and again, carefully applying a roller of blotting paper over what she had written to avoid smudging.

Meo sat in an armchair, holding on to the arm rests, his eyes wide open, his cap on his little round head and snot running down from both nostrils, taking in everything. He felt no fear or anxiety, for even at that age he could already sense vibrations in a room. The tone of a voice, the expression on a face, the positioning of a body and the speed of a hand movement told him everything, perhaps because he had spent his first three years living in a one-room hut with a drunken grandmother. The vibes he could feel that day were definitely positive. These women dressed in gray and white smell so clean. Their large, stiff white hats look light as a feather. Their faces are kind. They won't hurt us. And the white woman with the big nose also has a moustache, like the old one who opened the gate with a bunch of jangling keys. Above their heads, a ceiling fan with large wooden blades turned slowly, churning the air in the room and cooling them down. It was the first time he had seen an electric fan, and it fascinated him. The one thing that jarred this picture of peace and serenity was the sight of a huge cross hanging on the wall, above the white woman's head. It was that bleeding white man again, but instead of lying down this time he was standing. It looked as if he was tied to a cross. His arms were spread out, his head drooped, his long hair hung across his chest, his feet seemed pinned together. There were traces of red on his hands and feet. This was Meo's second introduction to the bleeding man and the more he looked at it, the more horrible it looked. Why is there blood on his feet? Grandma never had blood on her feet. Always on her face.

As for the Mother Superior, twenty-five years of overseas missionary work had taught her to read between the lines, and she knew, as did Sister Hue, that Cinnamon was making up parts of her story. But the Mother Superior had learned an all-important lesson in her missionary work in central and northern Africa, before coming to Asia. That lesson was that truth was a matter of perception. And if this young woman had willed herself to believe that this version was the truth, then that was the version the Mother Superior was going to build on. But before anything could begin, mother and son would have to be checked for diseases and parasites. This was done at the Pasteur Clinic nearby. Meo was found to be in good health although underweight, and would be de-wormed anyway. Cinnamon had weak lungs, which meant that she was predisposed to consumption, a common enough ailment in the countryside, where people seldom ate their fill, but there was no sign of tuberculosis at that stage. And so on the day that they had arrived at the convent, they were both cleared to enter that abode of peace and cleanliness. On the second day, Cinnamon was taught about convent life by Sister Hue, whom she had to address as *Ma Soeur*. Of paramount importance were the necessity of attending prayers; the timetable of such prayers; the Vietnamese wording of the different prayers; silence and cleanliness. On the third day she was shown her workstation, a large roomy hallway where other seamstresses worked. For the first time, Cinnamon saw modern sewing machines. Within a week, she could operate one all by herself and within the month she could produce work of the quality required. There was never any shortage of work because the convent took in sewing work from the French settler families for a fee, part of which went into the seamstresses' kitty and paid for their medical expenses. On the fourth day, the Mother Superior called Cinnamon in and asked her to pick a Christian name for her son. Cinnamon not only didn't know any Christian names, she felt so intimidated by the cleanliness and silence of the convent she could barely speak when spoken to, even by other peasant women like herself who had taken refuge there.

Finally, the Mother Superior said kindly, in Vietnamese, "Meo means cat. We cannot have animal names here, we must have a Christian name. Do you like the name Robert? That's my brother's name." Knowing how important in Viet Nam the naming of a child was, Sister Hue repeated the question. Completely lost, Cinnamon nodded. This is the second time Meo is being given a name by somebody else. You want to call him Hai, now that you can't call him Bach, but that isn't French. All these foreign names sounded the same to her but she could see that all the convent children had French names. She already attended prayers regularly and had managed to mumble her way through them, standing up and kneeling down at the right time. Her grim determination to do whatever was the right thing told her to keep her mouth shut, her eyes and ears wide open and perform all the required rituals religiously, however meaningless they were. As she told Meo later, much later, if this was the price for staying on in the convent, she was prepared to pay it in full. She was determined they would stay in the convent for as long as they could. She well remembered what the Head Nun had said about hiding from the evil stars in places where people didn't believe in stars and what the chicken seller, old Mrs Tam, had said about hiding from the pimps and low-lifes in Ha Noi.

Thus, in less than one week after they had left Phu My village, Cinnamon had joined the seamstress workforce at the convent and Meo had become Robert Ho. Pronounced the French way, with a silent "h", Ho sounded like *eau*, water. His mother had laughed at first, saying "Ho means lake anyway, so that's near enough." But try as she might, she couldn't pronounce Robert with an R instead of an L and she called him *Lo-Be*, which, in Vietnamese, means "little oven".

8

Robert

Meo, now Robert, spent his first month getting used to his new surroundings. Everything had changed but he knew he liked his new life better. The first thing he noticed was the absence of noise. In the village, to speak in extra loud voices showed honesty and openness. It was well known that a man who spoke loudly had nothing to hide. At his grandmother's, screaming fits and lengthy vituperations were normal when she had had a few drinks. The noise of things being knocked over and the violent movements made by his grandmother when the neighbors were trying to pacify her sounded like a village fight going on as he hid in the dirt and dust under the reassuring presence of the teakwood *cai phan*.

The absence of strong smells was what he noticed next. Villagers were children of the soil, sweaty men and women whose breath changed depending on what they ate. The paddy fields alternately smelt of wet rice stalks and dry straw, the summer breezes and winter winds smelt of grainy dust and sweet rain, and the open spaces carried the faint but pervasive smell of human excrement in the air because night soil was used to fertilize the land.

Finally, there was the absence of dirt and dust. Armed with new brooms, little Vietnamese nuns swept every room and dusted every piece of furniture every day. He didn't know what they did with the convent's garbage, but he never smelt or saw any during the whole time he was there.

In this quiet, clean and pleasant smelling environment, he soon became one of the many children that attended the convent's day care center, which was set up at the back of the convent, looking out onto a huge garden. All the children had been given French names, and many had the names of Christian saints. Sister Tuyet, the sweet looking young nun who had opened the door to them on that first day, presided over the little kindergarten world, and he soon grew to love her. The children who arrived as infants could stay at the convent until they were three or four years old, after which they had to leave the convent and join their mothers. In cases like Robert's they could stay on until they were six years old. In the meantime, at the day care center, they were taught the French alphabet, colloquial French and how to do sums. There was a time for play, a time for prayers, a time for books.

Over the next four years, he made friends with other little boys and girls like him and grew up in the serenity and peace of the convent. Unlike in the village, they ate three times a day, every day, whatever the season. Besides Vietnamese food, they drank one glass of milk and had one *tartine* of bread and butter daily to make them big and strong. Like the French, little Sister Tuyet would say. They played games, they sang, they were bathed daily. Their hair became lice free and they learned to brush their teeth with toothpaste instead of using bamboo slivers as toothpicks. In toilet training, they were taught to wipe themselves with tissue paper instead of scraping their bottoms with sticks or leaves and then washing the rest off with water. Talking loudly, shouting, crotch scratching, spitting, burping, breaking wind and a dozen other things became forbidden, or at least had to be done discreetly. Nose picking and tooth-picking were absolutely forbidden. Filthy habits, said Sister Tuyet, and that was that. They attended morning and evening Mass, which were held in Vietnamese by foreign priests. At first, Robert couldn't understand why it was necessary to go through all that mumbling and getting up and kneeling down but he said nothing and did what everyone else did, under the guidance of Sister Tuyet. It was easier to simply go along with what everyone did than to try and understand who *le bon Dieu* and *le petit Jésus* were.

The part he enjoyed most was the magical world of books. Sister Tuyet taught him how to read the alphabet and he loved every minute spent on reading. Colorful booklets on children's rhymes and fairy stories fired up his imagination at a young age and he developed a strong desire to learn how to read and write and to know more about everything, traits that helped him educate himself later in life. Little scratches made with a pencil, when put together, became words. Words described things that existed all around them, or pictures in their minds, called ideas. Some of these ideas were important ideas that controlled their lives. The word love, for example, was associated with a warm feeling of protection, of good food, colorful books and enjoyable games. Later, because this word was constantly associated with *le petit Jésus* and *le bon Dieu*, Robert soon understood that if he wanted to continue receiving love he had to show his gratitude for what Jesus and God were giving them. He showed this gratitude by being good, keeping clean and, he now finally understood, by attending Mass, singing along with the others, kneeling down and standing up with the others and sitting quietly during the sermons.

The more French vocabulary he learned, the more he wanted to learn. Above everything else, he wanted to own a book. To this day he could not understand why he was so attracted to books, but perhaps it was because everything that happened in that convent started out with a nun reading something from a book called *la Bible*. His childlike mind saw in books the fount of all knowledge, and for some reason, perhaps because he was his father's son and had inherited his intelligence and curiosity, he just had to know more. He was hungry for knowledge and he wanted to know about everything, without any particular plan in mind, and he must have asked why more than a dozen times a day. Young Sister Tuyet soon recognized that Robert was mentally more alert than the others. She reported this to the Mother Superior one day, and he was told that if he could remember his French catechism and improve his pronunciation, *le père Noel* would bring him a gift. That Christmas, he received his first book, *Les Aventures du Petit Poussin*. It was in French, and it was for children aged six or seven. He couldn't read it yet, but that didn't matter. He slept with it under his pillow. It was his book, and he would read it later, when he knew how to read. Sometimes, when no one was around, he would take it out and pretend he could read it, mouthing out loud French words he knew, or reciting prayers he had learned in Vietnamese, turning over the pages every now and again to impress an imaginary audience.

9

Le Petit Jésus and *Le Bon Dieu*

At night, Robert slept with his mother in a large dorm at the back of the church. Each woman had a bunk and a mosquito net, and the bunks were stacked four high, with a small ladder running up the side. Before going to sleep, the women would sit around the lower bunks on each other's beds and gossip to their heart's content. Before long, from hidden caches native delicacies would appear, such as dried fish, sticky rice cakes with mung beans inside, all sorts of very sweet candies which had melted and stuck to the paper they were wrapped in, or dried fruits. All these forbidden delights had been bought at the market with the pocket money earned from sewing things for the church and smuggled in to be shared after lights out. Without the presence of nuns, the women reverted to the vernacular; the intensity of the gossip rose; crude words and familiar expressions flowed past Robert's ears like streams of water, carrying his mind back to the village life he had left. Everyone chewed with their mouths open, including his mother, slurping, sucking their teeth and smacking their lips to show appreciation for the delicacies that were forbidden during the daytime. Some women picked their noses or cleared their nostrils by blowing hard through one while flattening the other with a thumb, straight onto the floor. Others spat out seeds all over the place and then picked their teeth leisurely with bamboo slivers they kept hidden in their pockets, flicking off little bits and pieces found between their teeth as the conversation droned on. Yet others belched whenever they felt like it, and once in awhile one would let off a big fart, which everyone would pretend not to notice. These were not convent nuns talking, but real people, people like his mother when she wasn't pretending to be a Catholic. All the children being asleep, the women felt they could talk freely among themselves. Having learnt from the sisters in the convent that confessions purged the tortured soul, each woman poured out her story of loneliness and abandonment. They were not confessing to God, or even to Buddha, who perhaps listened but never did anything, but to each other, victims like themselves, where they could find immediate comfort. There was no holding back, unlike when they were confessing their sins to the nuns, which they did with great selectivity. Ignorant, illiterate, often pregnant when they were abandoned or chased out by their family or community, the women had drifted around the countryside before washing up in the capital. There, in their own time and in their own way, they had found refuge at the convent. As he listened to them, half-asleep, half-awake, Robert was sometimes reminded of the unpleasantness he had grown up with in his grandmother's hut.

Some of the women had decided to adopt the new foreign religion with fanatical fervor, and their eyes shone in the dark when they spoke in hushed tones about Jesus and his love for Mankind. They sounded like the nuns except for their coarse dialects. Inside Robert, however, all mention of *le petit Jésus* and his father *le bon Dieu* brought back the mural he had seen on his first day at the convent. He felt a sort of revulsion every time he thought of this long, white, bleeding body. Years later, when his mother and he were working as servants at the Saintenoix residence, he would often think back to those late night discussions in an effort to make sense of what he had heard. At first he told himself the convent women, like his mother, were all just pretending. It's alright for the Mother Superior, who's French, to believe in and to serve this foreign god, but why would any Vietnamese nun believe in him? After mulling it over in the silence of the night as he slept next to his mother in the Saintenoix kitchen, he began to see that there were actually three groups. One's really converted to Christianity although they don't understand it. The others, including mother, are seeking the protection of a foreign religion in order to escape from their bad luck, which they believe is repayment for sins in previous lives. With the Catholics, *le petit Jésus* has already paid for past sins with his sacrifice, and, by simply confessing your present sins every Sunday, you are a new man every Monday.

There's a third group, mostly older women, who don't believe in anything, whether Buddhist or Catholic. This group made a strong impression on him. Cackling in the dark, they said that men invented all these religions to better control women. Another repeated again and again that men come out from between our legs, not from God in Heaven, but when they grow up they kick us around like dirt and revere God who did nothing for them. That alone shows us how worthless men are, with their religious bullshit. One older woman repeated nightly that after death the body was buried and big white worms ate the meat to their heart's content. The more dead meat they eat, the bigger the worms became, she would insist in her raspy voice. Another woman was convinced that all this talk of souls was nonsense. What a load of shit, she would explode. Heaven is not big enough to hold all the souls that have died. Has anybody ever come back to tell us there are souls? This would always trigger a round of discussion about spirits, which almost everybody was convinced existed. There's no God up there, this woman would repeat night after night, and all the Devils are down here with us on Earth.

As for Robert, even later in life, he never quite understood what it was they were supposed to be saved from, although the nuns had explained many times that they were all sinners and that was why Jesus had died for them. Maybe the French sin a lot, but your mother and you never really sin. Maybe we do a few things wrong, like everybody else, but why on earth would Jesus want to save us? Or abandon us?

It took three years before Cinnamon could be placed with a French family, because she was illiterate and had asked to learn how to read and write basic Vietnamese as well as speak basic French. The Mother Superior had found jobs for her with Vietnamese Catholic families, but she had steadfastly refused to work for a Vietnamese family. She said that her experience with high-born Vietnamese families had not been good and anyway she wanted Robert to continue speaking French as much as possible. The Mother Superior and Sister Hue looked at each other meaningfully when they heard her mention that she had had experience with high-born Vietnamese families. They remembered she was from Thanh Hoa province, and the Trinh clan automatically sprang to their minds.

And so things stayed as they were until Robert was eight and Cinnamon was placed in the service of a French family called the Saintenoix.

10

Monsieur Saintenoix

The Saintenoix had six servants in their employ. With Cinnamon and Robert, that made seven and a half, said *Monsieur* Saintenoix, laughing. All the servants, including Nam the driver, were under the direct supervision of *Chi* Huyen, the cook, who had lived with a French soldier for many years and spoke fluent pidgin French. Cinnamon had been hired as a part-time seamstress and kitchen helper, while Robert was assigned two official tasks. One was to help the driver polish the gleaming family car every morning, the other was to feed, wash and clean up after the three large, fierce-looking German shepherds the Saintenoix family loved as if they were human beings. The male was called Tarzan, and the two females Dulcie and Lucille. Lucille was the daughter of Tarzan and Dulcie, but they were all of the same size. These dogs knew by smell the difference between a Frenchman and a Vietnamese and at first Robert was afraid of being bitten. He would always speak to them in French before approaching them, saying things like, "Come here, Lucille, come, come!" or, "There's a good dog!" He spoke as cheerfully as he could but with some authority in his voice, as he had heard *Monsieur* Saintenoix and his son Étienne talk to them. The thick furry ears would stand up, the dark, intense, intelligent eyes would lock on to him, unblinking, but the thick tails would remain still. This small two-legged human who smelled like a Vietnamese but made sounds like a Frenchman intrigued the three dogs. It took one month of regular feeding and brushing before they began to accept him, after which they became good friends.

For Robert, being friends with animals, especially dogs, was something new. In the village peasants loved only their buffaloes and their fighting cocks. They took care not to overwork their buffaloes, not to expose them to the noonday heat; they scrubbed them every evening, talking to them, feeding them freshly cut grass before nightfall. At dawn, they carried their fighting roosters like babies in their arms and walked about in the mist so the cocks could breathe in the morning dew; they fed them the best grain, better than the family ate, massaging their muscular bright red thighs, denuded of feathers, after exercising them, and building cages that protected them from the heat and the rain. On the other hand, dogs and cats, along with pigs, goats, chickens, ducks, geese, snakes, frogs, eels, fruit bats, birds and all sorts of beetles, were eaten regularly, especially on holidays, even though some people considered dogs and pigs dirty because they often fed on human excreta. In the Saintenoix family, however, Robert noticed from the first day that the dogs ate more and better food than most people in his village and left larger and more copious droppings on the garden lawns than villagers left in the fields surrounding their huts. After a few weeks of cleaning up after the dogs, Robert could tell how healthy they were by the quality and quantity of their turds.

One day, *Madame* Louise Saintenoix was gardening and asked him to look for the bag of fertilizer she had left in the gardening shed. He found it in the garage and brought it to her.

"Ah, I see you found it! I knew we put it in the garden shed yesterday when we returned from town," she said, smiling at him.

"Actually, *Madame*, I found it in the garage," he answered in French. He had liked her from the start, because she looked kind, was always elegantly dressed and smelt of an incredible fragrance. Much later, Étienne told him it was called Chanel. Her hazel eyes, the long auburn hair that cascaded over her shoulders and the incredible beauty and sweetness of her smile entranced him. She wore red lipstick all day long. He would have done cartwheels to impress her.

"What! Why the garage? I told Nam to carry it into the shed when we got out of the car," she said, mystified.

"Perhaps he forgot to do it, *Madame*," Robert answered, adding brightly "Anyway, it's not lost, and that's the main thing."

Accustomed to "Yes *Madame*, No *Madame*" answers, *Madame* Louise narrowed her eyes, sized him up and, perhaps for the first time, really saw him as a person. A little Vietnamese, but definitely a human being. She looked quizzically at his appearance.

Since his convent days, Robert had learned to brush his teeth regularly and comb his hair twice a day, always making sure the parting on the left side was perfectly straight. He had two pairs of shorts, two short-sleeved shirts and one old pair of wooden clogs. Like all country people, he never wore underwear, but he had learnt at the convent to keep his clothes neat and clean and to wash his wooden clogs every morning before putting them on.

"Hmm... well... I'll talk to the driver tonight." She paused, looking sideways at him.

"Where did you learn to speak French so well?" she asked.

"At the convent, *Madame.*"

"Very good. Do you go to school?"

"No, *Madame.*"

"What! Why not? School is very important, especially for young boys."

She doesn't realize that people like me cannot go to school like her son. She doesn't seem to know much about life here, but never mind, she has such a kind and beautiful face.

"Yes, *Madame,* it is. But my mother does not have enough money to send me to a Vietnamese school."

"I see. Would you like to go to school, Robert? Robert is your name, right?"

"Yes, *Madame,* I would like to go to school and yes, *Madame,* my name is Robert. I was given that name at the convent. I am a Catholic, *Madame.*"

He felt this small lie would make an even bigger impression on her, now that she had noticed him. Anyway, it's half true, more or less. The image of a long bleeding white body hung on a cross briefly flashed across his mind but he suppressed it at once. Small sin could be washed away if he confessed on Sunday. He had learnt that at the convent.

His mother had impressed on him many times that they had to be on their best behavior if they wanted to stay on at the Saintenoix's and he wanted to do everything to help her. He smiled brightly at the perfumed lady in front of him.

Madame Louise looked at him thoughtfully, and then laughed ruefully.

"I am doing charity work all year long," she said, talking aloud to herself, nodding her head, "for hundreds of children I never even see, and right here in my house is a deserving boy who needs help..."

Robert said nothing, not knowing what she was leading up to. But he already felt that something might come of it. He wanted to hurry to the kitchen and tell his mother about it.

"I'll speak to François tonight about this. We'll find some way to get you into a proper French school, you'll see," she promised, primping her lips, the fire of determination shining in her beautiful eyes.

One week later, when he was nine years old, Robert began attending primary classes at the *Lycée Albert Sarraut* during the day, resuming his role as a houseboy in the evenings and during the weekends. This school was named after one of the longest serving French Governor Generals and at first had been strictly for French students, but Robert was *un cas spécial*, reserved for people sponsored by families such as the Saintenoix', the Court families in Hue and the few Indochinese families that had become a part of French society. *Madame* Louise's interest in him led her to ask Étienne to help him out with his studies. Tall, angular, pasty faced and wearing glasses, he was two years older than Robert. A quiet, modest boy who spoke colloquial Vietnamese, Étienne had a biting sense of humor that was totally out of character. Completely irreverent about subjects that were sacrosanct in his house, he made quirky remarks about everything. From French history, Robert learned about *Liberté–Egalité–Fraternité,* which Étienne casually referred to by its acronym, LEF, always adding "PPT" under his breath every time he listened to his father expounding on the wonders of LEF to Robert. At first Robert thought Étienne was saying a prayer, like the Vietnamese nuns said amen and crossed themselves each time *Ma Mère Supérieure* mentioned the name of *le petit Jésus* or *le bon Dieu*. He had learnt at the convent that *péter* in French meant breaking wind and that this was dreadful sin, and he thought Étienne was just being rude, but there was an extra "p" there, and he wondered if it might stand for *petit péter*, a little fart. Finally, intrigued, he asked Étienne about it. The older boy laughed with delight before answering.

"PPT, *pas pour toi*, not for you! You haven't seen that there is no LEF for your people? Only for us?"

From direct contacts with French people outside of the Saintenoix home, Robert had become aware that most French people despised and even disliked the Vietnamese, whom they considered unreliable, lazy, dirty and dishonest. They said things like this openly, in front of the Vietnamese present, as if they weren't there. In the Saintenoix home, there was no obvious racism because it was a master-servant relationship, and Robert could relax, but he picked up undercurrents of friction between the Saintenoix that he couldn't understand at first. One thing that did become clear after a while from listening to *Monsieur* Saintenoix was that the French presence in Indochina was the result of enormous violence done to the Vietnamese and that France was quite prepared to dish out more violence if necessary. *Monsieur* Saintenoix talked to Robert as if the latter were French, as if he expected the boy to automatically understand the French perspective on everything. This made Robert feel both pleased and disturbed at the same time. He knew he wasn't a French boy and, even though he tried, he couldn't share many of *Monsieur* Saintenoix's views, which he often thought were insensitive, arrogant and hid a propensity for violence. *Monsieur* Saintenoix was a large man, with an imposing paunch, a thick mustache and the voice of a baritone. When he had time for Robert, he would tell him about what France had done for Africans, for Arabs, and for the Indochinese, whom he called *les annamites*. France, he would say, had brought them Christianity, had taught them how to dress, eat and work properly. The most difficult, he would say again and again, was trying to make them honest. All this had been done through the French language, which had made the *annamites* civilized persons. All these lessons had come after great military victories in which brave French soldiers had died so that the French way of life could be brought to these people. He said all this with great conviction, in a voice used to giving orders. He was so positive and final about what he said that he reminded Robert of Mother Superior Marie or even Sister Hue. Everything they said came directly from God and simply could not be questioned. It was The Truth.

It was only much later, when he was living with his adoptive father, that he learned how things worked in Indochina, which the Vietnamese like him always called Viet Nam. The French had three social classes, like the Vietnamese. The first tier of this brittle, artificial society was composed of French colonial senior civil servants and bankers, all very close to the government in Paris. The Saintenoix belonged to this class. The second tier included the French business and commercial managing directors and their immediate assistants, also French. Tiers one and two were part of what was called the Indochina Lobby within the government in Paris. Finally came tier three, composed of French settlers, the police and the military, ordinary working class, tax-paying citizens. France ran Indochina through a fourth tier, composed of elite Vietnamese civil servants drawn from the ruling families and clans. These were highly educated men from large, feudal clans at the apex of which was the Emperor. Robert's real father, a mandarin, was such a man. The Vietnamese elite played a vital if precarious role, being the indispensable link between the French masters and the Vietnamese masses. Until the French had arrived, these men had owned all of Viet Nam and had been feared as well as respected. Now they were merely feared. In turn, these leaders, by right of birth, ran the country for the French through a huge body of civil servants, civilian and military. Essentially, these men and women, collectively named government people, were poor people who had managed to secure a secondary education and could read and write. Finally, there was the sixth tier, the masses, a vast majority of the population, made up of common people, most of whom lived in the countryside, who had only received a primary education in village schools. This social class, graphically named *dan be co thap mieng* in Vietnamese, or "people with short necks and small mouths", represented the common people. When *papa* got to this part, Robert was able to see society as a whole for the first time, and he knew then that his mother and he belonged to this third Vietnamese tier.

Madame Saintenoix didn't fit into any of these social classes. She lived in a world of books, music and perfume. She always smelt nice and fresh, was always well dressed and her movements were always graceful. Étienne adored her and *Monsieur* Saintenoix, a large, forceful and pompous man, acted completely out of character when she was around, doing everything she asked of him, like a big dog trying to please its master. Occasionally, when she was displeased at something he had said, she would say something in French very quickly, too quickly for Robert to understand, something that always ended with "...*tes poules†*", which meant your chickens. But what chickens? Robert, a precocious boy with a good brain, suspected that her husband had been guilty of something in the past and now desperately wanted to be forgiven by his wife, hence his over-solicitousness. But what had this to do with chickens?

This wonderful woman would spend time with Robert in the evening reading stories to him from Victor Hugo. Sometimes she read him poems she had written herself. All her books came from France, and none of them concerned LEF or war. Robert often picked them up to smell the leather binding. Even the glue smelt nice. He vowed to himself that one day he would have many books too, to add to the one he had kept from the convent, *Les Aventures du Petit Poussin*. In his desire to understand more of what *Madame* Saintenoix was reading, he took to asking Étienne to give him a summary of the chapters his

---

† *poules*: French slang for chicks, prostitutes, mistresses.

mother was going to read next, and in this way he was better able to follow the story line. Étienne and he became good friends and the older boy took him along to play football at school. Robert soon became a good player, better than most of the French boys, because he was faster and the heat didn't bother him. He loved to outrun and out-dribble the French boys, especially as he knew many of them resented him attending a French school.

At night, he would sleep on the same cot that his mother used, in the servants' quarters. Before going to sleep, she would ask him, in whispers, about his day. She was so proud that her son, now called *Lo Be*, was going to a French school, playing football with French boys, and was invited by *Madame* Louise to listen to her reading French books. He could feel her chest inflate with pride as he talked, sense her eyes widen in her kind, soft face each time he related something new, however mundane, such as what *Monsieur* Saintenoix had said to him that evening, or what Étienne had given him. She mentioned once or twice that as long as they could stay in a French home the bad stars could not influence them because the French didn't believe in them, and Robert knew that she dreaded having to leave the Saintenoix one day. Preoccupied with more immediate matters, he never asked her about these bad stars.

This idyllic life came to end when Robert finished his tenth year. *Monsieur* Saintenoix was recalled to France and within a month they had packed their considerable belongings, to be sent by truck to Sai Gon for loading onto the liner *Le Cambodge* heading for Marseilles. The family and the dogs would go south—by plane. By plane! Robert couldn't get over it. His mother received a gift of money equivalent to three months' salary and he received some books from *Madame* Louise, a brotherly hug from Étienne, and a framed photograph of the Saintenoix family from *Monsieur* Saintenoix. In the corner, he had inscribed in French "*A Robert, un gentil petit garçon*".

11

The Railway Bridge

His mother, like the other servants, had hoped that *Madame* Louise would introduce them to *Monsieur* Saintenoix's successor, but it turned out that there would be none, as the post had been reassigned to Sai Gon. *Madame* Louise didn't have any friends in need of servants at this time. None of the other servants had jobs to look forward to either, and it was decided they would all check with *Chi* Huyen every now and again, as she was the most likely to find work first, being the most qualified. Desperate, Cinnamon tried the convent but was gently turned away.

"We can't take you in a second time," *Ma Soeur* Hue said softly, her manly face softening as she recognized Robert. "There are so many women here already... we have to think about them first."

Through the latticed doors they could see that the convent was indeed full of women and children, and his mother said she remembered the day they had arrived there some seven years before. She had been totally ignorant then, and Robert was still a tiny tot. At least we've had a few good years and you're almost grown up now. If we can hold on for a few months maybe we can find work with another French family. They began walking aimlessly through the bustling city streets, their hearts empty, their minds confused. All around them shops were doing business, markets were filled with people, the sidewalks were crowded and a never-ending river of bicycles, motorbikes, *cyclo-pousse*†, pushcarts, cars and ox-drawn carts flowed along the main streets. The noise level was ear-shattering and the smells were unbearable after the

† *cyclo-pousse*: rickshaws

peace of the convent and the cleanliness of the Saintenoix residence. They could see that in the streets life was being lived to the full every hour of the day. There were many poor people around, people like them, except that they all seemed to have somewhere to go to. Cinnamon and Robert were also walking, but with nowhere to go to, drifting from street corner to street corner like empty shells, bodies from which the life-giving spirit had drained away. The umbilical chord that had connected them to the Saintenoix household had been cut, and they felt as if they were floating in a sea of strange faces, neither friendly nor hostile but totally indifferent. Cinnamon didn't know what to say to comfort her son, and he was too afraid of the answers she might give to ask any questions.

They slept the first few nights in the courtyard of a Buddhist temple in the Vietnamese Quarter but were asked to move on eventually. At the central market place, his mother walked around the stalls looking for work, any kind of work, but there was none. They couldn't afford lodgings of any sort because, until she found work, his mother wanted to keep the money she had for food. Finally, on the advice of a group of vagrants who begged for a living near the fish market, they settled on the underside of a bridge near the central railway station. This bridge crossed a malodorous canal that demarcated the western side of the wet market in a suburb of Ha Noi, and was called the railway bridge. Below the bridge, it was muggy in the summer, cold in winter and dusty all year long. When the trains passed by overhead, it was like an earthquake, but it was dry when it rained and, above all, it was free. The problem was that there were other families of vagrants that had lived there for years, taking up all the best spots, and settling in was difficult at first. After much negotiating, they were sold a small space, the one right next to a garbage dump, at the back end of the tunnel. Further at the back was the city dump, a multicolored hill covered with large bluebottle flies, cockroaches and rats. Dozens of families, many spanning four and even five generations, were busy from dawn to dusk picking over this smorgasbord of detritus for items that were still eatable or saleable.

Cinnamon at once began cleaning out their hole-in-the-wall, while Robert hauled buckets of water from the filthy canal crossed by the bridge. Using a bar of French detergent soap she had kept from the Saintenoix, his mother scraped and scrubbed away the dirt and grime that had accumulated over the years, dug out the rats' nests, refilling them with crushed stones, and, using her clogs, killed all the cockroaches she could see. "I wasn't always as concerned about cleanliness as now", she told her son, laughing, "but I learnt a lot at the convent. Being sick costs money. If we want to stay healthy, we have to keep things clean". Robert found dry straw and tied it into a thick bundle. They sprinkled water over it, then lit it, then ran this ball of smoke around the concrete wall of their new home, driving out the fleas, the ticks, the insects and the microorganisms that lived in the cracks. They gagged at the smoke and their eyes ran with tears, but kept at it till their space was cleared of chiggers and parasites. That first night they slept an uneasy sleep on a hard board that served as a bed, under the old mosquito net *Madame* Louise had given them. His mother cleaned the little space again the next day, from top to bottom, until it felt right for her. Robert found wooden posts and cardboard slats, and rigged up a barrier between the cubbyhole where they slept and the garbage pile. This man-made wall deflected the breeze from the street towards the garbage dump and cut down on the stench of rotting garbage, allowing them to sleep better that second night.

The little community around them watched all this fuss about hygiene with disdain. They felt the newcomers obviously thought they were better than them, what with all that soap and insect-killing torches, perhaps because they had acquired *tay* habits, white man habits, and in the tentative discussions that followed Cinnamon had to assure them that she and her son were genuine Vietnamese, straight from the countryside.

12

Minh

In this environment, a French name was a distinct liability, and Cinnamon decided that Robert should have a Vietnamese name. For the first time, they talked seriously about what his given name should be, an important subject in the Vietnamese culture. She said that since his father hadn't recognized him, he would carry her family name, Ho, which meant lake and denoted peace. On the other hand his father should contribute something to his adult name, and she would take the middle word Xuan from his full name, Trinh Xuan Bach. Xuan meant spring and denoted hope. His given name, chosen by her, would be Hai, which meant ocean and denoted power. As soon as his span of bad luck was over, she said, he could become Ho Xuan Hai. You can then be proud of your name, she said.

"It's a very good name," she added, "and it will be known throughout the country when you become famous."

But, she said, this was not a propitious time for him to use his real name because he was still under the influence of the bad stars, and to call himself by his real name was like challenging them to do their worst. No, they would reveal his adult name to the world only once the *Liem Trinh* star took over. On the other hand, he couldn't return to being Meo anymore, being grown up. She thought for a while, then she decided on Minh, meaning intelligent, enlightened, brainy.

"You're really intelligent anyway, son," she said proudly, wiping his sweaty face with her face towel. "I know. Everyone at the convent told me so. And *Madame* Louise also said so."

She looked at him strangely, tilting her head, a perplexed expression on her face.

"What is it, mother?"

"Now that I think of it, it's maybe because of your father that you are so smart. I don't have any education, but he could speak foreign languages. Yes, that must be it. At least, he gave you something."

Robert, now Minh, didn't quite understand the part about the bad luck stars and *Liem Trinh* but he didn't ask. You're lucky your mother is there to think for you. Minh sounds alright anyway. Meo… Robert… Minh… what next?

They slept, ate and spent most of their time on a thin wooden slat, which, like the ubiquitous *cai phan* in the countryside, had became their bedroom, living room and dining room. The toilet was a small stream that ran nearby. A wall made of plywood, corrugated iron sheets and cardboard had been built between the bridge inhabitants and the stream and solid stakes had been driven into the ground along the banks, behind the wall. Hidden from public view, toilet users held on to these as they went about the business of emptying their bowels. The smell of the garbage took some getting used to, but it wasn't too bad when the wind was blowing away from the bridge. After a month or so, they became used to living in the streets, but after the silence of the convent and the refined serenity at the Saintenoix home, the noise level under the bridge took some getting used to. For the first months, the thunder made by the trains running over the bridge directly above them was deafening and unbearable. At first, they all sounded the same, bone shaking and ear rattling, but after some time, they were able to distinguish between the cargo and the passenger trains. Fine dust, bits of plaster and all sorts of insects and bugs rained down on them every time the heavy troop transport trains roared by, laden with armored cars, tanks and large artillery pieces, heading north to put down local insurrections. Many of the old timers grumbled that it wouldn't be long before the bridge collapsed on them, and at first Minh was so worried he started sleeping with one eye open, until he was overcome with fatigue and couldn't get up in the mornings. The passenger trains were not so bad, just noisy. The problem was that they came by twice a day and once at night. But after the first year, they hardly noticed that they had become hard-core vagrants living permanently under a bridge. They didn't hear the trains any more; it was as if they had lived there all their lives. Minh had stopped brushing his teeth, washing his hair and body daily and went for days without even washing his hands. He smelt sour all night long, and so did his mother. They were both black with grime, and they regularly picked lice out of each other's hair, like everyone else under the bridge. The homeless street people all around them now looked at them in a friendly manner, coming over for long chats. When asked where they had come from, Minh regurgitated a story in which neither the manor, the convent or the Saintenoix appeared. His mother and he had carefully worked out a background that was acceptable to the vagrants and they stuck to it all the time they were under that bridge.

While his mother was out looking for work, he watched their belongings, such as they were, and played with the other children. His mother ate sparingly so that he could have more, and her consumptive condition worsened. At the beginning, she walked far and wide through the Vietnamese Quarter every morning, looking for casual work in market places and down at the docks. Sometimes she found work, but it was always for half a day or a day at the most, and it paid very little. Increasingly, heavy taxation, paid in quotas of rice, drove peasants to leave the land and seek work on French plantations, where work was seasonal. During the off seasons, hungry, illiterate peasants gravitated to military camps and urban centers in the provinces to look for work. From there they drifted on to Ha Noi where they soon became beggars, prostitutes, petty thieves or low-level criminals. In the capital, day workers and casual, unskilled labor was always instantly available, often for a pittance. Many of the shops paid their casual workers with food instead of money. In this daily quest for work, his mother met up with all sorts of low life who asked for sexual favors, mostly oral sex, or who wanted to introduce her to future employers living "nearby", or offered her work on "plantations", always promising regular pay. They all wanted her to follow them somewhere. She shied away from these men and women, ever conscious that, tied around her waist, tightly wrapped in oiled paper, was all the money she had left from her service with the Saintenoix.

"No job is better than losing this money," she would say to him at night, tapping her wad. "There'll be no food then."

Even then, there was little food, and their main meal was around ten in the morning. It was often the only meal of the day, and when they were hungry, they drank water in which they had boiled leaves picked from nearby bushes. After chewing on the boiled leaves, they spat out the fibrous parts.

Minh noticed his mother often went to the pagoda and asked her why.

"It's too complicated to explain now, but I am praying so that our bad luck will go away. There are three stars above you that are holding you back and I don't know how to get away from their influence. The convent and the Saintenoix home protected us from them, because the French don't care about stars, but under this bridge we're in their grip again."

Although by now he was becoming more aware of himself as a person separate from his mother, and he knew that somehow these bad stars affected both their lives, he could see she didn't want to talk about it and so he didn't insist.

His mother was no longer the wide-eyed country girl she had been ten years before. She had learnt a lot from talking to the other seamstresses at the convent and the servants at the Saintenoix home. She had learnt all about men, about their sexual habits and vices. She had asked her new friends about the curious practice some men have of deliberately not ejaculating, and had been told that this was a Chinese sexual technique. Amidst general laughter at the question, one woman had said "They tickle your little clam until it opens up and releases the pearls. They collect these pearls to add years to their lives." Hoots and jeers followed, and his mother would blush all over, insisting all the time that she had only learnt about this from a friend of hers. It appeared that a certain sect that followed the *tao* way of life believed that a man could absorb *chi*, the vital life force, from the orgasmic secretion released by a woman. By bringing on an orgasm in her and at the same time holding back his own *chi*, a man could double his life force and live well over a hundred years. This worked especially in the case of virgins and young women who had not yet given birth. It now all became clear to her. The Diamond Son had been to China, had probably learnt the technique there and used young women to ensure longevity. That was why he never touches a concubine once she had had a child. You probably added ten years to his life. On the other hand, if he had held back every time you wouldn't have had little Meo either. As the Head Nun said, in unhappiness there is happiness. You just have to look for it.

13

The Railway Gang

All of the things that had happened to Cinnamon in her short life came out in the long evenings as she sat with her son inside the little cocoon formed by their dirty, sagging, patched up mosquito net. To help them forget their hunger, she would talk for hours, about everything and about nothing. He asked a lot of questions and gave his opinion on everything. She liked that, and he could see how proud she was that he could talk along like an adult.

"You're like your father, son," she would say, her eyes brightening in the darkness. "He talked so well and so do you."

Minh could see that whatever his father had done to her, he was very much in her mind all the time. Sooner or later, whatever the subject we start out with, mother brings father up, because of the way you look, talk or act. One night she says this, the next she says that, sometimes contradictory. Does she still love him or does she hate him? Does she want you to take revenge on him? From what he had heard, he felt they should both hate his father, but he wasn't sure that was what she wanted. Better wait and see what she expects you to do.

The most important events in her life dribbled out, event by event, during the long evenings under the railway bridge. Seen from outside the mosquito net, mother and son looked conspiratorial and secretive as they bonded, night after night, discussing matters deeply embedded in their minds in soft voices so as not to be overheard. His mother was no longer the same person who had taken refuge in the convent. She had changed a lot, and become more experienced in the ways of the city. On the advice of her friends, who all seemed wise in the ways of men, she had slipped a long, stout steel needle, its top embedded in a small green wooden frog, into the bun she knotted her thick black hair into. The frog stuck out, like a cheap bright ornament. She was quite determined to use this hatpin to defend her money. She had been taught how to defend herself, too.

"If he's on top of you already, wait until he's busy doing it and then find the hollow at the base of his skull at the back of his neck with one hand. With the other slip the needle into it, hard and quick. He'll be dead before he can pull his bird out." Shrieks of laughter would follow.

"Yeah, and if he's shagging you up against a wall, feel for his kidney with your left hand, then slip it in as deep as it'll go. Stand still, let me show you. Everybody's got two kidneys ...here ...or here ...got it?" More laughter and cackling.

"Then run like hell, don't stand around. He might have friends waiting for their turn. Start screaming as loud as you can and run like the wind."

After a year or so of living under the bridge on one meal a day, Minh had begun to accept that most well-to-do Vietnamese despised poor people like them as much as the French did. Even those who were not that rich didn't want to have anything to do with them. When they saw the bridge people approaching to beg for a coin, they instinctively veered away, their faces disdainful. The middle classes, like the government people, sometimes stopped and berated them mercilessly, calling them names and threatening to hit them. Knowing he would not get anything out of them, Minh would hurl the worst swearwords he knew at them and run away before they could lay their hands on him. When he stopped to catch his breath, shame and anger washed over him for running away and he would promise himself that one day he would become somebody who commanded attention and respect. You're not a nobody. You have been to school, you're a person, and so is your mother. You're not dirt, just poor, that's all. But he was beginning to realize that his mother, even though she was not cursed by bad stars like him, would not be able to become somebody unless he carried her with him on the way up. Not only her lungs are sick but she is also uneducated. You have to climb up the ladder for both of you. But how? You don't even exist. You're always hiding under some name or other, living in the shadows as if you don't have a real name. Even if you are clean and well dressed, people who look can't see the real you. One night he woke up in a cold sweat. He had had a dream in which he wasn't wanted by the Diamond Son because he was poor, by *Ma Mère Supérieure* because he couldn't remember his catechism, by *Monsieur* Saintenoix because he wasn't French, and by the vagrants under the bridge because he behaved like a white man, a *tay*. He hadn't come from anywhere, so he couldn't join any group, but when he insisted on joining, they wouldn't let him in because he had always come from the wrong place. This nightmare of not belonging and not being able to join any group came back night after night until he talked to his mother about it. She looked at him for a long time, her small dark eyes searching his large, yellow-flecked eyes, then told him that when the time came, he would be better than anyone else. Much better. She said this in a plain, matter of fact way, as if she was talking about the sun coming up tomorrow, as it does every day. From that day this recurrent dream went away, never to return.

The railway gang boys began to warm up to Minh after he started swaggering around like them, scratching his crotch, swearing all the time and spitting everywhere. None of these boys could find work and no one was going to give them anything so they had to steal to survive. Like rats, they hid in dark corners until they saw an opportunity and then they pounced. They were all small, grimy, hard as nails and smart as monkeys. They picked pockets in the daytime and stole at night to support their parents and themselves. Minh secretly admired them and, with two mouths to feed, he fell in with them. Every day the railway bridge boys fanned out across the city, taking up their assigned spots, sharp eyes wide open, looking for opportunities to come back at night to steal something from the villas in the French Quarter or from the rich Vietnamese families living in a belt around the French Quarter. They also regularly worked the central wet market, where housewives carried shopping money, and the central bus stations, always full of peasants newly arrived in the big city to look for work. Some days were good, and they ate well, some days were bad, and they went hungry. They also snatched bags and pick-pocketed targets of opportunity on the streets. Everything they stole, except for food, they immediately fenced at the central market and bought rice for the family. Getting enough rice for the next meal was their main preoccupation and they were proud on the days they did well.

Another preoccupation, one that was shared by all the denizens living under the bridge, was the pooling of money to pay off the police. Under the pretense of keeping the underside of the bridge free and clear, the police extorted money from the little community by threatening it with expulsion every now and again. The older women were in charge of saving a fixed sum of money from all the begging, pick pocketing, petty thieving and prostituting activities with which to placate the police, who would make a show of relenting and allowing them to stay on under the bridge for another few months. Even then some of the more abusive policemen demanded free sex with the younger girls or ganged up to beat up a couple of boys for no reason.

Minh was eventually taught to be the second man in a string of three pocket pickers. The first boy was the real star of the show, and the third had to have stamina. The snatching or lifting was always done at a street corner. Boy number one, moving north, brushed against the victim and lifted the wallet or purse or coins, instantly handing them to boy number two, Minh, who was moving south. Within seconds, he immediately passed the takings to a third boy who ran down an alley to the west or east. It was impossible for the victim and his friends to figure out which boy had the goods on him.

In this mean little underworld that he lived in, it was important to know how to take care of yourself. The railway boys were like a pack of mangy wild dogs, perpetually on the hunt, perpetually quarrelling. The first line of attack or defense was to know how to swear and he rapidly picked up the six most common insults, which were motherfucker or father fucker, cock sucker or cunt sucker, son of a dog and eat shit. At first it seemed that every second word had to be a swearword if you wanted to be respected as a tough guy. Straight talking was in itself an invitation to sarcastic remarks that would lead to a fight. In terms of age and size, he was somewhere in the middle, an ambiguous position that had to be constantly clarified. He noticed that once he became angry he wasn't afraid of being hurt and would swing wildly with his fists and lash out with his feet, really intent on hurting his opponent but having no idea of what to do next. You are not a coward, but you still lose most of your fights. Why? Then one day a smaller boy from another street gang knocked him out with a swift kick to the groin and he couldn't walk properly for weeks. When he recovered, he decided to adopt this technique from then on. Holding up his two arms to protect his head, he bulled his way in and kicked his opponent's crotch as hard as he could. When the boy fell to the ground clutching his groin, he followed up by kicking his head till he passed out. He soon became known as 'Minh the Nut Kicker,' and even bigger boys hesitated to jump him.

He also discovered that cunning and trickery were a lot easier than going toe-to-toe with someone. A bigger boy challenged him one day for having accidentally moved onto his turf while running away from the police and they agreed to meet at dawn the next day behind the garbage dump to settle matters. Minh knew the other boy was a habitual knife carrier so he rounded up the three closest allies he had made over his months as a pickpocket and they took up their positions well before sunup, armed with clubs. Like ambush predators, they sat silently in the pre-dawn darkness while a thousand mosquitoes feasted on their skinny limbs. When the big boy showed up, they jumped him and beat him bloody. They snapped his knife into two and then stood over him and collectively pissed on his face. When the boy recovered, he left the area and never returned. After that even the bridge gang's leader looked at Minh with respect.

Some of these gang leaders were particularly aggressive and many carried some sort of weapon on them. Once at the top, they lasted for a while until a second level toughie took them on and beat them senseless, after which they moved out of the gang, having lost face. Minh definitely didn't want to be a follower and be ordered about, because he felt that he was smarter than the gang leaders, who were generally a combination of stupidity and viciousness. For some reason, even at that age, he didn't want to stand out in a crowd, up at the top one day and chased away like a dog the next. He wanted to get what he wanted without being noticed and began working to become the gang leader's right-hand man. It wasn't difficult. Using his brains and ingenuity, he anticipated different situations and steered the gang leader in the right direction. Whenever they scored, he let him take the full credit for it, fading into the background. Whenever they failed, which was not often, he at once stepped forward and took the blame, earning the gang leader's respect. Over a period of time, this stratagem worked and his position in the gang improved steadily as both the leader and the followers recognized that he had brains. His mother heard of all this from their neighboring bed-spacers and hugged him with pride at night. "Everybody says you're already twice as smart as the others. I know you'll go far once we can leave this filthy place."

After a year or so of living under the bridge, his sexual education began. The gang he had joined was composed of boys more or less the same age as him, but they had lived on the streets all their lives and they seemed to know a lot more than him about everything. Although he didn't think any of them had actually had sex with a girl, they all insisted that they had. He didn't really believe them, because he couldn't imagine who they could have had sex with. Except for one, who called herself by a French name, Hélène, the girls in the gang stayed close to their mothers, besides having brothers to protect them. And none of the boys had enough money to pay for a prostitute. When asked if he had fucked a woman before, Minh at first thought of saying, yes, of course. Lying, brazening it out, putting on a thick face was all part of their psyche, and a barefaced liar was much admired, even if everyone knew he was lying through his teeth. But he wasn't called the Nut Kicker for nothing; he had already established his reputation of being a tough guy; he felt he could afford to tell the truth. Strangely enough, his honest if anti-climactic answer made everyone feel superior. He didn't know more than them, so he wasn't a threat. They decided to help him become a man, and took him at nights to the suburbs where, from well-worn tree branches they climbed, they could look down through the open windows of private villas. Over a period of months, he saw husbands and wives, masters and maids, drivers and cooks all doing it. He once even saw a rich boy, no older than him, trying to do it with a dog until, thoroughly exasperated, it turned and bit him. Standing on a branch, holding on to the trunk with one hand, they would masturbate furiously with the other. Then, in city parks, they would hide in the bushes and watch young lovers kiss and paw each other until, finally, the girl would recline onto the grass and her boyfriend would roll over onto her. As they rocked back and forth in urgent love, they babbled sweet nothings into each other's ears, unaware that in the darkness, hardly a stone's throw away, a silent audience of street urchins masturbated in unison, in absolute bliss. Minh gradually understood that self-gratification was the extent of his friends' experience with sex. Granted, they had seen a lot more than him, but none of them had actually done it either. He felt better knowing that.

The one girl under the bridge who had no mother to stick to and no brother to defend her was this Eurasian girl with a harelip named Hélène. An orphan a couple of years older than Minh, she was strongly built, with a fair skin. She looked like a French girl and had hazel eyes. She dressed like a boy, cut her curly brown hair short and would have been good looking if it were not for her deformity, which made her look stupid. This impression at first sight was reinforced by her voice, which she deliberately made frog-like when she was begging. Her nickname was Rabbit Mouth. She slept at night in a dark corner of the bridge with a group of professional beggars, run by an old woman named the Old Witch. Everyone under that bridge feared the Old Witch, an evil-looking old crone who dabbled in herbal medicines and magic potions. She had once publicly put a curse on a policeman who was abusing them and told him he would die the next day at noon at the food stall section of the market, which he visited every day for a bowl of free beef soup. He never paid for his snacks or cigarettes but no one dared say anything. The next day, with half of the bridge denizens watching, he had died of convulsions, right there in broad daylight, exactly at the time she told him he would die. Some suspected the Old Witch had poisoned his bowl of soup before he arrived; others marveled at her powers. After that, no one ever thought of crossing The Evil One.

For years, the old hag had taken Hélène along with the beggars in the daytime, especially to the French Quarter, where the girl's harelip and obvious French blood usually squeezed a few extra coins out of the French passers-by. Now that she had started menstruating, they prostituted her at night. Because of her face, it was preferable that the client be too drunk to notice, but she had been taught to hold a face towel in her hand, which she casually held around her mouth when talking to people, thus hiding her disfigurement.

Once or twice, Minh had caught her looking at him in a curious manner, as if she were wondering what he was doing there. He didn't know why but he had felt attracted to her from the first day he saw her. He felt sorry for her and anger rose in his chest every time he heard people call her Rabbit Mouth, which he thought was a cruel name. In his mind, he always called her Hélène. He felt she was also interested in him, and he wanted to talk to her, but he was afraid of the Old Witch and contented himself with sneaking looks at her when their paths crossed.

One night a group of drunken rickshaw coolies entered the area under the bridge to rape the women who slept there. These men, belonging to the lowest level of the urban working classes, pulled rickshaws for a living. Wearing singlets and shorts, they ran barefooted all day between the shanks of the rickshaw, their leathery lungs filling with dust and their skin burning to a crisp in the sun. Getting drunk and fighting among themselves was one of the few pleasures in their short and brutal lives. Looking for free sex was another.

Having already been attacked by roving gangs of drunks, the little community under the railway bridge rapidly rose as one to repel the outsiders. Torches and kerosene lamps instantly came alive so they could better see the attackers. Knives and iron bars came out from beneath filthy mattresses and everyone screamed defiance. Without being told, young boys immediately ran towards the police station to alert the authorities. One coolie fell through Minh's mosquito net onto his mother, knocking him aside. Before she could react, the man, reeking with alcohol, had ripped her pantaloons apart and was trying to mount her from behind. With one fist, he was pounding her on the back of her head and she had gone limp. Minh hit the man on the back with his fists and tried to wrestle him off his mother, but this was an adult, not one of the flyweights he was used to fighting. The rapist backhanded him in the face, and he saw stars and tasted blood in his mouth. Then he heard a sickening, crunching sound and the man went limp. He looked up and saw Hélène with an iron bar in her hand. In the kaleidoscope of lights that flashed around in the Stygian darkness under the bridge, he saw she was laughing. With her mouth wide open, her harelip made her look like the devil, except that her teeth were small, white and even.

"Let's drown him," she said. He noticed with surprise her voice was perfectly normal, even pleasant to the ear. While the fighting was going on, they grabbed the man by the legs and dragged him off his mother, over whom Minh threw a blanket before helping Hélène haul the drunk to the smelly canal a few meters from their cubbyhole. Once there, he looked at her, not knowing what to do.

"Push him in," she said in a clear, melodious voice, not at all the foghorn voice she adopted for begging.

"Is he dead?" Minh asked, hesitating. Why are you asking this stupid question? Why aren't you like her? She looked at him with surprise, then reached over, iron rod in hand, and smashed the man's head a second time. The skull caved in completely. "He is now," she said with a short laugh.

They pushed him in and the body slowly sank into the deep, stinking ooze. A few thick bubbles appeared which burst with audible plops. Behind them, the fighting was beginning to end, although the police had not responded to the calls for help. It was late at night, and they had better things to do than to get involved in street fights between rickshaw coolies and vagrants living under a bridge. Minh suddenly remembered his mother.

"Thanks," he muttered. "I'm Minh," putting out his hand. He had seen Frenchmen and women shaking hands when they met in the Saintenoix days, and he liked this open and frank way of greeting people.

She hesitated for a second and then said, "I know you," and shook his hand right back. She had a firm grip and, unlike his, her hand was dry. "You're the Nut Kicker. I'm Hélène. They call me Rabbit Mouth, but I'm more like a tiger."

At the time, it didn't register, but many decades later, when he was known as the Tiger General, he often had the occasion to remember what his tiger-like rabbit had done that night. He nodded and ran back to his mother.

She had recovered and was sitting up in the wreck that their cubbyhole had become. She looked dazed, but from the buzz of conversation that came from the other vagrants, she knew what had happened. Her head ached and her hips were bruised where the man had mashed them with his powerful hands. She hadn't been raped, however, although her pantaloons were in rags by now. Minh sat up beside her, pulling her head against him, massaging her head and shoulders. He suddenly realized how small his mother was. Or perhaps he had grown bigger. In the dark that night, he sat rigid, still trembling from the encounter, his mind racing wildly. You aren't a boy anymore and if you want to take care of your mother you'll have to be like Hélène. Fuck me... the way she cracked his head... just like that. She pounced on the man like a tigress. No hesitation. Just one blow and it was all over for him. From now on don't hesitate before you act either. Act immediately like she did, right or wrong. After a while, he fell asleep, the vivid picture of that one moment imprinted on his mind forever.

14

Chez Rose

On weekends, the railway gang often hung out in the Quang Ba district on the edge of the city, a red light district favored by the French soldiery. From the city limits, a large dirt road led towards an abandoned tea plantation a kilometer or so away. In between endless rows of stunted or dead tea plants, the surrounding jungle relentlessly crept back in the form of thick, dusty undergrowth, jealously reclaiming land that had been taken by French settlers. Small islands of space had been cleared of bushes and a string of dingy bars-cum-brothels had sprouted, each with its own bright lights, loud record player and large radio set, run by tough madams surrounded by their complement of pimps. Well-worn tracks, lit up with kerosene lanterns that had been strung along wires from branch to branch, led from one bar to another. Inside were small, young, pliable and warm bargirls. Fresh off the farm, they were willing to do anything asked of them for a few extra *piastres*[†]. To the low-life that hung around the old plantation, the huge French soldiers were easy pickings, especially when drunk. Their watches, neck chains, rings, pens and sunglasses were all very saleable at the Thieves' Market in central Ha Noi, not to mention their fat wallets, bursting with money saved up for a night in Quang Ba.

One Saturday evening, the railway boys had targeted a group of French soldiers who were settling down to a drinking spree at the *Chez Rose* bar. It was run by a tough old Vietnamese madam whose name, Hong, meant 'rose' in French. *La mère Rose*, the old biddy Rose, as she

---

[†] *piastres*: French colonial currency.

was known to the French soldiers that frequented her place, sold *bière 33*[†] in the front room while renting out small cubicles and young girls at the back for quickies. A woman of indeterminate age, born with a cigarette in her mouth, she could have been anything between forty and ninety, depending on the time of the day and how drunk you were. Her mouth was a red gash of lipstick; her eyes melodramatically dark with mascara; her cheeks white with powder, with graying hair piled up on top of her head. She wore huge falsies that often slipped around her bony frame and she would pull and tug them back into place as she chain smoked. The French soldiers who frequented *Chez Rose* were fond of her. Most were in their early twenties and could have been her sons. When they had overspent, *la mère Rose* gave them the *cai but*, the pencil, which meant they could sign for their drinks. Sometimes she lent them money when they were hard up.

She had had problems with the railway boys before and kept a sharp eye on them as they flitted in between the seated soldiers, hawking cigarettes, matches, cheap lighters, paper fans and dirty postcards. There were twelve of them that night, more than usual, and she felt uneasy. She nodded to her head pimp, a hoodlum with a scar running diagonally across his entire face, and Scarface casually walked out to the highway to hitch a ride into town, where he headed for the nearest French Military Police post. Saturday nights were always problem nights. It was better to be prepared.

Because it was his first time in Quang Ba, Minh had been posted as the lookout, the easiest job the gang had. He stood by the door, looking up and down the dirt lanes for Vietnamese policemen in civilian clothes. While pretending to patrol the area, they really extorted money from the beer bars, coming up with all sorts of city ordnances that were being violated. The boys feared their own police more than anything. In the Vietnamese culture, children were idolized as long as they were seen as possessing that ultimate Confucian virtue, filial piety. There was no pity wasted on children who disobeyed their parents or who ran away from home. No attempt was made to retrieve their lost innocence and they were chased off, like mangy dogs, when they were not brutally beaten to within an inch of their lives. Polite society had a term for them, *bui doi*, or dust of life, blowing here and there, always unwanted. Minh knew that he belonged to this group, but he was no longer ashamed of it. Nobody wants to help your mother and you,

---

[†] *bière 33*: local French-brand beer

except for Mother Superior and the Saintenoix, and they're all gone now. Now she's sick you have to do everything you can for both of you to survive. It isn't enough to be able to fight, to kick nuts and to masturbate. A man also has to be able to provide for his own family. You are now able to bring back rice almost every day. That's a good start but it's not enough. The Saintenoix money's gone long ago and your mother depends on you and your wits.

While he was on the lookout, a fight started at the bar between two French soldiers, a girl screamed and bottles went flying. The two, both big, strong farm boys, wrestled each other onto the floor, swearing and grunting as they pummeled each other, knocking over tables, chairs, beer bottles and ashtrays. The tiny bargirls stood around them, shrieking. The other soldiers milled around, *bière 33* in hand, shouting encouragement. Over the indescribable cacophony of swearing, screaming, yelling and the sound of things breaking the record player could be heard at full volume. Suddenly a friend of one of the men wrestling on the ground rushed forward and began kicking the other man. His heavy military boots, with metallic studs in the soles, thudded into the back and ribs of one of the farm boys. This attack triggered an immediate response from the other soldiers in the bar, and a general brawl began. *La mère Rose*, her pimps and her girls promptly jumped into the fray to break up the *mêlée* of strong, drunk and ugly French soldiers who were reducing the bar to a rubble heap.

This was what the railway boys had been waiting for. Three took care of the till at the bar, where *la mère Rose* usually sat, and five rushed to the back. Here they slipped under the cardboard partition of the private cubicles, snatched the occupants' pants off the chairs on which they had been hung while the owners were busy fornicating on the wooden cots. They whipped the wallets out and ran back into the bar. The other four boys, all star pickpockets, were busy working the brawl, lifting wallets, sunglasses and pocket pens, snatching neck chains and watches. They methodically worked the outer edges of the free-for-all, staying away from the powerful punches and kicks that the enraged French soldiers were throwing around.

La mère Rose, a veteran of bar fights with scars to prove it, was in the middle of it all, a cigarette in her red mouth. One drunken soldier had grabbed her by the arm and wouldn't let go. She screamed at him, calling him a *salaud* and a *cochon*[†] and tried to scratch his thick face,

[†] *salaud*: son of a bitch; *cochon*: pig

but he slapped her with a huge paw and she felt her teeth rattle in her head. So she just stood there, eyes gleaming with hatred, one large falsie hitched up under her chin, the other under her armpit, mascara running down her face, wondering what had happened to the Military Police she had alerted earlier.

Minh had turned to watch the fight, forgetting he was on watch duty. More soldiers had joined in, one bar girl was knocked senseless to the floor, tables and chairs flew around the room. Suddenly he felt a strong pair of hands grab him by the scruff of his neck. A glancing blow to the side of his head stunned him, and he literally saw stars spinning around. The next moment he was being hustled along away from the bar towards what looked like a black French police wagon. The man who was half-carrying him was so strong that Minh's feet hardly ever touched the floor. When they arrived at the police van, the French policeman put him down and he instinctively went straight for the man's groin. But this was no street boy. He had been trained in unarmed combat, and he casually blocked the short, vicious kick with one thick leg and Minh felt his skinny shinbone disintegrate. The pain was excruciating. The policeman then threw a massive punch straight into Minh's face, picked him up bodily and literally threw him into the van, where he landed with a thud that jarred every bone in his body. Soon the other railway gang boys joined him, as well as the teenage prostitutes and their respective pimps. Everyone had a swollen lip or a serious nosebleed or the beginning of a black eye. Many had large bumps on their heads. A third black wagon drew up and a dozen French soldiers, all protesting loudly, were unceremoniously bundled in. The sickeningly dull sounds of wooden batons thudding on shoulders, arms and bare heads, alternating with screams and grunts of pain, could be heard distinctly as burly French MPs, the *Police Militaire*, cleaned out the place in their own time-honored way. *La mère Rose*, looking much the worse for wear, could be heard screeching and yelling in execrable pidgin French that the soldiers hadn't paid their bills for the beers drunk and damage done. The MP sergeant told her, not unkindly, to accompany them to the station where she could file a complaint. From all around the hollow, other French soldiers appeared, a bargirl in one hand and a *bière 33* in the other, to watch the proceedings. Advice of all sorts was yelled at the girls, the pimps, the pickpockets and the French military as they sat in the MP's Black Maria wagons. Just before the doors slammed shut, Minh thought he saw Hélène, who was hanging onto the arm of a French soldier. One hand was casually in front of her mouth, holding a handkerchief that cleverly hid her harelip. He tried to stand up to call out to her but his damaged leg gave way under him as the van roared off towards the city.

Within minutes, the Quang Ba denizens had returned to their preoccupations. The night air in between the trees, bushes and stumps welled up with music, yells, screams, whooping and hollering as the soldiers and the bar girls let their hair down while the madams collected fistfuls of cash. Saturday nights were always lively.

15

La Police Militaire

Once at the station, they were separated into two groups and ordered to sit on the floor in different corners of the room. *La mère Rose*, her pimps and girls, many with torn clothes, cuts and bruises showing, squatted in one corner, and the railway boys, all whimpering and groaning exaggeratedly in an effort to win sympathy from the French policemen, squatted in the other. In Minh's case there was no need for exaggeration. The bridge of his nose was dead to the touch, he had a huge lump sticking out over his left ear, both his eyes were rapidly swelling and he just knew that he would never walk again.

The twenty-seven French soldiers netted in the raid were told to stand at ease along one wall. They formed up, hands joined behind them, knees slightly flexed. The ones who had started the fight whispered to one another to try and co-ordinate their stories. The MPs fanned out. Two blocked the door, the others positioned themselves around the soldiers. A couple smacked their heavy mahogany batons rhythmically into thick, muscular palms, their eyes sweeping balefully over the unhappy lineup. The sergeant sat down at his desk and looked expressionlessly at each group. The weight of his blue eyeballs, as they swiveled slowly around the room, was unbearable and absolute silence returned. Slowly, with measured movements, he opened a desk drawer and set out a ledger, a pen and an inkpot. When he was good and ready, he simply grunted at the nearest soldier, without even looking up. It was obvious he had done this before. The man snapped to attention and reported his name, rank and unit. It looked like he had also done this before. Many times, perhaps. After all the twenty seven names had been duly recorded, the sergeant asked who had started the fight. Two men stepped forward who looked as if they had survived a train crash. They barked out their names, rank and serial numbers and were promptly shoved into the holding cell behind the sergeant. The sergeant looked up and down the line. "You, you and you two," he said, and burly MPs hustled four more men into the barren cell, which could hold ten men standing up. They had been picked out because they looked as if they had been in the thick of the fight, with torn clothes, black eyes and bleeding noses.

"You six will stay here until you are returned under escort to your units tomorrow noon. If I hear one peep out of you, there will be some broken heads tonight," said the sergeant. Eyes downcast, the men rapidly worked out who would sleep where in preparation for a long and uncomfortable night. They looked like men for whom a weekend in the brig was not a new experience.

"Wait," said the sergeant, as the MP corporal was about to snap the huge padlock shut. "We may have some more guests for the night," he added, looking at the railroad boys. A collective shiver ran through them at the thought of being locked up in the same holding cells as six large French soldiers.

The sergeant then asked if anyone had any complaints against the madam, the girls, the pimps or the pickpockets. The twenty-one men left started checking their pockets. Five soldiers, who had been busy in the cubicles at the back at the time of the brawl, had lost their wallets. Seven others had lost various items, mainly watches. One had lost a gold chain. All this was carefully written down and these thirteen soldiers were ordered to remain behind while the other eight were allowed to leave. These men stepped up to the desk smartly, saluted the sergeant, wheeled around and marched out in line, with straight backs, chests out, stomach in, but as quietly as possible, delighted that they were getting off so lightly. Once outside, they burst into laughter, slapped each other on the back, lit up cigarettes and headed straight back to Quang Ba. The night was still young, tomorrow was Sunday, barracks cleanup day. After that, one week of dull, square-bashing days that was the lot of a soldier in peacetime. All that could wait. Now was the time for more cold beer and hot pussy. If only those two assholes hadn't started a fight, they said to each other, we would all still be there, a beer in one hand and the other over that most delightful piece of the Indochinese female anatomy, the hairless snatch.

Inside the MP station, the sergeant turned to the motley group of Vietnamese. "Anybody speaks French?" he asked. A large man, a ruddy, mottled face, a bulbous nose and pale brown hair. His blue eyes were flat and hard but his voice sounded bored. Ever alert in spite of his lumps, bumps and bleeding nose, Minh saw an opportunity. He had been feeling out his shins with both hands and now knew that the leg was not broken. His spirits had risen. "I do, sir," he said, his voice quavering, breathing with difficulty.

He then stood up, holding on to the nearest wall. His nose was bent out of shape, veering towards the right. It hurt like hell and only one nostril worked. All the railway boys looked at him, as if seeing him for the first time. The Nut Kicker could speak French! None of them had known this, a secret his mother and he had jealously kept from the railway bridge occupants. The sergeant looked at him carefully.

"Is your nose broken?" he asked. Minh thought he saw concern in the big man's eyes.

"I don't know, sir," he answered, fingering the strange lump on his face. It was totally numb.

"I'll have someone look at it later. Where did you learn French?"

"At the convent, sir, and also at *Albert Sarraut.*"

Minh looked around at his peers as he said this, and he could see their eyes widen and the familiar swear words slowly forming on their lips. He remembered how some of them had made it hard for him to join them, and a thrill of pleasure shot through him.

The sergeant's eyebrows furrowed as he mulled this new development over. Convent and *Albert Sarraut,* and now a grimy pickpocket in a bar in Quang Ba district. He shook his head in disbelief and snorted.

"Come here, boy. What's your name?"

"Minh, sir."

A corporal stepped forward.

"Sergeant sir, this is the boy I caught at the door of the bar, sir. He was their lookout, sir. He tried to kick me, sir. Here, sir." He pointed at his groin and then stepped back smartly.

Minh looked at him. Young, brawny, thick hairy forearms, huge fists. The fucker punched you straight in the face and threw you through the air into the truck. Fuck me… if only you could be strong like him!

"Alright, Minh, you can be the interpreter tonight. First, I want the wallets and watches and gold chain returned now, otherwise the boys go into that cell," he said, pointing to the first cell, "and the girls into that cell," pointing to a second cell that was much smaller and which contained a single military cot. He paused. "When I say everybody, I mean **everybody**!" he added, his voice raising in an ugly way, pointing to both the railway boys and the *Chez Rose* group. "Otherwise I'll transfer you all to the Vietnamese municipal police tomorrow. You know what happens in a Vietnamese prison."

Still holding onto the wall, Minh cleared his throat, looked around at everyone and then carefully translated what the sergeant had said. A heavy silence followed while the message sank in. The railway boys had now forgotten all about his prowess in French and were focused on more immediate matters. Across the room, *la mère Rose* and her pimps glared at the boys. The girls could stay back if the French MPs wanted to have some fun with them, even for free, but there was no way she and her pimps were going to spend the night locked up because of what the railway boys had done. If they didn't own up and everyone did end up in a small cell, the pimps would kill the boys during the night, and the railway boys knew it.

"Minh, tell them I don't have all night. In five minutes, either the goods have been returned or everyone gets locked up," the sergeant said, jerking his thumb over his shoulder in the direction of the two cells.

Slowly, a wallet appeared, followed by a watch. There was a pause, then the other missing items were laid on the floor. It was all there.

"Pick up what's yours, and check it," said the sergeant, addressing the soldiers.

They crossed the floor, took back their belongings and returned to their former positions.

"Anything missing, or damaged?" asked the sergeant. To nod meant filling out forms, filing charges and having to return to the MP post the next day. They all wanted to get out of that post as soon as possible, go to another bar, throw down a few more drinks before returning to barracks. All shook their heads emphatically.

"Good, that's settled then. You all can go home now. This report will be on your commanding officer's desk by Monday morning. You soldiers should be more careful when you go out, get drunk and make trouble."

Having disposed of the French soldiers, the big sergeant now turned to the Vietnamese groups.

"What else is missing?" he asked, looking at the railway boys. *La mère Rose's* eyes narrowed and her pimps half-rose on their haunches in anticipation. Wads of wrinkled *piastres* and piles of coins that had been stolen during the fight suddenly appeared from nowhere. Scarface scuttled forward on all fours and scooped it all up. He then stopped and glared at the gang's leader, who slowly pulled out more *piastres* from the inside of his khaki shorts. Scarface grunted, scuttled back to his corner and handed the pile to *la mère Rose* who stuffed the lot into her handbag.

The sergeant stepped forward.

"You boys and girls should consider yourselves very lucky I don't turn you over to the Vietnamese police. Now you," he said, looking at the madam, "I suggest you just go home and forget about the whole thing. Don't forget, you run a bar where there are thieves and pickpockets preying on French soldiers, and you sell under-aged girls, which is forbidden under French law. If you file charges against the soldiers, I have to file charges against you."

Minh translated all this painstakingly.

"Tell him I don't want to file charges," she answered in Vietnamese, with resignation in her voice and anger on her face. He repeated her statement to the sergeant, who nodded and smiled at her. After some hesitation, she smiled back at him. They had obviously known each other for some time now, and this was not the first time she had been invited to the station. He could see the sergeant had a soft spot for her. A tough old lady but a fair one. Many a time she had lent money to a French soldier so that he could buy back something he had pawned in order to have instant cash to court the new love of his life. Many a time she had treated a young soldier who had caught an unmentionable disease, whether *Chez Rose* or elsewhere, by applying a homemade lotion of herbs that killed germs and making him drink a bowl of dark, bitter, foul smelling concoction, to wash his insides. It was safe to say that all the military police officers knew *la mère Rose*, either personally or by reputation.

The sergeant walked up to the railway boys who had returned the stolen goods.

"**EVERYBODY OUT!**" he barked in parade voice, startling them out of their wits.

There was an instant scramble and Minh also began making a move, painful as his leg was.

"Except you," said the big French sergeant, turning to him. His heart sank and he looked at the big man with fear. Viet Nam was full of stories about how old Frenchmen often enjoyed the company of very young boys, and how there was nothing fatherly about it. He had heard the phrase "nice 'n tight" in connection with this, but he wasn't sure what it meant and didn't want to find out.

16

Sergeant Escudier

Everyone scuttled out, including *La mère Rose*, relief flooding their hearts. They couldn't believe that the military police had been so lenient. But as soon as they were outside, Scarface whipped out a knife, followed by the other pimps, all experienced street fighters. They surrounded the railway boys, grabbing them by their hair and jerking their heads back, holding shiny blades against their throats. *La mère Rose*, uttering expletives worthy of a French *Légionnaire*, swore at the immobilized boys and slapped them as hard as she could, scratching them with her long, filthy nails. She then spat on each of their faces and kicked them in the nuts as hard as she could. After she had finished, the pimps laid in with a few heavier blows of their own.

"The next time I see any of you boys in my bar I'll have my boys throw boiling water in your faces. Remember that!" she screamed at them. She then heaved her two falsies into place, primped her bedraggled hair, pulled her dress down to show a tiny waistline and marched off energetically, her head high, her dignity intact. The girls and the pimps followed in silence. Having been through such episodes before, they knew what would happen. The French soldiers would all come back next weekend, like overgrown schoolboys, sheepishly make up with *la mère Rose* and the girls, settle the bills for broken furniture and unpaid beers and the *Chez Rose* bar would become a big, happy family again. And, like cockroaches, the railway gang would come creeping back, one by one, when all was forgiven, and life would continue as normal. Until the next *fracas*.

Inside the MP station, everyone relaxed, except Minh. The sergeant had gone to the small toilet room near the second cell, where the splash of his urine resonated loudly. Minh briefly thought of dashing out through the doorway, now that all the MPs had put their batons down and were loosening their tight, broad leather belts in preparation to getting some sleep for the night. But you can't even stand up. Where the fuck could you run to? Oh my god, when everyone goes to bed where will you sleep. All sorts of rumors and bits and pieces of information he had imbibed from talking to friends in the railway gang came back to him now. The French are well known for their sexual appetites, especially the huge black soldiers, *les Sénégalais*, with scars on their faces. They do it with animals as well as boys and girls, and women too. Then there are the Arabs, *les Marocains*, smaller in size and brown in color. Insatiable, they do it all night, even with menstruating women. The younger white soldiers generally like drinking and young girls. They don't chase after young boys, but the older ones might. What's going to happen to you?

Finally, the sergeant came out of the toilet, sat down at his desk and called Minh over. He also called one of his men, a corporal who knew first aid. The man examined Minh's nose, gently bending it this way and that. "It isn't broken," he said, "and it will regain its natural shape eventually. You are still young." In the meantime, cold compresses and aspirins would ease the pain. Minh was handed a wet towel, and he held it over his nose as the big corporal looked on with concern. He then looked at Minh's shinbone, running his thick fingers gently up and down. "Nothing broken," he said, "just a bump." Minh was given two pills and a glass of water. "They're pain killers," said the medic, "to make you sleep better."

The sergeant, whose name was Escudier, asked Minh about his family, and he told him about his mother. He asked him about his home, and Minh told him about the railway bridge. He asked him about his education, and Minh told him about the convent and the Saintenoix. Escudier's eyes lit up at the mention of the Saintenoix name. He obviously knew of *Monsieur* François Saintenoix. He asked Minh what he wanted to do in life, and Minh told him he wanted to become somebody so he could take care of his mother. Escudier smiled when Minh said this, and the boy suddenly sensed that the older man was a kind man. His instincts, finely honed from the days of a drunken grandmother, told him there was nothing to fear from this man. He relaxed and began to feel comfortable sitting there in front of the French sergeant, answering his questions without even thinking. He felt he could trust the big man.

After a while, Escudier looked at him quizzically, his blue eyes penetrating deep into the boy's soul. He reached for a pack of *Gauloise* cigarettes and lit one up. The acrid smell of black tobacco instantly filled the room. He blew out a cloud of smoke in Minh's direction, looking steadily at him all the time.

"Well, Minh, this is your lucky day," he said finally. "You are a very lucky young man. You have two fathers. Your real father, whom you may not know, but whom your mother does. Whatever kind of man he is, or was, I am certain that he would love you today if he saw you. Men do certain things in certain circumstances, and we mustn't judge them too hastily."

Minh looked at the big man expressionlessly, his mind racing. *Your real father doesn't cares whether you're dead or alive, but better not argue the point. This good man wants to help. You real father doesn't want you or your mother because we aren't good enough for him. He's rich and educated and we aren't.* Tears sprang to his eyes. Tough as he had become over the last two years, and determined as he had always been, he often sank into bouts of self-pity whenever he thought about the situation his mother and he had been left in, although he always tried to control these moments of weakness in case anyone was watching.

"And now you'll have a second father," the sergeant was saying, nodding his head. Minh had no idea what he was talking about.

"Yes, I shall become your second father and you will become my second son. Maybe one day you'll find your real father again, maybe not, but in the meantime you'll have a father and your mother will have a home."

Sergeant Escudier then told him he would adopt him and his mother for as long as he stayed in Viet Nam. They would stay with him at *la Citadelle.*

"You remind me of my son," he said by way of explanation. "His name starts with an M, for Mathieu," he added, laughing. "Maybe it's a good sign. Also, whenever I ask him what he wants to do when he grows up, he always says he wants to become an important person so he can protect his mother. Just like you did."

Minh sat there nonplussed, not knowing what to say. *Your name isn't Minh. It isn't even Robert. But it was Meo, and that starts with an M, like Mathieu. Better not confuse this good man.*

"Pasquier," the sergeant called out to the corporal who had applied first aid, "check on my new son before you go to sleep, will you?"

Across the room, a young man who was undressing for the night answered "Yessir". Later, he walked over to Minh's cot and gently felt the bridge of his nose with his thumb and forefinger, then gave him a cold compress to hold over it. Next to him stood the young soldier who had punched Minh in the face. He looked with a wry face at the flattened nose and the two enormous black eyes and shook his head. He then put out his hand and, after some hesitation, Minh shook it firmly. They smiled at each other.

"Sorry," said the young soldier.

"It's OK," Minh answered. He knew the soldier was genuinely sorry. That's because you speak French. Otherwise they wouldn't be so kind to you. *Madame* Louise, Étienne and the sergeant were all friendly because you can speak their language. Lucky you started out your new life in that convent.

After a while the lights were switched off and the chit chatting between the policemen died down. Lying in the dark, floating on waves of guttural snores that came from all around him, Minh felt more relaxed than he had been for weeks. His nose hurt, his eyes were swollen and the middle rack of the three cross bars in the military cot cut across his spinal column but he didn't mind. A new door has opened. Our lives will change from tomorrow. No more filthy bridge. Mother can eat regularly, receive medicine for her lungs, maybe you can get a job. Even go to school again. Things are looking up. It was lucky that fight *Chez Rose* started. You are so lucky. He cracked a smile in the dark, even though it hurt every muscle in his face.

17

Papa's Radio

The next day they moved their worldly belongings into Sergeant Escudier's barracks inside the French Capital Military Garrison Command, known as *la Citadelle*. During the first few days, Sergeant Escudier questioned him some more about their background. His questions followed a systematic pattern, covering all the important points first, then zeroing on the secondary and tertiary points, slowly boxing a person in, leaving no stone unturned. After a while, he would return to the points already answered, but from another direction, to check for inconsistencies. Much later in life, when Minh worked in intelligence, he recognized this method of questioning but at the time he was surprised why Sergeant Escudier kept on asking about the same thing in a different manner all the time. He had no problem answering him, however, because he had decided simply to tell the truth. Escudier listened carefully, nodding every now and again. He smelt of leather and tobacco and, from close, the pores in the skin of his face were huge. His hard blue eyes, normally placid, narrowed to slits as he juggled the answers around, often returning to the first answer to confirm the veracity of the second.

Your new father is intelligent. Even cunning. He is a lot more educated than the other French military. His language is polite, none of the vulgar swearwords that the French soldiers use all the time.

As it later turned out, this remarkable man was a highly complicated and sophisticated person who led many lives, a fact that very few people knew at the time. He knew all about *Ma Mère Supérieure* and told Minh about her background, the good work she did and the very strong influence she had with the French government in Indochina. He also knew everything about *Monsieur* Saintenoix and explained how French society in Indochina worked and where Monsieur Saintenoix stood, at its very peak, with the *Gouverneur Général*. Through this exchange of information Minh was eventually able to piece together the last few years of his life, and he came to understand things about the convent and the Saintenoix family that he had missed at the time.

In the meantime, Escudier had his mother examined by a military doctor who at once put her on medication to control her TB. He said this was necessary because she would be handling food while cooking for Sergeant Escudier. This was the first time they knew there was a link between TB and cooking. Minh's crooked nose returned more or less to its original shape although he had problems breathing through his left nostril at night when he slept on his right side. The unusual shape of the nose, in addition to his globular, yellow flecked eyes, gave off an impression of calculating hardness, even wildness that was in complete contrast to the soft and polite way he spoke.

Minh was allowed to sit in at a military school that taught basic French and military subjects to Vietnamese levies recruited into the French forces. He sat quietly at the back of the class and no one paid any attention to him. At *Albert Saurrat* he had been *un cas spécial* thanks to *Monsieur* Saintenoix, and here he was, a special case again, thanks to *papa*, who had great influence over things in the camp. Both his mother and he had been told by Sergeant Escudier to call him *papa* from now on, to simplify matters. He always spoke in French to *papa* and his mother spoke her pidgin French to him, while between them they always used Vietnamese, which *papa* understood a little. There is no *p* sound in the Vietnamese alphabet and she couldn't pronounce *papa*, so she called him *baba*. This always made him smile, because *baba* is the Vietnamese name for a terrapin snapping turtle.

In *papa*'s kitchen sat an imposing radio set the size of a small trunk. It was made of polished wood, varnished in different shades of black and brown, had big buttons that one pushed and a large dial that one twiddled around to tune in to different stations. After the convent and *Albert Saurrat*, this *poste de radio* became the next step in Minh's education, with the railway bridge a dead period in between. The *Voix de L'Indochine* broadcasts out of Sai Gon could be heard daily in French and in Vietnamese every evening. News about Indochina and abroad came over the airwaves and opened up his horizons, making him aware about things he never knew existed. *Papa* subscribed to a number of magazines from France that devoted much space and photographs to historical, cultural and war stories. He thus learned how many horses Alexander the Great had in his army, how long it took to build the pyramids and how France's army had triumphed over Germany in 1918, at the time his mother and he had entered the convent. *Papa* also brought back a French newspaper every evening that he read avidly the next day between attending classes. Geography taught where men live, history taught what great men have done and newspapers taught what was happening around them. Above all he loved history. Words that he couldn't understand he looked up in *papa's* dictionary. As he soaked up these bits and pieces of knowledge, he acquired hundreds of new French words in the process. Between the radio, the magazines and the newspapers, he was able to begin to understand subjects and issues that had only been vague notions in his mind until then. He soon began to make a conscious effort to connect them into a whole. He had learnt from his convent and Saintenoix days that everything was linked to everything else and an educated man could connect things and use this knowledge to make himself more important and powerful. Having seen the fate that awaited people without an education, he became determined to pursue this understanding in order to ensure his future.

The first thing he learnt was that Ha Noi wasn't the center of the world. There were many important countries in the world, beyond Viet Nam, and even beyond France. There was Japan, which had a new Emperor, named Hirohito. Twenty-five years earlier, Japan had defeated Russia, the first time an Asian power had beaten a European power. There was a new Russia, where Lenin had died a few years earlier and a man named Stalin had taken over. Then there was China, where a revolution had killed millions. Its leader, Sun Yat Sen, had just died and his brother-in-law, named Chiang Kai-shek, had replaced him. Finally there was America, where President Coolidge presided over the "Roaring Twenties", a huge and rich economy that attracted millions of Europeans, including Frenchmen. He realized for the first time that the Vietnamese, like his mother and him and everyone in their village, had come from southern China thousands of years before. They resented their giant neighbor for its bullying ways but at the same time they secretly admired its sophistication and had adapted many facets of its culture to their customs and traditions.

The more he learnt, the more surprised he was at how things were connected. A push in Europe ended up in a shove in Asia, half a world away. When the Turkish Empire collapsed, France and Germany went to war and hundreds of thousands of Vietnamese were shipped to French factories to free up young Frenchmen for the battlefields in Europe. While France and Germany were near each other on the map, Viet Nam and Turkey were half-a-world away and he couldn't find Ankara at first.

Another thing he learnt was what colonization was all about greed. Strong countries raped weak ones while pretending that it was an act of love. Everything *Monsieur* Saintenoix had told him about France's conquests abroad came back. It all fitted in now, and he began to understand what the *mission civilisatrice Monsieur* Saintenoix always talked about really meant. It was about might being right. The man with a gun could impose his will on the man with a spear and then turn him into a slave under the pretense of civilizing him. He now understood why Étienne's expression had always turned ironic whenever his father lectured him on France's work abroad. But the French weren't the only colonizers. England had seized parts of China and all of India; the Dutch had taken Indonesia; the Belgians and Spaniards had grabbed dozens of countries in Africa and Asia. The Chinese had invented powder and used it as fireworks for merrymaking and keeping evil spirits at bay, but the whites had thought of using it in their matchlock muskets. A few hundred men with firearms could mow down thousands who still fought with bows and arrows, and it seemed that the men with guns were always white.

He also began to understand more about the limitations of Jesus and God, who had appeared all-important to him at the convent. Millions of Chinese, Africans and white men were not Catholics and yet they lived normal lives. They didn't know their catechism but they didn't go to Hell, because they didn't believe in Jesus in the first place. He concluded it was therefore alright for his mother and him not to believe in Christianity either. He felt better after that. It had been bothering him for some time, a sneaking feeling that perhaps the Christian gods were right and that everyone else but his mother and he would be saved when the time came. It was now obvious to him that France used Catholicism in Viet Nam to win converts to their way of life. They talked people into following their way of thinking, colonizing their minds. Religion had been the wedge in the door. Behind the Catholics came the traders, opening the door a little wider. Finally, to protect the Catholics and the traders came the Army, flinging the door wide open, guns at the ready, flying the *mission civilisatrice* banner high, and that was that. The seduction stage was over, it was time for the rape. He wondered if his real father was a Catholic. If he were, there'd be two reasons for hating him now.

As time went on, from listening to the radio and from reading *papa*'s books and newspapers, he began to see the duality that existed in everything. Where there was colonialism, there was resistance, called nationalism, the love one had for one's country. In Africa, China and India, the natives revolted every now and again. They couldn't shake off their white masters, but they didn't stop trying. Even in Viet Nam, many Vietnamese refused to accept being civilized by the French and were fighting back. Some nationalists went into self-exile abroad to find a solution to French colonization. The one the French hated the most was one Phan Boi Chau, who had escaped to Japan and had been writing political tracts against French rule. And radio news from Paris was full of details about peasant uprisings in the provinces of Nghe An and Ha Tinh in central Viet Nam. The French Army had crushed the rebels, who had tried to set up *soviets,* workers' parties; but in Viet Nam neither the newspapers nor the radio carried any news about this. He discovered he could learn more about what was going in his country by listening to radio news from France than from Sai Gon.

18

Papa's Perspective

As Minh's education at home advanced, questions came out of nowhere that needed serious answers, and even when he thought he had answered them he couldn't be sure that he was right. How do people become important and have power? Not Lenin, Coolidge, Sarraut and other really important world figures, not even middle level people like your real father or *Monsieur* Saintenoix, who are born rich and famous, but people from humbler beginnings who become powerful and respected. Like *papa* or *Ma Mère Supérieure*. How did they make themselves important in society? After much thinking, he concluded that the Mother Superior was important because she believed in Catholicism, *papa* in *l'armée française,* and *Monsieur* Saintenoix in his *mission civilisatrice.* They all believed in a superior cause and they had become a part of that superior cause. What cause can you associate yourself with to become somebody? Does simply joining a cause make you important, or do you have to work for many years at it before you become somebody?

You are a Vietnamese boy, your adoptive father is a Frenchman, a good man who picked you and your mother up from a rubbish dump and now treats you like real people, as if you were real family. But *papa* is a military. Thanks to his radio and magazines you now know how the French military took your country by force. There are many Vietnamese in the mountains, fighting against the French. Where does that leave you?

At fourteen, Minh felt he was a man already and he desperately wanted to give his mother a better life, but he had a hard time thinking abstract thoughts through to a conclusion. He felt he should ask *papa* about it but he hesitated for a long time. He feared the nature of some of his questions might make *papa* think he was becoming rebellious, that he wasn't grateful for his help. When he finally approached him, *papa* laughed and teased him about being so serious, but when he saw Minh was making a real effort to understand the realities of life, he got himself a beer and a pack of cigarettes, loosened his belt, relaxed and sat down at the kitchen table.

"I am always surprised at how like Mathieu you are. He's also so serious about things and always wants to become somebody important. I'm not sure what it is you are looking for but I am going to try to give you the benefit of my experience," he said, laughing, his big head thrown backward, and Minh settled down to the first of many such talks, drawn out over a number of months, with his *papa*—adopted father, mentor, teacher and friend all rolled in one.

Because Minh' questions were wide-ranging and often unconnected, *papa* couldn't stick to a logical presentation of facts and ideas, as he would have wished, being a military man, and Minh absorbed important things bit by bit, in a disjointed manner. At the time, he understood only half of what *papa* was saying, but well before the time Minh had become known as the Grey Tiger, it had all jelled together and he was able to grasp the full import of his *papa*'s pragmatism and wisdom. To this day, he still remembered word for word the most important issues they covered.

"The modern world is a family of countries," *papa* said on that first day, "made up of tribes that have something in common. In each tribe there are families that have something in common and in each family there are individuals, like you and me and your mother, who have something in common. Countries, tribes, families and people who have something in common tend to form groups in order to defend their common interests. Banding and bonding."

"What do they have in common?"

"Language, religion, geography, history and culture. A vision based on shared experience. They see things the same way, so they end up thinking the same way and then doing things the same way. When banding and bonding take place on a small scale, that's the beginning of a tribe, the nucleus of a nation."

Minh nodded. He had more or less come to the same conclusions although at that stage he couldn't figure out what tribe he and his mother belonged to.

"But I don't have a vision, *papa*," he said, crestfallen.

Papa laughed. "Like Mathieu, you're too young to have one right now, but later, what you know, what you want and what you think will create an image that you have of yourself. You will then have a vision of how your life should be. The more educated you become, the more knowledge you have, the larger your vision becomes. Education enlarges our world and makes our vision clearer."

"You're right, *papa*! My world was very small when I came here but your *poste de radio* is making it bigger every day," he answered, making *papa* laugh.

"Right, son. Imagine how ignorant we would be if we didn't have books to read or a radio to listen to. Education is very important, whether you get it from schools or in the streets."

"The streets?"

"Yes, like you. After a few years at the convent and *Albert Sarraut*, your education continued under the railway bridge. That's learning from the streets."

"Which is more important, learning at school or in the streets?"

"Both are important and they complement each other. You told me you played football at school, right? Well, whether you play football in a sports stadium or in the streets or in a field full of cow dung, what's important is that you play, because it allows you to learn how to improve your game. Education is not only learning facts; education is learning how to learn. Learning is a process that will only stop when you die, and you cannot stay in school all your life!"

On another day they broached the subject of control.

"Having educated yourself, having enlarged your vision, having found your place in the world, you will want to move ahead, to be successful. To do this, there are two laws you must remember: the strong will always seek to dominate the weak and the weak will do anything to survive. Everything in society comes from these two opposing forces."

"Why, *papa*?"

"Because life is based on nature, and nature is based on survival of the fittest, where every living thing struggles for a better place under the sun. The winners survive and the losers die so that the world can move forward. From this natural order, which is often ruthless and brutal, comes progress."

"How does a person become strong?"

"By teaming up with people who think like him, the banding and bonding we have spoken about. One man can do little by himself, but with the support of a thousand men he can move mountains and change the course of rivers."

"After we join a group of people who think like us, how can we dominate the others in the same group?"

"By showing a quality called leadership."

"What's that?" This was getting interesting.

"In the olden days, when we were monkeys, force was our main weapon. We used muscles. Today, we are half-men, half-monkeys, and we use a mixture of force and persuasion. Perhaps in a few thousand years, when we are completely men, we will use only persuasion."

Minh thought back to the railway gang days, not so far away. You were just a monkey then. So were the others.

"How do you persuade someone to follow your leadership?"

"Make him believe that your vision will bring him what he wants. Businessmen promise money, politicians promise power, priests promise eternal life. When people believe in your vision, you have control over them. Together, as a large group, you can then take over smaller groups, grow bigger and resist being dominated by larger groups." He paused, saw Minh's puzzled frown and looked questioningly at him. "What?"

"Persuading many people is very difficult because everybody wants something different. I know because I tried this under the bridge."

"Right, you cannot motivate everybody, but, with practice, you will find the one thing that the majority of the people want at that time, and you can start by focusing on that."

"How can we lead without leading? Without standing up in front of everyone and giving orders?"

"Aha! That's what you want, is it? Why, son?"

"I don't know, *papa*. I'm not timid and I can fight, but I don't like to stand out in a crowd. Maybe because of my background..."

"Minh, whatever your background is, it is a unique one, it is perfect for you and you have nothing to be ashamed of. But to answer your question, persuade the leader to listen to you. It is easier to persuade one man than many."

"How do I do this?"

"Same technique as the leader uses to persuade a group of people. Figure out what he wants, help him get it, become his adviser!"

Minh remembered having done this under the bridge, when he was trying to build his position in that hierarchy of vagabonds and delinquents. He was pleased to see that he had known what to do even before meeting up with *papa*. Things are falling into place. You are beginning to understand things.

"Is that what you are doing, *papa?*" he asked. He had meant to ask him this for some time.

His adoptive father paused a long time, his large blue eyes turning hard. He is wondering if he should tell me the truth or not. Finally he said "Yes, son, that's what I do. Officially I am a sergeant in the Military Police and I take my orders from a lieutenant. Unofficially, I work for Military Intelligence, the *Deuxième Bureau*, and I keep watch over our officers, over civilians like Saintenoix and over all kinds of Vietnamese activists who want to fight us. I report directly to my real superior, a colonel."

"*Monsieur* Saintenoix?" Minh asked, surprised. "What can such an important man be guilty of?"

"Yes, Saintenoix. He and many others like him manipulate the currency exchange rates and make millions each year, hurting the government in Paris," answered *papa*, his eyes twinkling. "He also has Vietnamese mistresses and the Church here asked Paris to replace him."

Minh took some time to digest all this. Now you understand *Monsieur* Saintenoix's behavior towards his wife. You had more or less guessed something like that. That's why he was suddenly recalled to Paris. *Ma Mère Supérieure* Marie had the ear of the *Gouverneur Général*. With the Church and the Government against him, no wonder *Monsieur* Saintenoix left so quickly when the time came. It's funny how bits and pieces of information and impressions are now coming back, making a whole. The more you talk, the more you understand. *Papa* knows a lot. That's why the officers respect him although he's only a sergeant. That's why no one ever picks a quarrel with him. That's why he receives visitors at home in a private room, why he doesn't go to work every day like the others.

On another occasion, causes and ideologies came up.

"Where do causes come from?" Minh asked.

"From the human mind," *papa* said, tapping his head with a thick forefinger. "First comes the idea. When people think that idea is perfect, it becomes an ideal. When more people support it, it becomes an ideology, then a vision, finally a cause. When there are enough people behind the cause, they make laws to strengthen the cause and to propagate it among mankind. These laws, called policies, make up a framework that can be used to protect a cause like Catholicism, or capitalism or democracy."

"Does each country have its own cause?"

"Not really. Most of the time, causes are universal, drawing together people and races from all over the world. Democracy, for example, is a cause that attracts many countries in the world. The way a cause is carried out, however, may differ from country to country."

"How do we know which cause is best?"

"In the end, they're all the same. Today this cause is the right one, tomorrow it's another. New causes replace old ones."

"Why?"

"Because a country renews itself every year with millions of new babies, while the men who dreamed up this or that cause die of old age and their visions eventually die along with them. Countries have to stay young so there must be change."

"How can we know which cause to support?"

"That depends on the individual. At the personal level, like for you or me, it all depends on our character. Each cause demands something from you, like total belief, or total obedience, or total sacrifice, sometimes all three. Each cause has its own policies which serve as a control apparatus, and these rules and regulations affect us directly. Everyone wants democracy, which came to us Europeans from Greece, but in practice today's democracy has become quite different, and it continues to differ from country to country. You must choose a cause that has policies you can live with, otherwise daily life becomes unbearable. Also, as you grow older, you tend to grow out of a cause. Since no cause is absolutely right or totally wrong, whichever you feel comfortable with is the best one for you."

"How about you, *papa*? What cause do you support?"

"Well, I'm French and I support democracy and social justice. In France, our ideology is expressed by the words *Liberté–Egalité–Fraternité*."

"Yes, *papa*, I learned about LEF at *Albert Saurrat*. Do you PPT?"

"*Pas pour toi?*" *papa* burst out laughing. "Where did you learn that? That's for the intellectuals and leftists who don't approve of our colonial adventures abroad. Like here, for example."

"I don't understand what leftists are, *papa*. Anyway, does the French Army support LEF?"

"Of course. It fights to uphold the LEF cause."

"Then why is PPT true? Why is there no LEF for us in Indochina?"

"There is some already, and more will come later. It took France five hundred years and many wars before it could become the democracy it is today. It can't be taught in one generation!"

Minh took some time to digest this. The longer the lesson, the more the teacher can steal from the student.

"I see. Are all causes good?"

"No, of course not. A cause has both good and bad in it, although very often one man can see only the good while another only the bad. Both are partly wrong but that is their choice and they will have to live with it. Remember, however, that a good cause can turn bad if its policies do not change with the times, and a bad one at the start can become good if its policies adapt to the times. It all depends on whether the people who support the cause are willing to change with the times."

"How complicated, *papa*! Can we know how a cause will turn out?"

"We can't. We just pick one we feel best answers our vision today and support it one hundred percent. If its policies become unacceptable, we must also change and find another cause to support. This happens a lot in free countries like France."

"So abandoning one cause for another is all right?"

"Yes, but choice is a luxury that exists only in really free societies. In countries where people have the right to choose what they want to support or to believe in, people can change religions, political parties and even nationalities. In many countries in the world people don't have that choice. They are told to believe in this or that, to support this or that and if they want to change they are punished."

"But how can progress be made if people change their minds all the time? How can a country get better?"

"From the clash of ideologies, which leads to discussions and negotiations or to wars and massacres. France is powerful today because hundreds of years ago great thinkers and great warriors sacrificed their lives for what they believed was right."

19

Patriotism

On other occasions, they talked about a person's duty to his family, his tribe, his society, and then broached a subject Minh had always wanted to bring up but didn't know how. Patriotism, nationalism, love of one's country. This must be the cause you're looking for. Banding and bonding based on a shared vision. You can band and bond with other Vietnamese like you to fight for your country, like *papa* is fighting for his. You now know what is going on in the world, not like before. You should have stronger feelings about your country, your people, but Viet Nam is called Indochina, belongs to France. You're not French, you can't love Indochina like *papa* loves France. So where do you stand?

Papa's frequent references to Mathieu gave him an opening.

"Does Mathieu love France or does he love Madagascar? Will Mathieu fight for France, like you, *papa,* or will he fight for Madagascar?"

"Well, Madagascar is not really a nation, it's more like a collection of tribes. And right now Mathieu is too young to know what he thinks, as I suspect you are too. But when he grows up, because he is dark skinned and his mother is Malgache, he may resent the way the French settlers treat the natives and he may decide to support the Malgache resistance. Whatever he chooses will be the right choice for him, whatever I think."

This was the opening Minh had been waiting for.

"So the Vietnamese nationalists who are fighting the French are doing the right thing then?"

He held his breath at the audacity of his question. He knew that it was an important question, a hurdle that colored everything between the French and the Vietnamese, maybe even between *papa* and him.

This subject had been niggling at the back of his mind him ever since *Monsieur* Saintenoix had begun lecturing him on France's enormous contributions to the natives of the world, delivered with a cross in one hand and a gun in the other. At that time, from talking to Étienne, he had learnt that a Vietnamese political activist in France had written an open letter to the Governor General, *Son Excellence* Albert Sarraut, highly critical of French colonialism. After writing it, he had had to run away to another country to avoid being arrested.

"The answer is yes. This applies to the Malgache natives who fight the French in Madagascar, the Gaul tribes who fought against invading Romans, the American settlers who fought against the English, the Khmer and Cham races who fought against Vietnamese colonization not long ago. They all did the right thing at the time."

Minh breathed in deeply, exhaling slowly. He immediately saw *papa*'s point, but he didn't care about the other examples. In the same way that it is all right not to be a Catholic, it is also all right to resist the French presence in Viet Nam. But...

"So if it is not wrong to resist, why do the French put them into prison and execute them?"

Papa laughed, and lit a cigarette. He drew on it, releasing a huge puff.

"We come back to what I told you a few months ago, when we started these interesting discussions. The strong always want to dominate the weak. To dominate, they have to control. Imprisonment and executions are measures of control. Life is like that."

"There is no justice for the weak then? They are condemned to be dominated for ever?"

"History is endless and there is no never or forever; only in our personal lives, which are very short. Remember the world is always changing, little by little every day. Each generation wakes up to discover that things have changed completely. If you look carefully, you'll see that the strong, the rich and the educated of today were the weak, the poor and the uneducated of yesterday. And today's oppressed will take over tomorrow, as soon as the pendulum swings their way. What goes up must come down. Once in power, they will become rich and educated, will forget their roots, oppress their fellow men and be washed away in a few generations."

Papa paused while Minh took in this measured analysis, which stood all his fixed notions of fairness on their head. He means 'to each his turn'. Progress comes from a constant struggle between the strong and the weak. Society renews itself like a snake changing skins, like you changing names, going from black to white and then returning to black again, until next time. On their own the rich don't make the nation progress, nor do the poor, but their endless struggle to dominate and to resist domination ends up making the world better. So there is a good reason for all these wars after all. You have to look at the big picture, take the long view. Draw back and see the past, then use it to guess what your future will be like. You must use your brains and never stop learning. But how? You still have years to go before you can escape from the bad luck in your stars. It's time to ask mother about this unlucky star business.

Don't bring it up with papa. He'll laugh at you.

Gradually, Cinnamon and Minh learnt more about Sergeant Emil Escudier. He was thirty-five years old, an only child, born on the island of Madagascar, a French colony in East Africa. He had joined the military at eighteen and had soldiered in French colonies in Africa, the Middle East, China and Indochina. He had married a French-Malgache girl named Melissa, in Antananarivo, the capital, and they had a boy of the same age as him, named Mathieu.

"He even looks like you, slim and nimble, with big eyes," *papa* said one night in the kitchen, "but his skin is darker than yours and he has crinkly hair, like the blacks."

He would then take out the photograph from his bedroom and show them his son and wife. They had very dark skins, almost black like the Senegalese soldiers. He often did this, so they knew his mind was always with his real family. He loved France, for whom he had risked his life for some fifteen years, but really didn't know it at all. He had never been to Paris. He felt he could get on well with the French from the mainland, but had developed problems with the French settlers in Madagascar, whose narrow-minded attitude towards the natives irritated him, especially now that he had married a local girl and had a son who was obviously a *métis*[†].

[†] *métis*: a half-breed

20

Hélène

In between attending military classes for the Vietnamese levies and helping his mother around *papa*'s small house, Minh often had free time for himself. Now that scrounging around for the next meal and foraging for things to steal were no longer his first priorities, he could afford to relax and walk around Ha Noi, which he hardly knew at all. But instead of exploring the capital as he had intended to do at the first opportunity, he found himself drawn, as if by an unseen hand, to places he already knew. He would walk up and down in front of the convent and look at the spotlessly clean walls and front gate. The mural depicting the long white bleeding body didn't bother him any more now that he knew what religion was all about. We have a fat smiling Buddha with slits for eyes, they have a thin bleeding Jesus wearing a crown of thorn, the Indians have a multitude of animals and gods with dozens of arms, all painted in garish colors, sitting on their temple walls. To each his own god. Who cares. That old lady at the convent was right. Believe or not believe, we all die sooner or later. Good or bad, no one ever comes back. The most important thing is to live well and to take care of your family. Strains of organ music floated out from the convent. The nuns and their charges are on bended knees, heads bowed, hands clasped together fervently, mumble mumble, stand up, kneel down, stand up. If you'd stayed on at the convent, you'd be a cleaner now, or a carpenter. Perhaps even a helper to one of the senior *ma soeurs*, and your mother a senior seamstress or cook assistant.

He would have liked to see *Ma Soeur* Tuyet and surprise her now that he was grown up and was going to school but he didn't dare pull on the cord that rang the bell. You never believed in this religion. You have no right to hang around here. You're just a pretender, like your mother and all those women. Catholicism destroyed Viet Nam, worse than French guns. You must turn your face against it. It's a foreign religion, not for us. Yet how kind the nuns and sisters were to mother and you, even though you were so different. They must have known you could never become real believers in *le petit Jesus* and his father *le bon dieu*, and yet they gave you food and shelter and treated you like human beings…

Papa had taught him that nothing was all black or all white, that good and bad lived together and to accept one was to acknowledge the other. The Catholic cause might be wrong but the nuns were good people who had helped them when they needed help. *Papa's* cause was nothing to crow about either, yet *papa* was a good man too. Understanding this dichotomy was an important step in his learning process and, much later in life, it helped him separate an ideology from the enabling systems used to propagate it.

Minh also walked through the French Quarter past the mansion the Saintenoix family had lived in. The lawns were as green as before, the flowerbeds bursting with colors, with gardeners trimming bushes here and there. Instead, a huge private car was parked in the driveway, much bigger than *Monsieur* Saintenoix's car. He fancied he could still smell the perfume *Madame* Saintenoix wore and her soft, lilting voice came back to him. No Tazan, Dulcie and Lucille though, and he looked carefully at the corner in the garden where the dogs always left their droppings. It was spotless. This was the French part of town and he didn't dare stand around the large houses in case the police picked him up for loitering.

Another of his not-so-casual casual walks took him to the railway bridge, where he could see that nothing much had changed. Grimy street urchins were still noisily quarrelling, though he couldn't recognize any of them. The homeless and the jobless were still sitting around staring vacantly into space. The smells had not changed either. He was hoping he would see Hélène but he didn't dare approach the bridge proper, and stood discreetly behind a tree, watching what was going on. He didn't want them to see him as he now was, all clean and properly dressed like a boy from a good family. They would have laughed at him, insulted him, and perhaps thrown mud at him. Then he would have had to fight them and get all dirty again. He shuddered when he thought of how miserable life had been under that bridge.

Minh went to the wet market to see if the Old Witch and her crew of beggars were still there, hoping to catch a glimpse of Hélène. The beggars were spread all around the market place, and he approached one old crone he thought he recognized. She was blind. Or pretended to be.

"Where is Rabbit Mouth, auntie?" he asked softly. He hated himself for using that horrible nickname, but nobody used her French name.

"Who are you?" she answered in a startled voice, her gray head turning in the direction of the sound. "What do you want with her?"

"I lived under the bridge with my mother a long time ago, auntie. I want to talk to her," he said politely, keeping his voice low.

"You don't sound like someone who lived under the bridge, and you sound too young to be her client," said the old woman accusingly. He could see now that she was really blind. A tiny girl, about ten years old but the size of a three year old, suddenly popped up from the sidewalk from underneath a dirty blanket where she had been sleeping next to the old beggar. She was in rags, and her arms and legs were covered with sores. The sound of her grandmother talking had woken her up.

"I remember him! I remember him!" she shrilled. "He's the Nut Kicker, the son of auntie Cinnamon who lived near the canal!" Her teeth were all rotten.

There was an awkward silence, while the little girl scratched herself energetically and the old woman digested this information. Finally, she reached out and pulled the little girl against her face, inhaling her cheek loudly, kissing her in the Vietnamese style.

"My grand-daughter knows you, so I'll tell you where Rabbit Mouth is," she then said. Her raspy voice was friendlier now. Minh winced at Hélène's nickname but he didn't want to interrupt the old crone.

"She met a French soldier in Quang Ba who doesn't mind her rabbit mouth, and she's living with him in the *Citadelle*. She's left us, after all we've done for her. She's making money and eating three square meals a day but she never brings us anything. To think I taught her everything she knows!" The old beggar was shaking her head in disgust, mumbling to herself. "Now give us a coin so we can buy some food for today," she ordered him.

He had a few coins in his pocket for his canteen lunch at the military school and he prepared to give her one. But when he saw both their hands reach out, palms up, he glanced at the little urchin and felt his chest tighten. He promptly dropped all of his coins into the wrinkled palm the old beggar was holding out, and turned quickly away.

"Is that all you've got?" the old crone shrieked after him. "Hey, you, come back here…"

Minh's lips trembled and his eyes misted as he hurried away. *We're so lucky papa took us in. Otherwise we'd be like this woman and her granddaughter, dirty, full of lice, hungry.* As he walked away, he felt all torn up inside and memories of the days they had spent beneath the railway bridge came rolling back like big chunks of an ugly nightmare, crowding his mind.

Once back at the Fort he quickly went to the area reserved for the troops. *Hélène can't be living with an officer boyfriend. A non-commissioned officer at the most. Let's start at the married quarters, at the back of the barracks, where there are brick ovens and open sewers for soldiers living with native women. She's probably registered as his maid, cooking his food or washing his laundry.* He looked up and down three or four rows before he found her. She was squatting over a basin, washing clothes. She recognized him at once.

"Minh! What are you doing here?" she cried out, standing up, her hand and arms covered with soapy suds, forgetting to hide her mouth. She hadn't changed much, but was perhaps a little taller. The harelip was still grotesque, showing pink gum and her two upper front teeth, not unlike a large rabbit. But she had filled out, with real breasts that showed under her thin, wet blouse. Her hips were larger, too. He had seen how soft and round they were when she was still squatting.

The Old Witch had placed her in one of the bars at Quang Ba as an assistant prostitute and her job was to help out on busy nights when the regular girls had more customers than they could handle. She was kept for the older men, who were attracted by her French features, and the drunks, who didn't mind her ugly face. She had met Pierre, who was only nineteen, and he had fallen in love with her. He had bought her out of the bar, given her pocket money out of his pay every month and she now took care of him, like a wife should.

"He's a good man. He never beats me like the other soldiers beat their local wives. But every time he gets drunk he forgets how much money he had in his wallet, so I just help myself," she said proudly, laughing at her good luck.

Minh told her about the *Chez Rose* incident and how it led him to *papa*.

"I always knew you were going places!" she said excitedly, "Even when I first saw you I thought you were different."

"What do you mean, different?"

"Different from the others. Not stupid. Nicer."

"Well," he said, pleased that she had noticed these traits in him right from the start, "I have never forgotten you either. That night. Remember?"

"What night? Oh, you mean the drunk who was trying to rape your mother."

"Yes, that night. I admired the way you handled him. I couldn't have done it by myself."

"Well, when you know men like I know men, you'll understand how I feel about rape. When I hit him, I was thinking about all those bastards who hurt me."

"Boy, you really took care of him."

"Yeah, well, that's me. Move silently, hit hard."

He looked at her with admiration and silently vowed that he would also always move silently and hit hard in the future.

The next time they met, she told him that she was pregnant by Pierre, but that she was going to abort the baby. Minh didn't know what she meant, so she explained the procedure, which involved drinking herbal potions and sticking a piece of wire into her vagina to hook onto the baby and pull it out. It sounded so horrible that he could feel the hair on his arms rising as she casually talked about it.

"Don't worry, it's not the first time. I'm too young to be a mother, and anyway I don't intend to stay here. A kid would just get in the way," she said, laughing her melodious laugh, holding her handkerchief in front of her lower face all the time, in a most natural way. It had become an instinctive habit, this covering up of her harelip, and he hardly ever saw it throughout the conversation. This was the first time he had heard about her plans and he asked where she would go.

"France, of course," she answered rapidly. "Pierre and I are going to get married and he'll take me home to his parents when his time is up."

Green envy churned his guts when he heard that. Always incisive, decisive, knowing exactly what she wanted. Again he saw the night she had killed the *pousse pousse*[†] driver under the bridge. That's how you must be. Tough, fearless, always in control, instead of always reading, thinking, asking yourself if you are right or wrong. She doesn't read anything, never listens to news broadcasts, she doesn't even know

[†] *pousse pousse*: rickshaw

where France is on a map. Her world is small, but she doesn't care because she controls everything in it.

"So you'll become a fat smelly French housewife, live in a nice home and put on airs like a lady?" he said with a smirk, repressing his jealousy with difficulty.

"Naah, none of that," she answered casually, paying no attention to the change of tone in his voice. "As soon as I get to France I'll ditch Pierre and go to Paris. I'll earn money and get my face fixed. I want to open a brothel for rich people. I'll have plenty of French whores working for me. If you ever get there, you must come and see me. We're like family now," she said, hugging him to her. The smell of her skin was fresh, fragrant even. He hugged her back half-heartedly, resentful and supportive at the same time. *She's poor like you, less educated, yet she knows what she wants. She has a plan to get it. You don't have a plan. You just don't know what you want to do. That really hurts.*

They continued to meet around noon whenever they were both free and soon became the best of friends. Minh eventually confessed to her his lack of direction in life and his fear that he would never amount to anything because he never knew what he wanted, besides becoming an important person and looking after his mother. She always laughed at this.

"Boys grow up more slowly than girls. Don't worry, in a few years you'll know what you want and then you'll shoot upward like a rocket," she said with conviction. Chuckling, she would grab his crotch lightly and shake it, saying "Wait till you get some lead in your pencil!" He would blush to the roots of his hair, she would laugh at his discomfiture, and he would regret having told her anything. Talking to her was so different from talking to *papa*.

To show her he wasn't a totally hopeless case, he wanted to tell her about his thirty-six year curse and how he was sure to prosper after that, but he didn't because he simply didn't know the details. In spite of his talks with *papa*, he had never questioned his mother about it. He felt that it was more bad news, and now that his life had returned to normal, he didn't want to hear anything negative.

Left alone in Pierre's room at noon, on Pierre's bed, happy in each other's company, their teenage bouts of laughter and horseplay once or twice almost led to sex, but somehow it never worked out and they decided to leave it for later, when they had both succeeded in life. He knew that she was experienced, and he thought of her as an older sister, and respected her, although he knew he was in love with her. At the same time, he was aroused by the smoothness of her skin and the fresh smell of her hair, especially when she absentmindedly let him touch her breasts and kiss her nipples through her blouse. He had often thought about having sex with her, but he didn't know to begin. Walking home, he was always relieved that they hadn't gone all the way, although he felt that it was bound to happen, and hopefully soon. Once, she had playfully fondled his crotch, causing an instant erection. Visions of carnal pleasure had flashed through his mind but, to his absolute mortification, he had ejaculated in his shorts almost immediately and she had burst out laughing.

Later, trying to make up for hurting his feelings, she had said "When we're ready for love, we'll have sex."

"You must have been ready for love many times in your life then," he replied, vexed by her laughter and wanting to hurt her.

"No," she answered seriously, hardly noticing his ruffled feelings, "I've never had love—although I've had sex since I was eleven." Then, pointing to her crotch, she said, "Many men have touched this, but," pointing to her heart, "not one has ever touched this."

He looked down, saw the bulge under her thin dress, then at her breasts, not knowing what to say. What about you? Have you touched her heart? Try and separate things to better understand them. Cause and policies are not always the same, love and sex also are not always the same. She saw the blank look on his face and burst out laughing again, holding the handkerchief to her mouth.

"Minh, I'll save this for you," she said in her lovely voice, pulling his hand in between her breasts, pressing it flat against her heart. He could feel it pulsing and his mouth went dry. A brilliant flash blinded him, followed by a silent thunderclap and then he felt they were floating in space, high above the trees, holding on to each other tightly, kissing each other hard. She had no hare-lip and he wasn't a boy any more. They were two of a kind, made for each other, lovers now and for ever, both talking at the same time, emptying their hearts. Then suddenly they were back on earth, in *La* Citadelle, on Pierre's bed. Nothing had changed except that the magic moment had ended. He drew back to look at her. He knew she had meant what she said. She would wait for him, forever if need be. She was beautiful, and he knew now why he was in love with her. She is like you. Life has pushed you around but it couldn't break your spirit. They abused her body but they couldn't touch her spirit. She is pure and she says she'll wait for you. You'll also wait for her, however long it takes, thirty six years or more...

21

The Sea

Minh had never forgotten that his mother always wanted to see the sea because, when she was still young, her father had told her that it was good for people with weak lungs. Her father had also told her to call her first son Hai, 'Ocean,' which connoted power, beauty and promise. Knowing that his *papa* had some in-country holiday time coming, he often hinted to him that his mother had never seen the sea but that she loved it. One day, at five-thirty in the morning, a military truck pulled up in front of their house and a French driver got out, a piece of paper in hand. He was looking for *Madame* Que, *Monsieur* Minh and *Sergeant* Escudier. Minh ran into the house, woke *papa* up, and within the hour they were being driven to the seaside. Once there, they stayed at the French military facility which fronted on the beach and spent seven heavenly days and nights there.

The French soldiers garrisoned at the Sam Son beach resort had Vietnamese wives and girlfriends and they partied every night. The Vietnamese women and girls roasted fresh fish, shrimps, clams and lobsters, the French soldiers drank beer and *schoum,* a potent fermented rice wine with an unpleasant aftertaste, while a portable record player blasted out French songs straight from Paris. *Papa* taught Minh and his mother how to swim, placing one large flat hand under their stomachs to keep them afloat while they learned how to co-ordinate their arm and leg movements without swallowing too much salt water in the process. They practiced until their arms fell off before walking barefooted along the white sandy beach, picking up shells and catching the occasional crab. They lived on the beach all day long, drinking fresh coconut juice and eating the meat inside, and took long siestas in the shade of banana trees when the sun was at its highest.

For the first time, Minh felt as if he belonged to a real family, with a father and a mother. Sometimes he half-regretted that there was nothing between *papa* and his mother, like between real parents, but this reinforced his opinion of his adoptive father. There is a real difference between *papa* and the other military. Self-control. He never gets drunk, doesn't chase around after women in bars and brothels, seldom raises his voice, never gets into fistfights. Never touches mother, and always treats you like a real son. His love and admiration for *papa* grew, especially when he saw how the other soldiers treated their girlfriends and local wives. My *papa* is no ordinary soldier. No ordinary man either.

At night, they slept in the open, on reed mats laid on the sand between the pine trees, under mosquito nets strung up between the tree trunks. Tired, burnt by the sun, they were soon lulled asleep by the endless rhythm of the waves slapping against the sands, hissing as they rushed aggressively up the beach before pausing for a moment and then pulling back in a bubbly mass, frothily skimming off millions of grains of sand each time.

His mother found herself breathing more easily, especially at night. The medication she took suppressed her cough, but she could feel her lungs were sick. They couldn't inhale fully any more, as they had when she was younger. Breathing out was automatic but she had to consciously breathe in that extra half-breath if she didn't want to become dizzy from lack of oxygen. After *papa* was asleep, snoring loudly, mother and son talked to each other.

"I should really stay here until I am well again," she said one night, "but what can I do here? Join a fishing village? I'd have to marry a fisherman. The villages seem so poor. In the seasons when there is no fish the fishermen have to go inland to look for work in the fields. And if I stay you will want to stay with me. You won't get regular food and an education here. It'll ruin your life. So let's take care of you first. Better go back to Ha Noi and we'll see what can be done about me in the future."

On their last night, they sat on a rock overlooking the sea. Far below the soldiers were partying with their women, as usual, and their shouting and singing could be heard faintly. The sea was calm, with only tiny wavelets washing ashore. The moon shone bright overhead and a breeze blew in from the Pacific Ocean. *Papa* put his arms around Minh's mother and him and began singing a French song. *Papa*'s voice was low, too low, and also off-key, and they felt laughter bubble up inside them. But Minh didn't laugh, and neither did his mother. Although they didn't know the song, they knew it was a sad song. They also knew he was not singing it for them, but for someone far away, maybe his wife and son. Glancing up sideways without moving his head, Minh saw tears glistening in *papa*'s eyes. He also felt sad and wanted to cry because his beloved *papa* was crying. He looked at his mother, on the other side of *papa*'s large chest. She was already crying, her face all broken up. Many thoughts raced through his mind. Papa really loves us. He's so good to us but his heart can never be completely with us. It already belongs to his own family. When Mathieu grows up he may have all kinds of problems because of the color of his skin, but at least he will have his *papa* by his side. You are in your own country, your problems are not the kind a Frenchman can help you with. When *papa* goes away one day, it'll be just be us two… again.

In 1931, after a little over three long and happy years, Minh and his mother had to move out of *la Citadelle*. *Papa* was being sent back to France for training, to the mainland itself, and he barely had time to pack before he had to board a military flight to Sai Gon. The transfer orders came as a shock to all three of them, and *papa* sat there for some time, somber and silent, orders in hand, before he looked up and in a low voice announced to Minh that he was leaving the day after. They were allowed to accompany him to the military airport outside Ha Noi in the truck that came for him and his luggage, and just before they left *la Citadelle* for good, Minh ran over to Hélène's place to say goodbye. She wasn't in, and he left a message for her with the girl next door, also a former Quang Ba bargirl, asking her to meet him at the central market at noon the following day.

At the airport, *papa* stood apart from the other passengers, with Minh and his mother holding on to him. The large linen handkerchief flew in and out of his pocket, his large nose was blown with increasing vigor, and his throat had to be cleared a few times. They stood there in silence, not knowing what to say. After the convent, they had felt apprehension at what would be expected of them at the Saintenoix home. After the Saintenoix had left, they had felt lost, abandoned. And now a mix of all those feelings returned.

"I'll be back after my training," *papa* said, "and I'll be in *la Citadelle* again. Just look for me there every now and then and before you know it you'll see me back here again." He spoke in comforting tones, holding Minh's head tight against his large stomach. He smelled of cologne and leather.

"I'll write to you care of the camp's Post Office. Just check with them every month and see what they have for you."

Finally it was boarding time, and *papa* solemnly took Cinnamon into his arms and kissed her on both cheeks, which made her wail even more loudly. Buckets of tears poured out, and this sight made Minh cry also. *Papa* hugged him and gave him one loud kiss on each cheek and smiled reassuringly before climbing up the ramp. The military transport plane taxied onto the tarmac, gunned it engines, gently ran down the runway, gathered speed and rose gracefully into the sky. Minh again felt a huge emptiness inside, like he had felt when the Saintenoix left Ha Noi.

The whole episode, from the moment *papa* received his orders, had taken less than two days.

22

Tam

*P*apa left Minh his radio set plus some odds and ends, and gave his mother enough money to find a place to live in until he could return. Cinnamon decided not to rent a room in the Vietnamese Quarter but instead to keep *papa's* money for food in case she couldn't find work. They promptly sold everything as soon as they left *la Citadelle* and divided up the money into two packs. Each wad was slipped into a sturdy sash that they tied around their waists. There was no work to be found anywhere, no matter where they looked, and after a week of walking aimlessly around Ha Noi and sleeping on the ground under trees in various pagodas, they decided to return to the bridge near the central railway station. This time, things were a little easier, because they had already experienced street living. With their money they bought a berth in the middle portion of the bridge, where it was warmer in winter and less smelly the year round.

There were many new faces, some of the old ones having died off, many of the younger ones having moved on. The railway gang boys had either been dispersed by the police or had grown up and moved away. Many of the older people with whom they had become friends had died or moved back to the countryside. The Old Witch and her retinue of beggars had moved directly to the central market and slept between the empty stalls at night. Otherwise, there was little change except that the city dump had grown noticeably bigger. The smell of garbage, the flies, the mosquitoes, the cockroaches, the rats and the dust was still the same, as if the curse that had been put on this malodorous little community could never be lifted. Before the last *Chez Rose* episode, they had reached a point where they hardly noticed the dirt and the smells any more. Now, after three years in the cleanliness and orderliness of *la Citadelle*, the filth and the smell of ripe garbage hit them in the face like a giant wave. They started cleaning up their space again, and could sense the derision and hostility exuding from their neighbors, but this time they didn't care. Minh was seventeen already; he was tough; he had received an education of sorts. The convent, the Saintenoix, *papa* and the military school for the Vietnamese levies had taught him how to think, to reason, to plan things. He knew what was going on in the world, and he knew that living under the bridge would only be temporary. They had some money and they had bought the best spot under the bridge. They pushed and shoved their way around until a natural pecking order was arrived at. It didn't make them popular, but it won them grudging respect. Minh remembered *papa*'s comments that the essence of human relationships rested on domination.

All the hectic activity on the first day made Minh forget the rendezvous he had set with Hélène, and on subsequent trips to the market he waited for hours in vain. He also waited outside *la Citadelle* on a number of occasions, but never saw her come out. He felt a terrible sense of disappointment, a hollowing out of his insides. Maybe she's gone to France already. You're in love with her, you want to see her again. Does she think about you like you think about her? He noticed that in his mind's eye he saw her without the harelip, perfectly normal, beautiful and with a melodious voice. He thought he would tell his mother about her and how he felt, but with the problems of settling in under the bridge he never had the opportunity. By the time they had organized things, new problems and opportunities had reared their heads and he forgot about telling his mother about Hélène, although he couldn't forget his new love, whose face popped into his head at all hours of the day as he went about his business.

While scrounging around for the French medicines his mother had been prescribed at the military clinic, Minh met a couple of hoodlums who had just robbed a French warehouse filled with medical supplies. He helped them read the French instructions on the notices that came with the boxes; one thing led to another and he soon fell in with the Buffalo Head gang, a grouping of adult criminals. Because he could read and write, spoke French, and was perceived as being familiar with official documents, he attracted the attention of the top man, Buffalo Head himself. A dark, brooding man with powerful shoulders, thick arms and a massive head covered with tight curly hair, not unlike the

African soldiers in the French army, he spoke slowly, in a drawl, as if he despised everything and everyone. His face was a mass of angry red boils, some of them tipped with yellow pus. He had the habit of squeezing them between thick, dirty fingernails and then wiping his hand on his trousers. His breath was bad and Minh had to move discreetly upwind of him whenever they sat at a table to talk. Having discussed Buffalo Head with his mother, Minh gave his name as Tam, because he was afraid Minh might link him to *la Citadelle*. Buffalo Head, of mixed Khmer-Vietnamese parentage, tried to check on the new recruit's background but no one carried identity papers in those days, photographs and fingerprinting were in their infancy, and only the French had birth certificates. Though illiterate, Buffalo Head was a cunning and violent man. To cross him was to die and Minh, now Tam, knew instinctively he had to be very careful when dealing with him. He won him over, however, when he offered to forge some documents that were needed. When Buffalo Head saw the results, he declared that Tam would henceforth be his secretary. His ability to read and speak French, to read military maps, to help program an operation, all learned in his three years at *la Citadelle*, made him a natural for that position.

The Buffalo Head gang worked for shadowy trading groups that specialized in stealing cargo from bonded warehouses. The trading groups, many of them run by first-generation Vietnamese from China, first scouted for buyers for goods they didn't yet possess but intended to offer. They then picked a gang out of the many that operated in Ha Noi and commissioned it for the heist. The gang stole rice from government granaries, French military *materiel* from *la Citadelle*, high-value goods from warehouses at the Ha Noi go-downs along the Song Hong river that ran through the city. Buffalo Head always asked for a mobilization fee, a down payment with which he rented trucks, pallets, hand-cranked forklifts, cables and chains. Forged documents were prepared to take care of police roadblocks, which were everywhere throughout the north because of continuing resistance to the French presence. Buffalo Head even rented private warehouses where the stolen goods could be temporarily stored, pending delivery. Again, forged papers were needed there, and Tam soon became an important member of the gang, although he was the youngest and had no operational experience. Without really having had to work for it, he found a niche in the gang next to Buffalo Head, where he was shielded from most of the gang members, some of whom were really vicious thugs, particularly a hoodlum named 'Hammer and Tong' Chanh. Mother and son still had some of *papa*'s money left, food was no longer a problem and Tam was able to buy French medicine and clean clothes for his mother, as well as a new bed, mattress and mosquito net. Now a member of an organized crime gang, his status under the bridge rose but his mother decided not to move to a cleaner place until he had made enough money for them to buy a squatter shanty in the suburbs.

On one contract that Buffalo Head had accepted, the gang had to transport about five tons of stolen rubber from a French plantation to the Laotian border, where another gang would take over the cargo. Trucks were hired, professional drivers were picked, an army of coolies was mobilized, all placed under the supervision of an army deserter who could use a compass and read maps. An evil-looking man, he insisted that he had been a staff sergeant and wanted to be called Sergeant Le, but everyone suspected that he had only been a soldier and called him Ratface behind his back. Tam's ability to read and write French automatically made him Ratface's right-hand man. Tam had to be present in case there were paperwork problems with one of the many French military checkpoints outside of the capital city.

The convoy set off early in the evening for a midnight rendezvous at the pickup point, a Michelin rubber plantation run by French settlers born and raised in Algeria, where they were known as the *pieds noirs*. These loud and violent men were imbued with a colonial mentality that was even worse than that of the Indochinese French settlers. The *pieds noirs* were ruthless in their treatment of the Vietnamese toddy-tappers on the plantation. It was said that many of these workers, who scraped the bark of rubber trees and collected the raw rubber sap, were buried between the rows of trees they worked on when they died. Death could be due to disease, old age or being shot by their overseers for small infringements of plantation regulations. Drinking cognac as if it were water, the *pieds noirs* supervisors roared around the rubber plantation in French army cars, with pistols in their belts. In between the endless rows of trees, they often abused the female rubber tappers, calling on them for oral sex in return for *un petit cadeau,* a small gift, usually a few coins.

On that night a roaring party was going on, and long lines of cars and limousines were parked around the general manager's villa. On the terraces, figures dressed in colonial whites could be seen dancing to the music of a ballroom orchestra located inside the main hall. Occasionally, peals of silvery laughter could be heard as some French lady, dressed to the nines and fired up by the free-flowing champagne, laughed at some witty remark from a man she was thinking of bedding down with that night. Lights were strung all around the front garden and from afar the scene was dreamlike.

Their convoy skirted all that feverish activity and headed for the back end of the plantation, near a small lake. There, in the dark, bale upon bale of processed rubber waited to be loaded. The sickening, mind-bending stench of raw rubber instantly gave Tam a massive headache. His responsibility was to make sure that the data shown on the authentic inventory documents and the false travel orders tallied. All the figures had to add up. Everything was in French, of course, and it was necessary to get things right so as not to be caught out by the first French NCO who knew how to read and how to count. It turned out that the papers Tam had been given did not match those that they had brought along, and it was impossible to go on with the heist. The first military checkpoint would have undone them. The coolies looked at the drivers, who looked at Ratface, who looked at Tam. Consternation was written all over their faces. They had planned to move out while the party was going full blast. The insiders, low level management personnel who had been bribed to organize the theft, could read and they stared blankly at the two sets of documents, which seemed totally unrelated. Then one of them jumped up, slapped himself on the forehead, swore like a trooper, and rushed off. Three hours later he returned, with a new set of papers, the correct ones this time. Tam went over the lines, one by one, while the loading of the cargo began. When he had finished, it was almost three in the morning. The party was ending, guests were coming out, singing drunkenly. Ratface was four hours late and couldn't move until the guests left.

One car, a large, shiny *Citroen 15CV*, drove towards the lake and parked some twenty meters away from their lead truck, now loaded with rubber, blocking their way. The car windows were wound down, and soon heavy grunting and groaning noises could be heard coming from the car, which rocked from side to side as the sound of passionate copulation rose to a crescendo. A Frenchwoman's voice, low and raw, could now clearly be heard, urging her man on. The truckers and the loaders stood still in the darkness, some trying hard not to burst out laughing. Tam felt an erection coming in spite of his fear that things had gone wrong and that disaster awaited them. By now he was all of seventeen, and his testosterone levels had risen considerably since his railway bridge days, although he still hadn't had a proper sexual experience. The first sojourn under the bridge had been limited to masturbating while watching others copulate, endless discussions about what each gang member had done and would do when the occasion came, followed by more acts of self-gratification. The *Citadelle* days were absolutely sexless, Tam's main focus then being the family life they were experiencing, the absolute ecstasy and joy of being like other children who had mothers and fathers. There had been brief moments in the daytime, with Hélène, while her boyfriend was otherwise occupied, when he had thought about doing it but somehow nothing had actually happened.

Finally, the noisy fornication in the car ended. The car door opened and a fat, well-dressed French gentleman stumbled out, his fly open. He rushed towards their truck and urinated copiously in their direction. He then burped loudly, let go a thunderous fart, readjusted his tie and jacket, buttoned himself up and staggered back to the car. On the other side of the vehicle, a tall, slim, well-dressed lady was squatting and pissing noisily. She then stood up, pulled up her underwear, fluffed her dress out, rearranged her hair and got into the car. In a few minutes, they were gone, leaving behind a gaggle of drivers and coolies who were peeing all over themselves with laughter. Ratface slapped the bonnet of the lead truck to bring back some discipline, and after one last check the convoy headed west. It was by now four in the morning, and as they drove at top speed towards the Laotian border they could only think that if they missed their rendezvous they would have to either hide somewhere until the next night or return the load to the plantation. Fortunately, the Laotian gangsters, not being addicted to punctuality like the French, had waited for them.

Months later, Tam happened to be walking down a main street he usually avoided, and found himself behind a well-dressed Vietnamese gentleman and a tough-looking man whom he thought he recognized. The toughie was a member of their gang, 'Hammer and Tong' Chanh, a man known for his brutality. Chanh was Buffalo Head's deputy and had had a few run-ins with Buffalo Head lately over the division of the spoils after a successful heist. To avoid an open rift, Buffalo Head had given Tam the task of explaining to Chanh the amounts that had been deducted from his share to pay for the overheads. This had made Tam Chanh's enemy, and he had threatened to gut Tam like a fish the next time he didn't receive his full share. From his bearings and the close-cropped hair, the other man was obviously from the police. Tam could smell them a mile away. The men, called the *auxilliaires* in French, were Vietnamese undercover policemen working for the French *Sureté* and were much feared by the Vietnamese population. They had no problem blending in with the locals and, more important, knew how the Vietnamese thought, which the French didn't. Tam followed them and saw them stop at a warehouse near the docks. They stood there a long time, talking quietly. The policeman looked at the warehouse carefully, examining the doors and windows.

Buffalo called Tam in the next day and handed him a sheaf of documents. A new operation was being planned and he had to familiarize himself with all the details. Later, he would ask Tam to read these documents back to him. Tam sat down in a corner near the window and began looking through the papers, some of which were in French. A large cargo of commercial goods destined for Hue had been hijacked and stored in one of the gang's warehouses preparatory to being trucked to Hai Phong port, from where it was to be loaded onto sampans and smuggled into southern China. Tam suddenly realized that the warehouse in question was the one where he had seen Chanh and the policeman the day before. A cold, clammy hand suddenly gripped his bowels, squeezing hard, and he felt nauseated. This was exactly what they all feared the most every time they took on a contract. Betrayal. A set up. Walking into a trap. Being caught red-handed by the French police, or, even worse, the French military.

After a while, he told Buffalo Head he thought the police were watching that warehouse, because he had seen some police officers walking around it a few days before when he had passed by it by chance, without knowing at the time that it would be their next target. He didn't say anything about Chanh because, frankly, he was afraid of him. Buffalo Head's face hardened, and his eyes searched Tam's. His pupils were like black agates, hard and flat. In a strange way, they had grown into an asymmetric father-and-son relationship, in the sense that Buffalo Head trusted Tam to do what he was told and Tam trusted Buffalo Head to protect him in times of danger.

"Alright, this is what we'll do. We have three more days before we move. You tell our people to go on with all the preparations, like usual. If there is a traitor in our group, he must not suspect that I know anything. If you're right, I'll call it off at the last minute, at midnight. If you're wrong, and there is no one watching the target, we'll go through with it as planned. Don't worry if you are wrong. Better be safe than sorry," he said slowly, gruffly. They were huddled together and Buffalo Head was breathing into Tam's face. His stomach curdled. Shifting as far away as he could without offending Buffalo Head, he smiled back weakly. The problem with these gangsters is that if you get something wrong and cause them to lose money, they usually kill you. After he left Buffalo Head he asked his mother if he had read that policeman right. She appeared puzzled at his question but answered that she hadn't felt any bad premonitions or she would have warned him. On the other hand, she added, she had been to the pagoda again and the horoscope predicted major changes coming soon, but more readings were needed to get the details. Tam knew then that whatever happened at the warehouse he would not be in danger. Over the years, he had come to trust his mother's divinations implicitly.

Two days later, on the morning of the day the robbery was to take place, Buffalo Head, his brother, his three most trusted bodyguards and Tam took up their positions around the warehouse area. At noon they saw undercover policemen carrying guns into the warehouse and a wave of relief swept over Tam. He had been right after all and he started trembling uncontrollably. Until then, he hadn't realized how scared he had been. By nine o'clock that night, Buffalo Head had already decided to scrap the operation but he didn't want anyone to know this. He sent Tam to inform the truck drivers and loading teams that nobody was to move until Buffalo Head himself gave the order. Midnight came and went. Buffalo Head and Tam stood waist deep in a small mud creek that ran along the side of the warehouse, watching the nearby streets. They had camouflaged their heads with branches from a nearby bush. The hours went by, a minute at a time, while the mosquitoes feasted on them and the foul smells of the rotting detritus in the mud slime enveloped them, penetrating their nostrils, settling on their hair, seeping into their pores. At three in the morning, some of the policemen in the buildings nearby walked across the street to the warehouse to confer with those inside. They were carrying rifles. About two hours later, when the first lights of dawn had begun to appear, a car showed up. A Frenchman, wearing a gun at his waist, got out on one side, while a Vietnamese got out on the other side. They recognized Chanh. The men talked to the policemen inside the warehouse. After a while, everyone went away and Buffalo Head quietly withdrew his men.

A few days later, a local newspaper reported that different body parts had been found around the city. A leg here, an arm there, a head with the tongue cut out wrapped in newspapers in the central market place. But there were many such gruesome murders in the Ha Noi underworld, and Tam didn't pay the article much notice until one day Buffalo Head showed him a newspaper cutting. It was the one he had read that day, and reported the death of a gangster formerly known as Hammer and Tong Chanh.

Buffalo Head grinned, scratched his pus-infected jowls, and spat on the floor.

"I fed his liver to the street dogs," he drawled.

Tam nodded, not knowing what to say.

"Oh, by the way," he continued, "you'll be my deputy from now on and you'll get his fifteen per cent share."

They shook hands and Tam smiled inwardly. Your future in the Buffalo Head gang is assured. This means plenty of food for us, plenty of medicine for mother, perhaps a small hut in the suburbs soon. As she predicted, you were not in any danger throughout the exercise.

Unfortunately, the French colonial police and its army of Vietnamese informants were also very active in the maintenance of law and order. Capital crime meant capital punishment and the guillotine in Ha Noi worked overtime to make Indochina safe for the French and their property. One particular incident put a final end to the gang's existence. A shadowy group of traders had intended to commission the Buffalo Head gang for a heist at the airport. Buffalo Head's quotation had been too high, and they had picked another gang. The heist went sour, and because the cargo was all French military equipment, the rich financiers and gang members were promptly executed by the firing squad. Radio broadcasts and the newspapers all noted that the Vietnamese businessmen executed had all been from prominent, land-owning families. French tax collectors then summoned the family heads and publicly berated them for late payment, fining them heavily and publicly to humiliate them. French police then swept through the homes of middle class and professional families, hauling off dozens of young men for military service. For many in the Buffalo Head gang, all from the working classes, this was a powerful argument for quietly taking up farming in the countryside again until the French authorities had calmed down. Thus, after one relatively successful year and two large-scale operations in what at first had appeared to be a promising line of work, Tam was unemployed again.

23

Reincarnation

Under the bridge, his mother had nothing to do all day long except sit around talking to their immediate neighbors. She could no longer walk around the city because she now tired easily. She stubbornly refused to continue with the French medicine Tam had been able to buy for her. Now that he was out of work again, she wanted to keep whatever money they had left for food.

"What's the use of spending money on medicine if I am going to die anyway?" she protested every now and again, with exasperated sincerity in her voice when he insisted, and, hard as it was, he could see the logic of her argument. He remembered Mrs. Tam the chicken seller standing at the convent's gate, answering Sister Hue on the matter of tying up the chickens too tightly.

"They're going to die anyway, so what does it matter?" she had asked in a matter-of-fact voice. Country people have a pragmatic approach to birth, marriages, sickness and death and tend to accept things as they are, not as they should be, and his mother was very much country. She had come from hundreds of generations of hunter-gatherers who had eventually morphed into hundreds of generations of subsistence farmers, people who never had anything and never expected to have anything, and to whom living was in itself a miserable experience, dragged out year after year until death, the inevitable, came to sweep them away, like a broom sweeps dead and dying leaves away. For many, to be able to give up the unwinnable fight was seen as a blessing, for with death came rest and, perhaps, a chance to enjoy life beyond. Tam could see this fatalism in her eyes and he knew she was not afraid of death. The main thing, she said to him one night, is to have prepared for it.

After a while, he stopped buying her medicine and they settled down to an easy relationship in which both accepted the inevitable. Her health rapidly got worse as full-blown tuberculosis rotted her lungs. Her long violent fits of coughing became unbearable to the ear and blood now appeared regularly on the face towel she held up to her mouth. On nights when he wasn't doing part-time work here and there, he boiled various herbs in her tea to ease her cough, and crushed garlic for her to inhale the fumes so as to loosen the tight membranes of her damaged lungs. They spent hours through the night sitting next to each other on their bed space, under the mosquito net. Lying down made it difficult for her to breathe and after they had talked, or rather after she had talked, they slept the rest of the night sitting up. Tam had rigged a wooden panel against the wall to support her back and he half-slept with his arm around her. She leaned against him, her head on his chest, her fingers doodling against his stomach. In between long bouts of coughing, the muted sounds of which racked his lungs, she talked in a quiet monologue, mostly about her past. Each time a train went by overhead, she would take a rest and start again when quiet had returned. He knew she felt she did not have long to live and she wanted to tell him a few final things. Sometimes he felt his eyes close and he drifted off to sleep, but never for long, and when he awoke he knew he hadn't missed one word of what she had been saying. It was as if the little girlish voice was speaking from inside of him, and he could hear her in his mind even when half-asleep.

In the streets nearby the traffic rumbled by, even late at night, and all around the garbage piles stray dogs fought, snarling and biting each other, the losers yelping as they rushed off into the oncoming traffic to cause chaotic accidents and more yelling and shouting. From the windows of the houses nearby came a steady stream of radio music played at full blast or incessant quarrels, also at full blast. But under the bridge, in between the trains, there was peace. It was like a closed, stuffy little world, a small island far away from the real world, full of shadows and echoes and smells, filled with pathetic souls who peered about, living mainly in their own minds in a cocoon of hopelessness and emptiness, lost under a bridge surrounded by a large city that ignored their presence.

Over the months, night after night, she dredged up debris from her past that, somehow, was also debris from his past. Quite often, as she spoke, tears would sometimes well up in his eyes and slowly roll down his cheeks, one by one, reaching his lips, tasting salty. He would clench his teeth tightly shut so as not to cry openly, and every time he breathed in he could smell her dry scalp as her head rested against his chest, just under his chin. As she talked about things that mattered to her, things that had become embedded in her mind over the years, he relived them all, as if what she had felt all these years had also been felt by him at the same time. In fact, much of what she told him was not new. He had heard it in bits and pieces, in one form or another, at night in the servant quarters of the Saintenoix house, then under the bridge during his pick-pocketing days with the railway boys, then later in *papa*'s comfortable kitchen at the *Citadelle*. But this time, it was different.

Because he knew she was dying a little more each day, her words burned deeper into his mind than before and the more he listened the more he was convinced that his mother and he were really one person. He had come from her, but he had never left her. Or perhaps she had never let go of him. Either way, everything that was inside her was also inside him.

"Your father is Lord Trinh Xuan Bach. He must be about forty-five years old now and is probably still abroad. I don't know why he goes abroad. He has a wife in Thanh Hoa, with two or three children. He also has a village wife there, also with two or three children. He has many other children with mistresses like me and you are one of them. He never recognized you, so you can't carry the name Trinh. I ran away from the manor because I wanted to shield you from bad luck. My mother was an alcoholic, my father left us, same as my brothers. I had no money, I didn't know anyone and I only knew how to sew. Luckily we found the convent, which gave you a good start. I don't know where we would be today if I hadn't been taken to a convent by that old Mrs. Tam we met on the bus."

"When that old chicken lady advised me to hide in a French convent I agreed at once although I was more afraid of the French than of ghosts. I thought it was the best way to avoid those three cursed stars. At the pagoda the head nun told me that if we could live among people who were not superstitious like us we could escape the attention of bad spirits. The French are not like us, they don't believe in anything, so I wanted to stay there forever. I dragged out the years at the convent by learning how to read and write as slowly as I could. Yes, I could have learned faster, it wasn't that difficult. I wanted you to stay in that convent until you were a young boy, and I tried my best to be as stupid as I could, but I could only manage a few years."

"I don't understand why people who don't believe in the stars are not affected by Fate but it's true. In the Saintenoix family and *papa's* house in the *Citadelle* you were protected from bad luck. Remember how happy you were there? You were able to go to school there, and a French one at that! Otherwise you would never have seen the inside of a school, any school. I think the years we spent with *papa* Escudier were the best years of my life, and I got to see the sea with you. If it hadn't been for you, we would never have met *papa*, and if you hadn't asked him to go and visit the sea, we would never have gone. You said you would take me to the sea, and you did. I can never forget that. I always wanted to name you Hai, the sea, and when you come into your own, you can wear that name with pride."

What she said about being affected by the stars only if you believed stuck in his mind. If you don't believe that your fate is written in the stars, that your life is predetermined, you can escape from bad luck. *Papa* doesn't believe in the stars. The French don't believe in horoscopes and life charts, and they all seem to sail through life without any worries. But what about the good luck that is also written in the stars? If you don't believe, you don't get any of it either. Is it better not to know your future, just plough on ahead in the hopes that everything will turn out all right, or is it better to know, and thus be able to turn away bad luck by doing the right thing at the right time, like my mother tried to do. Do you believe in fate, are you superstitious, or do you believe because your mother believes...

"Now, you have to do what you have to do. For us poor, life is like that. We have no choice. But after I die it won't be the same for you, because you are not poor. I am poor, and all these people around us are poor because we cannot become better even if we have the opportunity. That's because although our bodies grew, our minds didn't. But you, your mind was opened at the convent and it will keep on growing, along with your body. You're almost a man already, you are intelligent, you can speak French and you will become an important person. You can never be poor, even if you have no money, because all the money you need you already carry in your head."

"I saw it in a dream, many years ago. After three life cycles, you will become a very influential person. You will wear a uniform, like a soldier, but you will not be in the army. Your enemies will fear you, your friends will respect you."

"What three life cycles, mother?" he finally asked. "How long is three life cycles anyway?"

"It's all in your Life Chart. A life cycle is twelve years. Most people live five life cycles, maybe six. You will live seven life cycles, until you are eighty four. You are now eighteen, in your second cycle. I'm thirty-four, nearing the end of my third. On the day we met, your father's star was *Co Than* and mine was *Bach Ho*, both contradictory stars, because that witch Miss Fatty didn't bother to consult the horoscopes. Or perhaps your father doesn't believe in them. Anyway, this meant our union could not succeed, and it didn't. You were born under a very powerful life star, *Liem Trinh*, but there were also three bad stars in your Main House. These are life cycle stars, and their combined weight overshadowed your good star. They have to be purged separately, one after the other. You will have to live them out before *Liem Trinh* can rise and lead you to success. Once it stands alone in your Main House you will become an important man for as long as you live."

Tam didn't find much consolation in this explanation. Another eighteen years to go before he could become somebody important, known by his own name, feared and respected by all like *papa* was. Eighteen years more. That was like a lifetime.

"I am not afraid of dying now, because you have already become a man. In fact, I am glad I shall die soon, because I realize now that I have been holding you back. You have a great future in front of you, but you cannot achieve it as long as I am clinging to your belt. You cannot fight the world and take care of me at the same time."

"On the other hand, it was my fault you were born into very bad circumstances and I am determined to protect you until *Liem Trinh* can take over. When my body dies, I shall reincarnate in you and settle in your liver. My spirit doesn't weigh anything, so it won't be a burden for you. I can see ahead, I can warn you of dangers until your lucky star rises. Until then we shall be inseparable. I carried you when you were small, and now you will carry me when I become small again. Every time you think of yourself, you are thinking of me, and I shall smile with happiness every time your thoughts caress me."

"When we die, if we have been worthy of Lord Buddha, our soul enters Heaven. Everyone has a chair waiting for him in Heaven. When your lucky star rises, I shall return to Heaven and sit on my chair. For forty years you will be very successful, then you will join me. I shall make sure your chair in Heaven is next to mine."

"I want my body to be buried at sea. I dream of feeling my body float on the sea, then sinking into it and becoming one with the ocean. Thus my life will have ended perfectly, with my body in the sea and my spirit in you, Hai, my ocean. I know all this will happen, because I saw in a dream some time ago that you would take me to the sea and let me sail away."

"Last night I died for a few minutes, and I saw you becoming a very important man, a man with immense power. I was so happy when I saw this I wanted my body to die for good, so as to free my soul for its next life in you, but I was made to return here. My time has not come yet, but it won't be long now. Don't feel sorry for me, it's only my body that will need to be buried."

"When you become an important man, you will meet your father. I know that because I have seen you two together in many dreams. He will be very old and have many problems, but you will save him, whatever happens."

This was new and Tam's eyes opened at once. Over the years, at the Saintenoix and later at *papa*'s, he had always felt that his mother should hate his father for what he had done to them, although he also had a sneaking suspicion that she secretly still loved him for the kind and caring way he had treated her before her pregnancy, perhaps the only time in her life when someone had treated her like a human being. But he couldn't imagine why she would want him to help his father out of trouble.

"Why, mother?" he asked.

"Since I have been going to the pagoda I have understood the meaning and purpose of earning merit on earth to prepare for the afterlife. By paying a wrong back with kindness, we make merit twice, once for forgiving and once for extending a helping hand. We shame the wrongdoer and show him the Middle Path. By taking revenge, we have strayed off the Middle Path, will gain no merits and will have stained our soul. What happened to me happened and I don't want you to dirty your hands with revenge for something stupid that I did. I have brought enough problems on your head as it is. Instead, through your actions, you can make him realize that although I have no education, I know the meaning of harmony and compassion and am trying to make him a better man."

This explanation helped him understand what she had meant when she said that dying was not frightening "once you have prepared for it". She had cleansed her mind of all negative thoughts and experiences, had forgiven everyone. She was entering the afterlife with a clean slate.

"But don't you still hate him a little, mother?"

"No, my son, I don't. I understand that people like him cannot behave in any other way, because they grow up like that, arrogant and uncaring. But he was very nice to me before you were born, and I know he can be changed, even late in life. I know you will be able to do it because I have seen it all clearly many times in my dreams."

"Even when I was young I could see things in my dreams that came true. After I die, I can help you avoid fatal mistakes until you can reach the age of thirty-six, where success awaits you. Whenever you are in doubt, listen to your inner voice, because that will be me speaking to you. After *Liem Trinh* rides high I can take a rest in Heaven."

One evening his mother stopped breathing as she lay in his arms. Half-asleep, he became aware that she had died only when he felt a sharp pressure on his chest. He looked down, and saw that she was pushing down with her forefinger. Her fingernail had scratched his skin, breaking it. He knew instantly that at that precise moment her spirit had entered him, Hai, her ocean, like *chi* enters and leaves the body, effortlessly. She has to be in your liver already, which means we have become one. People will think you're alone from now on but you won't be. Everywhere you go you'll always be together.

But first he had to send her earthly body to the sea. He picked her up and walked up and down the length of the tunnel under the bridge, hugging her, pressing his face against her cheeks and inhaling strongly and loudly. She was as light as a feather, and still warm. The other vagrant families, mostly very old men and women in various states of poor health, looked on silently and he could see them thinking. She's finally gone. After all that coughing she's better off dead anyway. Wonder who's next. If the boy leaves the bridge we can take his space…

He wrapped his mother's light, limp body in a thick blanket from head to toe. He then tied the surprisingly small bundle with rope onto the wooden plank they had used for a bed. From nearby, he pulled out a four-wheeled wooden cart used to carry garbage. He had worked on it over the weeks, in anticipation of his mother's death, and had strengthened the wheels, scraped the inside clean and washed the whole contraption at the stream. Like his mother, he also believed in being prepared for the future. He carefully placed the wooden plank into the cart at an angle, with her head upright, wedging the bottom so it wouldn't slip. He reached over and pulled out the thick steel needle from the bun of her hair. This hatpin, worn day and night, had been an indication of her mindset all these years under the bridge. Always be prepared for the worst. He slipped it into his waistband, determined to also use it for self-defense when necessary. Gently, he then edged the cart out onto the road. It looked as if he were a delivery boy hauling a statue or some garden ornament.

At the end of the road he turned left and pushed the rough cart towards the river, which led past the city center to the other end of town. Suddenly it began to rain, the streets emptied and he started running, pushing the cart faster and faster, laughing like crazy. He felt an enormous joy welling up inside his chest and he shouted into the dark skies above "My mother died but she didn't leave me…she's here with me…she'll always be with me…she died but she now lives again…I love my mother and she loves me…and we'll always be together…this is wonderful…thank you Heaven…thank you ! "

He knew that his voice carried into some of the houses and that he sounded like a drunk or a madman running and shouting in the rain but he didn't care. His beloved mother's Calvary had ended, she suffered no more and yet they were still together. Years of watching her die little by little had ended. They were both free now. He began shouting even louder over the clattering of the trolley as his feet raced along.

By midnight he had arrived at the far reaches of the Song Hong, well outside of the city, but he pushed the cart on further, wishing to avoid the small communities that had settled on the riverbank. He had been planning this for some time, ever since his mother had expressed a desire to be buried at sea. Finally, he arrived at the spot he had picked weeks before. In spite of the rain, he was covered with sweat, and sat down to take a rest. He then pushed the cart into a clump of bushes that grew on the riverbank and returned slowly to the nearest community, made up of some three or four families that made a living out of ferrying people across the river. He had picked this community because they had many small boats moored to a homemade jetty and because they had no dogs. Walking out into the river, knee deep in the mud, he carefully unhooked a small boat from its mooring. There was no moon that night, and he climbed into the boat and paddled it quietly with his hands down the river until he reached the place where he had hidden the cart. He lifted the plank to which his mother was tied out of the wooden cart and slowly lowered it full length into the boat. The fit was perfect, as he knew it would be. Always plan ahead. Always plan ahead. Never be surprised. He sat there, in the mud flats, silently looking at the small bundle that was his mother. There were no tears in his eyes. You have cried all the tears in your body listening to her night after night. You will never cry again. And there is no reason to. Her body has left you after all these years but her spirit lives on in you as we sit here on a moonless night watching her body about to sail for the sea. After a while, he struck a match and lit one joss stick, which he wedged into the prow of the boat. Joining his hands in front of his chest, he said a short prayer to the river spirit, asking him to carry his mother's body all the way to the sea, where she wanted to be buried. Then he lit another incense stick and prayed to the wind spirit, asking him to help guide the small boat down river. Finally he lit the third stick, and prayed to the sea spirit, asking him to receive his mother's body and to let her rest in peace in his arms. After prayers, he bowed three times, then waded through the mud, pushing the little boat out into the river, where the current would carry it on downstream. Here you are, with your mother, sending her body down the river to the sea. You don't know if it will ever get to the sea but the main thing is that the sending off ceremony had been done properly. In your mind, her body will reach the sea the next day, and that is all that matters. It will sail out to the middle of the ocean and sink beneath the waves, becoming a part of the ocean, in accordance with her wishes. You have done what she wanted and her body has received a proper burial. He then waded back to the bank and walked back to the nearest boathouse, where he undressed and washed himself. He then washed his clothes free of the river mud and sat naked in the darkness of the night while they dried. The death of your mother has lifted a huge burden off your shoulders. Watching her die had ground you down and sometimes you felt you were dying along with her. It wasn't her slow death that was crushing you but the feeling of hopelessness, of not being able to lessen her suffering. Now you feel calm. Your destiny is all written out. Your mother said so and she could see into the future. You just have to be patient and be careful, to survive until the three bad stars leave and *Liem Trinh* rises, after which nothing is impossible. The rain had stopped, the clouds had moved on, and the stars were now visible. Looking up into the night sky, he said loudly to himself, "Tomorrow I shall go and see if I can find Phong." Weeks before, he had planned to do this.

Phong was one of the Buffalo Head gang members Tam had known, and he had mumbled something about there being plenty of work for those who loved their country when Buffalo Head asked Tam what he intended to do after their gang broke up. Tam had said that he would find something worthwhile to do.

An incredibly strong sense self-confidence welled up in him and he smiled to himself. Silently, he spoke to his mother. Don't worry, mother, all will be right from now on. As long as we're together things will get better, bad star or no bad star. You are my star, I'll follow you to the end of the earth. Nothing can hurt us any more. We've been hurt enough already.

PART TWO

AT THE CROSSROADS OF LIFE

24

The Recruiter

Phong had been one of the more secretive members of the Buffalo Head gang. He often drew out one member at a time for quiet talks although he had never approached Tam, perhaps because he thought him too young. When the gang broke up Buffalo Head asked each man where he intended to go, with a view to regrouping when the situation eased up. Tam answered he would look for work and Phong, who was standing nearby, remarked that true nationalists were never out of work. Buffalo Head looked at him with some exasperation but said nothing, which surprised Tam. He got the impression Buffalo Head knew Phong well but didn't like him, for whatever reason. Tam knew there were Vietnamese students and intellectuals from the educated middle classes who opposed French colonialism, who called themselves nationalists and were politically active in the big cities, but Phong was from the working class. Like you and the others in the Buffalo gang. What kind of work can he mean? He can't be one of these nationalists. He's not educated.

The problem was he couldn't find Phong anywhere. Even when he worked for Buffalo Head, Phong had always appeared and disappeared at will, like a cat, so Tam left word at all the Buffalo gang haunts he had known. One night, while asleep in the cargo hold inside the central station, he felt someone pinch his foot lightly. In the darkness he couldn't make out the man's face, but he could see the shape of a head. His hand slowly reached for his waistband, for the steel needle his mother had learned to carry in the latter years of her life. He was preparing to lunge upward and stab at the man's throat but the man spoke first.

"You looking for me?"

It was Phong. Tam grunted and got up, let go of the slim needle, slipped into his sandals and walked off with him to a small park nearby that was popular with lovers.

"Why are you looking for me?" Phong asked in a low but clear voice. Tam noticed later that everything he said was quiet and deliberate.

"My mother died. You said there was plenty of work for those who loved their country. What kind of work?"

"Aha, so that's it. Yeah, I remember now. You've grown up, haven't you? How old are you now?"

"Twenty." You're already eighteen. That's close enough.

"Hmm, that old, huh? A man already. You know what I do?"

"Yeah, you work for Buffalo Head. Like me."

"No. I work *with* Buffalo Head, but I am from the resistance." He paused while Tam digested this piece of information. "Buffalo Head knows I'm a recruiter and he knows we can support or disrupt his operations in the countryside so he allows me to be part of his gang."

They walked on in silence. Tam now understood the reason for Buffalo Head's uncharacteristic reserve when dealing with Phong.

"Do you know anything about our country's history?"

"Nope. We've been busy looking for food to eat all these years." No use telling him about your *Lycée* Albert Sarraut and the *Citadelle* classes. He probably hates people who work for the French as much as he hates the French.

"Good. You're the kind of people we want to recruit. When did your mother die?"

"Last week. Lung cancer." First time anybody shows interest in your mother.

"She's lucky. Those who die can rest, those who live must continue struggling. Want to hear something interesting?" Phong said, his eyes questioning Tam's face. Tam nodded.

"We have always been a feudal country. Warlords recruit armies of peasants and fight each other every few years over land. Win or lose, they continue to live like landlords while the conscripted peasants die like flies. The masses are born into anonymity and die in anonymity, generation after generation. All right so far?"

"Yes, yes, I can understand that." *Papa*'s books and his wonderful radio taught you about feudalism and all that. It didn't seem as if the people were suffering that much, but it's possible.

"Good. About a hundred and thirty years ago, the Nguyen warlord turned to the French for military help. He crowned himself Emperor Gia Long and changed our name from Dai Viet to Viet Nam. French influence grew and sixty years later, the French asked his successor, Emperor Tu Duc, for exclusive trading rights, having helped put his dynasty on the throne. The Emperor refused and fought a protracted war with France for twenty-five years, losing Da Nang, then Sai Gon and finally Ha Noi in 1883. All right?"

"Yes, I can follow all that." *Papa's* books and radio don't present things quite the same way but the names and dates are the same.

"Right. We've been a French colony for the last fifty years. To keep their properties and their fortunes, the Emperor and his squabbling warlords decided to co-operate with the French. The masses were poor before but are doubly poor now, because they have to feed two greedy masters instead of one. All right?"

"Yes. I understand what you say, even though I don't follow politics. We've been too poor to care what the French or the Emperor or the ruling families do."

"There are millions like you, and that's where we come in."

"We?"

"The resistance. Poor people like you and me. People who till the land but don't own any. The resistance is fighting to take back what is theirs."

"But the nationalists who are resisting France are all educated people, not like me and..." Tam's voice trailed off, not wanting to offend the recruiter.

"...and *me*," Phong finished the sentence easily. "But you are wrong there. I'm educated and so will you be if you join us. The rich deny us an education so they can oppress us, but we have set up our own schools where they cannot reach us. Far from French guns, we prepare the revolution."

"You mean throw the French out and bring back the Emperor?"

"No. Throw the whole lot out! The French, the Emperor and the Court families. Then take their lands and redistribute them among us. We want to bring social justice to the people!" His voice rose slightly at this point and Tam could hear the conviction in his tone.

"How?" he asked. He wasn't just being polite. Mentally alert, always easily aroused by new ideas, he really wanted to know. All the talks he had had with *papa* on the subject were coming back to him. But you were discussing the intellectual merits of the subject.

Ideologies. Causes. This man is talking about the application of these ideas. Big difference.

"Unity, leadership, sacrifice, those are the key words. We cannot have many resistance movements, each fighting the other as well as the French. We need one single resistance movement with one single leader, a good man who comes from the poor and understands the poor. A man like comrade Quoc. With one party and one leader, we must then be prepared to sacrifice our generation so that our children will be able to live in freedom, peace and plenty."

This was heady stuff and his graphic description of how it was to be done left Tam silent. Phong had been crystal clear. He didn't talk like a worker, more like a teacher. Mother, are you listening? I need guidance. I can't stay a pickpocket or a gangster all my life. If I want to become somebody, I have to find a cause I can believe in and fight for. Remember, that's what *papa* said?

"I wasn't thinking of making a revolution," he said tentatively. "I was just looking for work."

"You'll find work after we've trained you. You'll receive a good salary while working for the revolution."

"How do you find work if you're against the French? They control everything."

"Not everything. Many landowning families secretly sympathize with our cause. They help us find work. Once inside the system, we are exemplary workers by day. It is by night that we do our real work."

"What's that?"

"We study how the French and their lackeys work, we look for weak points, contradictions. Then we sabotage the system. A pinprick here, a pinprick there; a thousand pinpricks to weaken the system, then a frontal assault to crush it. But at this stage, the pinprick stage, we hide our hatred behind a smile, we resist by cooperating. You can only study your enemy if you can get close to him."

By now Tam knew, from having listened to the radio during the wonderful years with *papa*, that Phong was a *can bo*, what the French government call *un cadre communiste*, a trained activist who mixed with the people in the countryside, raising their political consciousness and organizing them into groups opposed to colonialism Always of peasant stock, they were charismatic speakers. Trained in the history of Viet Nam, they impressed the common people with their education and swayed them with simple, rock-solid arguments.

"Comrade Quoc told us we have a long journey ahead. Not all of us will live to see it through. The first step is to recognize that in our society there is no social justice for people like us. The second step is to act to change this society."

"How?"

"By joining up with others who think the same. By spreading the word, by recruiting, by becoming an example for others to follow. There's strength in numbers."

Tam remembered *papa* had said exactly these same words. Almost everything *papa* told you supports Phong's analysis of the situation. People with a shared vision, banding and bonding against a larger force, taking over, changing things, then being overthrown themselves. The world progressing from these clashes of ideas.

"Most people are selfish, and think only of themselves," Phong continued. "We ask them to think of the people, of the country. We ask them to work for the people, for the country. French guns can be overcome by the masses, but to run our country the masses have to be educated first. We need good men, men who can go out and motivate others. Educators. Do you get it?"

"Yes, I do," Tam answered thoughtfully. He wants you to join the resistance. That's what he was doing in the Buffalo Head gang. Persuading gangsters to abandon their selfish calling for a greater cause. That's why Buffalo Head didn't like him. Mother, are you listening?

Phong was speaking again. "Besides educators, we need good men who can do research work, who can work with the enemy and be our eyes and ears. The more we know about the enemy, the deeper the pinpricks."

They walked on. Tam marveled that this man, who looked like any of the hundreds of workers doing lowly jobs in the capital city. He doesn't look like an educated man but he knows so much and explains things so clearly without sounding condescending.

"Both the educators and the researchers must work in absolute secrecy, which means they cannot have a normal family life. They go where they are sent, when they are sent. They change identities like a snake changes its skin. They do whatever needs to be done to further the cause. They have no lives of their own any more. All the time they work within the enemy's system, they are part of that system. This is what we mean when we say 'cling to the enemy's belt'".

Tam found himself nodding in the dark. On the French radio broadcasts, the educators Phong was talking about were called political cadres and the researchers were called spies. The French police call them terrorists and murderers. As to having no personality, changing names and moving from place to place, you've been doing just that from the time you were born. Perhaps you're destined to become a resistance fighter, a spy, a man with many names and faces. Mother, are you listening?

Finally, it came.

"Do you want to join us?" asked Phong.

At that moment, Tam's stomach muscles cramped up and a tingling but pleasantly mild electric shock shot from his belly button up to the spot on his chest where his mother had scratched him before dying. It was all over in a fraction of a second. His mother's face appeared instantly in his mind's eye, her eyes bright with encouragement. The numbers three and six, large and white in color, appeared in his mind. This was what he had been waiting for.

"Yes, I do," he answered.

25

The Cadres

Later that night, he followed Phong through the velvety night to the edge of the city, where squatter colonies lived in between festering rubbish dumps, without running water or electricity. Groups of surly men, some drunk, sat around smoking. Haggard-looking women shrieked and fought over scraps from the dumps while dull-eyed children, dead to the world, slept in dingy shacks that were washed away after each monsoon rain. Packs of mangy dogs chased after huge rats through holes in the flimsy partitions that separated the clapboard hovels. They picked their way down soft muddy lanes lined with putrefying garbage. After a while, they arrived at a small hut. Phong whistled softly and Tam heard the latch on the door being pulled. A small kerosene lamp burned inside, around which two men sat smoking. The third man had opened the door. They entered the hut and sat down on a reed mat on the beaten floor, cross-legged, while the smelly lamp sputtered steadily in the center of the circle.

Phong introduced him as a new friend. The other men continued smoking, their faces expressionless. An embarrassing silence hung in the air until Phong reached for the teapot behind him and began refilling the dirty teacups in front of them. Everyone sipped his tea noisily, and one of the men asked Tam what he had been doing these last few years. From the tone of his voice it was clear that he was the senior man in the room, and that Phong deferred to him. A surly face, thinning hair, deep set eyes, thick lips and shiny black teeth, a real peasant and a brutal one, born with hatred written on his face. Tam repeated the story he had given Buffalo Head a couple of years earlier, since he was sure that this was what Phong already knew about him.

When he finished, the four men looked at each other, expressionlessly. The leading cadre, whose name was Quach, turned towards him.

"Young Tam," he said evenly, "I take note of the fact that you speak French. Tell me how you came to learn that language."

Thinking that speaking French was a point in his favor, as it had been with the Buffalo Head gang, Tam was about to tell him about *Ma Mère Supérieure* and *Monsieur* Saintenoix when he suddenly felt a sharp pain in his solar plexus, like a reflux of bile. A giant number nine, black in color, flashed through his mind and he paused. His mother and he had worked out a warning system. Thirty-six was the number of years he was cursed, and three and six equaled nine. Each bad luck star lasted twelve years, a combination of one and two, which together made three. Three such stars made nine. Nine is your black code, meaning you'll die early. Thirty-six is your white code, meaning that you will survive your curse. These men hate the French with a passion and they are suspicious about your ability to talk French. Clearing his throat, he swallowed hard and repeated the background story he had given the Buffalo Gang leader. His mother had worked for a Frenchman when he was still young and he had picked it up from playing with the Frenchman's children. He couldn't remember the name of the Frenchman, nor the address, because that was long ago.

"What were the children's names? Surely you must remember them?" asked Quach with irritation.

"Lucille, Dulcie and Tarzan," Tam answered, holding his breath. But there was no reaction from Quach or the others present, and he smiled inwardly. Peasants don't know one name from another when it comes to French. You can say anything to them. They're not smarter than you.

"But how did you become fluent in speaking and writing French? Comrade Phong says you were able to read French documents."

"My mother then worked for another Frenchman, a military, and he sent me to school inside the camp."

"Your mother seems to like working for Frenchmen. Was this military man fucking your mother?" Quach asked. He made an obscene gesture, smacking one open palm over a cupped fist, making hollow sounds.

"I don't know," Tam answered, blushing instantly. Anger flared inside him at the man's coarseness but he knew he was in the presence of dangerous men. "He treated me like a father and wanted me to be able to read and write French."

"Was he fucking *you*?" one of the men asked, snickering. Quach looked at him and he fell silent. Obviously, there was a pecking order in this group.

"Was he your real father?" said Quach. "You look very light skinned to me." His eyes were filled with contempt as he looked at Tam.

"No, not at all. When I met him I was already ten years old. No, my father is Vietnamese, but I don't know who he is. He died when I was still a baby." So many people die every day for one reason or another you're always safe saying that someone died.

"Was this Frenchman a policeman?"

"No, just a soldier. A corporal, I think. I'm not sure."

There followed a long series of questions about the name and age and facial characteristics of the military employer, the exact location of his barracks and why his mother had left him. It seemed Quach knew something about the layout of the camp. Again he asked Tam if his mother had been a whore. It seemed he got some perverse pleasure insulting him. As the pace of the questioning picked up, Tam began to sweat seriously. The smell of the kerosene lamps gave him a headache and he was beginning to regret having made contact with Phong. But the miserable bastards are not getting the better of you. You're easily fooling these coarse and brutal men. They don't suspect you, because Phong brought you in, but they can't get a grip on you, so they want to humiliate you. He sat up, the picture of injured sincerity, determined to win this unexpected contest of wills.

Suddenly, he felt bilious again. His mother moving inside him. A large black nine. She was looking at the door and visions of guns flashed by his eyes. "There are soldiers outside," he said quickly, interrupting Quach.

For a split second the four resistance cadres remained frozen, only their eyes darting about. Then they dived head first through a hole that had been cut out of the mud wall nearest them. This small bolt hole, which Tam hadn't noticed until then, had been covered with brown rice sacks and looked like a part of the wall. He followed without hesitation and they scuttled like large rats down into a ditch just outside the hut, climbing up onto a wet earth dike and disappearing behind a small brick factory. Behind them a double-barreled shotgun blast shattered the flimsy wooden door and soldiers burst into the smoky room, guns firing wildly inside the empty hut.

With Quach leading the way, they walked single file down one lane and turned into another and reappeared near a waterway. *These people know every inch of the neighborhood. That's why it's so hard for the French to catch them. If you join them you'll be like them.* They slipped down the muddy bank and Quach untied a small boat. They all climbed in and paddled their way down the river estuary.

Finally, Quach spoke.

"Duc," he said with finality. "Wondered why he didn't attend tonight."

The other two men nodded grimly in silent agreement.

"Why?" Phong asked.

"The reward money," said Quach, again in a voice that invited no comments. "I should have rubbed him out last month."

Everyone nodded except Tam. A long silence followed, broken only by the soft sounds of their paddling. He wondered where Duc was and what would happen to him when Quach and his men caught up with him. *Chanh the Hammer and Tong man's body parts littered Ha Noi soon after the cancelled heist. Maybe some lucky dog will get Duc's liver?*

Quach spoke again, and his voice carried a hint of friendliness in it.

"Young Tam, you have very good ears. The Party can use a man like you." The boat glided along silently in the moonlight. He turned to Phong.

"French speaking recruits are always useful. Send him to Z-47 for basic training. You vouch for him, I'll second your vote. The best place to use him is at the Fort, since he knows it already. Make sure no one recognizes him."

The boat reached a small jetty and they all got off. The other men disappeared into the night without a word. Phong took Tam by the arm.

"Well done, Tam, well done. I know a place we can sleep tonight and we'll leave first thing tomorrow. We have a long way to go. From this moment, you have become a different person. Forget everything about the bridge, about Buffalo Head. Don't make contact with anybody from your past."

26

Z-47

One week later they arrived at one of the resistance training camps high in the mountains and Tam was interviewed by the camp commandant in the presence of Phong. The atmosphere was very relaxed, so he guessed that the camp was located in an area far from French garrisons. The formalities didn't take long, since he had no past activities they could check on. Quach and his cell in Ha Noi had already cleared him and he was too young to have had any kind of anti-resistance background. All this information was duly noted and recorded, and he was given a new name, Van, which means intellect, since it was obvious he was educated, being able to speak French. He couldn't help smiling wryly when he saw that he had accumulated another new name. Meo, Robert, Minh, Tam. And now Van. But he had grown up since and he now felt comfortable with having a new name. For you, a new name is like another shield, more protection. To live like Quach and Phong it's better no one ever knows the real you. You're already like *papa*, a man with a public job and a secret personality. Maybe you were born to be a spy. Maybe it's your Fate to become somebody by being nobody.

He was told he would train for three months at this camp, designated as Z-47 and then for another three months at another camp, L-11, then he was to report back to Phong in Ha Noi for reassignment. They met up before Phong left the training camp. The older man looked at him expressionlessly and said, "See you next year", turned and walked off. That night with Quach, Van had noticed the impersonal manner in which resistance cadres treated each other. Blunt to the point of rudeness, they did not observe the usual social civilities, but were always precise when giving or passing on instructions, sometimes saying point blank, "Repeat the instructions" to make sure they had been understood. It was very different from the polite and tactful way they spoke to non-resistance people. Later, as he trained with the resistance and understood what communism was, he understood why there was no warmth in them. The speed of their escape, the very few words they ever spoke to each other, the wordless goodbyes indicated a dryness and grim focus that life in the resistance brought upon its men. It was Party policy to deliberately suppress all forms of human emotions that could interfere with the accomplishment of a mission. The system produced soulless cadres who lived only to serve the Party. They ate, drank, slept, defecated and washed their bodies like everyone else, but with greater care, because they wanted above all to stay healthy so that they could better serve the Party. To find enjoyment in friendship or sex or personal comfort was frowned upon, and those who couldn't tear themselves away from these *bourgeois* traits were quietly weeded out of the system because they were considered weak and therefore unreliable. He remembered Phong talking about total sacrifice, giving up family, friends and the comforts of home. The Party was an implacable taskmaster and demanded total loyalty, dedication and commitment. Only those who constantly demonstrated they were prepared to sacrifice everything for the cause would be used.

Van's first month at the camp was devoted to hard physical labor from sunup to sundown, with one hour of very basic political education at night. In the second month, the best performers were allowed to attend the bi-weekly advanced political indoctrination classes, which were held at night and lasted from three to five hours. It was during this period that he learned to sleep only four hours a night and to catnap during daytime for ten to fifteen minutes when possible, springing wide-awake when called. Looking back, he now understood that the revolution was in its planning stages and there was a lack of everything. Not enough instructors, not enough recruits, not enough training materials. It would be many years more before armed attacks on the French garrisons could become a reality.

He was in a group of seventeen recruits and volunteers who had arrived more or less at the same time. Three were adults, two men and a woman who had left their village to join up. The fourteen others were boys and girls of his age group, evenly divided into seven boys and seven girls, all walk-in recruits from small towns and cities. All were really poor, and the only education they had received had been at the village primary school. They were told to carry fertilizer up a steep hill to a farm that had been cleared on a terrace half-way up the slope. The base camp was self-sustaining and it grew all the rice and vegetables it needed. The three adults, all broad-faced peasants with callused hands and large, rock-like feet, took to the work like ducks to water, having done manual work all their lives. The fourteen younger recruits, including Van, were the products of city life. Hard physical work came as a shock to them and he quickly learnt the difference between being tough and being strong. One lived in the mind, the other in the body. Having lived on the streets, they were all mentally tough as nails, but after one week of strenuous uphill climbing their lower backs, hamstrings and calves rebelled while their soft bare hands became infected with the many cuts and lacerations received from grasping vines and bushes in order to pull themselves uphill. The fertilizer used on the farm was the night soil that had been carefully collected from the camp below. The resistance was known for wasting nothing and everyone, from the camp commandant to the newest recruit, squatted on two planks to empty their bowels into large oil drums that had been stolen from the French military. Each day the contents were ladled out into thick ceramic jars that were placed into bamboo slings, two at a time. These slings had straps through which the carrier slipped his arms. With this heavy backpack sloshing around on his back, the carrier climbed up the hill, aptly named Shit Hill, to empty his load as directed upon arrival. During the rainy season, the hill turned into a giant mudslide and each time a carrier missed his footing and fell down the slippery slope the semi-liquid load tipped out, more often than not onto the carrier walking behind. The camp instructors watched them expressionlessly, but were always ready to lend a helping hand when a carrier fell. The incredibly foul smells and the disgusting combination of excreta and mud didn't put them off at all. They told the new recruits this was a test of their resolve, and that if they failed, if they couldn't accept a life of hard work, they were free to leave the camp.

"The revolution," they said, "needs people who are humble, hard working and disciplined. Working on Shit Hill will separate the men from the boys."

The first three days were the worst for Van. He wanted to vomit every time his hands came into contact with the slimy texture of the excreta, the foul result of hundreds of bowel movements fermenting in large vats filled with shimmering waves of fat white maggots. At night, when he dropped off to sleep, he was nauseated by the smells that had seeped into his clothes, hair and very pores.

The seven girls made a pact among themselves and began out-climbing the seven boys, perhaps because they only carried one jar at a time. This was unacceptable, and the boys redoubled their efforts to wipe away the shame. After one month, they were taken off Shit Hill and given quarrying work on a rock pile. This was backbreaking work, even harder than climbing uphill, but it was cleaner work and by this time they had become a lot stronger. In the third month, they were put to jungle clearing, where they had to deal with snakes and mosquitoes, malaria and dysentery. They knew their fortitude was being tested and they knew they were making the grade. They couldn't help smiling secretly when they saw new recruits heading towards Shit Hill, their pathetic faces grimacing at the foul odors surrounding them.

"Now I'm going to tell you about what's happening inside our country. I will do this by telling you the truth," said Brother Two, their instructor, a young man who until recently had been working in the fields from dawn to dusk. At the start of their second month, this was their introduction to the many long political lectures that followed. Lack of social justice was hammered home first and foremost.

"The rich own everything, the poor own nothing. There is no social justice."

"The rich are always right and the poor are always wrong. There is no social justice."

"You plant and harvest mountains of rice, yet you are always hungry. There is no social justice."

"The rich have schools, the poor have none. There is no social justice."

There was little doubt the instructor was putting into words thoughts and feelings that had existed since birth in the collective minds of the peasants and workers seated cross-legged around him. These feudal truths had become embedded not only in their minds but also in their parents' and their ancestors' minds, since the beginning of time. But this was the first time these social injustices had ever been presented at any one time with such clarity. Knowing that repetition was needed to reach the peasant mind, the instructors and senior cadres hammered the same themes home again and again until even the densest minds understood. The instructors' patience and way with words wove a solid fabric that bound everyone together, making them think as one. Now, finally, they could clearly see that social injustice had always been their lot.

Next came the development of a collective anger, channeled towards a specific target, for a specific reason, while keeping the whole exercise simple, so as not to confuse people who had seldom been required to think about anything. There was no doubt that the rich were a bunch of bastards who had been sucking the poor people's blood for centuries, but who were these rich people? It soon became apparent that they were not only the French invaders but also the Vietnamese landowners, who had collaborated with the foreigners to steal land from the masses, the poor, the people. From them!

"The Emperor in his palace, the French in their mansions, the military in their forts. We built the palace, the mansion, the fort, but we live in hovels. They have stolen everything from us!"

Every recruit knew at least one landlord, and anger, like a fire tearing through a dry patch of undergrowth, built up rapidly. The embers had always been there, but, once lit, they were being expertly stoked.

"The French devils from the west, the *tay*, send their tax collectors to our villages. If we can't pay, they put us in jail. Their soldiers come into the villages to rape our women. These *tay* are like hungry wolves who have come from far away to feast on our country. They are robbing us blind!"

Anger doubled at these revelations. It was true. Not only were we the victims of the rich, fat Vietnamese landlords, but also the victims of the big, mean, strong smelling *tay*. They concluded there were two enemies, two separate entities that they should hate, but they were wrong.

"There is only one enemy. The landlords and the *tay* are one and the same. Both exploit the poor. Our revolution is total. Vietnamese or French, they have both stolen our land and taxed us to death. To get rid of one thief is not enough, we must get rid of both of them!"

The next step was to develop an aim among the recruits.

"We want many things, such as food, clothes and shelter, an education for our children, some money to spend at the Lunar New Year festival. We want to have medicines, so that our children can survive their first years. We want to have the right to leave our masters and move elsewhere. We want to be free from debts. But more than everything, we want land!"

There it was. The magic word everyone could understand. Land.

"If we own a piece of land, we will never go hungry again. If we own a piece of land, our children can be educated, learn to read and write. If we own a piece of land, we can be born on our land and die on our land, instead of being born and buried anywhere, like animals."

"The rich and the *tay* have used our land long enough, it is time they return it to us. If they don't, we will take it back by force!"

"We must solemnly swear that when we take our land back, we shall not forget those who have abused us, humiliated us and killed us for many generations. Death is too good for them! These monsters and bloodsuckers must be roasted over the fire slowly, for many years, before the blood debt can be washed away!"

Wild cheering and hooting always burst out at this part and Van joined in wholeheartedly. Your mind has been liberated. You are now educated, like the rich, like the enemy. You are not afraid of them any more. "When we win," said the instructor, "we'll take everything from these greedy bloodsuckers and kill them slowly. To commit a wrong is the way of nature, but to correct a wrong is the way of men. We'll roast them over a slow fire. That'll be the sweetest revenge of all."

27

The Resistance

As the backbreaking months wore on, everything that they were being taught fell into clear focus. The instructors, young peasants until they joined the resistance, were speaking at the recruits' level, using terms and examples that were familiar to everyone and they looked upon them as older brothers.

"Education is power, so the Party will give you an education so you can go out and educate others, spreading this power around until we have enough to take back our land."

"While we educate you, we give you food, shelter, clothes and medication. With the Party behind you, you can go out and explain the truth to our brothers and sisters, recruit them into the Party. The more we are, the stronger the Party becomes!"

"Some of you will receive military training because we will need an army to overthrow the French and the landlords. But before we can attack, we have to know everything about the enemy. We have to have eyes and ears in their camps. We will need spies who can map the road to our victory."

"Our fight, our struggle, may take many years, but there is no doubt that we will win because there are a thousand poor men for one rich man. Once the *tay* see us standing shoulder to shoulder, they will run away and take their running dogs with them. Under the leadership of the Party, we can then take back what is ours!"

The call to revolution was a solid argument, and it went down easily. At night, before he fell asleep, Tam realized with increasing dismay that he had lived through eighteen years of gross social injustice and had never, not even for one moment, understood anything. At the convent, learning how to read French books had been his main preoccupation and he had been confused by the presence of Jesus and God. At the Saintenoix, he had seen for the first time the difference between how the French and the Vietnamese lived but he had thought this was normal. At *papa's*, with his books and his radio, he had become aware of the social and political issues that swirled around them. You and *papa* even discussed some of these in depth, but at the end of the day, your mother and you ate three times a day and slept comfortably under a solid roof at night, so these issues hardly concerned you. Catching up on your education, enjoying a real family life, all selfish interests, were uppermost in your mind. Under the bridge, with the Buffalo Heads, in a life of poverty, hunger violence, your main concern was finding food for your next meal. Purely selfish interests again. The instructors are right; we think of ourselves, we forget our country. Lord Bach abuses your mother, the rich exploit the poor. Two classes of people, rich and poor, like two different races, the French being a third. Your mother and you met some good French people, they treated you better than your own people, but it's true not everyone had your luck. There are thousands of greedy and brutal French settlers in Viet Nam. Everyone knows that.

One night, something new came up.

"We cannot have social justice if there is no social equality. In our society, the first priority is therefore social equality. This means we do not use the bourgeois forms of address any more. No more "sir" or "madam", no more "lord" or "lady". Everybody is addressed as 'comrade'. Our leader is addressed as comrade Quoc, and he addresses each of you as comrade."

The idea that a peasant could go up to a landlord and address him as comrade ripped away layers of social conventions that had been laid one over the other through the centuries, until they had fossilized into a hard cultural bedrock. And now, to be addressed as comrade was a shattering concept. In one single blow, the Party had lifted the scales from their eyes and stripped tradition to the bare bone. Van's head was spinning when he heard this. At the convent letters had become words, things and ideas. French was important in your young life, and now Vietnamese. The use of the right words can bond people to you, increasing your power. *Papa* said that as mankind becomes more civilized it increasingly uses persuasion. The resistance certainly knows how to persuade people. Are they more civilized than the French? With one word, 'comrade,' the Party had wiped away thousand of years of social inequality. A stroke of absolute genius. A door had been opened between rich and poor, educated and ignorant and everyone had become equal. Using words, the Party was winning the hearts and minds of the masses, growing bigger and stronger in the process.

After indoctrination at Z-47, Van was sent to L-11, where he followed a series of courses that covered the basic skills a cadre has to have. Health was their first concern. Foreign medicines were expensive; trained cadres were invaluable; maintaining good health was all important. Sleeping off the ground in hammocks, using mosquito netting, drinking only boiled water and taking bitter herbs to strengthen the immune systems were the first line of defense against malaria and dysentery. Specific roots and plants controlled infections, fevers and joint pains. Deep breathing exercises regulated the functions of the four main internal organs: heart, lungs, liver and digestive system. Massage relieved muscular pains and headaches; a concoction of crushed roots mixed with saliva healed small cuts. Van and his colleagues were surprised at how easy it was to stay healthy.

Physical survival was their second concern. Heightened awareness and instant reflexes were the first steps. Everything flowed from there. A cadre was a man or woman the Party had invested time and money on, and it was important to the Party that he or she survive to fight another day. He remembered the ghost-like way Quach and his colleagues had evaporated into the countryside that night within seconds of his sounding the alarm. He was taught how to disable a man barehanded in the opening seconds of a fight; how to escape through openings in the ceiling and floor when the doors and windows were shut; how to run and walk, and run again, for an hour at a time through rough terrain. As he kicked, poked and chopped his way through hand-to-hand combat classes, he remembered the powerful French military policeman outside *Chez Rose* that fateful Saturday night. In his mind he used him as the target he had to cut down, and he wondered if he could really do it in real life. At night he dreamt of different fights he would have with that young MP, winning each time.

He learned to work in the dark, finding his way through the jungle and spending hours climbing ropes. At all times he kept his mother's hatpin in his belt. Whenever he rubbed his stomach he could feel the little green frog stopper at the top of the pin. His mother's smiling face would appear and he longed for an opportunity to use it.

Sabotage was their third concern. He learned how public utilities, military hardware and industrial equipment could be destroyed with the use of homemade explosives, and how commercial machinery and home appliances could be disabled. Since the resistance movement in the hills had no access to any of these targets, training was theoretical. Actual practice would come on the job. But it was first necessary to recognize them for what they were, and then to know precisely what their weak points were and for this they used pictures and drawings of the equipment as well as wood and mud mockups. Dynamite, fuses and igniters, blasting caps, ammonium nitrate and nitric acid were stolen from the many French mining companies in the north. The peasants knew all about Chinese gunpowder from their past and had made their own fireworks for generations, so making smoke bombs and crude explosives was not new to them. Sand in a vehicle's gas tank, a missing firing pin in a rifle or an antenna on a military radio and the enemy was temporarily stymied. Deep wells and guard dogs could be poisoned. The use of flammable materials for arson became an art and the lighting of wildfires in summer to keep the troops occupied while they raided private residences was a common practice. Pre-positioning small caches of rice and water in the bush under rocks or high in the trees allowed a man to travel light.

Then came communications. Van was taught code words to describe specific layouts, to compress this information into a few easily-remembered words for couriers to carry back. Also, how to safely cache this information until it was picked up by another agent. He was shown what torture techniques he could expect from the police, and given a comprehensive story he could safely give the police under torture. He was taught how to communicate with agents and couriers who would visit him regularly to debrief him.

Finally, he was shown how to handle French explosives and guns. At this stage, the Party depended on French weapons, stealing them from hit-and-run raids on small, isolated outposts. These stolen weapons worked better than those that were available on the open market from French deserters, who sometimes sabotaged the goods before selling them. He saw resistance mechanics, peasant boys and girls, using the crudest of instruments, efficiently rebuild hand grenades, landmines and even bombs. Repairing and refurbishing a rifle was child's play to them and yet, until recently, these young men and women had patiently walked behind a plough twelve hours a day or, holding on to a stout pole, pedaled an irrigation wheel that turned a number of wooden paddles that sent the water splashing from one rice paddy to another.

He noticed there were other camps nearby as he became more familiar with the training base. From talking with his instructors, he learnt they were camps for porters, the lifeblood of the resistance redoubts. On bamboo poles and on reconfigured bicycles, they hauled into the mountains tons of desperately needed materials from the lowlands. Dressed in rags, living on two bowls of rice a day, they worked in the open, at the mercy of the seasons. In winter, the tempestuous monsoon rains lashed their skin, turned the earth trails beneath their feet into rivers of thick, red mud that sucked at their thick rubber sandals at every step. In summer, heat strokes, brought by the merciless sun, cut them down without warning. All year long, plagued by a million malarial mosquitoes, these human ants walked up hill and down dale, cutting through swamps and jungles before starting to climb the sheer limestone rocks that led to the resistance hideouts. Burying their dead along the trails, using sheer muscle power and an indomitable will, they overcame all the obstacles in their paths and delivered the goods. Everything the camps used was brought in from the lowlands, and without the armies of porters that operated day and night the whole resistance network of training camps would have ground to a halt.

Another camp was for couriers and contained a lot of women and young girls, a fact that was of great interest to Van's all male camp. The resistance did not have radios like the French military and the regional headquarters were linked to the many cells spread out all over the province by a network of human couriers. Even much later, after the Korean war ended, when Chinese copies of Russian field radios became available, the resistance continued using human couriers because sophisticated American communications equipment used by the French could capture their signals. The couriers were for the most part peasant women, many of whom were young girls, most of whom worked part-time only. In their district, they went from one cell or one information drop to another, collecting the information and passing it on, usually to another woman. Written information was carried in their clothing, in their hair, sometimes in the more intimate parts of their bodies; eventually it reached district or regional headquarters before being sent to the Viet Bac region near the Chinese border. Whether carrying vegetables to the market, hauling cheap goods on buses bound for the cities, serving meals in country inns or city restaurants, working in brothels that catered to the French, or simply visiting each other, a network of thousands of women passed on information up and down the line, ensuring that orders from the center reached the men in the field. When caught, the younger couriers were automatically gang raped and tortured until they had revealed all their contacts. To limit the damage, they were taught to give the names of people who were anti-communists, people the resistance wanted to compromise.

28

L-11

Van's final month of training were spent in a small village not far from Ha Noi. Near the village well was a large banyan tree surrounded by dense bushes. Nearby, in the open, was a very small, rectangular opening that served as entrance to a tunnel that led underground. A rectangular lid, camouflaged with wild grass and dead leaves, fitted perfectly over the opening. His guide pulled the lid up and Van slipped down the tunnel entrance, which led to a large underground chamber. The guide swiftly followed, replacing the lid carefully, from the inside. The chamber had two emergency exits that led to a tree line of bamboo copses growing along the edge of a dike about one kilometer from the village. Tiny air vents had been cut into the tunnel every twenty meters or so. During his first month, he stayed underground for three days at a time to acclimatize himself, emerging for an hour or so at night to clear his lungs. The little air available down below was stagnant and had to be shared by many men, women and children. The men were in training, like Van, and the women were there to cook and wash for the men. The married ones had brought their children along with them. The idea was to learn to eat, sleep and work underground for prolonged periods of time. To cope, Van learned a breathing technique, originally from Russia, aptly called "mouse breathing", which consisted of many but very small inhalations and exhalations. This was not difficult to do, since there was little space in which to move and no great physical effort was ever needed. He learned to apply lemon juice or his own urine to areas that had come into contact with the chiggers that lived in the tunnel walls. These bloodthirsty insects, looking for fresh blood to dine on, latched on to the tunnel inhabitants as they crawled by on all fours. Van repaired old guns in the daytime, studied the works of Lenin in the evenings, slept in a hammock at night and emptied his bowels in large earthenware jars that were set flush with the floor of wall cavities and served as toilets. When full, these jars were sealed and buried in the same wall cavities, but the stench of human excrement permeated every nook and cranny of that tunnel and he gagged at first whenever he had to make use of these underground toilets.

Besides repairing damaged weapons, he was also taught how to field strip old French handguns and rifles blindfolded. This was easy for him, having attended military classes for the Vietnamese soldiery at *la Citadelle*. As a future research cadre, he wasn't expected to do any fighting, but all cadres had to be familiar with the enemy's weaponry. In the early days of the resistance, a cadre had to be a multiple-skill asset, capable of being used as a courier, a spy, a saboteur, a recruiter or a political education cadre. The dependable French MAS-36 rifle had the distinction of being the last general issue bolt action rifle to be designed; the MAS-38 submachine gun, a reliable little weapon, used a low-powered French 7.65mm cartridge no one else used. Much later, the resistance modified these to take a 9mm cartridge. The Mle 24/29 light machinegun, after many modifications, turned out to be a solid weapon that he saw in use by the French until 1950. Old and outdated as they were, these French weapons could do a lot of damage and were far better than anything the resistance had at the time.

During this period of living underground, besides analyzing what Lenin had said, he also attended night classes in urban recruitment and political education. The first hurdle was how to blend into a workers' group. He had to be tactful, accommodating, helpful and absolutely honest in all his dealings with potential recruits. He had to be obedient where the French supervisors were concerned. Next, he had to identify his targets, disgruntled workers who nursed a grievance, whether specific or general. This grievance was the open door through which he could enter the man's mind and plant the resistance seed. In their parlance, he had to "slip into the target's mind". If the target went along, it was a victory for him. If he didn't, he had to identify the mistakes he had made, determine at which point he had lost him and re-calibrate his presentation for the next target. This personal trial-and-error process came out at the criticism and self-criticism sessions resistance fighters attended regularly when the situation permitted. In this way, they were constantly honing themselves, like sharpening a blade to make the next cut easier.

As Phong had told him the night they first met, the resistance workers were exemplary workers in the daytime and were often commended by their French supervisors, sometimes becoming the unofficial foreman the French would rely on to get all the other lazy and incompetent natives working. But at nightfall they were to hunker down with the other workers over cheap cigarettes and rice wine to commiserate with them over the iniquities of their miserable lives. The resistance leadership didn't want its cadres to talk about communism to potential recruits except to say that communism was based on sharing land equally between the poor. If anyone brought the subject up, having heard French propaganda describe the resistance as a communist movement, he was allowed to give a brief comparison between feudalism, which benefited the Emperor, colonialism, which benefited the French and their puppets, and communism, where the masses owned everything and shared it out equally. The cadres were to welcome such questions, which gave them the opportunity to plant a seed in the questioner's mind.

In the tunnel, Van's everyday instructors were men who had survived fieldwork for at least one year. They had worked right under the nose of the French, they had been blooded, and the trainees respected them like they would have respected their own fathers. But sometimes they would receive the visit of a senior cadre, men of much higher rank before whom their instructors bowed. A senior cadre was a man who had been accepted into the Party after a series of exams and had the right to carry a Party card, with a serial number on it. There was no higher honor for rank and file resistance members than to be invited to become a Party member. Too long an exposure to the French *Sureté* was dangerous, however, and these high-caliber cadres were brought back to underground camps for a rest period, during which they recharged their batteries and passed on their experience to the instructors to pass on to the recruits. By switching its agents around and changing their identities regularly, the resistance managed to field new faces all the time, making identification more difficult.

Their instructors told them that connecting with malcontented workers was easy, and slipping into their minds was not difficult once they had mastered the correct approach techniques. But translating whatever enthusiasm had been developed into positive action was difficult because everyone was scared of the French and their *Sureté Générale* officers, who employed Vietnamese police officers, the *auxiliaires*, to deal with troublemakers, unionists, resistance recruiters and communist agents. The Vietnamese police officers had a feel for the situation that their French superiors did not, and regularly planted *agents provocateurs* among the workers. These undercover agents often broadcast the fact that they had serious grievance against the French, drawing to them inexperienced resistance recruiters who were promptly arrested. Under torture, which was systematically used in the French colonial police system, they would implicate others. On the other hand, the instructors said, not all the *auxiliaires* were blindly pro-French. Some were ambivalent in their approach to their work, reported problems selectively depending on their personal likes and dislikes, nursed their own doubts and grievances about the system they worked for, and were themselves potential candidates for recruitment. Turning one of these men was a major achievement for any resistance recruiter because it gave the resistance eyes and ears within the French police system. In some cases, if these men had family living in the countryside, pressure could be put on them. Pressure could also be applied if they had personal vices that were not acceptable to the *Sureté*, or owed a lot of money due to gambling debts. Van found this part of his training fascinating. It seems your destiny is to be a spy. An invisible operator. *Papa* talked about working in the dark, faceless in daylight, manipulating people and events, collecting facts that can be used as weapons. Finally, you've found the road you must follow to become somebody important and powerful.

29

La Citadelle—Again

Finally, Van's training ended and he reported back to Phong. His basic training had covered a number of related disciplines, and he had managed to qualify in all of them, some to a higher degree than others. He now understood the overall picture. The Party had not deliberately cross-trained him to become a porter or a researcher or a courier or a guerrilla, but to become available for any of these callings, having built in a high degree of resourcefulness and self-confidence. Expertise in any given field would come with on-the-job training.

He was fairly certain he would be neither a porter nor a guerrilla but in between these two lay dozens of activities and he waited with trepidation to be told what his first assignment would be. After three months in resistance camps, he knew that whatever it was, there would be a series of tests for him to pass, and the Party would be watching and evaluating his performance and loyalty every step of the way. This would be done through the three-man cell system the Party used to enforce discipline and protect against possible betrayal. The three cadres supported one another and at the same time kept watch on one another. Everyone had a minder. The cell was part of a pod that could include as many as twenty cells that answered to a district committee that reported to a provincial committee. The provincial committees reported to regional committees which reported to a national security headquarters, located somewhere in the forbidding mountain range separating Viet Nam from China. The national security headquarters was controlled by the Party's Central Committee. Human couriers served as links between the control centers and the operational arms.

Phong introduced him to a commercial catering firm that serviced the Officers' Mess inside the French fort, *la Citadelle,* and Van became a delivery assistant. It was finally clear. He was to be a research cadre. A spy. Three times a week he rode in a van that delivered the groceries ordered by the chief cook, a French sergeant, and checked off each item with him. He then collected the money, signed a receipt, and went over the next list, to be delivered two days later. At first he was afraid a French soldier or officer might recognize him as having been *papa* Escudier's adoptive son, but it had been almost five years since his mother and he left the camp, and he had changed a lot physically. He had filled out, looked like a man now and was sunburned almost black from his work in the training camp. Don't worry, you're safe. All Vietnamese look the same to the French.

Soon after his first week, Van had the driver go past the NCO quarters so he could have one more look at *papa*'s house. His heart beat like mad when the truck approached that small bungalow where he had spent the best three years of his life. He felt a distinct twinge in his stomach as he looked at the neat little garden, the white fence and the curtained windows, and he was aware immediately that his mother was seeing everything he saw. He felt she was smiling at him, and he smiled back before telling the driver to move on. Wonder where *papa* is now? They wouldn't let you in *La Citadelle* after *papa* was reassigned, so even if he sent you anything you wouldn't know anyway. Is he sick? Is he dead? Will you ever see him again? Will he want to see you again now that you're in the resistance? It might be all right for Mathieu in Madagascar, but maybe he'll think you betrayed his love and trust. How long ago it had all been, he thought dreamily as the van moved from one Mess to the other. He also rode by the back of the soldiers' barracks, where Hélène had been. Everything had changed, and he hardly recognized the washing area where they would meet at noon before going into Pierre's room. Her hazel eyes and light brown hair came back to him and he was saddened at the thought that he would never see her again. She's in France already. Her harelip had been corrected. With a normal face she would be quite beautiful. *Papa*, Hélène, mother, all the people closest to you have gone away. Your life has become quite different. You're a spy now. One mistake and that's the end of you, but you have finally found a cause to live for. Nationalism. Freeing your country from the French grip. If you play your cards right, you can become a senior cadre like Phong or Quach. Maybe even higher.

After a few weeks, because his French vocabulary now included military slang and common French swearwords, the chief cook and he became friends of sorts. He was always given a glass of wine, which he hated but couldn't refuse, before climbing into the van to ride off to the NCO Mess, which his catering firm also serviced. This Mess was at the other end of the camp. In between the two were a number of garages, workshops, covered hangars and open-air parking lots where military equipment was being repaired, stored or parked. His first responsibility was to memorize the different types of equipment, the models, the numbers and the exact location. Next, he had to plan the best routes for an infiltrator coming from outside to get to the equipment. Then he had to make a drawing of the layout of the camp, pinpointing the underground cables from the city's power plant, the pipelines from the city's reservoir, the ammunition depots, gasoline storage tanks and backup power generators. Finally, he was to note the density of people at various locations during his visit times. For example: two hundred soldiers in and around their barracks at ten in the morning; fifty personnel in the kitchen; twenty officers at their desks; two hundred Vietnamese local hires for the cleaning, cooking and washing necessary. He had to observe which parts of the camp these local hires were allowed to move through unchallenged during the course of their work.

At the NCO Mess, his face still red from the glass of wine at the last Mess Hall, the same procedure was repeated with another French sergeant. Finally, Van returned to the caterer, Mr. Thai, a sympathizer with the resistance cause who, at great risk to himself, allowed his firm to be used as a cover.

On his off days, Van was responsible for equipment spotting. With powerful, stolen French binoculars in hand, he sat in the dusty attic of the National Museum, a three-story government building a few blocks away from *la Citadelle*. From his vantage point, he counted French scout cars, trucks, armored personnel carriers, light, medium and heavy tanks, and towed artillery weapon systems that left and entered the Fort, noting the times of entry and departure. Access to the top floor of the Museum was arranged through a security guard who was in fact a resistance plant and a member of Van's cell. His name was Quat, and he had been trained as a future guerrilla. In the meantime, he worked for the National Museum and kept an eye on Van and the third member of their cell, a woman courier named Thanh.

Although he knew both his cellmates by sight he instinctively avoided any kind of personal contact with them and, in the first year that he spent at *la Citadelle* as an eye and ear of the resistance, he hardly said more than ten words to Quat. The senior cadres at training camp had stressed that all relationships had to remain professional. Personal bonding was considered a bourgeois weakness, one that could interfere with the carrying out of Party orders, and such attempts were to be reported. Not to report them would merit severe blame at the criticism and self-criticism sessions that were an integral part of their lives as communist cadres. For many, it was this fear of public criticism by one's peers that kept them on the straight and narrow path.

Their cell's control officer was in the countryside, and Van returned to a village outside the capital every two months to report in person. His previous reports were reviewed carefully, almost word by word. Thanh had passed some of these on verbally, the wording had sometimes been less than exact and he now had to correct the wrong impressions they had made. He pored over maps and diagrams with senior cadres, pinpointing exact locations and confirming schedules. It was on these occasions that he had to participate in criticism and self-criticism sessions. The Party relied on these cathartic therapy sessions as a psychological benchmark to evaluate the reliability of a cadre. He would be asked to critically examine his recent conduct, pointing out the correctness of his actions or the failures he thought he was guilty of. It was essential that he be honest in his self-judgment while projecting a humble attitude. His colleagues would sit in silence, wondering how they would present their stories when their turn came. Occasionally, a senior cadre would make a comment, everyone would nod, notes would be taken by the secretary for the records. After Van had finished, a silence that was louder than words reigned. Then someone would speak up, criticizing or praising him. This was usually the time when personal grudges came out, disguised as righteous criticism for non-adherence to Party rules and regulations. Finally, the senior cadre would speak. To be praised for having acted correctly showed he had understood the dictates of the Party. Everyone would clap and he would stand down. To be criticized for having acted incorrectly showed that he hadn't, and his mistakes were dissected right there and then, in front of everyone. He would then apologize to everyone for having failed to see the error of his way, promising that it would not happen again. Everyone would clap, and the meeting continued. There was nothing spontaneous about the clapping. Everyone present knew the pecking hierarchy inside the room and waited for the most senior man to clap before joining in. As soon as the ranking cadre stopped clapping, everyone also stopped. On a few occasions, some members, carried away by their desire to shine in the eyes of the senior cadres, continued clapping after the senior man had stopped, only to become aware of their *faux pas* when they saw the most senior comrade look at them pointedly while the other attendees looked straight ahead, keeping their eyes religiously averted from the over-enthusiastic clapper.

Along with the three-man cell system, criticism and self-criticism sessions ensured that everyone in the magic circle knew exactly at all times what was expected of him. At first, Van sometimes left these sessions drenched in sweat, although he hadn't received any criticism, but he soon realized that the correct use of Party terminology was the key to a successful presentation. At the convent, had the nuns used a colloquial form of Vietnamese, the refugees would have paid less attention to what they were saying. But they used words and ideas that came straight from the Bible, from catechism, and everyone had to pay attention to what was being said or be left out of the conversation. Van was talking to a working class audience made up of peasants and workers who would have sat back and relaxed had he used the vernacular they were familiar with. The indoctrination sessions in the mountains had added dozens of new communist terms to the Vietnamese vocabulary, some of which were code words invoking ideas and images that only people who had attended would recognize. The more dogmatic Van was the harder he hit home and he caught some of the senior cadres giving him strange looks on a number of occasions, as if they had doubts as to the sincerity of his too well-crafted presentations. He was talking so much like them they must have wondered if he was secretly parodying them. They reminded him of the sweet-looking Sister Tuyet at the convent. She had also thrown strange looks at Van, then Robert, who, while reading from the Bible, was consciously imitating her inflections and eye-rolling at certain passages.

As a junior cadre, Van regularly received his share of lectures about the sins of the flesh, about weakening in his resolve to serve the Party, about allowing the act of fornication to ruin his life and lead to his betrayal of the Party's ideals.

"When the Party thinks you are ready for marriage, you will be authorized to find a woman who is suitable," he was told again and again by senior cadres, who reminded him of hard, dry and sapless wood. Otherwise, men could apply for marriage only after thirty of age, and women after twenty-five. Sexual attraction or dalliance of any kind before that age or outside of officially sanctioned marriages was strongly discouraged, with the offenders made to suffer public criticism and ostracism.

In spite of this pressure-cooker atmosphere, or perhaps because of it, a distinctly non-professional relationship began to develop between Thanh and Van. She wasn't pretty but she was attractive, especially when she was listening seriously to someone talking. He could sense she was both intelligent and sensitive. Her smiles, when she did smile, were quick and he knew she had a sense of humor, unlike Quat and the control officers. He realized he hadn't been with people who liked to joke and laugh since he last worked with the Buffalo Head gang. Rough and brutal men, their sense of humor was coarse, but they were always ready to laugh at a joke, even when it was directed at themselves. Since then he had been surrounded by equally rough and brutal men with serious faces whose sense of humor had been deliberately cut out of them.

30

Thanh

Thanh was a small woman who sold vegetables at the local market and Van always bought his legumes from her, at which time she passed on verbal instructions from their control officers. She took the bus into the countryside every third day to stock up on her vegetables, at which time she met other couriers and played her role as one vital link in a network that covered the whole province. She was about twenty years of age and had an extraordinarily loud voice for someone her size, especially when she was hawking her vegetables. Every two weeks or so Quat, Thanh and Van met casually at the market place, drifted into a tea house and sat down at a table near the back exit. As a researcher, Van was the star of the show because he had something new to report every week. Thanh said little, being basically a runner. Quat, the sleeper, was the senior cell member and it was his responsibility to decide on what should be reported. But he was totally out of his depth where *la Citadelle* matters were concerned, and Van had to summarize what Thanh should pass on. To regain control of the proceedings, Quat would pretend to think about what Van had said before nodding importantly, to show he approved of his report, and then would launch into a pep talk aimed at raising the level of their loyalty to the Party. The necessity to be ever more vigilant than they already were was stressed by their cell leader, a man who sat on his backside the whole day in a dusty museum, his mind a total blank, while Thanh maneuvered under the nose of French roadblocks and Van entered a French military camp daily to spy on the activities therein. Quat would always end the meeting with an anecdote about Nguyen Ai Quoc, the hero and the leader of the Party. Van never knew if these stories were true or not, but he suspected Quat was making some of them up. He caught himself exchanging glances with Thanh whenever Quat's unimaginative stupidity became more than they could bear. Van found her eyes mischievous. She obviously shared his opinion of their cell leader. He began to wonder what sort of a life she led.

Thanh's eyes could turn flirtatious at times and her voice softened when she spoke normally. Her lips, small, well-shaped and always red, mirrored her expressions of amazement, doubt, disgust and pleasure. Her teeth, small and evenly set, were lacquered black and shone brightly when she laughed. He began looking forward to meeting her. Their fingers touched on a number of occasions, when he was reaching for his vegetables, and he felt a thrill run through him each time. From the way she glanced sideways at him, when she thought he wasn't looking at her, he felt she was also attracted to him. Since he did not smoke or drink, he was able to save most of his salary every month. After remitting twenty percent of it to the Party through Thanh, he still had more than enough for his modest needs. He felt that he wanted to befriend this woman, whose eyes and smile began to haunt him as he went about his work. Finally, in the full knowledge that what he was doing was wrong and that he could be severely criticized for doing it, he bought her a silver necklace. One night, when there were few people around her stall, he gave her his present, wrapped in brown paper. When she felt the hard metallic chain through the paper she looked at him enquiringly. His heart beat furiously in his chest and he felt giddy. He knew they were on the brink of committing an irreversible act. She was a courier, he was a research cadre, they were in the same cell and personal relations were strictly forbidden. Yet he had sensed that there was something between them and this something was stronger than obeying orders. Anyway, the die had been cast the moment he bought the necklace, an act of utmost selfishness. That money could have gone to the Party, which was giving them everything they needed.

"Nine o'clock tomorrow night by the river bank. The stone dragon," he whispered.

Expressionlessly, she put the package away in her bag, unopened.

"Will that be all, sir?" she asked loudly. Flustered, he nodded and turned away, hoping she had heard him right.

The next night he arrived at the riverbank early and walked up and down for an hour. His eyes always kept in sight the stone dragon statue near the temple. His head buzzed with questions; his heart beat unusually fast. Each time a boat glided by, its oars splashing the waters softly, the moon's reflection on the river broke into dozens of rays of light that rippled softly in ever larger circles until calm returned. His mind was anything but calm. Has she reported you? Is Quat watching you from the shadows? Will you be called in tomorrow and sent to another province to cleanse the disease of sex from your weak and unreliable mind? Will all this come up at the next self-criticism session? He cringed at this awful thought. If it does, you just deny everything. Always deny, deny, deny. Never admit to anything wrong.

He also thought about his mother. Does she approve of what you're doing? Why not? You're a man now, you need a woman friend. Anyway, she knows everything you're going to do. If there is danger she will warn you. Calm down. Relax. Breathe deeply. Relax.

At the appointed hour, however, Thanh appeared and walked straight towards him. She had obviously been watching him for some time, perhaps with the same thoughts in mind. She took his hand quickly, as if they had always known each other, and led him away from the crowd at the riverbank.

"Too many people here," she said.

They walked until they came to a turn in the river where the grass had grown high and there were bushes everywhere. She guided him towards a dark corner and they entered a little alcove, where they sat down on the dry ground. Through gaps in the foliage above their heads, rays of the moon bathed their faces in ghostly pallor.

"Now we can do whatever we want," she said, laughing softly.

She then pulled out the silver necklace he had bought and placed it around her neck, asking him to adjust the clasp at the back.

It turned out she was from a nearby province, had been married to an older man, a farmer, and had had a baby girl. Husband and daughter had been killed in a French army operation that had swept through their village in the dead of night. She had joined the resistance soon thereafter, at the age of eighteen. After a three-month stint at a camp as a cook's assistant, she had been picked for courier service and had worked in this capacity for one year before the Party put up the capital for her stall at the market. During all this time, she had been able to hide from her minders the fact that she was a healthy, active country girl, barely twenty, recently married, and that the puritanical restrictions of the resistance grated on her. Or perhaps they knew but pretended they didn't, hoping that the discipline required in resistance work would eventually impress on her the necessity of overcoming these *bourgeois* weaknesses.

"They're all hypocrites anyway," she said with contempt, her sweet little lips turned down in the semi-darkness. "They're all after me like dogs in heat. With all their sermons about the Party this and the Party that, their hand are all over the place when they think no one is looking. The worst are the senior cadres."

"Quat?"

"Him?" she laughed, "No, he's too stupid for that. They picked him for guerrilla work because he's brain dead. But your control officer, what's his name…"

"Huy. Really? You're kidding!" Elderly, frail, sanctimonious and severe. The last person you would have expected of having a sex drive.

"Yes, that's the one, the old he-goat. He fathered a kid in Nam Dinh province, and they moved him here as a punishment but he's too old to change. When he begged me for it, I told him my control officer was already doing me, which is not true, and I think Huy reported him, the dirty hypocrite. I heard there was a big stink at top level but I wasn't invited to these senior self-criticism sessions. If I had confirmed or denied what I had said, one of the two senior cadres would have been in for the high jump. So they discussed and analyzed the matter among themselves and I never heard about it again!"

She then burst out laughing and Van laughed along.

"After that the word must have come down and no one dared approach me and I was left alone to do my work."

The scales were falling from his eyes, and bits and pieces he had heard over the last two years came together. Communism or no communism, Puritanism or no Puritanism, men and women were going to indulge in sex whenever they could, whatever the Party said. He now remembered that, on a few occasions, he had stumbled unexpectedly on men and women cadres copulating like animals in the fields or in a supposedly empty hut. Although he had quickly walked away each time, he thought he recognized some of the men, his seniors. It was the same with the Catholics, who sinned blissfully all week long and then cleansed themselves on Sundays. Human beings, like animals, were creatures of Nature, and the procreating drive was the dominant trait. Thanh and he were just doing what everyone else was doing, or at least trying to. The main thing was not to get caught at it.

That night, expertly guided by Thanh, he had his first sexual experience. It was wonderful, better than anything he had ever imagined. The roots of his feelings and emotions ran riot and he lost his sense of time and place. His hands could feel her soft skin everywhere as he sank time and again into her firm and sensual body. An aura of musk and the incredibly sweet scent of a woman aroused rose from their sweaty bodies as they strained against each other, reaching for the pure happiness they knew was coming. When they finished, he didn't know where he was at first but after a short rest, they did it again, and the second time was even better than the first. She wanted him as much as he wanted her, but cautioned him against letting his emotions run away with him. She obviously had good control over hers.

"We live in difficult times," she said, "the future is uncertain for people like us. You found me, I found you, we like each other and as long as we don't become attached to each other we can be happy together. Let's just enjoy everything while we can. Don't make promises about tomorrow, because you don't know what tomorrow will bring."

He met with Thanh again a number of times, always in different places, some of his choosing, some of hers, and each time they made love as many times as he physically could. Always fresh, she was insatiable, and in spite of her words he felt that he was falling in love with her. Fleeting thoughts of suggesting they leave the resistance and get married crossed his mind more than once. They could move to another province and start a new life, even raise a family. But he never said anything about it to her, because he felt ashamed about being so weak that he had nearly forgotten his resolve to become an important and powerful person in society, to ensure his mother a better second life than her first one. And he also had to find his father and help him. All these personal considerations, on top of working for the resistance, precluded marriage and a normal life. And anyway Thanh did not seem to want to get married again. She seemed perfectly content to live this dangerous life, hiding her work from the French police and her private life from the resistance. Apart from secretly rejecting the ridiculously severe restrictions on her sexual life, she was very much dedicated to the resistance, a fact that he discovered when they talked about the Party, in between bouts of wild lovemaking. She was quite emphatic about it. The Party and its cause were absolutely right, and were not to be questioned; the French had to be thrown out; the landlords had to be exterminated; land had to be returned to the workers. She accepted the fact that some senior cadres were lechers and hypocrites, but she was convinced that most of them were good men, as dedicated to the revolution as she was. She saw absolutely no contradiction between serving the Party loyally and enjoying sex occasionally. Being independent and strong-minded, she carefully picked her lovers and savored them. He knew that he was by no means the first young man she had chosen, and nor would he be the last. So he left things as they were and they continued their delectable encounters until one day she did not turn up at the appointed time.

The next day he searched the market place high and low, but no one knew where she had gone. Her stall was shuttered. Perhaps she had decided to leave without telling him, to avoid a messy situation. Perhaps she had felt he was still young and emotional, if not idealistic, and might upset the applecart if he decided he was in love with her. Or perhaps their affair had been discovered by her control officer and, with the Huy *fracas* still in mind, she had been quietly reassigned to another province. If this is the case, you will sooner or later be called in for a severe reprimand. Or worse.

31

Fieldwork

As it turned out, he never heard any more about Thanh. A new courier appeared behind her market stall, an older woman named Quy, who sold free-range chickens she brought in from the countryside. She had been with the resistance longer than Quat, the cell leader, and this added to his sense of insecurity. His anecdotes about Comrade Quoc became longer and more complicated but neither Quy nor Van paid much attention to him.

After about one year of delivering groceries and convoy spotting, Van was asked his opinion of Mr. Thai, the caterer. He seldom talked to the man, but he had sensed from the beginning that he had developed a split personality. On one hand he was a nationalist, committed to freeing Viet Nam from the French grip, and was determined to help the resistance as much as possible. On the other, he had a wife and children as well as old parents, who all depended on the business he ran. He lived these two lives in constant fear that the French authorities would discover the truth and execute him. Van thought he was an incredibly brave man. His mind said the cause was right, his heart that it was wrong yet he managed to labor on day after day, probably knowing that sooner or later the odds would turn against him. That was what he said in his report and was pleased when his control officer congratulated him on his "very perceptive report". He was soon disappointed, however, when he discovered how his report had been interpreted. The control officer had immediately zeroed in on Thai's weakness: his family, completely overlooking his bravery and loyalty. That's the resistance's way. Always look for the weakest point. Very pragmatic people. If you score nine out of ten points they'll focus on the one point you lost and find ways of using it to enhance your performance or destroy you, depending on how useful you are to them at that stage. With them, people are dispensable. *Papa* said good control systems used in war can go bad when peace returns and vice versa. To his control officer, Van's analysis confirmed what the provincial committee already suspected, based on reports from other sources: Mr. Thai's reliability was limited, because of his love for his family. He still harbored *bourgeois* sentiments. Van was instructed to stand around the catering firm when he was not delivering goods, keeping his eyes and ears open and report on Mr. Thai regularly, especially on whom he met with and what they talked about. Van thought about this for some time. If they've made up their minds that Thai is a risk and your reports don't support their analysis, you're either protecting Thai or too blind to see the truth. After a few more reports on Mr. Thai, none of which had anything of importance in them, he was instructed to report regularly on Quat and his activities at the National Museum. He was asked if his cell leader had ever expressed doubts about the resistance movement, if he was losing heart at the time it was taking to succeed, having been stuck in his job as a security guard for two years already. Does the Party feel you can be trusted and is giving you additional responsibilities? Or does it think you have failed on Thai but is giving you a second chance with Quat? Wonder who's watching you. Perhaps everybody. Perhaps Quy. That's how they maintain solidarity and discipline, to make sure everyone moves as one towards the same target. The soft voice, the gentle guiding hand at the training camps is now replaced by a system of absolute obedience. Your best friend will unhesitatingly report you to the Party if he thinks you are breaking Party rules and regulations. Even children are being encouraged to report on what their parents say and do. No wonder discipline is so good.

After about two years of regular reports on *la Citadelle*, an incident took place that changed everything. Resistance guerrillas climbed over the walls of the camp in the darkness of night and penetrated one of the many hangars near the huge water tanks near the Officers' Mess. They sabotaged trucks and command cars, blew up five medium tanks, set fire to the whole complex of repair shops surrounding the hangars and destroyed the backup generators. When the military firefighters raced to the scene with their trucks, they found that all the hoses had been chopped up into small pieces. In the pandemonium that followed, the guerrillas all escaped. No one had been killed on either side. Van recognized the entry route they had taken as one of the two that he had drawn up some time before, and he was impressed at the extent of the damage they could do in so short a time.

Psychologically, it was a blow to French pride and the French military establishment reacted strongly, conscious that it had lost considerable face in a culture where *façade* was as important as substance, if not even more so. In private, the Vietnamese population openly laughed at the anger and frustration being shown by these outlandish Europeans, with their large noses and red faces. All that *tay* discipline, firepower, arrogance and pretension now lay in tatters. For a military bastion like *la Citadelle* to be brought low by a band of ragged resistance fighters from the mountains was something that secretly tickled every Vietnamese to death, not only those who worked for the French but also those who worked with them. The French sensed this, and their fury was almost palpable.

Since *la Citadelle* was a military fort, the *Deuxième Bureau* headed the task force set up within twenty-four hours to investigate the incident. Military Intelligence invited the Overseas National Intelligence Agency, *la Direction Générale Extérieure de Renseignement* and Special Branch Police, *la Sureté*, to join in the hunt for terrorists.

Senior officers were immediately relieved of their posts and flown back to France, junior officers and NCOs were court-martialed, and a complete overhaul of the security system was undertaken by the *Deuxième Bureau*, which employed a large number of Vietnamese intelligence agents and their civilian assets. As an immediate result, all Vietnamese nationals working inside *la Citadelle* were re-screened by camp security authorities and over half were fired the same week, forbidden to ever again apply for work at a French establishment. Things had become lax, and bar girls, prostitutes and homosexual boys had been able to gain entry into the garrison through soldiers and NCOs who brought them in under the guise of hired help. New hiring procedures were instituted, new lighting systems were put up around sensitive areas, mobile night patrols cruised inside and outside the camp perimeter, ready to shoot anyone found loitering within five meters of the walls. All the houses outside the garrison walls near the area where the sabotage took place were searched, and some explosives were found buried in the garden of one house. Detonating caps and wires were found in other houses nearby. Camp supplies were now to be picked up by military truck under the supervision of the two Mess sergeants. There was now no excuse for the delivery van to drive into and around the camp any more. Van wondered if they suspected him or if this was just a general precautionary measure. If they suspect you, you would have been arrested already. But, suspect or not, they probably have your name down on a watch list somewhere. It's best not stay around too long, but to leave in a precipitated manner will invite suspicion and eventual arrest. His dilemma didn't last long.

Phong decided that he should move on to his next assignment and he left the caterer's services after a decent interval. He could see that Mr. Thai was visibly relieved that his van no longer had to deliver the goods inside the garrison gates. Every time he saw Van in the shop his eyes grew larger and the color left his face. Van was the link between the catering firm and the terrorist attack, and Mr. Thai had sweated blood while the police investigation was being held. Every day that passed brought the possibility that the French police would establish a link between the catering van and the bombing, which would have meant the firing squad for him.

To kill two birds with one stone, the resistance had deliberately thrown suspicion on the Vietnamese community that lived outside the *Citadelle* walls. In the eyes of the communist resistance, puppet troops and their dependants were as much the enemy as were the French. Because the dependants lived in extended families right outside the French fort, they were branded camp followers and could be sacrificed to the cause. Once the explosives were found in one house near the walls of the fort, the family head, usually an old grandfather, was jailed and tortured into confessing crimes he had never committed. His sons or grandsons who soldiered for the French were arrested and executed. A dozen such family heads were found guilty of having aided and abetted the communist terrorists and died by firing squad. In fact, none of these people had had any connection with the resistance. If anything, with a son or brother serving in the French army, they were pro-French and feared the resistance. It was just their bad luck the explosives and detonator cords had been planted in their gardens. The ruthlessness of the resistance and its willingness to sacrifice innocents made a deep impression on Van. While he understood and accepted the need to act decisively, even ruthlessly, against an enemy, he was still young and believed that an enemy had to be an aggressor, an obviously evil entity. This was definitely not the case with these families, and, not really knowing how or why the resistance picked its victims, he felt nauseated that some twenty people who had little or nothing to do with the French had had their lives casually thrown away by a decision probably taken by a lower level operational cadre. Are you too soft to be a real revolutionary, too civilized to become a barbarian? Does the end always justify the means? Maybe the cause you've taken up... blundered into is perhaps more correct... is not one that you feel comfortable with. It can't be the cause itself, because you still believe that sovereignty is the most important thing for Viet Nam, but the means the Party is using to protect and further that cause. His talks with *papa* came back, and he remembered the difference between a cause and its control apparatus. It was easy to say that they were collaborators, traitors or puppets but, in reality, they were just ordinary Vietnamese like his mother and him. In the Party's eyes, because they had been to a convent when no one would help them also made them collaborators. *Papa* had talked about the contradictions between the head and the heart, how it was necessary to move on when these contradictions became unacceptable. All that ideological claptrap about building a worker's paradise, and they start by killing innocents like your mother and you. A paradise built on bones and skulls of innocents? Killing of military or civilian foreigners who are in your country by force can be justified, but killing your own people when they are non-combatants can never be right. Who makes these decisions to sacrifice this group or that group? On what basis? Low level cadres with grudges to settle? Senior cadres for secret reasons of their own? He thought back to his trysts with Thanh. Had one of her panting admirers suspected that Van had been successful where he had failed, he could have decided to plant the detonators and caps in Mr. Thai's shop and the French authorities would have shot both of them. It was a frightening picture, a huge black hole torn in the security wall he had mentally erected after his training in Z-47 and L-11.

Soon thereafter, Van was introduced into a small village called Ha Ngoc, situated just outside the capital. Artisans who specialized in the carving and sculpturing of quality woods and whose skills had been passed down through generations produced copies of Chinese furniture as well as Vietnamese originals for sale throughout Indochina. For years, sophisticated French diplomats and bankers based in Sai

Gon and Ha Noi had quietly visited this village to order exquisite pieces of furniture to send back to France, where they were worth one hundred times the prices paid for them in Indochinese *piastres*. Copies of Louis Fourteenth furniture, Louis Sixteenth carved wall panels and Napoleonic chandeliers were a favorite with this elite social group, and the creative, nimble-fingered artisans were provided with photographs, drawings and measurements down to the last detail. Recognizing a good deal when they saw one, French settlers had rapidly followed the diplomats and bankers, making a business of buying furniture from Indochina for resale by their families in France. For the handicraft workers of Ha Ngoc, the arrival of the French had meant a boost in sales unequaled in recent memory, and the village had grown rich.

Many of the artisans had bought land in and around the village and had become small landowners. It was difficult to persuade these villagers that the French were evil, and that the Vietnamese ruling classes were bloodsucking leeches that had to be overthrown. Phong didn't even try. The villagers knew he was a resistance cadre, a communist, committed to the overthrow of the French on whom their livelihood depended, but out of a confused mixture of fear and admiration they kept their mouths shut. Phong, pragmatic and professional, had been taught the virtue of patience in his indoctrination courses. He knew the conditions were not right for political education, and both sides left it at that. Poverty and population density tend to blur otherwise clear-cut issues, compromise becomes a necessity, live and let live a way of life. Thus, with the full connivance of the villagers, Phong used the village as a conduit for introducing communist agents into French circles to gain entry into their private residences. No villager ever reported him, and the communist underground never assassinated anyone from the village for working with the French. This ambivalent attitude towards the resistance by the peasants was replicated in thousands of villages across the country, giving the communists the invisibility they needed in order to extend their control over the population in the countryside.

The more Van thought about the plight of the peasants, caught between an immovable object and an irresistible force, the more sympathy he felt for them. Coming from Phu My village, his mother and he were closer to these peasants than to the French or the resistance. The only solution left open to people like you is to act deaf, dumb and mute, to obey everyone on both sides promptly but do as little as possible. This obtuse attitude makes all villagers look like village idiots to the French, reinforcing their patronizing belief that the

Indochinese are an inferior race, and that the only way to wake them up is to kick and slap them around vigorously. Ironically, this is the opening that resistance cadres need. They patiently pick away at the brutalized peasant, peeling away the layers of instinctive distrust and fear of outsiders that accumulated over the decades, winning him over to a Party that protects him and gives him back his self-respect.

Because of his fluency in French, Van soon became the favorite interpreter of most of the woodcarving shops in the village, and he was able to make friends with many of the buyers, who were mostly French housewives, with a sprinkling of diplomats. He would ride along to facilitate delivery and he discovered that he could now appreciate the beauty and functionality of French architecture, the luxury of uncluttered space, the blending of colors and the comfort of their furnishings. It was a different concept of life, where silence, space and an eye for beauty were important factors which made life more enjoyable. He sometimes caught himself dreaming he wouldn't mind living in such surroundings. His mother could then have the comfort and luxury she's never had while she was alive. Then he would tell himself to stop thinking the unthinkable. You're in the resistance and luxury is not for people like you while millions around you have no food to eat. But in spite of his self-discipline he could see that there was another world besides the one the resistance lived in, a world that created things, like Ha Ngoc village, whereas resistance only destroyed things. *Papa's* words about bad control systems becoming good if they could change with the times came back to him. Will the Party be able to change after you throw the French and the landlords out?

32

Phu My Village—Again

In 1936, when Van reached twenty-two, he was sent to Thanh Hoa province with two senior cadres, one of whom specialized in arbitration cases, where he acted like a judge. Fertile Cochinchina, where the commercial-minded southern population had always been more receptive to foreign influence, had become a French colony, administered by French civil servants. Industrial Tonkin, where the northern population had bitterly resisted the French forces, had been brutally pacified and declared a French protectorate, also administered by French functionaries. Rocky, typhoon-lashed Annam, where feudal traditions and customs hadn't changed in two thousand years, was declared a self-governing protectorate. Central Viet Nam was poor, mountainous and difficult to reach by road or by sea. The Emperor, sitting in Hue, was allowed to appoint Court officials, provincial and district chiefs. In the jungles and mountains surrounding the vast tracts of land owned by the Court, the communist leadership, with deliberate perseverance, had gradually set up a parallel government, quietly mobilizing the masses in a determined effort to turn central Viet Nam into the first liberated zone. The Nghe An-Ha Tinh peasant rebellions in 1930 had been brutally crushed by French troops using Senegalese infantrymen, but the French had left and the ant-like work of rebuilding an infrastructure was now paying off. In Thanh Hoa province itself, in Phu My village, where Van was born, a network of Popular People's Committees now linked the twelve provincial districts down to the hamlet level.

At issue was an irrigation system, built years before by the Trinh clan, the most prominent family in Thanh Hoa. It had been partly destroyed by a typhoon and now needed serious repairs. The *Département des Travaux Publiques*[†] in Ha Noi, the DTPH, had sent in French engineers and technicians, with an impressive quantity of modern construction equipment. The DTPH camp had been fenced off, with French military posts set up on the perimeters. Native labor was recruited from the two nearest villages. Repeated petty thefts and loss of equipment had taken place, and the resident engineer, in a fit of anger, had decided to fire all the local workers and replace them with new ones from another village further away. Bad blood between the two villages soon developed, which degenerated into daily brawls at the DTPH camp gates and, after a month or so, the brawls had taken on an anti-French tone, as all demonstrations eventually did, with demonstrators throwing rocks and setting fire to isolated huts. This was the last thing the resistance wanted: the underground parallel government, while taking roots, was not yet solid enough to withstand the vigorous French counter-resistance campaign that would inevitably follow a serious local insurrection that had political overtones.

The resistance cell moved from one village to another, quietly talking to the village elders, pointing out the gains the resistance had already made in the province and advising them to calm the hot-heads down before the French decided to take over the administration of the district. For the most part, the village chiefs understood the situation, but the younger men didn't. Unlike in Tonkin, where French brutality and savagery had been graphically demonstrated against badly armed and ill-timed insurrections, Annam had been relatively spared by the French. As a result, in central Viet Nam, local distrust and hatred of foreigners was not tempered by the fear of French firepower. Van and the senior cadres devoted considerable time talking with the hotheads and took note of the ones that they considered irredeemable. After much discussion among themselves and lengthy consultations with their immediate superiors, they came to the decision that four young villagers would have to be removed from the village before the dispute could be brought under control. For the first time, Van saw the resistance machinery at work. The communist leaders were very deliberate when it came to killing anyone. Executions without Party approval indicated possible petty

---

[†] *Département des Travaux Publiques*: Public Works Dept.

bourgeois weaknesses, such as personal revenge, jealousy, envy and other selfish indulgences. Anything that smacked of selfishness detracted from the total dedication required by the Party. A selfish man thought of his own wants; a Party man thought only of the Party's needs. To receive approval for a killing, a case had to be made for the senior cadres to deliberate upon. This took time, as all the possible ramifications were examined minutely, to ensure maximum results. The disputes between villages had to be stopped before the French sent in troops to occupy the area but at the same time the local population had to be taught that the Party was all-powerful. An outside team of professional snatchers was guided to the targets by local assets. The four stubborn young men were cracked on the head simultaneously while asleep in their hammocks, bundled into blankets and noiselessly carried out to the highway in the dead of night. A truck drew up and they were driven to another province where they were buried alive deep in the jungle. The villagers were told that these men had gone away but everyone understood at once that this was what happened when you crossed the Popular People's Committee. Things took time, but when they were done, they were done with finality. The villagers understood the message and did not report the missing men to the French authorities.

This incident, like the *Citadelle* bombing, made a deep impression on Van. He now knew the resistance didn't kill people wantonly, as he had previously suspected, but always for a practical reason. And when they did, they did so efficiently. They could make a man literally disappear from the surface of the earth. Yet it bothered him. A small group has the power of life and death. Who are they and who appoints them? If not appointed by anyone, whom do they report to? This led to another bout of soul searching that was becoming a habit with him. Is it normal for you to ask yourself such questions? Do you lack the single-mindedness needed to make a revolution? Are you simply too weak to be a resistance cadre, too complicated a man to understand the need for blind obedience? Why? Because your father was an educated person, or your mother independent minded? Because of your *tay* upbringing in a convent? None of your comrades seem to be in any doubt about the correctness of the Party's approach to settling its problems. *Papa* himself used to say omelets couldn't be made without breaking eggs. Are you afraid of breaking eggs? Hélène wasn't and you admire her above all. What if she had hesitated that night? Deep inside him, doubts and self-doubts had begun to grow about the direction the resistance was taking and his role in it, spoiling the satisfaction he should have felt at having accomplished his mission and later receiving praise for it at the inevitable criticism and self-criticism session.

One month after their cell had arrived, the village feud subsided. Work on the repair of the irrigation system continued, with the French blissfully unaware that the resistance had helped them.

Now that he had some free time, he asked around about the Trinh clan, which lived in the manor in the hilly countryside outside the town. This wasn't difficult to do as the resistance had been studying the activities of the province's ruling family for some time, and had gathered considerable amounts of information over the years. Van learned all about his great-grand-father, the Viceroy Trinh Dao Thang, a warlord of the old school, who had terrorized everyone at some time or another, had fought the French right from the beginning and had died in a French prison in Algeria at the relatively young age of fifty eight. Although a dyed-in-the-wool feudal landowner, the Viceroy was held in some respect by the resistance for having fought the French and been jailed by them. Then came his grandfather, Lord Trinh Xuan Giap, who died at seventy-nine of cancer in Vinh. He had been a fanatical supporter of the Court at first and of the scholar-revolutionary Phan Boi Chau later, when it became apparent that the French had succeeded in diluting the power of the Emperor by appointing a young puppet as his successor. He was also very much a warlord, in the mold of his father, and had terrorized the region in his youth. The resistance saw in him nothing but sheer evil, not so much because he hadn't fought the French openly but because he supported Phan Boi Chau, head of the Look East movement, which was opposed to communism in any form. Finally came his father, Lord Trinh Xuan Bach, a more moderate and liberal man, a Westernized man but nevertheless a dedicated supporter of Professor Chau and his constitutional monarchy platform, which meant he was also a dedicated anticommunist. Lord Bach had spent ten years abroad, mainly in Japan and China, trying to drum up support for Viet Nam's anti-colonial struggle. For the last eleven years he had been busy rebuilding the family fortune and had had some success in expanding his landholdings. He and his wife, the Lady Nhan, had built an excellent relationship with the French Governor in Tonkin, and, Van was told, under this colonial umbrella Lord Bach was now free to exploit and oppress the masses. The Party knew everything about the Trinh clan and bloody retribution would be wreaked on Lord Bach and his family when the time came.

Van listened to all this in silence. He understood the resistance's line of thought, but by now he was able to reason things out for himself. Nationalism, freedom and land were the banners held high to attract the peasants. Soviet style communism was the control system used to keep those banners flying. By banding and bonding they gained strength in numbers. Tomorrow they might rule the country, become powerful, exploit the weak. It was Nature's way. Exploitation of one man by another was how mankind climbed the ladder of progress. If it wasn't an army like the French then it was a party like the communists. Either way, people like his mother and him, the common people, the little people, just did what they were told. This in itself is not an evil system, *papa* used to say, sitting in the kitchen, drinking beer, smoking *Gauloise* cigarettes, while his mother watched them talking in French. This is a very natural system, made by Nature, and we have to understand it and adapt to it in order to survive, to climb our own social ladder. "If you cannot not adapt to it," *papa* had said, "you have to leave it and start again. Whatever you choose will be the right choice for you." He had had said this many times, his mind on Mathieu as he spoke. *Papa* himself had been disappointed with the French attitude in Madagascar and in Indochina, but not sufficiently to quit.

As to communism and the workers' paradise that the Party wanted to build, Van already knew what had happened in Russia after Lenin took power in 1917. He had read all about it in *papa's* books and heard many intelligent discussions on communism over the foreign radio broadcasts since. The fruits of communism were there for all to see. A small elite group of middle-class bourgeois had taken over, backed by a fanatical corps of urban workers, and they had turned the country into a giant concentration camp. Having seized power, the new leadership refused to change with the times and had stuck to its grim and relentless wartime policies. The state had kept control of all the land and one purge followed another. Having wiped out the rich, the educated, the landowners and the middle classes, they were now intent on subjugating the masses, the common man and woman, people like his mother and him. They had embarked on the killing of millions of peasants at a time. What is the guarantee that our Party's version of communism will be any better? But why are you asking yourself such questions? Why all these doubts and self-doubts? Are you having a change of heart?

In the village of Phu My, where his family had lived for generations, he looked for his mother's house. Under the bridge, she had described where their hut was, about 200 steps from the village deep well, next to the Skinny Lady's hut, near a very large banyan tree. Van thought he should feel something about the place but he felt nothing. The tree and the well were there, but there was an empty lot where the huts had been and the present villagers couldn't remember anyone living there. Thanh Hoa province had become one of the provinces most heavily infiltrated by the resistance, and he could move about relatively freely. The villagers knew who the resistance cadres were, but they kept their mouths shut. As he walked along the country road that cut through the village, and then down the alleys between the bamboo huts, and around the market place where his mother must have been at some time or other, he was smiling to himself in he knowledge that she was watching everything from inside him. She must recognize her house, her neighbor's house, the road she took to go and work in the manor where you were conceived. He walked around for a long time, to give her a better look at everything she had known. He felt happy as he walked, knowing that she was enjoying the sights. Strangely enough, the province wasn't one of the poorest by any means. It was well administered by the local authorities, there hadn't been an uprising for over ten years, and the people he came across were all reasonably satisfied with their lot. Finally, he walked through the fields to the manor, following a route that his mother might have taken when she first started working there. He walked slowly, looking right and left carefully, aware that everything he saw she was seeing too. She's looking at everything you're looking at. She must be smiling with joy.

The manor was a huge fort, built on a hill planted with pine trees, with high walls surrounding it. On top of the walls armed soldiers walked back and forth. The gates were open during the day, and Van could see some of the activities going on inside. Once, he saw a person of noble stature and dress being driven out of the manor in a French car. Although he had no idea of what his father looked like until then, he felt a tiny electric shock running up from his stomach to his chest when the car drove by and he knew in that instant that his mother was telling him that this man was his father. Her spirit was looking at the car through his eyes and he felt the emotions that must have raced through her mind in those few seconds. His body suddenly shivered with cold, his hands turned clammy and the glands in his mouth secreted an acidic liquid that he swallowed with difficulty.

Back at the resistance headquarters, he decided he would write a letter to his father and have it smuggled into the manor. He picked on a villager who was not in the resistance, a carpenter who had access to the manor where he repaired and reconditioned antique furniture that had been in the family for generations. The carpenter knew who Van was and was a little apprehensive at first. Van put him at ease, but explained that this was resistance business and that it would be best for him to keep his mouth shut. He gave the carpenter the letter and visited his house again that night, after the man had returned to the village. The carpenter said he had handed the letter to a maid who had handed it to Lady Nhan. Van impressed on him once more the necessity of not talking about resistance matters and left the next day for the South.

Phong had decided that Van would work on a new operation in Sai Gon, and in the two days it took to travel south they exchanged less than twenty words. They were so attuned to what they had to do there was no need to discuss anything. And since small talk was frowned upon as a sign of *bourgeois* gossiping, there was no need to converse.

33

L'Alliance Française

Sai Gon, the southern capital, throbbed with life day and night. Compared to it, Ha Noi was just a provincial town, Thanh Hoa a large village and Phu My a mere cluster of huts. Thousands of bicycles flowed in waves down the main avenues, opening into streams like shoals of fish to weave seamlessly into the side streets and disappear. Bullock carts, loaded with goods, clanked along the main streets, clogging up traffic. Hundreds of rickshaws bearing self-satisfied customers deftly weaved their way in between the carts and the parked cars, each pulled by an emaciated, haggard coolie who ran barefooted in the dust. Military trucks and commercial vans rumbled along day and night. Private cars were everywhere. The noise and the dust caused by the traffic confused and disoriented Van right from the beginning. And the crowds! Hundreds of men, women and children thronged every sidewalk, all busy going somewhere, all in a hurry, all talking loudly at the same time. In their haste, they spilled onto the street, nearly causing accidents with the swarming waves of bicycles, the slow-moving bullock carts and the brakeless rickshaws. For a boy from the north, it was mind-boggling and it gave him a culture shock.

Once seated, they ate their meal in silence, enjoying each hot and spicy mouthful. Phong was obviously waiting for something, and Van was in a daze. Weighing on his mind was the effect his letter would have on Lord Bach when he opened it. He was sure his father would make an effort to remember the girls who had pleasured him around that period in his life. Keeping track of illegitimate children and their status within the family circle was very important for rich landowning families. Many a warlord had been overthrown and slain in his old age by sons he hadn't acknowledged and for whom revenge had come with mother's milk.

The owner of the beef and noodle soup shop, an older man wearing a dirty singlet and even dirtier shorts, appeared and nodded towards Phong. He was one of the many resistance sympathizers who operated safe houses for communist cells in the Vietnamese Quarter of the city. Phong and Van went upstairs where three men sat smoking in a small room. The men looked at them expressionlessly and one of them handed Van some documents. No one said anything, as he had expected. He looked through the documents and saw that once again he had become a new person, with a new name, Don.

"Who's this?" he asked, laughing, when he saw the identification card with a picture of someone who looked more or less like him on it. Sai Gon was more advanced than Ha Noi in every way, and everyone carried an ID that had his photograph in it.

"I don't know," answered the cell leader "but Phong described you months ago, so we already had an idea of what you looked like. It's not bad, is it?" he said proudly, looking from the picture to Van and back.

The next two years flashed by as Van, now known as Don, busied himself as a clerk at the *Alliance Française* building in central Sai Gon. The *Alliance* was a bastion of French culture, and offered a comprehensive French language course for beginners up to advanced levels. All the teachers were French. It had a vast library that contained maps of the world as well as French magazines. These were very popular with the young southerners, who were far more westernized than the northerners. They didn't look to China but to France, were avid for a modern education and curious about Europe. As the principal promoter of French culture, the *Alliance* put on a regular monthly program of French plays, French films and French musical *soirées*. The movies in particular had a huge success with the southern students and intelligentsia, most of whom spoke passable French. The Director of Personnel was a French lady, but her assistant, a southerner, was a resistance sympathizer, and he made sure that Don would be hired. He didn't know why Don was being introduced into the *Alliance*, where he had already been told by communist cadres to hire half a dozen plants, and he didn't ask. He wasn't a communist, but he recognized that only the communists had any sort of long-term policy. For some indefinable reason, he didn't like them. There was something vaguely menacing about them, perhaps because they were always so serious, unlike the happy-go-lucky and carefree southerners.

For the first year, no research work was required of Don but in the first three months his handler taught him every weekend how to become a model employee. The aim was for him to win the trust of the French management. He had to be punctual, presentable and alert and always finish the work he was given. He had to look people directly in the eyes as he spoke to them because, for the Europeans, this showed sincerity and honesty. Don found all this quite easy as he went about his duties, which included some light administrative work in the mornings and looking after the library in the afternoons. This was the best part and he read voraciously the moment he had a minute free, learning more in one month at the *Alliance* than in five years up north. He made it a point to read up as much as he could on communism, now that he recognized that his faith in the Party had begun to waver. He soon saw how Stalin had corrupted Lenin's interpretation of communism, and how Lenin's version itself differed considerably from the writings of Marx and Engels. The more he read about communism, the more he realized that a cause, however well intentioned, was only as good as its policies, which interpreted and applied it. The best of causes had been used throughout history to mask the worst of policies. France's democratic *Liberté–Egalité–Fraternité* at home had turned into colonization abroad; the Soviet Union Party's dream of a socialist paradise had turned into a reign of mass mobilization and terror. It was incredible how these causes, either already flawed in themselves or else seriously degraded in their application, still managed to attract so many supporters. *Papa* is right. Say the right thing, use the right words, people believe you and you control them. The communists are word masters, no doubt about that. You must separate cause and policies, or control system. Causes stay good forever. Even today democracy is attractive to millions, but how democracy is implemented differs so much from country to country. Eventually, causes are often betrayed by their policies. The litmus test must be how these policies treat the common people, people like your mother and you, whatever the cause. Causes are for you, so policies must be for you too, not just for the cause masters, the leadership, be it colonialist Frenchmen or communist Vietnamese.

In the second year, he was asked to report monthly to a new control officer, a thin southerner with a face like a knife, who listened in complete silence while he talked about what he had done, what he had seen, what he had heard at the *Alliance*. The man's name was Long, he spoke French fluently and worked as a personnel assistant manager in the French brewery that produced the most well-known beer in Indochina, *la bière 33*. Given his position in the firm, Long interviewed many Vietnamese at length in his small but impressive office, with a view to hiring or firing them. Don suspected that quite a few of those interviews were actually debriefs of communist cadres working throughout the city. Long wrote many things down, and often nodded, but never made any comments until Don had exhausted himself, covering every minute of every day. Then he would open his mouth and Don felt that reality had returned. Almost every meeting followed the same format. It was all so cut and dried, like the year he had spent at indoctrination classes at the training camp when he joined the resistance. Sitting ramrod straight, Long almost always said the same thing. First he would congratulate Don.

"Comrade, you are a good observer, you have done good research work, and I have noted that down. I know we can expect a lot more from you."

Don would bow his head slightly, smiling in an appreciative way. That's the technique. A bit of sugar first to relax you, then a bit of lemon to get your attention, then finally a dollop of doctrine to whip you into shape. Inevitably, the lemon part came next. Mild, with a sting at the end.

"But you are also sensitive to music, especially western music, and to thoughts and ideas, especially western thoughts and ideas. This is natural, since you are still a young man, open to all things new. But an active intellect backed by a lack of experience opens the door to the insidious propaganda of the enemy, which will cause confusion in your mind."

Unlike the other cadres he had known, Long was well dressed and looked like a successful businessman. After the dose of lemon, he would pause and offer Don an expensive brand of cigarette and pour him tea from a large pale pink French ceramic teapot into elegant teacups decorated with blue leaves. Each cup had its saucer, also decorated, but with golden leaves. Sometimes he would reach for an orange from the fruit basket on his desk, put it on a small plate along with a small knife with an upturned blunt end and lay it in front of Don, who would peel the orange, which was always juicy and very sweet, offering half to Long and eating his half slowly. Obviously one of the other agents inside the alliance is watching over you. They know what you like to read, what you say, how much time you spend in the library, who you go out with on weekends. But that's to be expected in this system.

Then came the lecture, to set the confused mind straight.

"Western books in French libraries spread nothing but propaganda, giving the impression that capitalism is good and socialism is bad, but this is not so. If democracy means social equality and social justice, then capitalists and socialists are brothers. But in capitalist societies, there are social classes, and these rights are limited to the educated, the rich and the powerful. In socialist societies, there are no social classes and everyone can enjoy social equality and justice."

Seeing no reaction on his part, Long would continue, not unlike a professor in front of a class of none-too-bright students.

"In capitalist societies, the means of production and distribution of goods are controlled by a tiny rich minority from the private sector, and the result is a huge gap between the few rich and the many poor. The small middle classes live quiet, desperate lives, totally dependent on their jobs at factories owned by rich capitalists, and to be unemployed is to return to poverty. The very rich, on the other hand, live in luxury like the French over here live. You understand all this, of course?"

This time Don would nod affirmatively. More tea. Another orange. Or a cigarette. The control officer was amazingly well versed in the political makeup of French society. The communists really pick their people well. Train them well too. If he wasn't a cadre he'd be a laborer, a construction worker, yet here he is, teaching you things you don't know. He even speaks French better than you.

"In France, like here, there is a Socialist Party. Yes, there is a socialist party in almost every country in Europe, and they all want real democracy. This can only be done through the government owning and controlling all the means of production and distribution of goods so that these can be divided up equally among the people. If the country is rich, everyone will be well to do. If it is poor, everyone will be equally wanting. This is social equality and with equality for all you can have justice for all. But the rich don't listen. *Egalité, Fraternité* stops at the entrance to their banks."

Don had heard this line of reasoning many times, from many senior cadres who were able to repeat their arguments word for word, like he had had to learn his catechism at the convent.

"Overseas, in French colonies like Viet Nam, it is even worse, because there is no *Liberté* either. The French settlers live like kings and want the natives to believe they are kings. Already, rich Vietnamese families here want their children to live like the French. Soon, our middle classes will follow suit, and that will be the end of Viet Nam. It is our responsibility to fight this insidious propaganda, first by educating the people when we can, and secondly by destroying these centers of lies."

This last part always brought back memories of the recent bombing at the *Citadelle*. Were they thinking of doing the same here? At one meeting with Long, Don asked Long why he wasn't working in a cell. Strange the system isn't watching you, testing you, evaluating you. Not one single self-criticism session since your arrival in the south. The Party's grip isn't as strong as in the north.

"You are in a cell and your senior comrade has been watching out for you for over a year now. In the south, the French security services have people in all French government offices, including the *Alliance*. We prefer to keep our men apart. After two years, you'll be the senior man in a cell, you'll know the two juniors but they won't know you."

Towards the end of the second year, Don was given an unusual assignment. Report on the seating arrangements at the November concert at the *Alliance,* Long said. This was the yearly event at which the *crème de la crème* of Saigonese society was invited, with the Governor General of Indochina and his lady as guests of honor. The French directors drew up the guest list but, having become a trusted assistant secretary, one of Don's responsibilities was the filing of all documents at the end of each day.

The Governor General and his wife would be seated in the middle of the front row, with the Chairman of the *Banque de l'Indochine* and his wife on their right and His Excellency Ton That Dien, the representative of Emperor Bao Dai, on their left, with Mrs Dien. The Emperor, recently returned from his studies at *La Sorbonne* in Paris, had left for the south of France for a long rest to recuperate from his busy schedule at the Court. Don had been told by Long to stay away from the *Alliance t*hat night. This was not easy to do, as the local hires at the center were expected to stay until the end in order to help clean up after the show. He applied for sick leave after lunch and was allowed to go home. He noticed that three other clerks had not shown up for work that morning. Now you know who's been watching you. There has to be at least two established cells at *l'Alliance,* with newcomers like you forming the embryo of a third cell.

That evening, Sai Gon was a blaze of lights, like a society matron adorned with diamonds, preparing for a social function. The square was all lit up, filled with curious onlookers. The *Alliance*, all primped up, looked like a nervous star receiving the finishing touches of makeup before appearing on stage. Don knew that behind all this glitter and excitement, unknown to the crowds, shadowy groups of men moved about in a deadly game of cat and mouse, intent on murder. French military mobile brigades, heavily armed, had cordoned off the whole area, but stayed in the shadows so as not to alarm the population. Their radio communications exchanges could be heard crackling in the dark every now and again. Dozens of Vietnamese undercover policemen mixed with the crowds, blending in, listening to snatches of conversation, watching hand movements. Occasionally, they would pounce on a man and hustle him away out of the crowd into a back alley, while uniformed policemen busily controlled the crowds.

One by one, shiny black limousines drew up and well-dressed Europeans alighted, greeted each other with handshakes and kisses amidst laughter and smiles before walking into the lobby. There, the women were presented with a bouquet of flowers by the organizers, while the men were handed a large, beautifully printed program. Some of the older guests, obviously old colonials, arrived in their personalized, custom-made *pousse-pousse*, with plenty of shiny brass parts and fitted out with lanterns for night riding. These handcrafted rickshaws were pulled by barefooted coolies who ran in between the long spans in front of the carriage, sinewy calves and thighs rippling with muscles, bony shoulder blades glistening with sweat and large, callused hands gripping the shafts tightly. When the Governor's car drew up, a small Army band played the *Marseillaise* and a contingent of Senegalese troops presented arms. Governor General Lelouche, a fat old gentleman with watery eyes, smiled and waved to the crowd before entering the cultural center with his wife.

After the last guests had arrived, the *Alliance* doors were closed. A squad of policemen took up their positions in front of the doors and was soon joined by the drivers and the rickshaw coolies, who had parked their respective vehicles at the back of the building. The crowd was allowed to move in closer to the building, which was all lit up inside, but had to maintain a respectful distance from the policemen. The sound of speeches being made in French could be heard, thanks to a powerful public address system. Then came the sound of musicians testing their instruments, followed by more speeches, and, at eight o'clock sharp, the concert began. The French were famous for their punctuality.

34

The *Alliance* Bombing

According to eyewitnesses who saw the whole thing, the first bomb went off in the pit that ran like a trench around the stage, between the front seats where the Governor General was and the concert musicians. Half a dozen native workers, responsible for adjusting the loudspeakers, helping the conductor and the musicians set things up and carrying on and off the heavier instruments, were killed instantly. They had been crouching down in the pit, waiting for the show to end. The French concert musicians, all recently flown in from Paris, froze in their chairs, paralyzed, their mouths open. Some dropped their instruments, which clattered to the ground. All looked at the conductor. The poor man, who had a heart condition, had turned towards the Governor General, hoping for some guidance. His baton trembled in his hand as the pounding in his heart made him dizzy.

Jean-Pierre Lelouche, the Governor General, was an old colonial hand who had survived a number of bizarre situations in the French colonies of Central and North Africa. Nothing could surprise him. Having accepted the fact that a bomb had gone off but hadn't killed him, he unceremoniously dropped to the floor, along with his wife, another old colonial hand. On their hands and knees, they crawled energetically along towards the exit sign, their large posteriors swaying in unison from side to side, like the humps of camels traveling across the desert. The Chairman of the *Banque de l'Indochine*, also an old colonial hand, slipped to the floor with his wife. Both being lightly built, they decided to crawl under their king-sized chairs, and lay wedged between the stout carved legs, breathing heavily, their eyes darting about, not unlike a pair of large, resentful, white snails that had slipped into shells

that were uncomfortably tight. The representative of the Emperor, His Excellency Dien, was a tiny man even by native standards. As with most Vietnamese, he was extraordinarily nimble. Almost before the reverberations of the first bomb had died away, he had shot over the back of his seat. He ended up in the second row, in between the legs of a very startled guest, who thought the bomb had thrown up a dead body that had now landed at his feet. Mrs. Dien, even smaller than her husband, burrowed head first deep into her seat, her arms and legs tucked under her, in a perfect circle, with only her small bony posterior showing. Covered with smoke and dust from the explosion, she looked like a small beach ball someone had left behind.

Within seconds two more bombs went off inside the concert room. Panicked into action, the guests now hurled themselves towards the exit doors. As if on cue, a violent fire broke out and black smoke blanketed the hall. Screams and swear words filled the air as distinguished guests fought desperately to get through the doors which, for some incomprehensible reason, wouldn't open. Outside, in the streets, the crowds rapidly grew in size as everyone rushed up to the Alliance building to see what was happening. The policemen were grimly hacking away at the heavy doors with fire axes, especially at the chains that someone had bound around the sturdy handles. Finally the doors were smashed open and the guests poured through, screaming and crying, their clothes torn, their faces blackened, their eyes wild with terror. All semblance of European dignity and superiority was gone. They rushed into the street, in torn and tattered clothes, calling hoarsely for their drivers and private *pousse pousse.* Some of the French men, their faces distorted with hatred, rushed forward into the crowd throwing punches and kicks at startled Vietnamese onlookers, closely followed by their wives who screamed insults at the crowd. Absolute pandemonium reigned, with the police trying in vain to drive the crowds back so that the cars and the rickshaws could reach the front steps of the *Alliance.* From the building thick black smoke poured out of the ground windows and many of the lights had gone out. The Vietnamese crowds watched with mouths agape. They had never seen anything like this.

The military soon cordoned off the whole square, driving the crowds back with gusto. The fire brigade then appeared and began hosing down the building. By then the last guest had gone, and the only Frenchmen around were grim-faced men from the *Deuxième Bureau* and senior officers from the *Direction Générale Extérieur de Renseignement* and the

Sureté. Don casually moved away, with mixed feelings in his heart and conflicting thoughts racing through his head. All this research that is being done on everything French is certainly paying off. They know exactly where and when to strike. You remember Long's face. Sharp as a knife. He said the propaganda centers had to go, and this one certainly is going. Do you feel bad about those people inside the concert hall? Not really. You've never liked the French anyway except for *papa*, who isn't really French any more. Arrogant and abusive people, always kicking and slapping everyone around. It was time they got some of their own medicine. Do you feel happy the resistance has succeeded? Not really. Cold meretricious calculating people. Always suspicious of everyone and everything. This is becoming a war between two ruthless groups who are determined to kill each other. Neither side has any time for people like your mother and you, and there are millions of people like you who don't attend concerts, don't throw bombs at people, but they never say anything while the French do this and the Party does that as if you didn't exist. You're on one side today, perhaps on the other side tomorrow. Maybe there won't even be a tomorrow. The French are going to arrest every Vietnamese working at the alliance. They have to know it was an inside job.

The next morning he showed up at the *Alliance* as usual, and was promptly picked up by the police. At the central police station, sitting in one large cell, were all the Vietnamese staffers except for six, including the three who hadn't reported for work the previous day. Now you know why. They did all the inside work. Your role was a minor one; you are still being tested. Interrogation started, and they were questioned one by one by French police officers, assisted by Vietnamese police interpreters. Don didn't have much to say. He described his duties at the center, the French teachers he knew personally, the Vietnamese colleagues he socialized with. He told them he knew nothing about the bombing and that he hadn't been present that evening, having gone on sick leave that afternoon. He produced a doctor's prescription for an upset stomach. Long, who obviously knew a thing or two about police procedure, had advised him to get one the day before. He was told to sit in the corner of the room while the next man was interrogated. From where he sat, he could hear snippets of conversation as the police officers talked among themselves. The six who had not turned up for work that day were prime suspects, with the three who had not reported for work the previous day topping the list. Don was also a suspect, but the fact that he had a doctor's certificate and had reported for work the following day worked in his favor. One of the officers scrawled "To be watched" on his file, and he was allowed to return to work that afternoon.

The terrorist attack on the *Alliance* center had killed fifteen Vietnamese and seven Frenchmen, wounded seventeen French guests and destroyed the main hall of the building. The Governor General had been spared, as had the Chairman of the Bank and the Emperor's representative and their respective wives. The government immediately announced that it was the work of communist terrorists and vowed to track down the perpetrators. In the meantime a curfew would be in effect in Sai Gon from ten at night to six in the morning. A number of suspects had already been arrested. The Emperor, in Cannes for some unspecified medical reasons, had sent a note to the President of the French Republic and another to the Governor General of Indochina, expressing his total outrage at this barbaric act. He intended to return to look into the matter personally as soon as the doctors allowed him to travel. Within hours of the incident, Paris had promised that heads would roll unless tangible results were shown and had set a deadline. Two senior police generals flew into Sai Gon the same week. One was *un Normand*, with hard blue eyes, blond hair and large shoulders, the other *un Corse*, with piercing dark eyes, a permanent five o'clock shadow and pomade on his hair. Their cold eyes and unfriendly mien indicated that they had come for scapegoats. The Alliance was a civilian office, and the Indochina *Direction de la Sureté Générale* headed the task force immediately created to deal with the bombing. Included were the *Deuxième Bureau* and the *Direction Générale Extérieure de Renseignement*.

They harnessed their most trusted and most competent senior aides, Vietnamese police officers without whom they would have been totally blind and deaf. The task force was given two responsibilities. One was the capture of the terrorists who had planted the bombs, the other was the uprooting of the communist infrastructure that had been allowed to grow in the southern capital through "laxity on the part of the authorities". The *Sureté* Director and his colleagues knew, from the wording of the task force's terms of reference, that their careers depended on immediate results. Un-characteristically warm and friendly, they huddled with their eyes and ears, the senior native *Sureté* officers.

These auxiliaries, all seasoned senior police officers, in fact did most of the work for which French police officers received bonuses, decorations and promotions. They accepted this fact of life in return for substantial pay packages by Vietnamese standards, and were content to remain out of the limelight. But this time, things were different. The French Governor General was frantic. The auxiliaries saw in this crisis the opportunity to make a killing, both personally and professionally. They listened carefully to the promises being made. Bonuses, promotions, free schooling for their children, free medical coverage for their families. They rapidly worked out their assignments, drawing up in the process detailed budget requirements that involved large cash advances with which to jump-start the information flow, followed by more large cash advances to accomplish the mission. They made sure that these large cash advances, which could never be covered by receipts, would address their own personal needs. An opportunity such as this didn't happen very often, and for many of the senior auxiliaries, retirement was just around the corner.

For the next few months, intense pressure was put on the communist underground by three French security groups that had gone berserk. Vietnamese agents of the Special Branch Police, Overseas National Intelligence Agency and Military Intelligence worked twenty-four hours a day to flush out dozens of communist cells spread around the city. It helped that most communist cells were composed of northerners or centrists, who had different accents from the southerners. It also helped that, by and large, southerners do not like centrists and northerners, whom they look upon as poor cousins. What helped most, however, was that the Vietnamese officers were much more familiar with the resistance underground networks than their French superiors knew, or would ever know. Now that the proverbial iron was hot, they intended to strike it as hard as they could, intent on making as much hay as possible while the sun shone. Within hours of the bombing, the military had set up a ring of steel around the greater Sai Gon area, using thousands of Vietnamese soldiers under the command of French officers. It had become impossible to slip into or out of the city, even by using secret routes through swamps, canals, jungle trails and riverbank tunnels. With each passing day, the police and the military dragnet tightened further, bottling up the communist infrastructure in the southern capital. The rat hunt, known in police circles as the *ratisserie,* now began in earnest.

To become invisible to the authorities, communist agents have to blend into the population. Generally speaking, this population was made up of poor people, most of whom wanted to stay clear of any involvement with the authorities. They were prepared to see nothing, hear nothing and know nothing. The sea in which the fish swam was a sea of silence. Once this silence was broken, however, the sea dried up, the curtain rose, the floodlights came on and all sorts of bottom dwellers were caught out in the open. The auxiliaries quietly approached family heads and community leaders in districts they suspected had been infiltrated. Money talks, and people talked. With large amounts of cash in hand, the auxiliaries stripped away layer upon layer of a communist infrastructure that had taken years to put into place. To these auxiliaries, ferreting out communists and their sympathizers was not particularly difficult because, unlike their French superiors, to whom all Vietnamese looked alike, they could instinctively smell a dissident. The four bombers were caught hiding in basements of vacant warehouses in the suburbs and the iron shackles placed around their ankles were welded on the spot, an indication of their future fate. They were from a province in the Delta, and none had ever worked at the *Alliance*, but they had been guided every step of the way by the six *Alliance* staff members who had not reported for work that day. These had also been captured, and, within hours of what the police called tactical interrogation, had revealed everything. Their ankle bracelets were also welded, to be buried with them when the time came. Orders were telegraphed north for the guillotine in Ha Noi to be loaded onto the next train heading south.

"The Slicer" arrived in the southern capital in perfect working condition, as was expected, and was put to work at once, cutting off six heads each working day. It took about an hour and a half per execution, and three were done in the morning, three in the afternoon. The procedure each time was identical, and, because it had to be done properly, it took time. The prisoner had to be brought out, his face had to be clearly shown to all present and the official photos taken. The charge against him had to be read in French and Vietnamese, while the mechanics of the execution were prepared. This took about half an hour. After the head had dropped into the basket, the body was removed, the blood on the guillotine platform wiped off while the blade was winched up and locked into place in preparation for its next descent. The head was then picked out of the basket, sometimes held up for the audience to see once again that the right man had been executed before being dropped into a thick brown rice sack that turned dark red after the second or third head. Hundreds of fat blue bottle flies latched onto the sacks containing the severed heads. Prison officials present then had to sign a number of documents attesting to the fact that they had indeed witnessed the execution of so-and-so, writing out the exact time and place. This took about an hour. Try as hard as they might, six a day was the best the execution team could do.

The vast police-military net, working with grim efficiency, slowly but inexorably closed in on the communist leadership in the southern capital area. Before the deadline set by Paris had been reached, the ranking cadres of the Sai Gon–Cho Lon communist underground movement had been captured and twenty-four three-man cells put out of action. The two police generals from Paris, now smiling and in a backslapping mood, promised commendations, toasted the local French officers with champagne and flew back, congratulating each other on a job well done.

The Vietnamese *auxiliaires*, the architects of this stunning government success, returned to anonymity. The wives quietly began looking around for properties to buy with their husbands' newfound bonuses. In the suburbs, a large number of poor families and communities that had cooperated with the authorities counted up the crisp new bills they had received and made plans for their use over the approaching New Year, the *Tet*. Unfortunate as the bombing of the Alliance had been for the victims, it turned out to be a blessing in disguise for the government, which used the incident to clean out the communist underground infrastructure, and for many poor families, who received unexpected windfalls. For the communist infrastructure, however, it was a major setback and the time had come for a serious review of the situation. Failure meant blame and blame meant punishment. Heads would have to roll, new networks set up and a maximum effort made to regain the momentum that existed before the successful bombing of the *Alliance*.

Perhaps because the police report had not cleared him entirely, Don was called into the *Alliance*'s Security Office just before *Tet* and told that his services were no longer required. The Security Officer was a Frenchman, and his attitude seemed neutral. He neither believed nor disbelieved that Don could have been part of a plot to blow up the *Alliance*. His deputy, however, was a retired Vietnamese auxiliary police officer. His name was Nam, meaning "southerner", and he had a visceral hatred for northerners and centrists. After his superior had left the room, Nam looked around to where his secretary sat. The young girl had gone out. He rearranged a few papers on his desk that were already perfectly aligned and began toying with a pen. During all this time he avoided eye contact. Now he looked steadily into Don's eyes. Now you know what Death staring at you is like. The whites of his eyes were yellow and there were specks of black in them. Don's stomach convulsed and he saw his mother's face flash before him. She looked pale and frightened. He saw the number nine float by his eyes, just like when he was being interviewed by Quach in the smoky hut.

"We're Vietnamese, you and I, and I know that you know I know your kind, even if these French people don't, so you can stop playing innocent. I'm retired but in my days we killed a lot of communist spies, especially Northern ones. Young ones like you, who don't know what they are doing in the South. More than I can remember. I still have many friends on active duty who think like me. Don't ever let me see you anywhere near the *Alliance* from today or I'll have you picked up and we'll make you disappear, you piece of filth."

Don sat in silence, looking at the security officer. He remembered a picture of a cobra staring at a rat in one of the colored photograph magazines in the *Alliance* library. Nam was the cobra. The only reason why the rat is still alive is because you remain perfectly immobile. The moment you move one whisker, indicating the intention of escaping, the cobra will strike. Don sat stock still, hardly breathing, every pore closed.

"I know where you sleep, I know where you eat at night. So far, I have traced your background back to Ha Ngoc village, where you were used to spy on French houses. If you were staying on, I would have Mlle Laurence report you to the French *Sureté*. You're lucky you're leaving today, you filthy little bastard."

He stopped talking and looked at every pore in Don's face. Finally, he held up two fingers, pointed them at his eyes and then at Don and said, "I am watching you. Come near here, we'll cut your throat."

The hatred in his eyes was frightening. Don knew Nam meant every word he said. There was no doubt in his mind this quiet and intense man and his friends had killed quite a few people when they were still on active duty. For these professionals, getting rid of him would be child's play.

"Now fuck off," Nam said quietly.

35

A Change of Heart

On the other hand, the *Alliance's Directrice du Personnel*, *Mademoiselle* de Laurence, a French woman with strong leftist tendencies, was a close friend of the Governor General's wife, another opinionated woman. This gave her a privileged position in Sai Gon's elite society of government officials, bankers and plantation owners, and *Mademoiselle* de Laurence didn't hesitate to speak up for *les Asiatiques*, having taken a degree in Asian Cultures at the Sorbonne. She liked and admired the Vietnamese race and wasn't afraid to say so. Very few people agreed with her views, but they kept their opinions to themselves, at least in public. Don had always looked neat and presentable, and she felt sorry for him. She quietly arranged for him to receive a month's salary as separation pay, and personally handed him a letter of commendation that would help him find work with a French-run enterprise. She didn't believe for one moment that the bombing had been an inside job. *Mes petits vietnamiens,* my little Vietnamese, as she called her staff, are simply incapable of such action, she would say. Like many of the better-educated French people Don had met through the Alliance, *Mademoiselle* de Laurence showed an extraordinary degree of naïveté in her dealings with the Vietnamese. Her innate dislike and contempt for the French police and military was well known and the fact that six of the *Alliance's* local staff had been executed by the police simply reinforced her opinion that France was demeaning its image abroad through the use of such incompetent and brutal personnel. Used to dealing with colleagues who were suspicious of their own parents, Don found this misplaced trust very appealing. It was like dealing with the average, normal human beings again, although Don knew that he himself no longer qualified as one.

He went back to the room he rented in the Vietnamese quarter and waited for Long to make contact, but neither Long nor Phong did. He thought of making contact, but had been told never to go to his control officer until called for. The following month, just before his savings ran out, he found work at the Lamy Café, a popular place that catered to Europeans and was well known for its *patisserie*. Don noted with satisfaction that the Café was near the river, in another part of town far from the *Alliance*. The owner, *Monsieur* Lamy, was a professional *patissier* who worked in the kitchen all day with his two Vietnamese assistants, while his fat and strong-smelling French wife ran the place and Don served the clientele, taking their orders, collecting payment and making change. In his new job, in between frenetic bouts of activity usually associated with lunch and dinner, he had a lot of time to himself, though he had to stay within range of *Monsieur* or *Madame* Lamy's voice in case he was needed. In between chores, he would sit by the huge bay windows and look out onto the world around him, at the hundreds of passers-by of all sizes and shapes, all busy going somewhere, their minds focused on everyday hopes and dreams. Some were even nodding or shaking their heads as they walked along, talking to themselves. As he watched this endless stream of people, his unconscious mind returned to everything he had learnt at the convent, at *papa*'s, in the resistance, everything his mother had told him under the bridge. It was all coming back to be reviewed, re-analyzed and re-concluded. He knew that something was wrong somewhere, something needed re-thinking. He knew he needed to take control of his own mind, which he had placed in the hands of his superiors when he joined the resistance.

He started with Sai Gon and Ha Noi. Having now seen both, the difference between north and south was startling. The north was cold and rainy, people were reserved and somber. The south was warm and sunny, people were smiling and outgoing. Two different countries, really, and he knew one thing for certain: he liked the south better than the north. Why were they so very different? The north displayed the red peach blossom at lunar New Year, the south the golden apricot flower. Why don't they have the same flower on such an important day? If the ancestors had wanted red and gold, they could have grafted the two, or chosen a national flower that grew both in the cold north and the warm south. Why insist on being different?

He remembered his long discussions with *papa*, after his mother had fallen asleep, in the little kitchen where *papa* loved to eat bread and *saucisson*. They had been speaking of the different policies that leaders adopted in the furtherance of a national cause, policies that formed an ironclad framework in which systems like tribalism, feudalism, colonialism, fascism, communism, socialism and capitalism could thrive. At the end of the day, all these systems, good or bad, would clash with one another, *papa* had said, because they were different. And furthermore, each system would have internal clashes too, because, the freer the society, the greater the division of opinions. From these clashes, whatever the outcome, came a better world each time. After each war, the world improved because problems had been solved and society was rebuilt on sounder foundations. After each earthquake, each flood, the world emerged a greener and cleaner place. Countries had long and enduring lives, like history, and could take any punishment that Nature or Man could inflict on them. But for the individual, life was short and people should try to live a happy life during that time. To do this, the right cause, or, to put it more simply, the right kind of work, had to be chosen. In this light, your first priority is not to take care of a cause, but of your mother and you. If your vision coincides with the cause you support, then heart and mind would meet. If it doesn't, then you would follow the heart rather than the head. Long's disappearance is a Heaven-sent opportunity to cut your ties with the Party. The next step is to find work that will allow you a greater degree of control over your life. He thought of police work, like being an *auxiliaire*. When a crisis arose they took over from their French supervisors; they were well respected by their superiors and they played an important role in society. He had twelve more years to go before *Liem Trinh* could reach down to anoint his life with its magic powers. His mother and he had received protection from the three malevolent stars during their years at the convent, the Saintenoix household and *papa*'s, so they hadn't done too badly, although they had suffered in the years under the bridge. His mother had been right all along: Fate really existed, and by knowing in advance what it held in store you could deflect bad luck and maximize good luck. When Phong had invited him to join the resistance, she had encouraged him because she knew the resistance people were not superstitious. They believed in the Party, not in Fate. The Party would make their Fate. And she was right: he had lived through the many dangerous years in the resistance without a scratch. He knew he had to do his best to survive until his thirty-sixth birthday, chopping and changing lifestyles, rolling with the punches and ducking the blows that life handed out. His years with the resistance had started well, and he had been full of enthusiasm at first, but the more he had seen the less he had felt comfortable. The resistance cadres are no different from the French colonists. They look upon poor people like you like they look on cattle. There to be manipulated, to be used. At least with the French there is hope of democracy later; with the resistance you'll just get more oppression. Like in Russia today. Now is a good time for you to break away. Working for the French police is a good idea, but what if one of Nam's friends recognizes you?

Madame Lamy came in and asked him to help her with the drying of the tablecloths, and he went out back and hung them up carefully. It would be another hour or so before the first customers came in for an *appéritif,* followed by the ever-popular steak and French fries, a glass of wine and *un quart de fromage.*

The months wore on. Breakfasts, lunches, afternoon teas and dinners followed one another like clockwork, while French customers flowed through the Lamy Café like wine and he began to despair of ever being able to find work that he liked and at which he would be good enough to earn a degree of control over his life.

36

Capitaine Godot

One day, a French customer who looked familiar came into the café for lunch. He sat down, opened up a newspaper and started reading. Don circled around the large, pensive looking man who reminded him of his *papa* from the *Citadelle* days. Could this be Sergeant Escudier, the man they had seen off at Ha Noi airport a lifetime ago? They had never heard from him, and if he were, he had changed a lot. This man was thinner, was beginning to go bald, and his full, ruddy face was heavily lined. Also, he now had a thick mustache. It was like looking at the brother of an old friend. There were similarities but they weren't the same. Like you. You must have changed beyond recognition yourself. After a few more looks, from different angles, Don became sure that this man was his former *papa*, and he approached him, asking him what he wanted to drink. The man lifted his head, looked directly at him. For a couple of seconds, it didn't register. All he could see was a smiling young Vietnamese waiter in a French café. Then he jumped up, knocking his chair over backwards and shouting in the vernacular "Minh! Good God! What the hell are you doing here, son?"

His *papa* stood up, still tall as ever, and hugged him to his chest, kissing him loudly on both cheeks. Don stood there limply, his arms hanging down, embarrassed at this public display of affection. *Papa*'s bristly jowls scratched his cheeks, and he could smell the once familiar mix of tobacco and shaving lotion. He thought for a brief moment of hugging him back, because he was really overjoyed at seeing him again after all these years, but he hesitated and let the moment pass. Having heard the commotion, *Madame* Lamy came running out and stood there open-mouthed, fat and sweaty, wiping her hands on her apron. The other customers, all regulars, looked on with interest. Adult customer kisses young waiter, calling him by a different name. That was interesting. A whiff of scandal, perhaps? Nothing new in Sai Gon, the Paris of the Orient, a wide open city where anything could happen. And often did. What could it mean?

Escudier let go of him and turned around, facing *Madame* Lamy.

"This is my adopted son, whom I left behind in Ha Noi many years ago! I've just returned to Indochina, and the last person I ever thought I would meet here was my son! Madame, a bottle of champagne for my table and a glass of wine for everyone who comes in for lunch today. This is my lucky day, and we must celebrate!" he said loudly, hardly able to get the words out of his mouth fast enough. He looked ecstatic with joy, but she could see tears glistening in his eyes. He pulled out a large handkerchief and blew his nose loudly, then wiped his eyes carefully. Finally, he sat down and pulled Don onto the next chair, forgetting that he was a waiter. Don looked up at *Madame* Lamy and she nodded, turning away with pinched lips. Having lived in Indochina for some time, she was no longer surprised at the antics of French people just off the boat.

After work, he joined his *papa* in a *bistro* nearby, so that they could talk in private. Back at the Lamy café their meeting had set off a wave of rumors, and *Madame* Lamy was having a hard time coping with all the questions her customers were asking her. Everyone wanted to know the secret link between this stranger and her waiter, *çe beau garçon*. Someone had heard that this man, Godot, was the new *Directeur de la Sureté* of Cochinchina, and passed on the information in a low voice, with pursed lips. All his listeners nodded gravely, as if they had also heard the same from their own sources. But one customer disagreed. He had heard that Godot was from the Finance Ministry in Paris, interested in the foreign exchange anomalies being practiced by the French settlers. *Madame* Lamy and a few others present began to worry about the black market deals they engaged in monthly, changing French francs into *piastres* through Indian *bric-a-brac* shops rather than through the *Banque de L'Indochine*. A woman claimed she knew all about this new police chief but couldn't say anything because she had been sworn to secrecy. Sai Gon's French community was small and clubby, and the voluminous amount of gossip and rumors that emanated from this well-to-do social class daily was known as *Radio Catinat*. Dotted with well-known cafés, boutiques, restaurants and hotels, Catinat Street had been named after *Marechal* Nicolas Catinat, and it was here that anyone who was someone gathered for afternoon tea and *patisserie*, to comment on the day's events, whether it be political, financial, social or, most titillating of all, sexual. Many a good reputation had been mangled beyond repair over an afternoon tea of *café au lait, profiteroles, meringues* and *milles feuilles*.

After they had settled down in a quiet corner, Don described to *papa* what happened to his mother and him after they had seen him off, leaving nothing out. *Papa* hunched forward with intense concentration at the part about the communist training camp episode, and his involvement in the *Citadelle* and the *Alliance* bombings, but he said nothing throughout the long recital. As Don talked, *papa* drank beer and smoked, as he used to at the *Citadelle*. His face, which had aged, looked somber, and anxiety grew inside Don's mind. When he related how his mother had died and been buried, however, he saw tears appear in *papa*'s eyes. Out came the large handkerchief, the nose was blown and the eyes dabbed. More beer was ordered. Finally, Don stopped talking. There was a long silence, and he feared the worst. But in his mind he was resigned. What has to be, has to be. *Papa* treated you well, like a son, and it is therefore your duty to behave like one towards him. He has experience and is wise, and if he thinks you have done wrong and deserve punishment he will punish you. Mother is dead, *papa* is the only one on this earth who cares about you. Even if he beats you or sends you to jail it will be because he cares for you.

Papa stubbed his cigarette out with finality, drank a long draught of beer and leaned his elbows on the table, crossing his thick fingers in front of him. He looked at Don searchingly, sensed his apprehension and smiled to put him at ease. He reached across the table and ran his fingers roughly through Don's hair, a gesture that Don usually hated when people did that to him, even friends, but this time he positively loved it, growing ten feet tall as he felt *papa*'s stubby fingers against his skull. His *papa* then began talking earnestly and Don knew everything was going to be all right after all.

"First of all, Minh, you are like my son. I think of you as I think of my Mathieu back in Madagascar. We all have to survive as best we can and nothing has changed between us. I will help you all I can from now on. Secondly, as soon as I got back to France, I attended a special training course and was ordered to sever all contacts with Indochina. I could not write or telephone even my family from that place, let alone Indochina. But when I graduated, I sent you many letters, some of which contained money. I suppose that by then you had stopped going back to the *Citadelle,* right?"

Don nodded, looking at his *papa.* He hasn't changed at all. He's a large man, but his heart is even larger. He's a man of his word, and you know that if he didn't write at first it was because he couldn't. Don felt sorry for his *papa.* He has problems of his own and you are adding to his problems.

"Thirdly, son, I want to tell you how sad I am to hear about the way your mother passed away. She was a good woman, I could see that the first day I met her. And I could see how she loved you."

Out came the handkerchief, the large nose was blown one more time, the eyes wiped dry, the throat cleared, and a swig of beer drunk.

"Now I have a new rank, captain, but I wear civilian clothes all the time. I work at a desk, analyzing incoming information for my boss, Colonel Perret. He asked for me when I was still posted in Algeria. Strange to say, brain work is very tiring. When I was in the Military Police and physically active, I weighed ninety-five kilos. Now that I am over fifty and sitting at a desk job all day, I weigh only eighty kilos!"

He burst out laughing, and drank more beer.

"Oh, and I also have a new name, Pierre Godot. Yes, like your people, we also switch personalities, especially in new posts. Master Sergeant Escudier is gone, *pouff!* just like that," he said, snapping his fingers loudly, "and *Capitaine* Godot is here! *Voila!*" he exclaimed, spreading his arms dramatically.

Don looked at him, flabbergasted, but before he could say anything, *papa* said, "Now, let's get serious. What do you want to do? How can I help?"

Don swallowed hard, breathed deeply, sending the air all the way down to the pit of his stomach. He had to calm his mind. Today had been a series of amazing events. He knew his mother was listening. This is what they had been waiting for. He saw her small, sweet face turned towards him. You have done almost twenty-four years already, two life cycles. The year of the Tiger's coming up soon for the second time. Maybe *Liem Trinh*'s powerful rays are beginning to pierce through the last bad star? Maybe your good luck will start early?

Papa's question hung in the air for some time. They looked at each other in silence. Don picked up his glass of *grenadine,* emptied it and set it down. He stared at *papa,* his heart beating fast. After the change of heart he had experienced following the *Alliance* bombing, things were becoming clear in his mind.

"Well, first of all, I want to be called by the name my mother chose for me. I have been Meo, Robert, Minh, Tam, Van and now Don and that's enough. From now on I want to use my real name, Hai. My mother gave it to me because she loved the sea. My middle name is Xuan, from my father's full name and my family name is my mother's, Ho. So I want to be known as Ho Xuan Hai from now on."

He paused, and saw a strange look cross *papa'* face. But his adoptive father was nodding in a supportive manner, and, now that he was finally Hai, he felt emboldened This is an important step. It establishes once and for all that you are a person in your own right, as good as anyone else. Now that you can think clearly, the most important thing is for you to move back into your own skin.

"I don't want to return to the resistance. My mind is with the nationalist cause, but my heart is against the communist application of that cause. I have read about communism and I have seen it at work in the resistance and I know they don't care about people, only about the Party, about themselves. Their policies are killing people, people like my mother and me. I know world history now, and many other countries have regained their sovereignty without using the communist system, so why can't we? They also made war, but became free and democratic, with leaders chosen by the people. I have made up my mind. I will fight communism, but not as a soldier. I want to work in the police, in any capacity that you think will suit me. I don't need to be rich, because there's only my mother and me, and we are simple people. I just want my mother's spirit to lead a happier life than she led when she was alive."

He paused, wondering if he had said too much, or had said something stupid and *papa* was going to laugh at him. But the older man didn't laugh. His eyes narrowed, his mouth puckered, his mind deep in thought. Suddenly he stood up and threw some money on the table.

"It's late, Hai, and I've got to work tomorrow. I have to check a few things out first. Let's meet again in a week or two and we'll talk about what I may have for you. Oh, where Hai is concerned, for me you'll always be Hai from now on but for the time being you should remain Don until you have a new, official identity," he said, putting his arm affectionately around Don's shoulders.

When he heard his *papa* call him Hai, Don felt he was walking on air and was hardly aware that they were leaving the café and saying goodbye to each other until his *papa* hugged him and then, in a surprising gesture, extended his large hand for a formal hand shake. Don's heart soared as he returned to reality. He already treats you like a man, shaking hands like that.

37

Intelligence Asset

Within the month, *papa* had returned to the Lamy café and they arranged to meet at his office the following day. He gave Don his official calling card, which read *Capitaine P. Godot, Chef de Bureau DGER, Ministère de la Défense Nationale, République Française*. When they met at his office, he locked the door from the inside, switched on the overhead fans and brewed some coffee, talking all the time.

"Intelligence agencies are neither military nor police, but something in between. The Ministry of National Defense has two intelligence arms, one for military affairs, *le Deuxième Bureau,* and one for civilian matters, the DGER, la *Direction Générale Extérieure de Renseignement.* Until recently it was called the DGSS, *Direction Générale des Services de Sécurité.* With each new administration we tend to change government office titles, to give the impression of a new dawn having arrived. In fact, nothing much changes and it just confuses everybody," he said, laughing, setting out the cups, spoons, sugar and milk. "In Indochina we work closely with the *Deuxième Bureau,* because the line between military and civilian matters is not clear. My specific job is to weed out resistance spies in the government. There are many and the number is growing." He laid a tin of biscuits on the table, paused and looked at Don, his eyes questioning. Don nodded, to show he understood what *papa* was saying. "In our organization, one group specializes in intelligence, one group in counter-intelligence and one group in coding. I head counter-intelligence. Our work is often of a political nature. Besides spies inside the system, we also keep an eye on resistance sympathizers, inside or outside the system. We also keep an eye on a number of people who can harm us. There are many Japanese nationals here being used by the Japanese secret services. There are also Frenchmen here who will do anything for money. Among the Vietnamese, there are basically two resistance groups, with different ideals, but they both want us out of Indochina. The communist resistance is made up of peasants in the countryside and workers in the cities. The leadership mobilizes and educates the masses, Soviet style, and they have plants everywhere, but you already know that. Their agenda is violence. The non-communist resistance, the so-called Nationalists, composed of students and intellectuals, have a political agenda. They have formed dozens of political parties, some with the support of the Socialist party in Paris, and have been giving us problems abroad and at home for the last fifty years."

He paused, sipped some hot coffee, looked at Don.

"Surprised?" he asked.

"Yes and no, *papa*. You told me a long time ago that you were involved in some sort of secret police work. I often thought of you when I was with the resistance and we were analyzing the French police system," I replied.

He smiled, pointed to Don's coffee, which he had left untouched. Don picked up his cup and drank some. *Papa* leaned his two elbows on the table, his face about thirty centimeters from Don's, who could now see every pore in *papa's* cheeks, and the bristly hairs of his mustache near the lips, some of which had been burnt by the cigarettes that he smoked all the time.

"I'm going to hire you to work for me, as a special intelligence asset. This means only my boss and I know about your identity and your responsibilities. Your official name will be Ho Xuan Hai. But because you will be doing undercover work, you will have an operational name, Le Van Loi. The communist resistance represents the main threat to us. Without Russian communist training, comrade Quoc and his cadres would be no different from Phan Boi Chau and his VNQDD movement, with plenty of wind behind the sails but no rudder. But, my son, because of your past, I have to stress that by helping you, I am putting my career and perhaps even my life into your hands. I have absolute faith in what you have told me. I know you wouldn't lie to me any more than I would lie to you. Do you understand the situation we are both in once you start to work for me?"

Don sat up, filled with pride and determination. *Papa* loves you as no man has in your life. He gave you and your mother a new life, and is now helping you start a new career. He trusts you as no man has ever done. The situation is clear. It is your duty to help *papa* in any way you can, even if you have to die in the process. A new name doesn't matter now since you have to pretend to be someone else so that you can rise in the world. Anyway you are still under the influence of the bad stars, though working in a French agency will lessen the bad luck.

"*Papa*, I understand everything very clearly. I told you about the night my mother died and her spirit entered me. You are talking to my mother and me, and we promise you that as long as I live we will do everything we can or must in order to help you," he said. It came out more solemnly than he had meant it to.

Papa sat back with a smile, obviously convinced. He lit up, exhaled a cloud of smoke, half-closed his eyes and asked him why he had joined the resistance.

"Because I had no money and no work," Don answered at once. It was the truth. "And I was attracted by their cause, nationalism," he added.

"That's understandable. Why did you leave them?"

"I didn't. After the *Alliance* bombing my group broke off contact. They went underground and I never heard from them again. Perhaps because I was still a junior cadre. Or perhaps our control group was wiped out by the *auxiliaires,* I don't know. Anyway, after a long silence, I began thinking things over and decided not to work with them any more. I had already begun losing my faith in the system, in the Party's policies, before I came south. By the time I met you at Lamy's my mind was made up already. Even if they had contacted me, I would not have returned."

"Do you still feel something for the resistance cause, son?"

Don knew that this was the main question, on which hinged everything else they had talked about. But he had examined his soul thoroughly since the bombing, in fact since 1935 when he had helped negotiate a truce with the DTPH in Thanh Hoa, and he knew what to say. The truth.

"Yes and no, *papa*. I think that all Vietnamese want to be free from foreign domination. Having had some education and after seven years in the communist resistance, I know very few people in the countryside understand the difference between nationalism and communism. Resistance against foreign aggression is purely Vietnamese but communism is as foreign to us as French colonialism. The senior communist cadres are cleverly using anti-colonialism to gain control over the masses, hiding the fact that they want to replace feudalism with communism. What the Party stands for sounds glorious and noble, but I know what is happening in Russia."

Papa nodded. "Very clear thinking, son. You have grown up! You are right, what's happening in the Soviet Union is not a pretty sight. Here, we watch both nationalist and communist targets and I'll use you against purely communist targets. That way we can be sure any ambivalence that still remains in your mind won't be put to the test," he said, smiling good naturedly.

38

First Target

In January, Don resigned from the Café Lamy and started on the required paperwork to become a DGER asset. This involved fingerprinting and having photographs taken, as well as filling in long and detailed forms on his past activities. *Papa*, now reborn as Captain Godot, made sure only one copy was made and this was kept in his desk, under lock and key. Don signed his real name, Ho Xuan Hai, talking to his mother at the same time. Look at my signature, my new name, my real name, the name you gave me. This year is a tiger year again. I have to survive only one more bad star. Perhaps *Liem Trinh* is already beginning to shine through. I can see you smiling. He closed his eyes and saw her face appear in front of him. She looked young and sweet, as she had been when they were still at *la Citadelle*, her eyes opened wide with pride and admiration when she watched him talking to *papa*.

The DGER targets included men from the educated middle classes, professionals who worked for the government in key positions or successful businessmen who worked on government contracts. Many of these men were ambivalent in their attitude towards the French and some actively helped the communist resistance by passing on key information. All had socialist leanings, and to what extent they realized that the resistance was in fact communist was not clear. These sympathizers were not only inside the system, they were part of that system, as *papa* had said, and it was difficult to get close to them unless you also behaved like them. Don, now Loi, would have to socialize with them, and become friends with them. To mix with them he would have to show a certain degree of social sophistication, more than was needed when he was a resistance cadre approaching disgruntled workers. He was confident that he could out-think and out-talk any resistance sympathizer on the merits of communism, socialism and nationalism but his problem was how to rapidly develop a cheerful, friendly personality, having spent the last few years in the shadowy world of spying. He had to be less reserved, less "northern" by nature and be more outgoing and relaxed, like the southerners were. He had to learn to enjoy life, to drink, smoke and talk about sex, like all men did, and not recoil at the thought of taking a bribe or of giving one. Without realizing it, he had gradually become robotized over the last seven years, except for the wonderful hours spent with Thanh, and now he had to thaw out and return to being a less-than-perfect and therefore a perfectly-normal person, warts and all.

"It's all one big game. Undercover agents must develop two separate personalities. One is pleasant, normal, even stupid at times, like the rest of the boys. The other is the policeman, alert and observant. The trick is not to show both at the same time. Rent a studio in the Dakao area of town," said *papa*, "where we have a number of safe houses scattered around and security is good. Your cover is all in this folder. Study it carefully and we'll discuss it later. Given your experience, I'm open to suggestions."

His first assignment was Doanh, a senior land surveyor at the *Bureau du Cadastre*, the Cadastral Survey Office, who had access to official maps on which government facilities and French military camps appeared in great details. Fluent in French and well liked at work by his French supervisor, Gamecock Doanh, as he was known, ate lunch at a small noodle soup stand at the back of a pagoda in the suburbs during the week. He had been spotted meeting with known communist agents here. DGER auxiliaries had deliberately allowed the cell to operate, hoping in this way to identify more sympathizers, especially those in the civil service. Now it was time to latch on to the target.

Like many southerners, Doanh liked gambling, especially cockfighting, hence his nickname. He attended cockfights once or twice a week, sometimes losing heavily. First, Loi checked on his sources of income, almost always a sure indicator of a man's affiliations. His wife and children lived on his salary, so his gambling money had to come from the resistance. They were buying him. To blend in with the cockpit crowds, Loi rapidly learned all about betting at cockfights. He thought this would be a useful exercise in more ways than one, since he was now in the process of re-inventing himself as a normal, friendly, next-door-neighbor type. He visited gamecock farms to recognize the different breeds and the characteristics that cock-fighters looked for in a bird before placing a bet on it. He picked up the jargon of the sport, and began frequenting the cockfight pits that Doanh visited. Inside the pit, the level of noise and the heat were unbearable. Raw emotion swept over the audience in waves, followed by the sour smell of hundreds of sweaty bodies crammed into a small arena. One bird after another stumbled drunkenly to the ground after having had an artery slashed by an eight centimeter steel gaffe affixed to the left leg of his adversary. Noisy jubilation mixed with screams of despair as small fortunes changed hand, with the colorful bet takers always popping up at the right time and the right place to take a bet or to settle a payoff, never forgetting a bettor's face or the amount involved. Loi struck up a friendship with Doanh by standing next to him, asking him for tips and betting on the same birds. He once borrowed a small amount of money from his newfound friend to cover a bet, and promptly repaid him after the next fight. He had by now become used to drinking beer, though he still found it bitter and unpleasant, and they went out for a beer and grilled dog meat snack. As he drank the foul tasting *biere 33*, he had to eat sandwiches along with them in order to control the effects of the alcohol. Doanh said he had lost a large sum of money lately but that this did not affect his family, to whom he religiously gave his salary every fifteen days. On one occasion, Loi flashed a wad of bills and Doanh asked him what he did for a living. He told him he was with the PTT, the Postal Telecommunications Department, was not married and received a good salary. Within weeks, they had become good friends and Doanh confided in him that it was getting more and more difficult to sustain his secret vice. They met at Loi's rented room in Dakao to talk it over. The room had been wired by counter-intelligence. It turned out that while Doanh basically sympathized with the underground resistance, as many southerners did, he was not a communist and didn't really hate the French. Somewhat apolitical, he had at first accepted resistance money mainly to feed his cockfighting habits. Later, he said, he regretted this but couldn't break away from his handlers, whom he feared. If they gave him to the French police, he said, that would be the end of him and his family.

"No more cockfights, no more wife and children," he said dramatically, drawing his index across his throat. The problem was that he was running out of material they were interested in, and he was being pressured for new documents that he didn't have access to. It was getting more difficult to get money out of them.

Loi offered him a regular sum to replace the dwindling resistance money, and Doanh accepted. He had guessed by now that Loi was not just a simple telephone technician, but he didn't care. Southerners have a tendency to live for the day and not worry unduly about tomorrow. Loi arranged with Captain Godot for the *Bureau du Cadastre* to make available new material to Doanh, which reinforced his position with the resistance cell, and contacts between them increased. With two sources of income, Doanh's self-confidence grew, he became a heavy bettor, more often than not winning large sums. In return, he unwittingly helped Loi identify more resistance cells, more sympathizers and the courier system linking them. After a successful seven months of surveillance, Doanh disappeared without trace during one of his survey trips in the provinces. His body was never found. Loi remembered the four hotheads in the DTPH dispute in Phu My village. They had also disappeared without trace.

"They're not totally stupid. They must have caught on to the false documents we gave him," said *papa* laconically. Loi's jaw dropped. It was the first time he heard that the documents he had passed on to Doanh were not genuine. This is no game, everyone is playing for keeps. Poor Doanh, he was out of his league, and you have to make sure you aren't out of yours. The same day Doanh did not report for work *papa*'s men moved in and cleaned up the nest of vipers Doanh had revealed and Loi was officially congratulated on his first success.

Professionally speaking, the first step in intelligence and counter-intelligence work starts with the information gathered. Generally speaking, the more information, the clearer the picture. Information came from two sources, written material and verbal reports. Loi's spider's web of eyes and ears within the civil service and the military was to be made up of people from all different walks of life, some of whom were more reliable than others but none of whom he could trust completely. He lied to them about his motives, and they lied to him about what they knew, and in the middle of all this deliberate but acceptable deception and subterfuge lay a kernel of truth. The second step now involved the interpretation of this truth or that hard fact. The third step was the most complicated: what to do with this valuable information? Plans had to be drawn up, some overt, some covert. Some plans had plans within them. Agents had be briefed on their roles, deployed and supported. Whether the operation succeeded or failed, absolute silence had to be maintained at all times, to avoid giving the enemy an indication of how the system worked. It was a surreal world, full of half-truths and lies, a constant battle between people who had many faces and who were quite ruthless in how they accomplished their mission.

He had always been an avid reader, and he read and re-read old files until he could identify patterns that fitted into a matrix that was growing in his mind. This framework of reference helped him evaluate the raw information that came in and prepare for new twists and turns in this complicated world of make-believe. Slowly but surely, with *papa's* help and advice, he built up a small group of informers and undercover agents who reported to him. He also began to target communist agents, a tougher and more dangerous breed than sympathizers. So focused was he on the games of cat-and-mouse that he had grown into that he completely lost track of what was going on outside his lethal little world of stealth.

Through poring over existing files and talking to his colleagues, it came to Loi's attention that a communist cell was being formed inside the *Ministère du Transport,* the Transportation Ministry. Mr My, one of the two deputies to the minister and outwardly a staunch Catholic, secretly sympathized with the communist cause. He had hired as assistant an expert in rolling stock who had been suggested to him by a ranking communist cadre. Together, they had linked up with another government official in the same Ministry's shipping division, who was a communist plant. It was obvious the communists wanted an insider at the highest level in a Ministry that controlled national transportation at airports, ports and railway yards. Loi arranged for the telephone lines of Mr My and his two cell mates to be cut, at different times, over a period of three weeks. The PTT was called for repairs and he turned up to check the circuits, placing a tap on the targeted lines. In this way, he learnt when and where they would meet and discreet surveillance could be set up ahead of time. After a few months of shadow play, he pounced on all three at their rendezvous, using the regular judicial police as arresting agents to make it appear it had been a lucky arrest resulting from a chance tip off. The judicial police system was riddled with communist plants and sympathizers, and the nascent Viet Minh infrastructure encouraged a number of ranking government officials with leftist tendencies to intercede at police headquarters level for the release of the three. Had the arrest been made by the *Deuxième Bureau,* the communists would have sat on their hands. The government officials who came forward were identified and discreetly weeded out of the system. Loi's deft handling of an operation at ministerial level led to him receiving a decoration from Colonel Perret, *papa*'s boss, a hard-nosed veteran who had earned his spurs in Algeria. Colonel Perret had liked him at first sight, having heard nothing but good things about Lieutenant Ho Xuan Hai, code named Le Van Loi, from his subordinate, Captain Godot. The meeting was convivial, and Perret opened a bottle of champagne, another beverage that Hai found sour, acidic and undrinkable, but as they talked of this and that he could sense that his superiors had their minds elsewhere.

It was late 1939, and the clouds of war in Western Europe were already clearly visible. Like many ranking French officials posted in Indochina, Godot and Perret spent long hours listening to the radio, their faces anxious, their lips pursed. The French dailies brought nothing but bad news. For Colonel Perret and his team, the communist infrastructure in Indochina had become secondary in importance to Germany's intentions in Europe. After Germany and the Soviet Union divided up Poland in September of the same year, Britain, France, Australia and New Zealand declared war on Germany, but in fact there was no fighting between them, only political and military posturing.

On June 22, 1940 Marshall Pétain of France signed an armistice with Germany and opened negotiations with Japan on Indochina. France was now an ally of Germany, and Germany's other ally was Japan. The status of the French colonial regime in Indochina had become very unclear. For Frenchmen who could not accept France's abject surrender, the only option was to desert their posts and rejoin a little-known French colonel named Charles de Gaulle, who was in England, calling the Free French to his side.

39

The Japanese Occupation

The Americans had been shipping supplies through Hai Phong port to Chiang Kai Shek's troops in Yunnan province, and the Japanese Imperial Army High Command in southern China asked the Vichy government to allow Japanese troops to cross into north Viet Nam to put a stop to this. The dithering over this request by a regime allied to Japan's ally, Germany, and therefore now technically also Japan's ally, infuriated Tokyo and on September 22, 1940, Japanese troops from China attacked a number of French forts on the Chinese border, killing eight hundred French troops. Two days later Japanese aircraft bombed Hai Phong port and Japanese ships landed troops which marched on Ha Noi. The Pétain government in Paris capitulated without any further ado and Japan took over control of northern Indochina. Within the week, high-ranking Japanese military intelligence officers from the Kempetai had arrived in the northern capital to supervise the takeover of French military installations, including *la Citadelle*.

Primarily concerned with supporting the Japanese front against Chiang Kai-shek's Kuomintang troops in southern China, the Japanese Imperial High Command at first had little time for Viet Nam. While making a half-hearted effort to oversee the French administration in Tonkin, they gave the French a free hand to rule Cochinchina. But it was an uneasy situation: the French resented the Japanese presence and took malicious pleasure in playing tricks on the "yellow monkeys"; the Japanese, infuriated by the determined resistance they met in southern China, looked at their French "allies" with barely concealed contempt; the Vietnamese population, sensing a change of leadership, took advantage of the situation to humiliate the French.

John Havan

In Sai Gon, Colonel Perret and Captain Godot continued to work as before, reporting to their offices every day. But in fact they were preparing to desert their post. Huge quantities of dossiers and files, amassed over the years, were systematically destroyed; reports to the Vichy government in Paris were doctored and reports from Ha Noi were given the full bureaucratic treatment and sidelined. As *papa* told Hai, with a wicked twinkle in his eyes, it was vital that Vichy collaborationists, Japanese fascists and Vietnamese communists not get the better of French colonialists.

Perret and some of his friends, all ex-paratroopers who had served in Algeria, methodically prepared maps and medicine for an escape on foot through Laos and northern Siam into Burma, where British colonial troops were still in control. *Papa* would sail to Singapore from Can Tho, a major port in the southern Mekong delta, on a friend's yacht. It was now all a question of timing. Everything had to be done in great secrecy, as they couldn't trust their own people. The French community was divided into rightist officers, such as Colonel Perret and *papa* on the one hand, and the *collabos,* a generic term for all collaborators, such as the Governor General, His Excellency Jean-Pierre Lelouche and his staff on the other. In the middle was a large body of confused and fearful French settlers, many with Vietnamese wives and Eurasian children. Hai's concern was for *papa*, whom he didn't see as a Frenchman, but as a human being, a good and kind person. His adoptive father was now in great danger and had to run away, and he couldn't help him. He wished he could go with him, but he realized that he would only slow him down. What will you do in the British army *papa* intends to join?

In December 1941 Japanese planes and submarines attacked Pearl Harbor and Japanese tanks and infantry swept through Thailand, Burma, Malaya, Hong Kong, Singapore, the Philippines and Indochina in a series of well-planned tactical campaigns. Overnight, in Viet Nam, French administrators and policemen were arrested and locked up, and the French military restricted to barracks. Japan had taken over Indochina, and, as promised in the Greater East Asia Co-Prosperity Sphere propaganda broadcast hourly on the radio, would give Viet Nam its independence in gradual steps. An all-Vietnamese government, essentially the same one as had worked under the French, was installed and the Emperor was invited to return from his mansion in Cannes to once again sit on the throne in Hue. The Japanese civilian and military administrators who replaced the French now milked the

Vietnamese cow around the clock to support the Japanese war effort in China. Famine soon resulted in the countryside, especially in the north, and peasant revolts broke out regularly, which were brutally and efficiently dealt with by superbly conditioned Japanese troops.

One morning in late 1941, Captain Godot summoned him, Lieutenant Hai, to his office. The Vichy government had just agreed to the second back down and Japanese were now to take direct control of south Viet Nam as well. He had been advised to prepare to receive Colonel Tomohiko and his staff the following day, to "coordinate the management of intelligence affairs from that time onward". The memo was signed by the Governor General, The Honorable Jean-Pierre Lelouche, and addressed to his superior, Colonel Perret. They stood shoulder to shoulder, leaning over his desk, reading the memo together. *Papa* then spoke rapidly.

"Son, the first thing I did this morning was to destroy the original of the documents you signed when we hired you. There is no record of a Ho Xuan Hai or a Le Van Loi ever working here. I never made any copies for France. Besides Perret and me, no one knows your background. You can become whoever you say you are, there is no way the Japanese can check. I have left a few sensitive documents in my drawer you can use anyway you want. In about one hour, I shall leave for Can Tho. From there, my friends and I shall sail for Singapore. At least the British are fighting back. You have nothing to fear here. I suggest you stay in this building and continue to work for French intelligence, under Japanese supervision. The whole world is breaking apart, I don't know what is going to happen to my family, to me or to you. We have to be brave, to keep our eyes open and to seize whatever opportunity we see."

He clenched his ham-like fist in the air, to show how an opportunity was to be seized. Tears welled up in his eyes and he hugged Hai, his adopted son, to his chest. Hai was crying openly too, and he hugged *papa* back vigorously, kissing his bristly cheeks. He remembered the scene at the Lamy Café when his *papa* had recognized him and had kissed him on both cheeks. He had felt he should also kiss his *papa* back, but was too embarrassed to do so. It was simply too French for him. But this time things were different. There was no need to hold back now that he felt that he would never see him again. They heard a loud knock on the door, and *papa* wiped his face, blew his nose and opened the door. His executive officer appeared, pale and sweaty.

"I'm sorry, *mon capitaine*, but the Japanese are already here, "he reported, saluting. "They arrived earlier than expected," he added, apologetically.

Captain Godot thanked him and quickly closed the door. He looked at Hai for a long time, then stood to attention and saluted. Hai saluted him back smartly, putting everything in this military gesture of respect, knowing that this was the last time he would see him. He felt his mother move inside him and he knew she was also looking at this good man who had done so much for them. For a second, Hai saw *papa* and his mother and him standing at Gia Lam outside Ha Noi after the *Citadelle* days. *Papa* was going away again, but this time his mother had already gone. Both men knew they would not see each other again this time. The advent of World War Two had changed everything. They stared at each other for what seemed an eternity; *papa* then slipped out of a side door that was hidden behind a curtain. A narrow corridor led him out into an empty antechamber. He crossed this and walked out into bright sunshine, towards the motor pool where his private car was waiting, with spare tanks of gasoline in the back.

Hai stood alone, momentarily lost. He then walked behind *papa*'s desk and sat down on his father's chair. He pulled open the drawer and took out a thick folder. He glanced at the files inside. They were all about communist and opposition plants inside government ministries. He placed the documents in his briefcase and walked out of *papa*'s office. Once outside, he sat down on a bench to wait for the Japanese delegation.

Five Japanese officers soon arrived, their swords slapping against their boots. He had seen Japanese before, mostly small-time traders, fishermen and photographers, but this was the first time he had seen the Japanese military. They were small men, much shorter than Frenchmen, about the same size as Vietnamese, but more compact and hairy. Their brown uniforms were well cut, their boots shiny. They looked purposeful, their eyes taking in everything at a glance. They gave the impression of being professional soldiers and it was hard to imagine a group more unlike the casual and relaxed French officers, with their long hair, rumpled uniforms and cigarettes permanently dangling from the lip. The Japanese were escorted by Captain Godot's executive officer, various French police officials and translators. They saw him sitting still outside Captain Godot's door.

"Who's that man?" asked Colonel Tomohiko, in Japanese. A Vietnamese translator repeated the question in French.

"He's Captain Godot's special assistant, sir," answered the *aide-de-camp*. This was translated into Japanese.

"Tell him to come into the office with us," said Tomohiko. He was a stocky man, very white of skin, with a perpetually turned-down mouth, above which sat a small moustache. His head was shaven clean and he smelt of soap and leather. A long sword dangled from his left hip, the tip of the shiny black scabbard dragging on the ground when he took his left hand off the handle. After a short look around Captain Godot's office, Tomohiko and the group went into Colonel Perret's office. Tomohiko promptly sat down on Perret's chair, looking around at the large office and its modern furnishings. The Japanese officers stood at attention, and everyone imitated them, not knowing what the proper etiquette was in Japanese military society. One young Japanese officer began moving around, sealing all the file cabinets and desk drawers with yellow tape on which Japanese characters were written. He then removed all the pictures, decorations and the paintings from the walls and stacked them neatly in a corner of the office. From his leather satchel he pulled out a small Japanese flag and taped it to the wall just behind Colonel Tomohiko's head.

The Colonel swung around, glanced up at the flag, turned back to them, shot up and roared something in Japanese. For a small man, his voice had a raw power to it that rocked them all back on their heels. What made it all the more surprising was that he hardly opened his mouth. The Mongolian set of the face, the heavy lidded eyes, the intensity of his stance were something new. Hai had never seen body language like this before. This short, paunchy man in the tight uniform was like a coiled spring. He exuded an aura of violence. The translator, pale as death, stammered the order in French and Vietnamese in a squeaky voice. The Colonel had told them to bow to the flag. Quickly recovering, they all bowed, inclining their heads to varying degrees. The Colonel roared out another order, and the anger in his voice shredded the inner tissues of their ears. He rushed out from behind his new desk and stood looking at them, his face filled with contempt. There was blood in his eye and his right hand hovered above the hilt of his sword. Then, with a visible effort, he composed himself, turned towards the flag on the wall and then ceremoniously bowed from the waist, very low, eyes looking at the ground, arms held rigid by the side, palms against the outside of his thighs. The translator did not have to say anything. Everyone had understood perfectly. Tomohiko returned behind his desk, and they all bowed again, properly, Japanese style, to him and to the Japanese flag.

Later, when he had taken down all their names and titles, the Colonel sat back and spoke to them through the interpreter.

"Since Bey-rey and Go-do-tu have deserted their post, they have become fugitives. When caught, they will be executed. This office will be mine and all French officers working directly under Bey-rey and Go-do-tu will report to me after lunch today. You," he said, pointing to Hai, will report to my second-in-command, Captain Watanabe. What is your name and rank?"

"Tran Van Xuan, lieutenant, *Deuxième Bureau*, Colonel," Loi answered, bowing in the proper manner. Xuan had been his research assistant until the day before, when he had asked to be relieved from duty now that the Japanese were taking over. He wanted to return to the province to take care of his family. It's funny, this is the first time you are picking a name for yourself. He bowed deeply, impressing Colonel Tomohiko. Heaven alone knows where all this is going to lead to. You had almost become Hai with *papa*'s return, now you are Xuan. Thirty-six years before you can live under the name your mother gave you. Funny, for a few minutes when *papa* returned it felt as if the bad luck stars had forgotten about you and moved on because you worked for the French. Imperceptibly, he shook his head. Another nine years to go, and under the Japanese this time. Every time you get a new name... whoosh... it's like a whole chunk of your life just disappears down the drain. You get reborn, again, each time.

"All Vietnamese working in these two offices will report to Captain Watanabe. They must prepare an up-to-date report of their activities. I shall then give them their instructions," Colonel Tomohiko said, in a matter-of-fact voice. He had a problem pronouncing the names of Colonel Perret and Captain Godot, and the translator didn't understand what he was saying at first. Finally, in a quavering voice, he managed to get Colonel Tomohiko's message out. Everyone present nodded officiously, as if nothing had changed. In fact, from the moment that little cloth flag had been taped up on the wall, a whole era had died a silent death, never to return again. That little flag is your introduction to Japan. You're about to be reborn—again.

40

The *Kempetai*

For the following six months Hai, now Xuan, worked as special assistant to Colonel Tomohiko's deputy, Captain Watanabe, who was in charge of Japanese counter-intelligence. Watanabe sat in *papa*'s office, and Xuan sat in a corner in the same office along with Watanabe's team of interpreters and translators. The Japanese were nothing if not thorough in everything they did and by now he could speak colloquial Japanese, having spent four hours a night attending the language class Colonel Tomohiko had set up right from the beginning. Although the Colonel was always accompanied by an interpreter when he addressed the Vietnamese staff, he had a small Japanese-Vietnamese dictionary permanently in his pocket. He would often whip it out and find the one word that he felt summed up what he had said. He would repeat this word emphatically, in a loud voice, and everyone would bow each time. On a number of occasions, because Vietnamese is tonal while Japanese is not, the mispronunciations were hilarious but nobody dared laugh. They all stood there rooted to the ground while laughing gases roiled around riotously inside the coils of their intestines until they were ready to burst at both ends like ripe watermelons. Tremendous anal muscle control had to counterbalance intense mental focus as they fought to keep a serious face while bent double. When he was in a good mood, which thankfully was not often, Colonel Tomohiko tried to enhance Japanese-Vietnamese relations by using the formal Vietnamese way of greeting a group of people. In Vietnamese, the word *cac* is used to denote plurality, meaning "all" and is commonly used when addressing more than one gentleman or lady or *mademoiselle. Chao cac ong, chao cac ba, chao cac co* mean "greeting

216

all gentlemen", "greeting all ladies", "greeting all young ladies". The word *cac* is pronounced as a long syllable with a rising accent, but the Colonel pronounced it as a short syllable with a heavy accent, as most Japanese words are pronounced, and it came out as "testicles". Word quickly spread around the compound that anyone who laughed at Colonel Tomohiko's testicle greetings risked having his own testicles sliced off on the spot, and Herculean efforts were made to stop belly laughs erupting madly every time the Colonel smiled and showered everyone with his testicular greetings. They all thanked God for the mandatory deep bows, which hid their faces and undoubtedly saved a lot of lives, although the good Colonel must have wondered why there was so much unnecessary bowing and scraping going on every time he spoke Vietnamese. He probably thought this was in gratitude for his graceful gesture, not knowing he had been nicknamed Colonel *cac*, with the heavy accent.

Captain Watanabe was a younger man, thin, in his mid-thirties, with a sharp, aquiline nose. He rapidly acquired enough basic Vietnamese to make himself understood most of the time, but as soon as he had difficulty with a word, out would come his well-thumbed little dictionary, a replica of Colonel Tomohiko's, also printed in Tokyo. Apparently, every officer in the Japanese army of occupation had been issued with such pocket dictionaries. As were most of the Japanese officers that Xuan met during the Occupation, Watanabe was by nature polite, methodical and patient to a fault. Every detail had to be recorded, evaluated, authenticated, annotated and cross-indexed with other relevant details until a pattern appeared. Watanabe spent all day and most of the night analyzing this massive amount of data, some of it in Vietnamese, some in French, but most of it in Japanese. The Japanese had long been studying Viet Nam in secret, and they knew to the last centimeter the depth of every major port and its tide patterns. Their businessmen, itinerant traders, photographers, tourists, agricultural experts and herbalists had mapped every major waterway that irrigated the Mekong delta, the height of every hill and mountain in the region and even the number of villages in the areas they were interested in. It was ant-like work and it must have begun well before World War Two. In many ways, in their humorless dedication to their work and the intensity of their focus on the problem at hand they reminded Xuan of the communist resistance cadres he had worked with.

Over the next year or so, as he worked diligently for the *Kempetai*, he watched with interest as the social pendulum changed from black to white, or rather, as he concluded with a laugh, from white to yellow. French government administrators, police officers, military personnel, overlords and masters until recently, had been returned to their former posts but now Japanese supervisors and Vietnamese translators peered over their shoulders all day long. Japan was obviously in full control and the long-simmering Vietnamese hatred for the French was now allowed to bloom in full force. French settlers were ridiculed openly and often attacked in the streets, with Japanese troops looking on in amusement. French women who used to flaunt large breasts and pop-up behinds under short thin cotton dresses now wore shapeless nondescript clothes and no makeup when they had to go shopping at the market. At the urging of the Japanese authorities, most of the Vietnamese servants had left their employers, and now white faces were seen regularly at the smelly central markets and cluttered little Vietnamese shops, all located in the Vietnamese quarter, far from the French quarter with its huge acacia trees and well-kept parks. The French women hated being followed by hordes of street urchins who jeered at them, singing popular jingles that coarsely described bouncing buttocks and swinging tits. French men now went out in groups, ready to help each other in case of attack. The usual arrogance had disappeared and they avoided making eye contact with the Vietnamese. On the city streets, the sidewalks now belonged to the Japanese, officers or troops, and both the French and the Vietnamese deferentially stepped down into the street to let them pass unhindered. Until then, the Vietnamese had always had to step aside to let French men or women go by. French children stayed at home, all the French schools having been closed. When they did venture outside, Vietnamese urchins chased after them, throwing stones and hurling insults.

The French community, pro-Vichy or pro-de Gaulle, suffered all this in silence. Their fear of the Japanese was real, for they had recognized in them a race even more ruthless than their own. Except for a few highly educated Japanese officers, many of whom could speak French fluently, the Japanese as a whole disliked whites and treated them with contempt and brutality. One unfortunate word, one vexing gesture, one misunderstanding and they were mercilessly slapped by men who were half their height. To the Japanese military, slapping symbolized domination, superiority, contempt and punishment. It established an immediate pecking order. Japanese officers slapped non-coms, non-coms slapped soldiers, older soldiers slapped new recruits and all the Japanese military slapped the French and the natives. The slap was hard, almost always accompanied by the same mildly insulting adjective, "bad man" or "stupid man", since the Japanese language lacks really vulgar swearwords. Within the military, an innate discipline of steel existed, and the man being punished would bow after each slap, salute and bark out "Yessir"! With civilians, however, at the first sign of resistance, such as not bowing deeply, out came the swords, four foot long and razor sharp, to confirm domination. To survive, the French had to do what the Japanese did, and formally bow at each slap.

The way the population now behaved towards them vindicated the French in their belief that all the natives were basically treacherous and ungrateful. In their minds, the French settlers saw themselves as saviors, men from a superior race whose sense of duty had forced them to try their best, but they had failed, mainly because of the inferiority of the material they had had to work with. All that kindness, all that effort at civilizing the natives, and now they were biting the hand that had trained them with firmness and even love. They were now surrounded by "yellows", "rice-eaters", "monkeys", none of whom liked "whites". Some yellows were communists, some rice-eaters were fascists, but the worst monkeys were the formerly servile natives. Many whites wished they had had the foresight and the temerity to leave, like the rightist officers had done before it was too late.

It was around this period Xuan read with interest that Nguyen Ai Quoc had returned to Viet Nam after some thirty years of self-imposed exile. A nationalist who had deliberately chosen the Leninist version of communism, he set up camp in Cao Bang province and adopted the pseudonym of Ho Chi Minh, rapidly becoming known as Uncle Ho. The communist resistance movement he had founded since the early '30s, and which Xuan had joined, changed its name to *Viet Nam Doc Lap Dong Minh Hoi,* known as the Viet Minh for short. His guerrillas, led by a teacher-turned-military named Vo Nguyen Giap, emerged from their jungle lairs and mountain caves to attack the occasional Japanese barrack, the Viet Minh forces being too weak at this stage to do more than harass the new masters of Viet Nam. To help them become more effective, the American Office of Strategic Services began air dropping supplies and modern weaponry to these newfound supporters of democracy and the Viet Minh gained stature in the eyes of the general population as the only viable Vietnamese resistance movement, helped by no less than America, which was certainly not communist and not even socialist. In the countryside, the peasantry saw in the Viet Minh movement the renaissance of a new and sovereign

Viet Nam. This nationalistic image, totally divorced from Leninism and Stalinism, which the peasants had never understood anyway, was later carefully cultivated in the countryside by Uncle Ho in his war against the French.

The Japanese Imperial Army officer corps despised Caucasians, be they French, Dutch or British. Racism in reverse, Xuan noted. This hatred for the whites, common enough throughout Asia, was made worse by a peculiarly Japanese concept of loyalty and honor. *Bushido*, a warrior's code developed in the thirteenth century by the *samurai* classes, had gradually lost its fervor at the time of the Meiji restoration, when samurai swords were confiscated and destroyed, but had been revived and adopted by the Imperial Japanese Forces at the start of Word War Two, when samurai swords were mass-produced in Ministry of Defense factories, serialized and issued to all officers (long version) and non-commissioned officers (shorter version). An enemy was expected to fight to the death, as the Japanese were prepared to do. In *Bushido*, to die fearlessly at the hands of an enemy who was stronger was in itself an act of great heroism. Japanese tales abounded of a fallen warrior who asked the victor to unmask himself so that he could see the face of the man who was about to kill him. On the other hand, an enemy could be spared and even shown respect if he showed fearlessness in the face of death. Great beauty and poignancy were attached to the act of fighting without fear until the end. When Japanese officers found that Westerners and Asians in general preferred surrender to possible death, they concluded that these people were spineless cowards who did not deserve to be treated like human beings. Thus, when they were taken as prisoners of war, they were treated with contempt as a matter of course. This mindset often led to bestial brutality when these less-than-human prisoners had the temerity to demand this or that privilege in relation to their rank, or because of something they called the Geneva Convention.

Since the new national government had been put in place by Japan, to spy on it now was to spy on Japan, and the *Kempetai* turned its attention towards communist and nationalist spies inside the Vietnamese administration. With an army of well-paid and well-coordinated informers, the Japanese effortlessly cut through the communist infrastructure in the villages, towns and cities, driving the communists back into the jungles and mountains. Torture followed by beheading was the order of the day for agents caught in the *Kempetai* dragnet. There were very few prisoners in Japanese jails at any given time and, outside the prisons, everything ran like clockwork. Prisoners of war were usually divided into groups of ten. If one managed to escape, the other nine would be beheaded the following day. The population feared the Japanese and therefore obeyed them. Absolute discipline, readily enforced by the sword, allowed a handful of Japanese to dominate millions of Vietnamese and thousands of French still in Viet Nam. But the Japanese didn't rely solely on brutality to overcome the enemy. A strange mix of Asian guile and European inflexibility, the *Kempetai* were at times wilier than the Viet Minh and more practical than the French. Their approach combined a judicious mixture of strategic thinking and tactical execution. When Xuan got to know them better, he saw that these were highly disciplined men whose individual genetic makeup, he suspected, must have been identical. His former comrades in the resistance had been as different one from the other for having come from different provinces and speaking different dialects. They had had to be ground into dust, sent up and down Shit Hill, denied any form of sex, reformed and shoehorned into the unique Party mold through a long and detailed indoctrination program. To a lesser extent, French military recruits underwent the same process. The Japanese, on the other hand, must have been born alike from the first day, like ants, and it made them superior in the world of fighting and aggression. Watanabe told Xuan once "You are like sand, each grain beautiful and shiny. When mixed with water, each grain floats away. We are like mud, ugly and dull, but when mixed with water we solidify into one."

Hai's understanding of the Japanese grew over the first year as the Captain, who allowed himself two hours of rest in the evening hours at the office, taught him how to play an incredibly subtle board game called *go*. Originally developed in China thousands of years before, it had been modified by the Japanese to adapt it to their peculiar mindset. This was Watanabe's secret passion, and it made him what he was, a powerful strategic thinker who could react tactically within seconds. Over the years, as the Viet Nam saga dragged on and the Japanese were replaced by the French, the Americans and finally the communists, Xuan often thought back with pleasure to the many games of *go* he played with Watanabe during the occupation and he was convinced this complex game contributed greatly to his ability to think and act seamlessly at a time when everything was breaking up around him.

Militarily, the Japanese Imperial troops were as different from the French Colonial Corps as night was from day. They relentlessly pursued the enemy into his hideouts and exterminated him to the last man. They excelled in night patrols and no guerrilla dared to sleep in Japanese zones of operation. Any civilian, man or woman, caught with a weapon in hand or a radio was beheaded. Yet in spite of this absolute ruthlessness, a throwback to the days of the Mongols, the communist-led resistance continued to be active, day in day out, famine or no famine. For every man killed, and many were killed each month, two new ones were recruited. As the years wore on, both the *Kempetai* and the Japanese Imperial Army came to recognize that the Viet Minh were also dedicated and fearless fighters. In the *Bushido* mind, this was an enemy worthy of fighting, whereas the Vietnamese government they had set up merited nothing but contempt. For the vast majority of Vietnamese, having been dragooned into working for a new overlord who treated them with contempt while secretly admiring the enemy, this attitude was extremely confusing. Gradually, when things became clearer, the secret hatred the Vietnamese population had felt for the French grew to encompass the Japanese as well. To be treated with contempt by whites was hateful but to be expected, but to receive the same treatment by Asians, by rice eaters like themselves, was not only hateful but also unacceptable.

As Xuan's spoken Japanese improved, Watanabe's trust in him grew and he was given undercover work in the countryside, where the Viet Minh infrastructure continued to grow despite, or perhaps because of, Japanese brutality. The documents he had taken from *papa*'s desk had given Captain Watanabe the impression that he had been a high-ranking counter-intelligence agent in French military intelligence. Watanabe decided to use his expertise in the field, where Japanese intelligence wanted to ferret out communist resistance agents and their supporters inside provincial capitals. His responsibility was to sift through all the information gathered and discern trends and patterns which would allow the *Kempetai* to preempt American OSS and communist resistance plans and projects. After one year in the field, Xuan was transferred to Cam Ranh Bay, a deep warm water port that the Japanese were particularly interested in developing. The communist infrastructure in the area, having been built up during the years when the French ran the port, was well developed and the *Kempetai* office in Cam Ranh itself was as large as the one in Sai Gon. He was assigned as a liaison officer between Captain Tomo and the Sai Gon office. Tomo headed a large contingent of informers who weeded out the communists, real or otherwise, from surrounding villages and townships, as well as from Cam Ranh town itself. Xuan's work was to collate all the Vietnamese reports, comment on them, and send them down to Sai Gon weekly by Japanese courier. Watanabe would then read through the translations and issue instructions to Tomo. The work was tedious and necessitated a great deal of deduction and interpretation and translation before the Vietnamese assistants and their Japanese superiors in Cam Ranh could agree on what to send to Watanabe. Xuan's line of work was dangerous as he often had to come into direct contact with the communist agents who had been arrested. Once or twice he thought he recognized a face or two from his days of doing research work in the north. As an analyst, he didn't wear a hood like the informers did and the prisoners could see his face. The ones who live will remember you. The Viet Minh already have a list of everyone working for the *Kempetai*. When the Japanese leave it will be death for you to be caught in a communist-controlled zone.

In 1943 the first American planes began bombing the Japanese in Viet Nam. Ownership of a short-wave radio was absolutely forbidden by the Japanese, the penalty being instant execution, and many Frenchmen had already been beheaded. But Xuan could listen to Tomo's post, and he was able to follow the course of the war. Japan had not been able to bring China under its control, the American navy and air force were beginning to penetrate the Japanese homeland and throughout Asia indigenous commando forces under British command were sabotaging Japanese garrisons. Things were not going well for Japan.

In early 1944, Colonel Tomohiko called everyone in to brief them on a new development. General de Gaulle's Free French forces in Britain had set up the *Direction Générale des Services de Sécurité*, the DGSS, the French Intelligence Service, which had its headquarters in Calcutta, India, under Major Boucher de Crèvecoeur. The Free French major had in turn set up a special operations unit in Kandy, Ceylon, called the French Indochina Section, the FIS, which reported to Force 136, the Asian and Far Eastern arm of the British Special Operations Executive, the SOE. The FIS numbered forty officers and one hundred and eight other ranks, including twenty-seven Vietnamese. With logistics and training support by the SOE, the FIS had infiltrated twenty-four agents with large quantities of arms and explosives. It was now more important than ever to identify and root out spies and informers already in the system. In the meantime, to nip in the bud any idea of a French uprising, the Japanese army launched full scale attacks on all the French garrisons on March 9. In Tonkin, the French fought to the last man, some troops escaping into China, where Chiang Kai-shek's troops promptly arrested them. But in central and southern Viet Nam some fifteen thousand French troops were disarmed and confined to barracks under heavy Japanese guard, while all the civil servants were imprisoned.

The Allies did not attack the Japanese forces in Viet Nam, but after Germany surrendered in Europe, the handwriting was on the wall. The US firebombing of Tokyo, on March 9-10, 1945, signaled the end of an empire. The Greater Co-Prosperity Sphere was imploding, and it disintegrated altogether five months later when America dropped two atomic bombs on Japan. Xuan heard on the radio that one hundred thousand people had been killed and one million wounded.

On August 14, 1945, Emperor Hirohito declared the unconditional surrender of Japan.

41

Étienne Saintenoix

In Viet Nam, the Japanese High Command kept its guns but handed over power to the Viet Minh, arguably the only credible existing political organization in the country. Secretly, the High Command admired the Viet Minh for their determination and bravery, qualities they saw as being quintessentially Japanese. Perhaps even more important, the Japanese recognized in the Viet Minh an Asian movement that was inherently anti-white, and that fitted in with the Japanese mindset. With the Japanese studiously looking the other way, Ho Chi Minh's fledgling troops promptly seized Ha Noi and created a National Liberation Committee to form a provisional government. In Sai Gon, communist liberation committees had sprung up in every district of the huge city, and everyone waited to see what would happen next, now that the French were gone, the Japanese were going and the Viet Minh had re-appeared, like ghosts out of nowhere.

Xuan was not one of those waiting to see what the future had for him. After his stint with French intelligence and the Japanese *Kempetai*, he knew he was marked for death by the Viet Minh. In his favor was that fact that he didn't have any relatives or friends to care for. He carried his mother's spirit in him and all his worldly possessions could have fitted into the knapsack on his back. He had loads of experience but traveled light, moved silently and hit hard, like Hélène had advised him that memorable night under the bridge. At thirty-one years of age, he felt he was already faster on his feet than any Viet Minh spy, French *2ème bureau* agent or Japanese *Kempetai* officer. He stuffed rolls of cold rice, slabs of dry meat and a bottle of water into a backpack and went down to the Sai Gon docks on the night of the Japanese surrender. After waiting for things to settle down, he walked up to a sailor who was urinating against the wall in a corner and struck up a conversation with him. At one point, he produced a thick wad of notes he had taken from the *Kempetai* safe in Watanabe's office and the sailor handed him some identification documents enclosed in a waterproof plastic envelope. He looked at them. His new identity was Mercier, André, seaman first-class.

"You can see from the photograph he's a Vietnamese, though he has a French name," said the sailor. Xuan nodded, and a little later they walked together up the gangway and he climbed into one of the lifeboats.

The *Cambodge* was one of three liners belonging to the *Chargeurs Réunis* line that plied the Saigon–Marseilles route. As soon as it reached international waters, seven stowaways emerged from their hiding places and asked to be put to work in return for bed and board. After a tongue lashing by the French captain, they became unpaid deck hands. Once in Marseilles, they were offered a choice. They could face arrest, jail time and eventual deportation, or they could sign on for five years as merchant seamen, third class. It wasn't much of a choice, and they all signed on, some quite determined to desert at the next port. Life as an unpaid deck hand had been hard, and a small salary was not going to make much difference. Xuan, now Mercier, was a slightly different case in that he had an acceptable identification document. He was assigned to the ship's kitchen after it was discovered that he spoke good French. Wearing a uniform and a cap he served the ship's officers their three meals a day. In between, he helped the chefs prepare the food for the guests, officers and crewmembers. In the process, he learned how to cook Vietnamese, European and Arab dishes, discovered he had a natural bent for cooking and eventually was appointed assistant cook.

On the world stage, as he could hear from the radio sets in the kitchen and in the Officers' Mess, General De Gaulle had returned to Paris in triumph, General Leclerc had arrived in Viet Nam to reclaim "France's patrimony", France having regained her seat at the superpower table. Washington and London had given Paris the nod over its former colonies, and De Gaulle was determined to take back Viet Nam, Laos and Cambodia. Six eventful years after the world had erupted in war, the balance of power was swinging back to its old position, with a number of differences here and there. One of those differences was that the communist movement in Viet Nam had implanted itself solidly in the countryside; another was that the charismatic Ho Chi Minh had morphed into Uncle Ho, a nationalist hero in the eyes of the peasantry. After some fifteen years of research and indoctrination, the Party that Mercier had once belonged to was now prepared to carry the war to the French.

After two years on the ship, André Mercier was given three weeks' leave and he decided to take it after they docked in Marseilles. Having remained on board from one port to another, and he was flush with money. This time, he rented rooms near the port area with his friends. He enjoyed his first week in the sleazy, raucous, cosmopolitan back streets of Marseilles, for centuries a melting ground for seafarers from North Africa and the Middle East. Towards the south, the whole city smelled of *couscous*, an Arab dish made with semolina, vegetable soup and greasy chunks of mutton. Mercier's Greek, Turkish and South Sea island seaman friends were far more adventurous than him and knew where all the best brothels and bars were. They promised to fix him up with an Algerian girl named Fifi. He was told again and again that Fifi could "suck a bull dry in one minute flat." Never having seen a bull being sucked, he didn't know quite what to expect, but he was certainly determined to go through with it. As it turned out, Fifi was everything his friends said she would be, though he was taken aback when she first appeared. She was considerably older than he had imagined. But she knew what a man wanted, and she played him like a master guitarist strums his instrument. Mercier soon realized why it was that almost everyone he knew talked about sex all the time, and he regretted having missed so much of it over the years. He mentally vowed to engage in this exquisitely pleasant pastime as often as he could from then on. The third time around, Fifi's wig had fallen off. Later, she took her false teeth out to wash them in a glass and he almost threw up when later, after a wild bout of sex, he felt thirsty and almost drank from that glass.

One afternoon, sitting at a bar, eating peanuts and drinking *un piper soda*, a cooling and delicious concoction of peppermint and soda, he was idly leafing through a newspaper when he saw a name he recognized. "Banker receives award for war services", the title read. The article was about a *Monsieur* Étienne Saintenoix, a director at the *Banque Nationale de Paris*, being decorated by *Président* De Gaulle at the Elysées for his work "during the dark years when the soul of France lived across the ocean".

Mr. Saintenoix was now the deputy Director General of the BNP in Paris and would leave for a visit to Indochina soon, the article went on to say. Mercier promptly ripped out the page and returned to the ship. He took out all of his back pay, changed into his best clothes, packed a small bag and headed for the railway station. He bought a ticket for Paris. At the BNP branch nearest the central railway station in Paris, the teller had no idea who Mr. Saintenoix was and referred him to a supervisor, who wanted to know who he was and why he wanted to meet with Mr. Saintenoix. It's obvious you don't look like the sort of person Saintenoix associates with. Nevertheless, perhaps because he spoke good French in spite of his working class appearance and rough hands, the supervisor made a few phone calls to BNP headquarters in downtown Paris and put him on the phone. The lady on the line was a secretary who wanted to know his name and address, so she could take the matter up with her superior and call back. Mercier gave his name as Robert Do, pronounced without accent the French way, his convent name, and said he would wait by the BNP phone, not having found a hotel for the night. After an hour, the lady rang back to say that Mr. Saintenoix was at his country residence near Fontainebleau and would return to Paris the following week. Mercier was stunned. He had found Étienne. In a tight voice, he asked her for the address of the country residence or the phone number. He could not believe his luck when she gave him both. He then rang through to Étienne's home and a girlish voice answered that daddy was out walking the dogs, but that he was coming home soon for lunch. Mercier walked about the station, eating his lunch in a café. At one in the afternoon, he called again. A man's voice answered.

"Saintenoix", it said. It didn't sound like Étienne at all.

"This is Robert, the boy who worked at your house in Ha Noi from 1922 to 1924. Your parents hired my mother and me, and you tutored me at home. We played football together," Mercier said rapidly, afraid that Étienne might hang up on him.

There was a long silence. It had been over twenty years.

"Robert? Where are you calling from?"

"From Paris, Étienne. I am here on a visit."

"Robert? Is that really you? It's been a long time. Your voice doesn't sound the same. Excuse me, but what was my mother's name?"

"Louise, *Madame* Louise. The German shepherds were called Tarzan, Dulcie and Lucille. Your father gave me a photograph of all of you before he left Viet Nam. Your mother used to read to me from Victor Hugo's novels, sitting on a yellow rocking chair, in the corner of the sitting room, near the green table light with a painting of a naked woman on it," he said. There was another long silence, and he thought Étienne had hung up. But he hadn't.

"Oh my God! It's really you! How are you, Robert? Don't answer that, we can talk later. You must join me here today, and we can spend the weekend together. I have a wife and two children now…"

"How do I get there?" Mercier cut in.

Directions were given, and by nightfall he stepped out of the train at Petit Fleuris station, near Mouans Sartoux village, in Fontainebleau district. Waiting at the door of the tiny station was Étienne, a large man by now but still pasty-faced, with glasses, flanked by a pleasant looking woman and two children.

During that long weekend, they talked, ate and drank from morning until late at night. François Saintenoix had passed away ten year before, followed by Louise shortly after. Étienne had taken up banking on the advice of his father, had married and was now "dabbling in politics", as he put it. During the war, he had joined De Gaulle immediately, taking his family with him. As it turned out, it had been the right move. He was now one of the right-hand men the General depended on for financial advice and, officially, had been tasked with coordinating the French armaments industry's efforts to increase defense sales, the aim being to rival America's within ten years. Étienne looks sideways when he says this, as if he's trying to remember the lines he should say. He is either lying to you, or hiding something from you.

During the weekend of talks, he had probed Étienne as Étienne had probed him, and he had had the distinct impression that Étienne's real job was not to help sell warplanes and tanks.

"What a fascinating life you've had," said Mercier.

Étienne's next trip to Indochina was to inspect the BNP chain there. "Would you like to join me?" he asked. Mercier promptly nodded, glad he had talked at length about the Escudier and the *Citadelle* periods of his life, leaving out the railway bridge and the Viet Minh training camp episodes. He explained how Escudier had became Godot and how he had worked for him. Étienne seemed particularly interested in this part. Mercier had also explained why his name was now Mercier, and Étienne had clapped when he heard this story.

"Wonderful, wonderful! You're really an original!" he said. "I always knew you were different from the other *Annamites*. Even when we were kids. God! I remember the millions of questions you used to ask me! Tutoring you was hard work!"

"And what would you like to do now?" asked Étienne on the last day. They were preparing to return to Paris by car.

"I'd like to work for French intelligence again, but I don't know where Captain Godot is," Mercier answered.

"Not a problem," said Étienne. "Give me some time and I'll track him down for you. I know quite a few top military men in General de Gaulle's entourage, and if your boss is around, we'll find him."

Mercier thought briefly he should ask him to track Hélène down too, but dismissed the thought instantly. Obviously a man like Étienne would hardly be likely to know a person like her, whatever she had become since arriving in France.

Seven months later, Étienne and Mercier met in the lobby of the Metropole Hotel in Ha Noi. Étienne was on an official BNP visit and had asked for two deluxe rooms. Mercier had resigned from the *Chargeurs Réunis* shipping line, with a little help from Étienne, who had prodded the Chairman of the company to release "my very dear friend Robert Do, a.k.a. André Mercier".

Étienne brought with him good and bad news. Captain Godot had joined the Australian forces as an intelligence advisor and had been killed during the war on an operation in East Timor, where the Australians were trying to dislodge the Japanese. Colonel Perret had been captured along with the British commando force he had joined in Burma. He was executed shortly after capture. On the other hand, General Touquet, head of the *Deuxième Bureau* in Indochina was ready to receive Robert Do in private, having been advised to do so by a senior adviser to General de Gaulle. It was decided Étienne would take him in to meet with General Touquet. That's how things are done between important people. A phone call here, a discreet whisper there and a whole organization readjusts itself to accommodate the will of the leadership, of the important people, of the movers and shakers. In one minute he's done something that would take you years to achieve. That's power and influence for you. That's being somebody important. That's what you're going to be.

Later, Mercier talked to his mother about the death of *papa*. There was not much he could say, since he knew that she already thought the same things he thought. He observed a moment of silence and mother and son thought back to the good times they had had with that wonderful man who had been a father to both of them. He felt that he should pray for his soul, but he had never taken up a religion and the only prayers he could remember vaguely were those he had learned at the convent, so he mumbled a Christian prayer for *papa*, whom he knew had been brought up as a Catholic. He also said a prayer for Mathieu and for *papa's* wife and as he mumbled his way through the prayers he tried to imagine what pain and sorrow they must have felt at the loss of such a wonderful father and husband. *Papa* had been only a part of his world, but to his wife and son he had been their whole world. He wondered if *papa* had ever told his family anything about his family in Viet Nam.

One evening, while Étienne and he were having dinner in the hotel restaurant, he thought he saw a face he recognized among the waiters. Pretending he had to go to the toilet, he approached the man discreetly and took a good look. Without any doubt, it was Long, his control officer from the *Alliance* days. Mercier, now back to being Robert Do, didn't let himself be seen, and sat down again with his back to the kitchen door, from which waiters poured in and out. He was now a grown man, and one who had had more than his share of adventure, but nevertheless his heart was beating fast. Long was like a ghost from the past, a past he would rather have forgotten. As he ate with Étienne, he reviewed his options. On the eve of returning to a world that he knew and enjoyed, he couldn't let Long, or anyone, throw a spanner into the works. He came to the conclusion that he would have to kill him at the first opportunity, and, without thinking, his fingers caressed the little green frog at the top of the thick, sharp needle in the waistband of his trousers. Later that night, in his bedroom, he decided to open the window to get some fresh air. Looking out, he heard two men talking quietly in the shadows on the next balcony. He switched his lights off and returned to the window. One man was a Vietnamese, the other was Étienne. It was too far away to hear what language they were talking in, or what they were saying. They spoke softly, and both nodded their heads quite a lot. Finally, Étienne turned to go back into his room, and the man followed. The light struck his knife-like face as he walked by. It was Long. Lying in bed that night, Robert's mind ran riot. *Étienne knows Long. Who's using whom, or are they on the same side? Where do you fit in? What does Long know about you and Étienne? Does he remember you?*

After they had met with General Touqet, Étienne took him to his BNP office and sat him down. It was their last day together, as Étienne was flying back to France that afternoon.

"Robert, I think General Touquet will find you the post that you want. He's a good man and he obeys his superiors, even when he doesn't understand what it is they want. Most military are like that," Étienne said matter-of-factly, handing him a cup of coffee.

"I have to tell you something that must be kept a secret between us. I am a banker, and my friends and contacts funded General de Gaulle's campaign during the war. I now head this group, and we work for the General. Because father was an old Indochina hand, the General wants me to re-immerse myself in the affairs of this country, to get an understanding of what is really going on. The communists are everywhere now, and we are looking at a long war that France cannot fight by herself. The General does not want to be dependent on American aid forever, however, and wishes to keep his options open."

Étienne paused, looked at Robert, one eye cocked.

"Do you have any idea of what I'm talking about?" he asked.

"I think I do. Your high-level friends in the government want to open a back channel with the Viet Minh. They don't want to use the SDECE. It has to be completely unofficial, completely deniable if it blows up," Robert answered, adding, "In fact, you have already been talking to the enemy."

Étienne sat still, stunned. Finally, he said: "I see your time with Captain Godot has been well spent. Yes, you are perfectly right, and you said it before I even brought it up! I can see that we're going to work well together." He paused and looked at the floor for a moment. Then he looked directly at Robert, his face serious now.

"Without going into the details at this stage, my friend, I have to explain something to you. Our group, which shall not be named for the present, reports directly to the General's inner council at L'Elysée. Excuse me, I should call him the President. General makes us sound like a banana republic," he laughed briefly and then became serious again. "We may make use of the other two ministerial level intelligence services but we do not share information with them. General Touquet answers to two masters, the Chief of Staff of the *Corps Expéditionaire* in Indochina and the President's adviser on political matters, with whom I work closely. Touquet has been picked because he is willing to compartmentalize his two roles. Whatever you tell him he reports to us and to us only. What *Deuxième Bureau* tells him goes back to his Chief of Staff and from there to the Ministry of Defense in Paris. Our group has no official name, and its activities are always conducted within the shadow of plausible denial. You understand what I am saying?"

42

CODEX

After Étienne had left, Robert returned to Sai Gon to await a call from General Gilles Touquet, the new commanding officer of the *Deuxième Bureau* in Indochina. With money in his pocket and time to spare, he spent his days at various libraries, reading voraciously, picking out books on modern and ancient history, biographies of the lives of great men and books on the two World Wars. Two weeks later, he was instructed to contact a Mr. Herment at the Continental hotel, on Rue Catinat. This was a very large and luxurious French hotel, often referred to as *la grande dame,* built in the colonial style of architecture. At different times, it had received foreign kings and queens, presidents and prime ministers, and was the epitome of old European, upper-class comfort and service. During the Japanese occupation, the Japanese High Command had commandeered the grand old lady for an extended four-year stay. Accompanied by Captain Watanabe, Robert, known as Xuan at the time, had seen the Japanese infantry, in full battle dress, chasing the foreign guests out at bayonet point, and the royal suite was then reserved for General Mutukoshi Homma, to whom Colonel Tomohiko reported. After the Japanese surrender, the French management ripped the wallpaper off, room by room, changed all the drapes and carpets, repainted the interior from top to bottom after having washed and scraped everything thoroughly with *eau de javelle* detergent.

"We've got to get rid of that Japanese smell," said Mrs. Ortoli, the wife of the Corsican owner, her face contorted with disdain.

As it turned out, Mr. Antoine Herment was not from the police, or even from intelligence. He was a high-ranking civilian official from the Ministry of Foreign Affairs who reported directly to the *Palais de L'Elysée*. It soon became clear he outranked everyone in the French chain of command in Viet Nam, which was perhaps why he was putting up in a suite at the Continental Hotel. A small, tired looking man with a pointy nose, Herment had a soft voice and delicate hands. A staff of four French officials attended to his every need. He invited Robert to sit down in his suite, and tea was brought up.

"Mr. Saintenoix has briefed our group and I think your background is exactly what we're looking for. We are working together on a sensitive project and are looking for people who can do liaison work with certain elements in the communist resistance movement here. As a key link on the ground, the liaison officer's evaluation of the situation will be very important, which means he must be able to understand the issues involved. Do you follow what I'm saying?"

"Yes, of course," Robert answered. "Étienne discussed my responsibilities with me, privately and in front of General Touquet. Étienne then briefed the General, in front of me, on the nature of our first project."

"I see. That's good. Touquet is not from our group but he reports to us. He will process you into the organization but won't give you an office and a title. At no time can you ever become an official member of anything you are engaged in. But at all times communications between us will go through Touquet. Alright?" he asked, his sharp nose slanted sideways, his eyes quizzical. Robert nodded.

"Right. After you've settled down, we shall send you an assistant of mine, Jean Blanchot, and he will go into the details of your first operation. We shall take you into our confidence stage by stage. When we feel that you are the right man, we'll confirm to Touquet you're working for us from then on. If we judge you are not the man we want, we'll tell Touquet we've abandoned the project and he can use your experience and talent for his own ends. Whether we confirm your appointment or not, you'll still be employed by Touquet. That's what Étienne wants. We know that from your work with Captain Godot you understand the Viet Minh. It's just that our work has a political slant to it and we want to see if you can adapt to it before we take you on permanently. Is all this clear?" smiled Herment.

"Perfectly," Robert answered. He's more relaxed now. He'll fall out of his chair if he knows how well you understand the Viet Minh.

"Do you know anything about the SDECE?"

"Well, when I worked for Captain Godot, it was called the DGER, *Direction Générale Extérieure pour le Renseignement.* Before that is had been called the DGSS. Whatever it is called, it has a pretty wide ranging scope of work. I got to know some of its officers quite well but I've never worked with them. We were in the *contre-espionage* faction and my scope of work was limited to communist sympathizers already inside the government infrastructure."

"Excellent. Your strong point, where we are concerned, is your knowledge of the communist infrastructure. And also the fact that you know Étienne personally. In this kind of business, that counts for a lot. I think we'll get on well in the future, work-wise."

"One question," Robert said.

"By all means," Herment readily answered. "We've got to understand each other very well before we get started."

"If a high-level contact with the enemy is required in case something important needs to be said in a hurry, there is already one between the *Elyseés* and Moscow, so I presume that our link with Ha Noi is being set up to clear up the details."

Herment nodded, tentatively.

"Can you give me an idea of what these details might be?"

"Certainly, once you've been confirmed in your post. In the meantime your responsibility is to open this link and keep it open so our people can meet their people in absolute secrecy. In a way, this secondary aspect of the operation is more important than what we could be negotiating about, because if our operation becomes public the government falls and there will be no negotiations whatever on any subject."

He paused and looked at Robert heavily.

"Will I be working as part of a team?" Robert asked, thinking of Long.

"In time, perhaps. But the immediate nature of the work is such that you will not be required to work with or to co-ordinate your findings with your colleagues. We would rather you work on your own, coordinating closely with your communist counterparts and reporting only to us. The more of these communists you get to know the better. You don't discuss your work with your colleagues. In this way, if something goes wrong, damage can be minimized."

Herment looked at him, his light brown eyes quizzical again. Robert nodded. Herment smiled and he smiled back. Compartmentalization. They have others besides you, all doing the same work. They want to hear different versions of the same story, to better evaluate things. The Viet Minh and the Kempetai do that too. All intelligence services are basically the same.

"I have a dinner this evening and have to see some people here before that, so I cannot spend more time with you. I leave for Paris tomorrow morning. Good luck, Robert," said Herment, extending his small hand, which Robert shook carefully.

As he stood up, he suddenly remembered something. His face lit up and he pointed to his neat little head.

"I forgot to ask you," he laughed. "What do you think of our project? Is it a good idea or not?" he asked.

"It is a good project but it will achieve nothing," Robert answered promptly.

"Oh, and why's that?" he asked, consternation written all over his small, quizzical face.

"The die is cast. The Viet Minh were ripe for discussion with America right after the Japanese surrender in 1945, especially after having received OSS support. With France out of the picture, they were ready to abandon the Soviets. By allowing the French to return in force, Britain snubbed them and America rebuffed them; they could not turn to China, the traditional enemy, so they re-committed themselves to their original sponsors. Uncle Ho cannot change course until he wins this war, whatever you offer."

Herment's face froze and he looked disconcerted. Then he recovered, nodded his head and they shook hands again. Robert left the room, suddenly uncertain about his future, walking slowly down the carpeted halls. Maybe you should have kept your mouth shut. But, one week later, Herment's man made contact and he knew everything would be all right after all.

Jean Blanchot was quite different from Herment. Of medium height, rugged, a man of multi-faceted personality, he could turn on the charm when he wanted to and he could turn into a bully when he needed to. A cunning peasant, used to handling men, this man was more of an intelligence control officer. He knew how to persuade people, to develop their enthusiasm, to recruit them. They spent three days together, mostly in one of Touquet's offices. He started off by telling Robert to forget the *Deuxième Bureau,* the DGER, now renamed the SDECE, or any other intelligence service he had had contact with.

"Our project is one-of-a-kind," he said, "and it had nothing to do with the ministries of the Interior or Defense."

"It goes all the way to the top," he said, pursing his lips knowingly. Robert nodded along. That means the president, his security advisers, his financial backers, like Étienne. Blanchot said many things and Robert asked many questions, but it all basically came down to three things.

"First, you have to work with your counterpart to ensure that these secret meetings remain secret. The French press is our greatest enemy," said Blanchot. He spoke in short sentences, for maximum impact.

"Leaks can come from only two sources. The French media, especially the leftist press, which is always looking for shit to stir up. Then the Vietnamese nationalist resistance, who would sell their mothers to embarrass France. Touquet and his team here are always on the lookout for nosy journalists and photographers. But you have to watch out for the nationalists, who also have eyes and ears everywhere."

Robert looked at him. He's certainly put his finger right on it. Even the *deuxième bureau* employs Vietnamese assets who are resistance sympathizers. There are even some in the DGER.

"Second, you have to work with your counterpart to make sure the agenda of these meetings are acceptable to both sides before they meet. These communist bastards are inflexible and take months before they can confirm anything. Our man is coming from half-a-world away, and we don't want to waste his time because the commie in front of him hasn't been cleared to discuss all the issues on the agenda."

Robert nodded.

"All that is basically organizational, but we need someone we can trust who really knows the communists and speaks their language. After you're confirmed the focus will shift to the subjects being negotiated. Sound out what your counterpart or counterparts think about the talks. Dig deep, look for opportunities. What we are really after will be communicated to you through Touquet."

"I can't dig if I don't have a shovel," Robert said.

"Very true. I was coming to that. With these cold bastards it's no use playing the personal relationship card. And money won't work either. Threats are out since they are our bed partners, more or less. They'll only exchange hard info for hard info. After confirmation, we'll feed you stuff you can give them in return for what we want to know."

There it was, in a nutshell. Secrecy, contacts, intelligence. A big meeting was coming up. The nameless project turned out to have a name after all, CODEX. Robert asked Blanchot what the name meant. Nothing, he was told, just a name. He nodded. You are working unofficially on a nameless project whose codename means nothing. If you succeed you will have achieved nothing. If you get killed in the process, you'll die for nothing.

Blanchot gave him the names of his counterparts on the Viet Minh side and he started working the very next day. He noticed Long's name was on the list. He had been hired as a special consultant on security to the *Deuxième Bureau*.

43

Liem Trinh

The first three years passed by in a blur, thanks to a heavy and complicated workload accompanied by massive bouts of frustration. Robert's work was not compartmentalized into day or night, weekday or weekend. He was always on duty, always ready to respond to secret instructions from Paris routed through General Touquet or to discreet feelers from the communist side routed through a number of couriers. He took his days off whenever he could but a holiday of any kind was out of the question. On the other hand, he enjoyed working in the shadows, with minimum supervision, assuming heavy responsibility, dutifully reporting everything to the best of ability, agonizing over his analysis of the proceedings, as he had done in Cam Ranh with Captain Tomo. But he couldn't help feeling frustrated as endless talks and meetings came and went after months of intensive preparation. CODEX wasn't getting anywhere and he was being pushed one way and shoved the other in the grim fight between the French and the Viet Minh. He felt he was always waiting for something to happen so that he could react to it. After he was confirmed in his post by the Saintenoix-Herment group he did less security work and more intelligence work, delving into the minds of his counterparts. But the little bits and pieces of information he was given to exchange with his counterparts resulted in equally meretricious tidbits of information that were often worse than useless. Your backers don't really trust you enough yet to give you a real shovel, and the result is like spooning up breadcrumbs on the table after lunch. Or perhaps someone else, working parallel to you, is getting the important stuff while you are limited to being the sideshow. In this business, overt operations almost always masked covert ones, one inside the other, like the Russian wooden dolls.

Then, in 1950, Robert turned thirty-six and within a week everything changed. Thinking back, his work with the Viet Minh, the *Direction Générale Extérieure de Renseignement* and the *Kempetai* were like digging out a series of dark and dirty tunnels deep inside an old mine without the help of a map or a compass. The foul smelling tunnels ran haphazardly all over the place. At all times, you could only see as far as the battery operated torchlight, worn on your head, allowed. Over the years, small mountains of serious doubts, self-doubts and questions without answers had accumulated in the recesses of his mind, exerting an arthritic effect on every nook and cranny of his brain. He had devised a number of tricks so that he could navigate the tunnels without stumbling over mounds of moldy skeletons and headless zombies, but he couldn't imagine a day when his mind would be clear and relaxed, when the tunnels would run unencumbered and lights could be seen at the end.

Yet in the space of a few days after his birthday, his mind cleared as if by magic. He went to sleep one night and woke up the next day to a new world around him. It was as if he had drunk a cleansing potion and all the toxins had been flushed out of his system. The tunnels in the mine were wide and dry, ran symmetrically, were well lit and well aired, and had been cleared of all obstructions. Massive self-confidence infused every millimeter of space inside his skin, like air being pumped into a football. Within the week, he radiated energy. Mentally and spiritually he had finally become the man he felt he was always destined to be, a man with a simple and crystal clear vision of things around him, a man of strong convictions backed by a decisive mindset. He was like a snake that had changed its skin, emerging clean and new, hungry and aggressive, absolutely fearless. He could now foresee problems, think out solutions and act without hesitation. He was finally like Hélène had been on the night she cracked the rapist's skull, able to act without a second thought, to take charge and not worry about being right or wrong. He could make omelets now, and he was looking forward to breaking as many eggs as he could. You've become Ho Xuan Hai, you've entered your own skin, you've become somebody important in the scheme of things, a person who can and will impose his will over events and people. Your guiding star, *Liem Trinh*, has finally stepped out from behind the three Evil Ones, sending them screaming like banshees into the outer horizons of space, and now it will spread its powerful, golden light over you and everything you touch. Your time has arrived, finally.

He had been waiting for this miracle for a very long time and on the eve of his thirty-sixth birthday he had a long talk with his mother. He saw her appear in his mind's eye. She was standing by the stove in *papa*'s kitchen, as she often did when *papa* and he were busy talking about things. She now stood there, a kitchen cloth in her hands, looking in his direction but not at him. Unlike in the past when she was communicating with him to warn him of a danger or to support a decision he had made, she no longer looked into his eyes, she didn't smile and her lips did not move. She spoke without speaking and they conversed without conversing. He knew what she was saying even if she didn't actually say it. She was there, she was aware that he was there, but she was no longer a warm human spirit living in his liver. She had become an indelible memory who now lived in his mind. She said she had done her share and he was well capable of taking care of himself from then on. She was over fifty, she said, it was time for her to take a rest. *Liem Trinh* would protect and guide him from now on. It was time for him to step out, to claim for himself the place in the sun that he deserved. She said he should just move ahead and not be afraid of anything any more, because whatever he did would turn out right. Her chair in Heaven was assured and she would keep his ready for him.

Over the following three month period, his personality changed so much that both his CODEX colleagues and Viet Minh counterparts made remarks about it.

"What have you been eating lately," joked General Touquet after one of their sessions, "you seem to be bursting with new energy! Tell me the secret, Robert. This war is grinding me down. Look at my hair, it's almost all gone now!" They had become friends and Robert was having dinner at his house, with his wife and daughter.

"Comrade, you have become a man of steel," said Long. "Do you sometimes remember what Uncle Ho used to say in the earlier days? 'In war, the outcome is not determined by weapons but by the fighting spirit, the strength of the heart'. Things are not getting better for the French, but you seem to have become twice the man you were," he said one night at a safe house. They had eventually met again, soon after

Robert started work on CODEX and it had been a total anti-climax. Long never mentioned the *Alliance* days, talking to him as if they had never known each other. He was still a Viet Minh cadre, a high-level one, and he was being truly professional. Robert treated him as an equal and they were at all times correct and formal, totally focused on the work at hand and their responsibilities. They both knew that they needed each other, although Robert was sure that Long had no more idea of what they were supposed to achieve than he did.

With *Liem Trinh* reigning in his Career House and the three evil stars banished for ever from his horoscope chart, Robert moved quickly to put his stamp on the proceedings, gradually assuming greater control over the timing, format, length and subject of these endless negotiations. He remembered his conversations with *papa* on how to make himself important to the leader of his group, and not only to his own group but also to the opposing group. He knew what both sides wanted and he dangled the possible prize at every opportunity he was given. You are now in control of your life, your mother and you have become important people, to be treated with respect and dignity. Your thirty-six year curse is over and, instead of waiting for instructions, or asking for clarifications, you should simply organize things the way you think they should be done. Instead of reporting back everything, carefully select what you want to say. Instead of telling your counterparts everything you have been instructed to tell them, pick out what you want them to know. It is impossible for either side to double check.

Robert had become his own man. In his fourth Year of the Tiger, the tiger in him had stepped out of the shadows into the sunlight.

After being confirmed in his post by the Herment group he had been informed by General Touquet in a very private meeting that the crux of these secret talks was the acceptability of a deal in which the Soviets would retain their influence over the north while the south would remain in the French sphere. The fly in the ointment was Ha

Noi, which was now being wooed by Mao's China, which had serious ideological differences with the Soviet Union. It was important to find out how close Ha Noi and Peking were, so that differences between them could be exploited, and that was where CODEX came in. Secret and direct talks with Red China would start once the Chinese had indicated a desire to talk. So far, they hadn't, but Robert was to begin putting out feelers on the Viet Minh side.

After *Liem Trinh*'s appearance, his new and innovative approach revived the secret talks and made them more meaningful. They reached a point where, even at his level, he could clearly see the rupture between the pro-Moscow and the pro-Peking factions within Ha Noi's men on the ground in South Viet Nam and he suggested to Paris that they develop a two-pronged approach by setting up CODEX 2, which would focus on the pro-Moscow supporters while CODEX 1, with him at its head, would continue to play the pro-Peking card. Herment sent him a message through Touquet. "Noted. Congrats your recommendation. Already in the works. CODEX 2 Long". Robert was not surprised by this development, having always been aware that no intelligence operation puts all its eggs in one single basket, but he was taken aback to discover that Long had offered to work with the French. He had had the impression that Long truly hated them. Then he remembered Ho Chi Minh's words back around 1946, when he was accused of betraying Viet Nam by offering to co-operate with the returning French forces. In the vernacular which he was famous for, he had said, "I would rather smell French shit for a few more years than have to live with Chinese shit forever."

Ironically, at this juncture of his life, when everything began going well for him, the situation on the ground began souring for France. The new French army in Indochina, the *Corps Expéditionaire*, helped by America, fought tooth and nail for every inch of territory, convinced that Indochina belonged to France by some divine right. The communist resistance, solidly backed by the Soviet bloc at the United Nations and openly armed by Red China, was in no mood for compromise. The political education phase that had started in the '30s, the one Robert had joined under the name of Tam, was now over. The masses had been sufficiently mobilized and guerrilla forces equal to battalion strength had begun to attack French military bases in the countryside. In the mountains and along the Cambodian-Laos borders, although no one wore any insignia of rank, a professional officers' corps trained battalions of regular army troops, supported by thousands of militiamen backed by a nation-wide logistical network of porters and couriers. Everything that had been predicted in his days with the resistance was now happening. The seedlings had grown into innumerable trees that formed vast forests of little red flags with a five-point yellow star in the middle. Throughout the north, small men wearing green Viet Minh pith helmets were slowly bottling up the French in major towns and cities. The military situation looked increasingly grimmer each year and, as the war intensified, excess American World War Two *materiel* poured into Viet Nam from US bases in Germany and Japan, along with American financial aid from Washington to pay for the French Expeditionary Corps. At the White House, increasingly, the French war in Indochina had lost its colonial taint and was being reinvented as an anticommunist crusade. It had now become a good war, for a just cause. The French, often derided in the American press as colonizers simply trying to reclaim their former colonies, had now become defenders of American-style democracy. The Viet Minh, who had been America's allies during the Japanese Occupation, had now become the enemy.

A stalemate ensued in which neither side was able to get the upper hand. Gun for gun, the French, with their American weapons and Vietnamese levies, had initially wielded greater firepower. But with the Korean war drawing to a close, Chinese guns and ammunition now poured into Viet Nam, cutting down the French advantage. Man for man, the Viet Minh troops were now like an army of ants surrounding a single colony of large, hard-shelled dung beetles. Uncle Ho had said prophetically "You can kill twenty of my men for every one of yours that I kill, but in the end you will have to leave Viet Nam," and he wasn't simply mouthing a threat. Lenin's forceful vision and Stalin's pragmatic ruthlessness, combined with the tribal fanaticism inherent in all Vietnamese when it came to racial sovereignty, produced a mindset that was irreversible. To win, the communist leadership was prepared to accept a twenty-to-one kill ratio, or even higher.

As they worked closely together, Robert and Touquet became more than good friends and on many occasions he was invited to listen to the latter's headaches, the foremost of which was OPX1, one of the many "black operations" he handled. Back in 1946, under intense pressure from Europe and America, France had announced with great fanfare its intention to relinquish its monopoly of the opium trade in Indochina. By 1950, however, to break the military stalemate resulting from American guns being matched by Chinese weapons smuggled across the border, it became necessary to recruit, train and arm the hill tribesmen in Laos and northern Tonkin to cut off Chinese supplies to the communists. These paramilitary forces, made up of primitive mercenaries, would operate as counter-insurgents behind communist lines, fighting what amounted to a secret war in Laos while conducting cross-border raids into Burma, Cambodia and even southern China. The problem was that it was impossible to use American aid money for this change of tactics, and in Paris the war in Indochina was becoming a political issue of major importance, with the military budget being scrutinized *centime* by *centime* each year. The obvious solution was to have the SDECE, using *Deuxième Bureau* facilities and personnel, revive the opium trade in order to fund the secret war, and Operation X1 was born. The *Groupes Mixte de Commandos Aéroportes,* the GMCA, would be made up of French NCOs and officers from the Special Forces. The Meo, Man, Mong, white Thai and black Thai tribesmen, all ethnically non-Vietnamese, would be equipped with French weapons and paid out of purely French-controlled funds. Washington, secretly pleased that the French were making an effort to pay for their share of the cost of the war, turned a blind eye to this imaginative use of the poppy fields as well as to other Operations X, codenamed OPX2, OPX3 etc.... For Touquet, these massive headaches had to be kept out of the French and international press at all cost, a task that would have felled a dozen generals.

44

The Mandarin

As CODEX dragged on inconclusively, Robert was given access to the voluminous files French intelligence had compiled over the decades on anyone who was perceived as being remotely important, whether as a friend or a foe. In between doing his official work, he quietly began doing research on his father and the Trinh clan, partly because of his mother's request, but also partly out of curiosity. The more he read, the more he found himself empathizing with his father, whose life story read like an adventure novel. It was easy to see that his father had been quite a man, much more than simply a lecherous, pleasure-loving nobleman. A highly educated scholar in the classical tradition, born into the ruling caste, Lord Bach had nevertheless remained a moderate man. His wife Lady Nhan was a charming, westernized woman. His best friend was a Japanese officer, formerly a high-ranking intelligence official in Tokyo, whom he had met and befriended while in China. His second best friend was a Frenchman, formerly the Governor of Tonkin but now the General Manager of Michelin Plantations. His closest Vietnamese friend was a southerner, Mai Huu Hoang, his business partner and the president of the *Tout Va Bien* conglomerate in Sai Gon. At the Court and in the northern capital of Ha Noi, Lord Bach was respected by his peers, men who headed the elite families that discreetly ruled the land from behind the French façade. He was obviously a man among men and as Robert read on he felt secretly proud he had come from him.

But things had changed over the last twenty years. The Second World War had turned things upside down. Everywhere, colonial regimes were beginning to crumble. In the Vietnamese countryside, the peasantry, comprising nine tenths of the population, tacitly supported the foremost anti-French resistance movement, the implacable Viet Minh. In this quagmire of a situation, where nothing was clear-cut, relationships based on blood, marriage or social affinity cut across ideological lines. Ambiguity existed at all levels, and it was impossible to know who believed what or supported whom. A classical case was Lord Bach, who had been anti-French, pro-nationalist, anti-communist, was now pro-French yet had had a son who had worked for the Viet Minh.

In 1954, Robert arranged to meet his father and his step-mother, Lady Nhan. The first meeting took place at the Continental Hotel in Sai Gon, where Lord Bach was staying. As a director of the TVB Group of companies, he often traveled to the southern capital to attend board meetings and visit with his business partner, Mr. Hoang. After the shock of the introduction wore off, a rather stilted conversation followed. They remembered the incident of the letter Robert had written years before and which he had signed Ho Xuan Hai, but they couldn't understand what it was he wanted from them. He told them he wanted to help them move away from Ha Noi when the time came. They wanted to know why they should move anywhere. He told them the French were about to lose the north. Apparently, they knew the situation was serious but didn't believe it was critical. That was the second shock that night. They asked why he wanted to help them. He told them he would answer that question after he had done it. He told them to think his offer over and promised to make contact again in the near future, leaving a highly puzzled elderly couple sitting at the table.

A few months later, when the situation was verging on terminal, they met again, at the Metropole Hotel, in Ha Noi this time. By then, a number of things had happened that convinced Lord Bach that the north was about to be lost and that the Trinh clan's considerable fortune should be moved south. They were talking about some eight coffin-sized containers filled with gold, jade and precious jewelry as well as banknotes. Added to this were some twenty relatives who could not be left behind. They made plans there and then and by the time they parted, the die was cast. The plan was for Lord Bach to throw a giant celebration at the manor on the occasion of his seventieth birthday. This three-day bash would mask the departure of Lady Nhan and the gold. During the first night, Robert would move her and the closest relatives and the family fortune to Gia Lam airport, from where all would be flown south, where Mr Hoang awaited them. The next night, while the party was still going strong, he would pluck Lord Bach from the manor and have him flown south. His position within the Saintenoix-Herment group gave him operational control over a number of seats on military flights, and he could move who or what he wanted from province to province with a minimum of paperwork.

At midnight of the first day of the party, while a massive fireworks display lit up the manor and its surroundings, a number of catering vans and trucks carted away a number of people and boxes as planned, heading for the airport outside Ha Noi. After his men had confirmed that the plane had landed at Tan Son Nhut airport in the south, he phoned Lord Bach at the manor to let him know the first part of the plan was completed. The second part of the plan was to begin in the early hours of the second day. But something went wrong here and Robert learned from his sources inside the Viet Minh infrastructure in Thanh Hoa that Lord Bach had been captured during the second night and taken to a 'liberated zone', the communists' term for Viet Minh-controlled territory. The news came as a shock to his sense of professionalism. He didn't like being trumped by the enemy at the last minute, especially after he had successfully fooled them over the disposition of the Trinh fortune. But he still had any number of aces in his arsenal. Since his thirty-sixth birthday, the tunnels in the mine all ran in a straight line and finding his way around wasn't that difficult any more. The French military still ran the country, the Vietnamese civil service still ran the government and the communist resistance, while a clear and ascending menace, was nevertheless still in a weaker position. He held in his hands the lives of some fifty high-ranking Viet Minh cadres, a few of whom were linked to the highest leaders of the revolution by blood or marriage. He controlled a number of deep penetration assets inside the communist's provincial infrastructure and could evaluate their constantly shifting priorities. He had working for him a number of sleeper agents inside the so-called liberated areas, whom he reserved for the day when the north fell, should it ever fall. He was in a strong position, and unless Lord Bach was executed within the first days of his capture, he should be able to negotiate his release and score a few more points in the bargain. And, above all, he had been told by his mother that he would succeed in helping his father, and he believed in her predictions implicitly. It was written in the stars. However, what happened over the next few days was beyond his control. In fact, it was beyond anyone's control.

The battle of Dien Bien Phu had become a nightmare for the French and it ended earlier than anyone had expected, in the only way possible. The communists won, the French lost. In the blink of an eye, this changed everything. By destroying the French will to fight, the Viet Minh had not simply won a battle but the war for north Viet Nam. The red ants, or red termites as the French called them, had patiently cored away the inside of the colonial infrastructure, which stood like a mountain on the flat plains and rice fields of Indochina, and it was now imploding. Washington and Paris mourned, Moscow and Peking celebrated, while the Vietnamese on both sides counted their dead. War now gave way to politics, and within twenty-four hours, a Conference on Indochina had been convened in Geneva. For weeks, there was no-one Robert could negotiate with because the necessity for negotiation was not clear. If the Viet Minh were going to win all of Viet Nam at the conference table in Geneva, there would be no need for negotiations at all. Winners don't negotiate with losers.

Quietly, patiently, Robert forced himself to remain calm and keep open the communications channels he had developed, waiting for his counterparts to show signs of life. All the while, he kept one eye on Ha Noi and the other on Geneva, where lions and hyenas fought savagely over what was left of a dying buffalo carcass, with jackals and vultures yelping and screeching on the sidelines, waiting for their turn to feed on the scraps left. The Stalinists in Moscow, protectors of the workers of the world, didn't want to see the Viet Minh being awarded all of Indochina. They thought it might tip the balance and lead to an outright US-Soviet conflict. The silent agreement, in Viet Nam as elsewhere, had always been to bleed each other until one side gave up and withdrew, not to win an outright victory. The Maoists in Peking, promoters of Asian communism, didn't want a unified Soviet Vietnamese state on their borders in 1954 any more than they had wanted a unified American Korean state on their borders in 1953. The Americans, promoters of world democracy, sat on their hands, shell-shocked. Mystified since birth by the complexity of European politics, they didn't want to become involved in this heady mix of European *and* Asian politics. Washington felt that dealing with countries that had a two-thousand year civilization was already difficult and no one had the stomach to deal with ethnic groupings that had been around for five thousand years. The French, protectors of the French cultural mystique, were busy cutting their losses, even if it meant abandoning the Indochinese empire. Into this complicated imbroglio slipped the silky Chou En-lai, Mao's Minister for Foreign Affairs, with his unique blend of skill and tact. As he had done in Korea, he again proposed a compromise solution. Indochina, like Korea, would have to be cut into two parts. His argument was that, for France and the Viet Minh, half a loaf was better than no loaf. What he didn't say was that for Red China half-a-loaf in Korea and another half in Viet Nam offered ideal buffer states, even if the truncated countries distinctly felt they had been sold down the river.

Finally, the acrimonious Geneva Conference debates came to an end. The Viet Minh would be awarded the north and the French could retain the south, subject to national elections that would be held in 1956.

The same day it was announced, Robert's counterparts made contact with him. Denied total victory on the field of battle, the communist leadership, long-term thinkers and supremely pragmatic, knew that the time to talk had come around again. Within twenty-four hours they had begun discussing possible prisoner exchanges. He offered Colonel Nhon three communist cadres against three nationalists. Lord Bach was included in this number. On his list was a man French counter-intelligence teams had caught by chance, a northerner named Tien. He had been carrying a letter from the Viet Minh leadership to the shadowy communist party headquarters in Sway Rieng, Cambodia, in the south. There was a strong possibility that Tien was a close relative of Pham Van Dong, Ha Noi's Minister for Foreign Affairs and Ho Chi Minh's right hand man. Given the way political activists on both the nationalist and the communist sides changed names and identities every few months, it was always difficult to establish anyone's identity with any certainty. His source of information, however, had lived in the same house with Tien in the past, and Tien had once confided in him that he was the nephew of Uncle Ho's "right hand man". At the time, the only leader of the communist resistance whose name was well known was Ho Chi Minh himself, and the names of his closest assistants, such as Vo Nguyen Giap and Pham Van Dong didn't ring a bell anywhere. But it had all been written down, as everything is in the field of intelligence, and Robert, as a voracious reader of files, had come across it. Now, many years later, that 'right hand man' label fitted the Minister of Foreign Affairs. After much polite but at all times deadly serious haggling, Nhon and Robert agreed that the three Viet Minh cadres would be exchanged for an extra three cadres, bringing the total to six. An intuitive and cunning man, Nhon had sensed that Robert's pressure point was Lord Bach, and had asked for a greater number of communist agents in exchange, but decided to stop at six after Robert casually informed him that Tien, the communist colonel's pressure point, was dying. This was not true, but he had decided to make it come true if Nhon broke off the negotiations. Nhon sensed his mindset on the matter and stopped at six cadres.

Finally, Robert was able to recuperate his three exchange prisoners and he flew his father to Sai Gon, where he was hospitalized for over a month before the doctors would release him to his family. During that time he was able to talk to him a number of times, and they became friends. He liked the old man, and he could see his father was proud of him. Robert went into the details of his mother's reincarnation in him and why she had wanted him to help Lord Bach, as well as her conversion to Lord Buddha. Lord Bach asked him if he really believed that his mother could reincarnate in him. He answered that he believed everything his mother had ever told him. He told him that through his eyes she was looking at him that very instant. An indescribable expression came over his father's face. His face flushed with blood and his eyes sank into huge circles. Robert and his mother leaned forward to look deep into these deep wells, at the bottom of which they could see the old man's soul, and they saw a good man, a man they could be proud of having known. The wells filled up with tears and Lord Bach cried silently. Robert took his father's hand in his and stood there by the bed, saying nothing. There was nothing to say, really, because he knew at that instant that his mother and he were now one with the old man. He had accomplished her wishes. For her, the circle had closed; for them, it was now possible to move on.

PART THREE

BRIDGING
THE SINKHOLE

45

The Three-Legged Duck

By 1954, the Allied Powers had broken up, pitting Red China and the Soviet Union against Britain and the United States. In Asia, Mao's 'Little Red Book' held sway over one fifth of the world's population. In Europe, Stalin's Iron Curtain had slammed shut around the Soviet Union, imprisoning millions. Nationalist China and France, bit players from the start, were now sidelined, with Chiang Kai-shek taking refuge in Taiwan while de Gaulle turned his full attention to Algeria, where a replica of the Indochinese war loomed. In Washington and London, the bogey of international communism was all too real and pragmatic despair reigned at the Geneva Conference on the future of Indochina. The little green *bo doi* in pith helmets and sandals made of old tires had knocked everything askew and time had to be bought at all cost.

On July 21, Chou En-lai's proposal was accepted. In the North, the Democratic Republic of Viet Nam (DRVN) would be formed whose leader would be Chairman Ho Chi Minh. In the South, the State of Viet Nam (SVN) would be formed whose leader would be Prime Minister Ngo Dinh Diem. Both men were from Central Viet Nam, both had spent their adult lives fighting French colonialism, both were men of implacable will. But, having come from opposing ends of the social spectrum, each had his own solution to the country's problems now that the French were on their way out. To Prime Minister Diem, from a prominent Court family, sovereignty meant protecting feudalism from both communism and democracy, while to Chairman Ho, from a poor but respectable family, sovereignty meant replacing colonialism and feudalism with communism. As with all mirror images, their dreams for a new Viet Nam were diametrically opposed and it didn't help that their respective sponsors, Washington and Moscow, also had confrontational agendas.

Robert breathed a sigh of relief. In one fell swoop, the Geneva decision had isolated the communist cancer to the North and given the South, his adopted home, a chance to shrug off the French embrace and emerge as a sovereign state. Given the vast differences in racial characteristics and temperament between northerners and southerners, the chances of the two new sovereign states clashing again was a distinct possibility, but both the North and the South needed a breather first and the Geneva Conference had bought everyone some time. He tried to remember what Churchill had said over the radio during the dark days of World War Two, when he was still Xuan, working for the Japanese, something to the effect that failure was never final and victory never permanent. He felt that was definitely the case today.

On July 25, General Touquet ordered Robert to Ha Noi to destroy sensitive dossiers and arrange for French staff and assets to board a destroyer in Hai Phong harbor. It was of vital importance to the new Mendes-France government in Paris that all traces of CODEX be completely erased.

"It never existed, do you understand?" said Touquet tersely, holding him by the arm, looking him straight in the eyes, his lower lip trembling. "For both of us, no, for all of us, CODEX cannot have **ever** existed!" His tension ran through Robert like an electric current. He could smell the fear in the general, could see it in his eyes. They had become good friends by then. He squeezed the older man's shoulder, smiled reassuringly, saluted and walked out. In retrospect, there was nothing to say. Like many brilliant initiatives he had worked on over the years, it had seemed a good idea at the time. Now it was like the bubonic plague. You're lucky you only have CODEX to worry about. Poor Touquet's got a dozen Operations X to worry about, any one of which can drown the new *République Française* in a sea of slime and end his career.

Since the Viet Minh were not scheduled to take over control of the capital until mid-October, the French army was able to organize an orderly departure program for its personnel. This operation was carried out under the inscrutable gaze of boyish-looking infantrymen with thick rubber tire sandals on their feet, green cork helmets on their heads and short, business-like AK-47 assault rifles slung across skinny shoulders. To prevent the French from sabotaging what was now "the people's property", the Viet Minh had posted small contingents of soldiers to stand watch over public buildings. For the people whose property was being protected, however, the sight of the now famous *bo doi* in green uniforms in the streets of the northern capital had started a panic. The coastal highway going south had been cut by the communist insurgents at various points but the highway to Hai Phong port east of the northern capital had been left open. It was now clogged with a million people heading for French and American navy ships that would take them south. The first wave was composed of refugees who had worked for the French and who now feared arrest for collaboration. The second wave included staunch Catholics who followed, lemming-like, because their priests had told them the Virgin had gone South. The third wave was made up of ordinary citizens, neither civil servants nor Catholics, who feared being left behind and fought ferociously for space at the Hai Phong docks.

In the capital, panic ran like a live electric current among the French military intelligence community. High ranking officers from the *Deuxième Bureau*, the *Service de Documentation Extérieure et Contre Espionage*, the *Groupements Mixtes de Commandos Aéroportés* and sundry smaller intelligence organizations sneaked about, tight-lipped and formal, avoiding eye contact. They had all worked on covert operations whose existence now had to be denied at all cost. The North was lost but there were still careers to be rebuilt in the South. Sensitive files had to be burned, important dossiers had to be packed, high-level Vietnamese agents had to be quietly released from their contracts, large sums of money had to be moved and, finally, reassignments in Cochinchina, in the south, had to be negotiated. No one wanted to return to France, where revolving-door governments were looking for scapegoats with which to satisfy a public that felt humiliated and betrayed by its leaders. To be in any way connected with any of the super-secret Operations X that the French High Command had run up to the fall of the North was a ticket to instant career disaster.

Robert soon found himself completely on his own. Now holding the rank of captain in the DGER, an organization which no longer existed and for which he had never worked, he was left to do what he wanted because absolutely no one wanted to know anything about CODEX. After he had destroyed all the documentation relating to this operation, he came across millions of French francs and American dollars in the main safe, contingency funds amassed from the sale of opium for the super secret operation that never existed. Without hesitation, he arranged for the contents of the safe to be boxed up in metallic containers and flown south as military intelligence cargo. He then opened three small separate foreign currency accounts in Sai Gon and one large one in Hong Kong, using different names. He had already decided he would not ask for reassignment in France and he wanted to use the CODEX money to insulate himself against the difficulties the new Republic of Viet Nam could expect to face. As it turned out, this was one of the wisest decisions he ever made.

In the north, Chairman Ho was at first acclaimed as a popular hero of what the Viet Minh called the French war. With tacit support from the Soviet Union and Red China, he immediately imposed on his people a rigid, top-heavy bureaucracy similar to Stalin's. The center of power was the Politburo, whose authority flowed through the Public Security Ministry, which vetted everything and everyone. Under the pretence of land reforms, blood-thirsty purges, pogroms and kangaroo courts eliminated some 100,000 so-called landlords, many of whom owned tiny plots that barely fed their families. It was payback time, and memories of Robert's instructors at the training camp came back to him as he listened to the daily news broadcasts. Some twenty years before, they had promised humiliating and bloody retribution and, at the time, innocent that he was, he had thrilled to the thoughts of killing off fat French and Vietnamese landlords. As it turned out, all the fat ones had escaped to the South, leaving their poor, skinny tenants behind to face the wrath of the revolution. But the Party had promised blood, and blood there had to be. Waves of public executions raged from province to province, rivers of blood ran red on the ground while millions of landless peasants watched in open mouthed horror as thin, emaciated peasants like themselves were labeled landlords and beaten to death in public in the village square. For the Party, the land reform atrocities were necessary not only to eradicate the landlord class but also to instill absolute obedience through fear in the working class. When peasants refused to work, workers struck, revolts flared and famine loomed in different parts of the new republic, the Party immediately deployed the same fanatical *bo doi* infantrymen and security cadres who had crushed the French at Dien Bien Phu. Within two years popular support was replaced by sullen obedience as the dead hand of communism tightened its clammy grip around the nation's throat.

In the South, things developed completely differently. The new republic was promptly nicknamed the three-legged duck by the southern population, freak animals being seen as harbingers of bad luck in the countryside. Appointed by Emperor Bao Dai, Prime Minister Diem's first year in office was chaotic, with quasi insurmountable problems piling up by the month. His generals had all been French-trained and resented a Vietnamese Commander-in-Chief. Two heavily armed fanatical religious sects, the Cao Dai and the Hoa Hao, deeply rooted in the Mekong Delta, the South's rice bowl, refused to pledge allegiance to Sai Gon. The Binh Xuyen, a heavily armed urban mafia controlling the port area of the capital, openly ran gambling, prostitution and drugs rings in Sai Gon's sister city, the Chinatown known as Cho Lon.

In the second year of his appointment, however, the new Prime Minister saw the appearance of the real problem he would have to live with, a nightmare he would have to endure long after he had tamed the Army generals, the religious sects, the Binh Xuyen gangsters and a restive Buddhist population. Ironically, the source of his problem came from the source of his political support. Well-meaning but ignorant and arrogant US advisors at all levels of the administration insisted on micro-managing the new republic, now renamed the Republic of Vietnam (RVN), down to hamlet level. In theory, on paper and in accordance with the Geneva Convention decision, the State of Viet Nam was a sovereign entity, entirely capable of making its own decisions. In fact, the remaining French forces had the guns, the newly arrived Americans had the money and the newborn RVN had nothing but problems. Hence the three-legged duck nickname.

A stubborn nationalist and a born political in-fighter, the new Prime Minister deftly sidestepped this chaotic situation by using CIA funds to set up a secret political party, the Can Lao, made up of a cross-section of union leaders, politicians, scholars, industrialists, military and security officers who had sworn personal allegiance to him. "Diem's men", as the Can Lao men were called, began to spread out through the national spectrum, serving as the eyes and ears of the Prime Minister, gradually tilting the balance towards the embattled Diem. They represented the first leg of the abnormal duck.

The second leg was represented by French civil servants, military and settlers who had governed the north until the debacle of Dien Bien Phu. *Les Tonkinois,* as they were called, had regrouped in the south, with egg all over their face and sabotage on their mind. With the RVN a sovereign entity, their status was unclear, which increased their paranoia. Would Cochinchina, a French colony until now, become a French protectorate, as Tonkin had been? Or, horror of horrors, would the baton slip from French hands into American hands? The French mystique had lost its shine and the presence in Sai Gon of *les Tonkinois* generated general embarrassment all round. To the military, having lost more than 92,000 men over an eight-year period, this was an unacceptable situation. Large quantities of French military equipment and ammunition recently received from the Americans mysteriously disappeared into Binh Xuyen, Cao Dai and Hoa Hao hands and what was left was carefully sabotaged before being officially handed over to Diem's fledgling new South Vietnamese armed force.

The third leg was represented the Americans, whose USN ships were busy ferrying successive waves of northern refugees to the South. Large American civilian missions sprouted like giant mushrooms in Sai Gon, taking over the best real estate in the most prestigious quarters, headed by larger-than-life country directors waving Washington-backed programs in one hand and bags of greenbacks in the other. After six years of the Japanese Occupation and eight years of the first Indochina war, the South had been drained of energy and at first the free-flowing US dollars were welcomed as a timely blood transfusion. But American blood was too rich for South Vietnam's deflated veins, and as the flow continued unabated, the cure began killing the patient. Pimples became boils that turned into carbuncles that rapidly became open, purulent sores, not unlike those seen on lepers. Within two year, armies of prostitutes, pimps and beggars had filled the major towns and cities, congregating around the enclaves where Americans lived, played or worked. Among the middle and upper classes, a reserved, conservative Asian mindset gradually degenerated into naked greed. Unable to have a say in their own country, and deluged with a shower of greenbacks, taking the Americans for every last dollar became a perfectly normal and worthy occupation for every self-respecting Vietnamese citizen.

Driven by the universal law of survival, the weird-looking national duck paddled ferociously, with each leg pulling in a different direction, to the consternation of the passive, predominantly Buddhist southern population in the countryside.

46

Chaos and Confusion

By 1955, Robert was forty-one years of age and had worked in the field of intelligence for the Viet Minh, the *Direction Générale Extérieure de Renseignement*, the *Kempetai* and the *Service de Documentation Extérieure et Contre Espionage*. By now he knew his trade well. He loved it and couldn't imagine himself doing anything else. After thinking seriously about his future, the future of his mother and of their chairs in Heaven, he finally made up his mind and applied to join the Republic of Viet Nam's National Police Directorate. The NPD was being set up by the CIA for the Prime Minister and, right from the start, everything went wrong.

From the day it was born, the NPD had become one more bone of the many bureaucratic bones being disputed between Washington and the RVN. The CIA had proposed the wholesale integration of the French-trained Vietnamese *auxiliaires* from the *Deuxième Bureau*, the *Sureté Générale* and the *Police Municipale* into a General Directorate of Police and Security Services that would report to the Interior Ministry. It was a very American plan; simple, practical and expedient, a plan for people who were in a hurry to get things done. Like most American plans, it didn't take into consideration the social and cultural issues involved. Diem had no love for the French and no trust for the Americans. He could accept the *Police Municipale* but didn't want the *auxiliaires*. He knew the loyal ones would remain French in their minds while the greedy ones would switch over to the Americans; none would come over to the new Prime Minister. Unable to say no to his CIA advisors, he quietly asked his brother Nhu to set up a parallel security force within the Can Lao party to counter-balance this development.

Ngo Dinh Nhu, a thin, handsome, ascetic intellectual with a penchant for intrigue, immediately and expertly complied, drawing on the many loosely controlled CIA budgets readily available to the RVN. Thus, from day one, the stage was set on the RVN side for the birth of two national security forces, both generously funded by America, programmed to work at cross purposes.

To make things worse, a battle was shaping up on the American side between the Military Intelligence Service (MIS) and the CIA over the collection and interpretation of intelligence on the communist infrastructure that Ha Noi had left behind in the South after the Geneva Conference. This was a carry-over from World War Two, when the Pentagon and the OSS, the forerunner of the CIA, had already clashed in Europe and Japan, and it was essentially a battle between military and civilians. In the RVN, American Army MIS advisors sat besides Vietnamese field officers, while CIA advisors flanked RVN ministers, the NPD chiefs, province and district chiefs. Their conflicting suggestions had the force of commands, since America now funded the very existence of the new Republic. Their Vietnamese counterparts found this situation confusing and turned to the Palace for clarification.

To protect its fledgling administration from heavy-handed US intrusion, the Palace discreetly set up invisible firewalls at province, district, city and township levels. A nationalist first and foremost, the Prime Minister instructed key RVN officials, civilian and military, to listen politely to American advice and to agree with everything but to do nothing until they received Palace clearance. If deemed to be against Vietnamese interests, American advice was to be ignored, but always in the most oblique way, to save American face. Key officials who accepted American money or took American advice without prior clearance were summarily replaced, with no reason being given. Diem had concluded that the Americans were like overgrown children who couldn't agree among themselves on anything and whose priorities changed by the day. Unknown to the Viet Minh, the Americans and even to the southern Vietnamese, the new Prime Minister, a cold, calculating and stubborn man, had spent all his adult life working towards this moment. His first priority was the destruction of all internal opposition to his rule. His second priority was to replace the Emperor's Nguyen dynasty with the Ngo dynasty, his own. His third priority was dealing with the communist republic across the 17th parallel, which he would do in his own time and in his own way. He gave himself two years, maybe three, before Ha Noi could become sufficiently stable to become a major threat.

Looking back over the years, Robert had to admit that the new Prime Minister had his priorities right and that his American advisors didn't. Historically, in feudal countries, the leader has to control his internal enemies before he can deal with external enemies. He remembered from his reading sessions at *papa's* that Alexander, Hannibal, Genghis Khan all ruthlessly molded the surrounding tribes into one whole before striking out abroad. In the north, Chairman Ho was doing just that. If the Soviet Union had been a Western-style democracy and had insisted on elections while he was fighting a war, Ho would have been overthrown. In the South, however, Diem was unable to assert his authority in the Vietnamese way and was never able to gain control of the situation. He ended up pulling against his backer, who was adamant things would have to be done the American way.

In this madhouse atmosphere, Robert was re-assigned to the *Sureté* arm of the South Vietnamese NPD under his real name, Ho Xuan Hai, with the rank of captain. Its first Director was General Chuc, formerly a junior lieutenant in the *forces auxiliaires* in charge of housing and transportation in the French *Sureté Générale* in Ha Noi. His four-rank promotion to this all-important post had been made personally by the Prime Minister. At NPD Headquarters, General Chuc was flanked all day long by Colonel de Villepin, formerly the head of the *Sureté Générale* in Tonkin, and by Major Milkie, an American security advisor from the Military Aid and Assistance Group (MAAG), which was responsible for coordinating the activities of all American agencies in Viet Nam. Not sure of how much authority he could actually exercise on his own, General Chuc suffered from a massive inferiority complex whenever he dealt with the iron-willed Colonel de Villepin, an older man who had sowed terror in the Viet Minh ranks right up to the fall of Dien Bien Phu. In his youth, as a sergeant in the militia that served the Diem family at the Court, Chuc had received only a primary education. His spoken French was minimal and his grasp of security matters was rudimentary. With Major Milkie, his problem was compounded by the fact that the American major spoke neither French nor Vietnamese. A translator was needed and most of the time it was de Villepin, fluent in both Vietnamese and English, who fulfilled this role. To escape from these two demanding men, who preached vastly different doctrines, General Chuc spent most of his time at the Palace, in full dress uniform, sitting outside the Prime Minister's office, hoping to be called in for instructions in a language he could understand, delivered by a man he was ready to die for. In his absence, the NPD divisional heads sat on their hands, awaiting orders from their superior, who was 'at the Palace'. All attempts made by the CIA to wean General Chuc away from the Palace failed miserably, as did outright attempts to buy him. "He's too dense to be bribed," one American advisor told Robert.

Within the NPD, Captain Hai was at first assigned to the Research and Documentation Bureau (RDB), a vital agency with an innocuous name through which the CIA kept tabs on the Army of the Republic of Viet Nam (ARVN), its Military Intelligence Service, province chiefs and the Prime Minister's domestic foes. The RDB centralized on microfiche all security and intelligence records, an activity that placed it at the heart of the national security and intelligence network. His superior was Major Du, a northerner and a Catholic. Holding the rank of sergeant, he had formerly been an interpreter in the *Sureté* in Ha Noi. He showed Hai that the official appointment dossier was in the name of Ho Xuan Hai. Hai saluted. This is the name your mother always wanted you to have. It's been a long wait, but now you're not only your own man but you can work under your own name.

After formally taking office on July 7, 1954, Prime Minister Diem began a series of maneuvers to crush internal resistance to his rule, and in this he was directly advised and supported by Edward Landsdale, a highly controversial CIA colonel. Formerly a Madison Avenue advertising executive, Landsdale espoused a program he called "psywar", a new notion at the time. The first step was physical: the identification, isolation and neutralization of the enemy. He had devised this approach while attending Army intelligence courses. The second step was psychological: co-opting the population into believing it was being offered exactly what it wanted. Making full use of the national and cultural quirks of a race, he often said, it was possible to sell people anything. He had learnt this from his time on Madison Avenue.

For the first three years of its existence, Ed Landsdale aggressively ran the new republic through the Prime Minister's Office. Diem's new national army surrounded and attacked two major southern religious sects that controlled vast tracts of land in the Mekong Delta, killing some of them and driving the rest into the arms of the local communist insurgents. Next, Diem's new national police force took on the Binh Xuyen, the river pirate gang that had worked hand-in-hand with the French SDECE in the trafficking of drugs. The Binh Xuyen had also bought control of the capital's police and national security force, having negotiated this arrangement with the French just before the fall of Dien Bien Phu in the north. Binh Xuyen gangsters, with the signature gold tooth, chest tattoos and shoulder-length hair, patrolled the streets of the capital in police uniforms, intimidating the population. Their leader, Lai Van Xang, a former pimp and enforcer, had promoted himself to general rank. The aristocratic new Prime Minister saw this as a revolt of the working classes and he launched a pitched battle for control of the capital. Brutal fighting erupted through the streets of the capital and its sister city, Cho Lon, as heavily armed forces unloaded point blank at each other with rifles, grenade launchers and mortars.

In April 1955, when the house-to-house fighting began, Hai had been in the RDB barely six months. One afternoon he was leading a platoon of combat police when they were surrounded by Binh Xuyen troops in downtown Sai Gon and bottled up in a large office building. An American observation helicopter, piloted by an American advisor with a Vietnamese pilot seated behind him, hovered overhead, keeping tabs on the Binh Xuyen movements as they maneuvered through the besieged capital. Determined to finish off the novice RVN police units, the river pirates hammered the building with mortar fire, taking out one room at a time. The standoff lasted a day and a night before a battalion of ARVN Marines loyal to Diem was brought in from the provinces, where they had been fighting religious fanatics. Within the week, they had cleared the gangsters out of the capital. Hai had lost six men, was down to a few clips of ammunition and had received two bullets through his left thigh. No bones were broken and after one month in a military hospital, he was released, as good as new. Major Du recommended him for a medal and they met in his office.

"Between us, I know you understand the situation. Upstairs," the Major said, glancing at the Prime Minister's picture on the wall, "you know what they think about the *Sureté* boys. The RDB is subject to dual control, American and Vietnamese but the Palace is gaining the upper hand. That's why you were not promoted to major upon being re-assigned to us, although you deserved it. You were holding a captain's rank in the French DGER when we were only sergeants in the *auxiliaires* but that's the way it is. You can stay with us as long as you want, but I have been told that there will be no promotion, and it is even possible that eventually you will be weeded out. But the CIO is a good opening for you. Also dual control, but the CIA has the upper hand there. I advise you to jump at this chance."

This was a new organization that was being organized, a Vietnamese replica of the American CIA. Colonel Landsdale's ever-fertile brain had been promoting this new project, among many others, since his arrival. Hai applied, his transfer papers were processed and within the month he was welcomed into the CIO, promoted to major, given his own office and a secretary. On the door, a sign read: "Major Ho Xuan Hai, Assistant Supervisor, Department of Analysis, Central Intelligence Organization." Every time he saw that sign, he knew his mother saw it too, through his eyes, and he couldn't help smiling. There had been many ups and downs, and they had come a long way, but this sign showed what *Liem Trinh* could do now that it had returned to its proper place in the firmament.

47

Acclimatization

After he joined the CIO, Hai's English began improving, thanks to a series of language courses developed by Michigan State University for MAAG, whose first priority was to wean the RVN's military and police away from the French doctrines of war and security and train them in the American way. A common language was necessary, and as early as in 1955 MAAG had set up TRIM, the Training Relations and Instruction Mission, to implement the training of South Viet Nam's officer corps. TRIM would lead to the setting up of AFELS, the Armed Forces English Language School, where selected officers would be taught English, sent to the US, return and become instructors themselves. It was in this way that Hai met an American who would become a lifelong friend and the younger brother he never had. His name was Jonathan Winthrop, Jr., a Yale graduate in Political Science and a specialist in Asian languages who had joined the State Department. At his own request and by using a lot of political pull, he had been seconded by the State Department to the CIA in Sai Gon as an intelligence analyst.

Jonathan, who spoke, read and wrote Vietnamese as well as Mandarin and Japanese, was the son of the Senator from Maine and was one of the few that had been accepted into the CIA because of his language skills. Although the need to interface with America's new client was a high priority, Vietnamese speakers on the American side were rare throughout the war. Jonathan's Embassy cover was that of a language instructor at the AFELS and he had to put in a few hours as an English instructor every now and again. Born with the proverbial silver spoon in his mouth, Jonathan was a tall, athletic, handsome and adventurous young man. He had joined the State Department on the recommendation of his father. Fresh out of university, inspired by what he saw as America's new role in the world, he had volunteered for this new assignment, against his father's advice. When he first landed at Tan Son Nhut airport in 1957, he had looked around him and taken a deep breath. Smiling in a friendly way at the Vietnamese around the tarmac, he had pressed his palms together in a typical Buddhist gesture and greeted them in Vietnamese. He received blank looks in return, though some older people crossed themselves and bowed. He didn't know it at the time, but his heavily accented Vietnamese made him sound like one of the Catholic or Protestants missionaries who worked in the countryside. Basically, he had expected to be welcomed, to be liked in return. He knew America wanted to do the right thing by South Viet Nam, and he was convinced his contribution could make a difference. Within months of his anti-climactic arrival he had realized that his government knew little about the situation on the ground in the South and cared even less. With the massive arrogance that came from having massive power, Washington intended to 'clean up the French mess' in six months; show the Viet Minh that America wasn't France; show the Soviet Union that the US could not be pushed around; and show Red China, like it had in Korea, that there were limits to Mao's Little Red Book. All this was to be done with minimum consultation with the Vietnamese counterpart, who was deemed too slow and deliberate in the decision-making process—they just didn't do things 'the American way'. As a result, the US Embassy in Sai Gon was misinterpreting signals from the southern Vietnamese population and was itself sending confusing signals to the new Prime Minister, his Chief of Staff and his Interior Minister. With growing dismay, Jonathan saw that every American mission, starting with the Embassy and including his own, the CIA, had rapidly become an island unto itself. Each Mission Director was an untouchable, with his own set of political connections in Washington. Each had his own budget, drew up his own plans, designed his own hiring policies. Determined to build their own empires while the going was good, the mission directors spent the American taxpayers' money like water to feed their overweening egos, soon becoming legends in their own minds. As he said to Hai after they had become friends, the green dollar in the South achieved in two years what the green men in the North had taken nine years to accomplish, effectively cutting off at the knees what had been a traditional and cultured society and turning the population into a nation of beggars where everything was for sale.

In the first months, Jonathan desperately wanted to learn more about the country before he could sit down to correct this slide into disaster. He felt he had sufficient contacts in Washington, through his father, to get to President Eisenhower. Jonathan was certain that the President, a man of experience, used to handling non-Americans, would understand. Jonathan also recognized that he simply didn't know enough about the country at this stage, and that he needed to find a mentor who not only knew how things worked but why and who could explain them in terms an American could understand. When he first met Hai at AFELS, he felt he had found his man. On his side, Hai was surprised to see this high-level American official take to him so rapidly but he welcomed it. The military and police are being Americanized and a personal American friend will help you no end. After Jonathan invited him to a few dinners at MAAG and a few movies at USOM, they discovered that they really enjoyed each other's company, in part because they were both young at heart and in part because they could progress their language skills by leaps and bounds.

In 1958 Hai was sent to America to be retrained in police work at the International Police Academy at Georgetown University. Working with a mix of FBI and CIA instructors, he was taught the American approach to counter-insurgency, criminal investigations, interrogation and agent handling. A massive culture shock scrambled his brains during the first three months. He had seen Marseilles, Paris and different ports of call during his self-imposed exile from Viet Nam after Dien Bien Phu but none of those held a candle to America. The skyscrapers; the network of highways; the number of cars; a telephone in every room; air-conditioning everywhere; America had to be seen to be believed. The country was made up of large, self-confident, well fed and well dressed people who talked business all day long. Then there was instant communication between offices in different cities; the speed with which decisions could be made; the ease with which things could be done. From force of habit, Hai headed for the nearest public library to read up on America, looking for the key to America's startling success after only two hundred years of existence. Strangely enough, he found most of the answer in the streets, from mixing with ordinary Americans. All these discoveries came in bits and pieces, a jumble of impressions, feelings and facts that revealed themselves as time went on, gradually forming a pattern, a mental picture of what America was all about.

At first he saw the obvious signposts of a dynamic and free society. Among the white population, social equality was plain to see, with every man convinced he was as good as anyone else, whatever his station. Professional competence was important. Working hard, holding down a job was a matter of pride, whatever the job. A free press, a national radio and television network kept everyone well informed. Laws were enforced without fear or favor and he read many times about influential people who ended up in jail in record time for breaking the law. Everything worked and if it didn't it was soon fixed. But behind this host of values there existed an indefinable mindset that he failed to see at first and which, when he found it, didn't fall into any of the "–isms" that he had read about in his attempts to educate himself at *papa*'s, or the *Alliance* or in later libraries. President Calvin Coolidge is reputed to have said, "The business of America is business" and this sentence reverberated through his head as he hunted around for his own definition. For lack of a better expression, he decided on 'a culture of prosperity', a vibrant way of life based upon job flexibility within a matrix that included integrity, work ethics and high levels of productivity. Making money within a clear framework of laws was what America was all about. Much later in life he had the opportunity to compare America to Europe, especially Old Europe. He saw how the Protestant ethic had turned dormant states into progressive ones in Europe before arriving in America, where it bloomed in the wide-open, fertile native soil from the first day. Every man was expected to work; hard work was revered and material gain was seen as proof of a man's success in life.

Americans had wrenched themselves free from old, conservative European values, represented by a culture of rigidity, of preserving the past. She had built a new system based on this culture of change, with hard work as the road to riches, using the rule of law to level the playing field. The key to keeping capitalism vibrant is transparency, and this is ensured by the American constitution. *Liberté–Egalité–Fraternité,* interpreted the French way, with Étienne's famous *pas pour toi* following it, has fallen flat on its face: a vibrant cause betrayed by its policies. As to Chairman Ho's Socialist paradise up North, after only three years it looks more and more like a poor version of Stalin's

Hell on earth. And our half-hearted attempts at building Western style republicanism are simply pathetic, all show and no substance. You have now seen how the road to democracy lies in the practice of capitalism within a framework of fair and just laws. You now understand that the average citizen can only band and bond with the common good in mind once he has been freed from poverty and hunger. The American-style constitution, suitably adapted to Vietnamese conditions, must become the role model. Like the Chinese, the Vietnamese are a disciplined and mercantile race, so the rule of law and a free market are not new concepts. But rule of law must be fair, not skewered in favor of the elite as it must always be in a feudal society. The key is that the constitution and the laws that uphold it should be prepared by a body of men selected by the people from the people and not just the elite. At night, before falling asleep, Hai explained all this to his mother. He was really explaining it to himself, but he didn't want her to think that he was always chopping and changing his mind, going from the Viet Minh to the French and now to the Americans. He then discussed it with his *papa,* whom he knew would understand the meanderings he had had to take in his search for a cause he could commit to whole-heartedly. He also knew that it would take some time before Vietnam could wash away the culture of feudalism ingrained in its collective mind, and that this could only be done after the coming threat of war with Ha Noi had been dealt with. But, he told himself, win or lose, now or tomorrow, he had to have a vision in mind, something worthwhile to focus on and he had chosen a dynamic, free and open society based on hard work and productivity.

Towards the end of his stay, he was approached by well-dressed men who introduced themselves as CIA recruiters. They explained that within the CIO was an office called the Counter Intelligence Bureau, the CIB, and that they were assessing potential recruits. A number of discussions followed at various private offices during which they went into the details of what the CIB was supposed to do. One day, out of the blue, the senior man in the group, Jim Donovan, asked him why President Diem hadn't yet been able to establish effective control over the southern population, even though he was receiving plenty of American support. This is a loaded question. They're putting you on the defensive. Counter-attack. Just tell them the truth, regardless of the consequences.

His spoken English wasn't that good at the time, and he began by apologizing for his strong Vietnamese accent and lack of vocabulary. Donovan nodded, the others smiled deprecatingly, as if saying 'no problem', a phrase very popular with Americans and very indicative of their go-getting mindset.

"After Geneva Conference," Hai then said, "Diem fifty-three, Ho sixty-four, both old nationalists, both fight French. North South have same problems. Country bankrupt, many refugees, peasants cannot grow rice, demonstrations in countryside, labor strikes in cities. Ho and Diem from old Viet Nam, have same attitude for masses, big stick small carrots as you say. Russia no interfere with Ho housecleaning, he use big stick, no carrots, he control North within two years. Americans want Diem operate American way, plenty carrot, small stick. Diem has stick but must ask Americans for carrots. If Diem take American guns and money to use his way, he can control South quickly. Human rights, social justice and free press all important, for Vietnamese same for Americans, but must come after war, not in middle."

After he had said this, an uncomfortable silence fell on the little group. The voice-activated recording machine came to a silent stop. An unpleasant truth had been spoken, and the audience was groping for a correct reaction. You've stunned them. Switch from counter-attack to attack, as they do in *go*. He remembered the *Kempetai* days, when Captain Watanabe would deftly turn the table on him with one deft move in a corner of the board far removed from the center of the ongoing 'land grabbing' battle that is *go*.

"I ask you questions. If Washington want democrat, why pick Mr Diem? He from old Court family, he feudal. If Washington want popular president, why pick Catholic for Buddhist country? If Washington want reformer, why Mr Diem? He monarchist, he no want change, he support Emperor system. If Washington want to pick anybody, why not ask the people first? Washington have plenty money, plenty contacts. If you fly one thousand South Vietnamese family heads to America for one week discussion it cost less than Sai Gon budget for one day."

No one made any attempt to answer.

"Enemy not superman, like in American movie. He not bigger not stronger than us. North masses no understand communist ideology, same like South masses no understand democracy. But communism is good system for making war, for destroying. Make people think of group, not self. Capitalism not good for fighting war, make people think of self, not group. Both sides Vietnamese, same character, same fanatic, same fatalist. Can endure great sacrifice for cause. Ho and Diem spend twenty five years looking for solution for Viet Nam problems. They spend five years fighting Japanese, nine years fighting French. They have big patience. Discipline, self-sacrifice and patience inside Vietnamese blood three thousand years, in North and South. Ho and Diem fearless, willing to sacrifice everything for national cause. The Vietnamese fight many wars already but they only know how to fight Vietnamese way, not American or Russian way."

He looked at his audience. Not a smile, not a facial twitch, but four pairs of burning eyes fixed on him. You've nailed them. Keep going.

"Finally, one big problem coming. Russia give military support but don't send Russian soldiers fight in Viet Nam. Russia give financial support but no Russian *ruble* in Ha Noi. Everybody use Vietnamese *dong,* everybody live like poor, even communist leaders. Correct decision. Too many American soldiers and politicians in South no good. Too many American businessmen in Sai Gon no good. Too many American dollars in the street destroy society. If American soldiers kill Vietnamese people like French soldiers, very big problems for my government. This is Asia. Asians kill Asians is OK. Foreigners kill Asians, north or south, is not OK."

The recruiters sat there flabbergasted. Finally, one of them cleared his throat in an exaggerated manner, and they all stood up and went to the canteen for lunch. The recruiters felt they been punched in the stomach. As insiders to the thinking in the White House, they knew that it was just a matter of time before US combat troops would be sent to Viet Nam.

48

Growing Pains

By the time he returned to Sai Gon, Hai had been secretly hired by the CIA to head the CIB and copies of his file had been sent by courier to the US Embassy. He moved into the new CIB headquarters on Vo Tanh street, was given a new secretary and an office staff and settled down with his first American advisor, James "Buddy" Grindell, prepared to do serious work. Instead, they both found ourselves doing little if any work at all during his first year because of the intense intra-murals between the American hawks and the doves within the CIA, a new imbroglio hidden within with the perennial fight between the CIA and the Army's MIS. They waited for things to get better, but they didn't. The Americans equated spending money with making progress and settled the intramural problems by throwing more money at both antagonists. The Embassy, USAID, USIS, USOM, MAAG enjoyed their power to fund new plans and programs and this led to another problem when the senior Vietnamese executives employed in American missions caught on to these free-spending habits. Having made themselves indispensable to their American employers, as the *auxiliaires* had made themselves indispensable to their French employers, they obliged them by coming with up with new suggestions whenever budgeting time came around. The mother lode had been found, it was time to tap it to the full, and soon the tail was wagging the dog.

The dust caused by these inter-agency disputes on the American side never settled, but a *modus vivendi* was arrived at in 1960, four years after President Diem had repudiated the national elections envisaged at the Geneva Conference. By this time, the Viet Minh regime in Ha Noi had resurrected its network of agents and guerrillas in the South. The new resistance forces were controlled by COSVN, the Central Office for South Viet Nam, which the CIB knew was headquartered just over the Cambodian border. Ha Noi called them the NLF, the National Liberation Front and Washington called them the Viet Minh until a USIS official realized that the term Viet Minh connoted solidarity and was associated in the Vietnamese mind with a successful nationalist revolution. He then coined the derogatory term Viet Cong, or Vietnamese communist, which was promptly adopted by the press and shortened to VC. Within a couple of years, a VC presence had emerged in all of the forty-four provinces that made up South Viet Nam.

In 1959, General Ly, the CIB commanding officer, was arrested and executed by General Chuc, his commanding officer, for passing sensitive information to a communist contact. Hai had known he was a plant from the beginning but he was an untouchable because he was linked by marriage to the President's family in Hue. Jonathan in the CIA and Hai in the CIB had been watching Ly's actuations for some time and they decided to anonymously tip off the Director General of the NPD, who still spent more time in the corridors of the Palace than at his desk. They knew that a formal approach by the CIB through the CIO, backed by the CIA, would get nowhere because the President trusted none of them. They felt that General Chuc's connections to the President would act as a counterbalance to General Ly's ties. The President's reaction was immediate. Obviously, national security overrode family considerations if the information came from someone the President trusted. The result of all this was that Hai was officially confirmed head of the CIB, on the strong recommendation of the US Embassy, speaking for the CIA. At the Palace, in the presence of the Interior Minister, the Director of ARVN MIS, the new Director of the CIO and the CIA station chief, President Diem personally conferred on him the rank of Lieutenant Colonel. As he pinned the rank on his epaulette, the President said quietly in Vietnamese without moving his lips "Try to remember whom you are working for." Startled, Hai looked at the President, whose face was only a few inches away. The small, dark eyes were expressionless; the heavy, fleshy face was closed. It was as if he hadn't said anything.

49

Grey Tiger

The culture of change that Hai had fallen in love with in his Georgetown days, when his first impression of America had hit him with the force of a meteor impacting the Earth, was beginning to pall. As *papa* had said many times, even great ideas turn sour if they are wrongly implemented, and change for the sake of change had become 'Standard Operating Procedure'. *Papa* had said once that every fool can under-do, and every idiot can over-do, but it took a wise man to do just enough to make things work. That was like the Buddhist 'middle road', the road of moderation. If the European model had seemed archaic and at times arthritic, the American model moved with the speed of a loose cannon, missing its target more often than not and causing real damage to both friends and foe in the process. With unlimited additional budgets falling out of the sky, plans, programs and personnel appeared and disappeared at bewildering speed while in-fighting muddied up the fine lines delineating fact from fiction. It was like sitting in a giant roller coaster that had left its tracks and was careening through space while the riders squabbled about the seating arrangements.

Amidst all these bewildering developments, the one positive development was that the working relationship between Jonathan and Hai had turned into a solid personal friendship. This became known within Embassy circles, where the detractors of "the Winthrop faction" within the CIA seized on this overt fraternization with a ranking member of the RVN to attack Jonathan and the conclusions his team arrived at after analyzing inputs from the field. For different reasons, it was bruited about that Hai was President Diem's plant in the CIO, which could compromise CIA operations. This was somewhat ironic, for both Jonathan and he knew that the Palace considered Hai a CIA plant in the CIO. In the streets, the coffee shop and noodle stall rumor mills had it that Hai was a deep penetration agent, using his position at the CIB to protect other communist agents, which was one reason why Ha Noi often seemed to know Sai Gon plans as soon as they appeared on the drawing board.

None of this bothered Hai. In the light of the mutual suspicion and distrust that had grown between the US Embassy and the Presidential Palace from the beginning of America's involvement in the war, this was par for the course. In fact, he rather enjoyed the reputation of being distrusted by everyone. It built up his mystique as conspiracy theorists tried to work out why he was still being kept on if he were really a traitor, a double agent, a spy and a plant. Rumors flew thick and fast, many of them contradictory. When asked about them, he deliberately kept a straight face, never making any comments, thus reinforcing the rumors.

Abstemious and reserved by nature, Hai didn't drink or smoke and lived for his work. He seldom met with anyone outside of his immediate circle and never allowed photographs of himself to be published. He never married, had no mistress and slept at the office most of the time. He had no family, didn't own a house or a car, didn't belong to any sports or social club and was seldom seen on the official cocktail circuit. With the CODEX funds behind him, he did not need to extort money or accept bribes from large business concerns and public personalities in return for police favors. He could afford to stay away from the ever-growing drug trade, which had rapidly sucked in ranking American and Vietnamese officials in the same way it had sucked in ranking French and Vietnamese personalities in the recent past. Within the CIB, he dealt with corruption in an unequivocal manner. The accused was placed on an equal footing with an enemy agent for having deliberately undermined the people's trust in the agency. The charge was always national sabotage, which in wartime carried the death penalty. But while he did not allow incompetence and corruption on his own turf, he religiously refrained from criticizing NPD colleagues guilty of these shortcomings. It was an upside down world where doing wrong was seen as normal and doing right was seen as hypocritical or, even worse, as betraying one's peers, and he soon realized that he couldn't change the world. He wanted to focus on the communists and didn't want to have his colleagues shooting at him at the same time. Not burdened by religious or spiritual concerns, he simply saw corruption as a disease, a silent killer. Like a cancerous growth, replicating out of control, it killed off all the honest cells one by one. Hai was determined the enemy would not inject this cancer into any organization under his control.

For the few people who knew him personally, as Jonathan of the CIA did, he was either very ruthless or very professional, perhaps both. As CIB Director at first and as the little-known midwife of the *Phoi Hop* program later, he was instrumental in making a large number of communist agents, NLF cadres and sympathizers disappear without trace over the years. To be certain that he was not doing what the communist resistance had done, he made sure he only targeted professional agents, men or women who had committed themselves to the communist cause and knew what the price of that commitment would be. He religiously avoided touching non-combatants, camp followers, people that he saw as 'civilians' in his mind, people like his mother and he had been. He had never believed that prisons could reform or rehabilitate agents of the caliber he was dealing with, and if he felt that a man was beyond the turning he paid him the ultimate tribute a warrior could offer another by burying him standing up, his dignity intact. Like Hai, the man had made his choice, he had fought the good fight in the belief that he was right. Unlike Hai, he had failed and now he had to pay the price for that failure. Hai admired bravery in a man, even an enemy, and at times he thought he might have learnt that trait from the *Bushido* code that Captain Watanabe had painstakingly explained to him in the days of the Japanese Occupation. He knew from his mother that he would end his days peacefully somewhere abroad, but if her prediction turned out to be wrong, he would have welcomed the same treatment at the hands of his captors. Having learnt his lesson from CODEX, no written records were ever found, even after the fall of Sai Gon. Fortunately for him, in the bitter, brutal and divisive multi-billion dollar war that ranged from the assassination of minor RVN officials at hamlet level through acts of urban terrorism by suicide bombers to the carpet-bombing by USAF B52s, his swift and discreet dispensation of justice didn't stand out sufficiently to be noticed by the international media.

The enemies of the Diem regime took to calling him the Grey Tiger after an enterprising opposition newspaper in Sai Gon coined that label. Since President Diem's enemies encompassed a wide segment of the population which included communist agents, Buddhist monks, student activists, southern opposition politicians, various quasi-militant organizations and the American doves at the US Embassy, the Grey Tiger appellation quickly became notorious from Ca Mau to Ben Hai. In Viet Nam, as elsewhere in Asia, the tiger is admired as the king of the jungle, renowned for his ferocity, courage, resourcefulness and raw power. In village lore, however, once a very old tiger turns grey with age, he becomes an object of fear and hatred. Too old to hunt deer and boars, he turns into a man-eater, lying in ambush along country roads and at the edge of the forest in the late afternoon. His grey coat blends in with the evening mist and by the time the woodcutter hears his roar it is too late. Sometimes grey tigers come into the village at night, enter thatched huts whose door has been left open and snatch sleeping children from their cots. Radio Ha Noi, in its nightly propaganda broadcasts to South Viet Nam, soon used the term as an adjective to qualify the killing of civilians by Diem's police, such as "…last night, in the village of Dong Xuan, Diem fascist forces engaged in grey tiger executions of thirteen men, seven women and fifteen children, burying their bodies in shallow graves near the village pond…" or, "…grey tiger activities were reported in Phuc Loc village when ARVN forces swept through on orders of the US Army to raze the district…"

To those Vietnamese and Americans who opposed the communists, however, Hai was portrayed simply as a tiger, neither fawn nor grey. He became the Tiger Colonel, then later the Tiger General, a nickname that stuck to him as his reputation for ruthlessness grew in size and the long arm of the CIB grew in reach. In Vietnamese, it had started with a play upon words, and the switch was easy. Ho, his family name, is pronounced with a falling accent and means "lake". When pronounced with a falling-rising accent, it means "tiger".

These appellations sometimes amused him, at other times flattered him. A cat for thirty-six years, a tiger in nine. What's next, a dragon? But, in his more reflective moments, the Tiger label bothered him. The truth was that he could see the war settling down to a steady grind of maiming, killing, burying, without any end in sight, with him in the middle of it, doing his share of the butchering. Increasingly, they were reliving the endless French nightmare, which had revived the fatalism and fanaticism inherent in the Vietnamese psyche, dormant until then since the Vietnamese had overthrown the Chinese colonizers one thousand years before. On both sides, north and south, the sole aim in life was now to keep fighting and to keep destroying, blindly, without any clear sense of purpose. By 1960, the Vietnamese carnage had lasted fifteen long and bloody years. Brutalized by incessant warfare, with half a million dead on each side and no sign of peace ahead, northern communists and southern nationalists flailed away at each other, like punch drunk boxers fighting on instinct, unaware that in Paris and Geneva their respective puppet masters, sitting comfortably around large conference tables, surrounded by attractive secretaries, were working on diplomatic ways of disengaging before repairing to a five-star restaurant for sumptuous lunches washed down with dry martinis and vodkas.

Beset with Buddhist problems throughout the South, gross corruption within his immediate family, a feudal mindset and an innate inability to get on with his only backer, Washington, President Diem gradually lost American support. Ironically, his style was in turn too dictatorial for the doves at the White House and too pusillanimous for the CIA hawks on the ground in Viet Nam. Although the American ambassadors, MAAG chiefs and the ubiquitous Colonel Landsdale by and large recognized in Diem a man of personal integrity and a gutsy fighter, their supportive reports carried little weight in Washington, where the culture of change had gone into over-drive. High-level White House political advisors and secretaries demanded a new approach and a larger budget every other year, which meant new faces as well. As President Diem had often said to his political confidants back in the late fifties, the Americans had no patience. They tried everything out for a short time until they hit on the right solution, often by luck, regardless of the costs involved in terms of money and personal lives. "Act first, think later is the American way," he had often said, shaking his head in disbelief.

By 1963 Washington had hit on a new solution to the Viet Nam problem and the first step involved getting rid of a recalcitrant President. He couldn't do anything right and it was time for him to go.

50

Phoi Hop

Maneuvering between the two uneasy allies and coordinating between his own squabbling agencies had become so time-consuming that it interfered with getting the CIB work done. Over the first six years, Hai had built a team of dedicated professionals who worked eighteen hours a day building up nation-wide files on VC agents already inside government agencies. Using money and more money, the CIB had turned many of these moles, but close supervision at every step was needed to ensure the continuity of their newfound loyalties. In the forty-four provincial capitals, CIB agents worked with the province chiefs and the Regional NPD Special Branch police chiefs to keep track of the VC infrastructure. Hai felt that his small organization, properly supported, should do more than simply identify and turn enemy agents. Without fanfare, he had begun a program of infiltrating the VC, starting at the village and hamlet levels. Given the terror and hatred that the armed VC propaganda teams inspired at village level when their orders were not obeyed, this hadn't been as hard as he had thought it would be, and he was soon working on counter-infiltration at district level. Twenty out of forty-four provinces were critical and needed full-time attention, twenty-four hours a day, and he had neither the time nor the manpower to devote to them.

Every six months, he sat down with his friend and now de facto control officer, Jonathan Winthrop, for a long and often cathartic discussion in which they brainstormed each other and allowed themselves to let go of all their suppressed tensions. Jonathan was an analyst, part of the Directorate of Intelligence (DI), and he was not supposed to handle foreign agents, which was the work of the

Directorate of Operations (DO), but, after nine years in Sai Gon, it was known that Jonathan Winthrop was being groomed for bigger and better things. The US Ambassador had approved this arrangement because Hai had been hired in the US and Jonathan had been designated Embassy liaison officer to the CIB. As usual, they spoke in a mix of English and Vietnamese. Hai's mastery of English grammar and vocabulary was by now almost complete although he couldn't get rid of his Vietnamese accent.

After a brief review of what had been happening, he concluded that they were in a big mess and that it was time to change some ground rules or face disaster. It was nothing that Jonathan hadn't heard before or didn't know about but it was the first time he had heard it put all together so bluntly.

"We losing this war?" he asked.

"Intelligence-wise, yes. Politically, we're halfway down the drain. Militarily, nothing but gloom and doom ahead."

They were both sitting in Jonathan's office, which was wired. Everything they said would be picked over by his American colleagues and would cause messy fights between the doves, the hawks and the dodo birds. Good, someone's got to say it sooner or later and it might as well be you. With your reputation, it's to be expected anyway.

"I'll start with three under-cards and talk about the main event last. First, a hostile media on your side. No matter what your Government does, it's wrong. If they saw your President walking on water the headlines would be screaming 'The President can't swim!' This war has become a TV circus and the enemy's cornered the high ground. Diem is portrayed as a corrupt and brutal fascist while Ho has become a nationalist, even if politically misguided. Does our case stink so badly that it is totally unpresentable, or is your government simply clueless in the PR field?"

He could see Jonathan squirm in his chair. This was sensitive ground. Press freedom is enshrined in the US constitution. For him to even think of attacking this sacred cow was to commit political suicide. They sat there like two lead soldiers looking at each other, knowing there was no solution to that one. Having made his point, Hai moved on.

"Second, regime change. Let's think the unthinkable, mention the unmentionable. Our man is no longer acceptable to your side, and it is inevitable that he must go. The signs are already there, it's just a question of when. Your people probably have their eyes on a new man already. By bringing the CIO and CIB into the picture with the new man early in the game, we can develop trust between us right from the start and avoid having a situation where the top man doesn't trust his own intelligence agencies. We don't want the new man to set up his own version of the Can Lao, do we?"

He was watching his friend closely as he talked. Jonathan involuntarily glanced at the cupboard on his left, where the invisible surveillance camera was.

"Wow! Hold on, my friend, hold on," he said rapidly, holding up his hand. "I don't feel comfortable discussing this sort of thing with you at this stage. Let me find out who is the right person for you to talk with. Let's meet tomorrow on this, when I'll know more. What else can we discuss that's less contro...uh...that's more feasible?"

Hai looked at him. Very strange people indeed. They want to overthrow a man they handpicked, but have no idea who to replace him with. What do they want to do? Organize democratic elections in the middle of a war? He shook his head slowly, his eyes locked on Jonathan's. Then he breathed out, decompressing.

"Third, survival. In nine years, the CIB has turned 1,700 of their men, disposed of over 4,000 and scared off 2,000. We are at the top of the list on every VC assassination squad, as you know from your own reports. They don't want just to infiltrate us, they want to kill us off, one by one, period, especially in the provinces. My men are all individually targeted for assassination, as I am, and so far I've lost 97, all highly trained professionals. Takes about a year to replace each man."

"Right. What can I do?"

"I have a list here," Hai said, reaching into his briefcase. "It is the same list I've been forwarding through CIA channels for the last two years. Early this year I sent another copy, marked O'Leary, and nothing came of that either. This time I'm giving it to you. I've updated it since. More guns, ammo, two-way radios, motorbikes, cars and trucks. More training and refresher-training facilities. Modern communications equipment to link up the provinces. A doubling of our present strength, to total three thousand men. Air America support in moving our personnel about the countryside. And a quadrupling of the kitty we use for buying information."

"Wow! They don't call you Tiger for nothing! That's what I like about you, Hai. No beating about the bush. You're like an American!" said Jonathan, reaching for the list.

Hai thought about this remark. Four or five years ago, when you were desperately trying to become American, it would've been a compliment. Now, having seen the Americans at work...

"Anyway, you can relax now. I promise you'll have everything you require within ninety days. I can get all this crap and more but three thousand men, that's three battalions! Are you planning a sneak attack on Ha Noi?"

"No, on the VC infrastructure. I've been working quietly on a project that coordinates our Special Branch police, CIB and ARVN MIS activities on a district basis in four provinces. I was able to do this by persuading the military and police officials involved that this approach would fast track their chances of promotion. I told them the Palace was behind it. That's not true, but who's going to double check?"

Jonathan sat up. This was new.

"What project is this? Who's funding it? Do we know about it?"

"No, it doesn't have an American name for the present. I call it *Phoi Hop* in Vietnamese. It was initiated by a Captain Minh in Special Branch. He's an egghead type that I have since hired into the CIB. I'm using CIB funding at present and no, the CIA knows nothing about it."

"Hey, that's initiative for you! How's it working out?"

"On a small scale it's been quite successful. If we stick to a small-scale operation on a province by province basis we can overcome the first hurdle we always meet, the resistance the police gets from the military in the field, where all of our suspects come from. Once we can coordinate police and military we can produce a hybrid paramilitary team that can do research on the NLFI, arrest key men, obtain intelligence from them with which to infiltrate or degrade the enemy."

"This sounds like a prototype program, small in size and scope, based on your personality and influence in the scheme of things. Why do you need to beef up CIB personnel?"

"To cover 44 provinces and 250 districts. Some are safe and we can maintain a permanent presence, others are not and we fly our boys out at night. The CIB needs to be seen wherever there is an enemy presence. Sitting in air-conditioned offices in Sai Gon and the provincial capitals is not going to do it. No use focusing on the towns if the surrounding districts fall one by one under enemy control at night."

"You're right there. I like the name, *Phoi Hop*. "Combine, coordinate". Good name. How's it going work?"

51

CIB Problems

"First, we do away with the smorgasbord of intelligence agencies in the capital running dozens of operations on a national scale, and replace them with small, highly specialized intelligence groups adapted to provincial conditions, which means dialects, family ties, culture, the whole caboodle. Everything they learn is then centralized at regional level. Field CIB evaluates the data collected and passes it on to a paramilitary field force to take corrective action after copying CIB headquarters."

"The first part sounds good but what's this field force? What field force?"

"We build one, using mercenaries and such. Quality intelligence is given to a paramilitary force that's built for the kill. It is super secret, highly paid, highly motivated, heavily armed. It can move in and take a cadre out at a moment's notice. It can blow up a COSVN camp sitting in Cambo."

"Wow! What would you call these units? Who would control them?"

"Security Field Forces, operating at provincial and district level. Our side would control them. Either NPD Special Branch or CIB. Your side would pay for them. Can't have Americans killing Vietnamese extra-judicially, can we?"

"Right, ha ha. What kind of units would these be? Who'd volunteer for them?"

"Army deserters, criminals, returnees from the other side, Nung mercenaries and Montagnard tribesmen. Anyone who's tough and wants to earn what an ARVN colonel earns. Officers would be CIB or NPD men."

"Wow. You've certainly thought this one out. How can we sell *Phoi Hop* to the CIA?"

"We don't. If you people get hold of it, it'll become a multi-million dollar program run by multi-million dollar managers who'll turn it into another multi-million dollar national mess. Within the year it'll have been taken over by some hotshot manager straight out of Washington, with the Vietnamese relegated to the sidelines. The moment American-controlled mercenaries start killing Vietnamese VCs, that's when the shit hits the fan."

Hai liked that American idiom and used it often when among friends. It's so graphic, and just right for your situation. There wasn't one fan during your stay in the US, but here you've got millions of fans everywhere, and a lot of shit too.

"Well, if you want US funding, you'll have to sell the concept to the Embassy at least. The Ambassador, with positive CIA input from me, sells the idea to Washington, which then budgets for it and tells MAAG and CIA here to support it. But you'll still need an American interface right here."

"It could be you."

A long silence followed.

"Can it be done?"

"I think the answer is yes. It sounds feasible but I have to find the right man to take *Phoi Hop* to Washington. Until then it'll have to stay your baby. Jesus, Hai, how did we get into this mess?"

"It's difficult for the whale and the minnow to swim in unison. To tango you both have to be the same size."

"What about Ho and the bear? He seems to be doing all right."

"Yep, he is. He's small, like a dung beetle, but he doesn't have the Soviet elephant sitting in his living room, shitting everywhere and crowding him out of his hut."

Jonathan burst out laughing, and Hai laughed along with him. It was good to be able to laugh with each other. There hadn't been too much to laugh about lately and they deliberately milked the laughter for as long as they could, knowing they were only putting off the return to a painful discussion.

"OK, Tiger," Jonathan finally said. "Leave it with me. You'll get your *materiel* very soon this time and I'll look high and low for the right sponsor for *Phoi Hop*. Boy! With under-cards of this magnitude who's got time for a main event, but anyway what is it?"

Now we were finally getting to it. Hai glanced at the cupboard and smiled.

"Since the Soviet Union got the atom bomb, the two super powers have been engaged in play-fighting, using conventional weaponry in locations outside their territories. Neither side wants to win conclusively, which might force the losing side to resort to nuclear weapons. The idea is to drag it out, to bleed each other, to bankrupt each other while testing each other's military strength and political resolve in far away places. Korea, Cuba, now Viet Nam. There will be others. Take your pick, Africa, the Middle East, Eastern Europe. In our particular equation, North is allowed to attack South in our garden and we are allowed to defend it while our respective backers stand by to supply increasingly heavy weaponry. But there are no plans to attack the North. Can you see what this Moscow-Washington arm-wrestling match in my garden is doing to my house?"

Jonathan sat stock still. The peripherals, the under-cards as Hai had called them, had all excited him and elicited a reaction. The crux of the problem, what Hai called the main event, now crushed him. Intelligent as he was, he had probably never seen things quite that way. Unlike Europeans, American are by and large convinced that their governments are incapable of devious action. But Hai had laid it out graphically. Unless the South attacked the North with the aim of taking over their territory, there didn't seem to be any light at the end of the tunnel, no matter however many millions of American dollars and South Vietnamese lives were thrown into the grinding machine below the DMZ.

"We both know the Pentagon is only too pleased at this on-the-job training opportunity, which allows it to develop new strategies, try out new tactics, deploy new weapons systems and replace stocks of World War Two ammunition with New Age explosives, the kind that would be needed if push came to shove in eastern Europe," Hai continued but Jonathan held up his hand and he stopped. They had already covered this particular issue many times before and they both realized that, in their own ways, they were both just pawns in the game that was being played out in South Viet Nam.

By 1963, Washington had decided to get rid of President Diem, who was now seen as a stumbling block to victory because of his unpopularity and his obstructionist policies where the American vision was concerned. He had been asked to abolish the Can Lao party but he had refused to do so, claiming it represented the true nationalists in Viet Nam. The CIA, with the full support of the new US Ambassador, Henry Cabot Lodge, quietly arranged for a *coup d'état* to be mounted by a group of top ARVN generals. President Kennedy agonized over every report that arrived at the White House, hour on the hour. What had to be done had to be done, but it was important that President Diem not be harmed in any way. It was felt that the image of America, The Land of the Free and the Home of the Brave, had to be protected at all cost. But the carefully laid plans went tragically wrong and the President and his brother Nhu were assassinated inside the APC that was bringing them back to ARVN headquarters. Photos surfaced the same day showing that both men had been hogtied before being shot in the face. The American media went wild. Three weeks later, Kennedy was assassinated in Dallas, and the media went ballistic. Hai didn't know it at the time, but the twin assassinations had ushered in a new phase of the Viet Nam war.

Meanwhile, in spite of Herculean efforts, Jonathan hadn't found the right sponsor for the *Phoi Hop* project they had so enthusiastically discussed. There was plenty of money allocated to intelligence, but it had to be run and controlled by Americans. New American-run programs continued to be launched every year, new acronyms appeared, new reputations were made and the bandwagon rolled on, impervious to common sense and originality of thought. Hamletization Programs were followed by Pacification Programs, then Vietnamization Programs, Rural Reconstruction Programs, Revolutionary Development Programs, ICEX Programs for intelligence-coordination and exploitation, intelligence gathering programs masked as Census Grievance Programs, *chieu hoi* Returnee Programs, Public Safety Programs and a host of others. The Palace, ARVN and NPD were deluged with new programs bearing new names and logos every year. Remember the first time you walked into one of the super-marts in the States, where dozens of attractively designed cans, all standard size and weight, sell basically the same luncheon meat at different prices, each rationalizing the extra cost due to the inclusion of one superior ingredient? Each program is designed to make life better for the peasants, yet nine out of ten end up killing more peasants, creating more refugees.

"You know us," Jonathan said to Hai one day. "Although we usually end up doing the right thing, we have to try out all the wrong ones first. But don't give up on me. I'm still working on it and it won't be long now."

Hai remembered that President Diem had also said something like that, minus the first part.

The three years following President Diem's assassination saw ten South Vietnamese governments relay each other in a series of bloodless coups and counter-coups by ambitious generals. Each coup maker received immediate American approval and support, however briefly. Finally, after Ambassador Lodge's replacement, General Taylor, dressed down the leading coup makers like a teacher scolding schoolchildren, there was one more lightning *coup d'état* and things settled down, with General Nguyen Cao Ky becoming Premier in June, 1965. The same year Hai was appointed major general and the CIB grew in size and importance.

52

Decision Time

In early 1967, Hai saw a pattern appear in the CIB data bank on the VC infrastructure. Until recently, communist cells in Sai Gon numbered 162 professional cadres, some 300 active supporters and over 2,000 sympathizers labeled as Class A, B and C. But five major cells out of twelve had mysteriously left the city, leaving seven behind. The largest stay-behind cell was composed of seven senior cadres, headed by a man named Linh, who worked for an American Protestant publication, *The Awakening*. The other cells averaged three to five men. One of these included a man named Tuan, who had undergone training for a suicide mission and was presently on a familiarization course in the capital. Apart from the agents, 120 Class A sympathizers who were under surveillance had lately made no attempts to meet with their handlers. Twenty-four known couriers who linked the cells with one another and with the sympathizers had suddenly gone to ground, including a woman named Lan Lan. At the central market, usually a reliable center of information, rumors had it that a major attack was being planned and that Sai Gon was included in the plan. Hai ordered his moles in the North to focus on the People's Army of Viet Nam's plans for the coming Winter-Spring campaign.

From a military viewpoint, the VC guerrillas effectively controlled the population in the provinces west of the capital by day and by night. North and south of the capital, they controlled only the night. MAC-V, the old MAGG under a new name, continued turning out positively upbeat reports, with an ever increasing number of VC bodies being counted, more districts pacified and enormous progress being made in the fields of medicare and humanitarian aid to the thousands of families who had fled the USAF saturation bombings and flocked into RVN refugee centers. The ARVN General Staff went along with MAC-V, although the Vietnamese Corps Commanders knew exactly what was the situation on the ground. The President of the day and the American Ambassador at the time joined in the chorus, allowing the American Defense Secretary to report to President Johnson that the war was being won. Whistle-blowers and poor team players, American or Vietnamese, risked being instantly weeded out of the system. It was quite useless asking the MIS, American or Vietnamese, for information on a potential attack. Hai needed reliable information and there was one communist plant who might know. His name was Tuat, a special assistant at the Presidential Palace. He was a Northerner and his background had been military. He had figured on the CIB list for some time but the Palace was out of CIB jurisdiction. Now, with the worsening situation, there was no more time for intramural games. Hai made a phone call and the spy was contacted by a double agent asking him for a meeting that evening at a coffee shop near the Palace. Unsuspecting, Tuat walked over to the meeting place, crossing the huge park in front of the Norodom Palace. As he walked in between the huge acacia trees the French had planted centuries before, a man approached him to ask for a light. When he reached with his right hand for his lighter, another man hit him from behind.

Two days later, Hai was clearer as to what was happening. The moles had reported that the PAVN, the People's Army of Viet Nam, was planning a Winter-Spring offensive that would target most of the forty-four provincial capitals. Attacking in divisional strength, PAVN would seize territory below the DMZ and hold it, to draw American forces up north. VC regular units, recently re-armed in Cambodia, would attack in battalion strength and overrun all the provincial capitals in Central Viet Nam. The southern provincial capitals would be shelled and harassed, including the capital. They couldn't yet pinpoint any dates. Tuat, for his part, had been persuaded to give some numbers. The PAVN could throw between 10,000 to 15,000 regular troops into the battle for control of the DMZ, while the NLF could put up between 80,000 to 100,000 regulars and guerrillas to attack 36 provincial capitals, 64 district capitals and 20 US airfields, the main target being Hue. Hai's men had been unable to get anything out of him on Ha Noi's plans for Sai Gon. Hai looked at Tuat, who was very much the worse for wear. After drugs, electricity had been used, and there was a faint smell of burning flesh. He kept on asking for water.

The CIB men looked at Hai, their eyes questioning. The last thing he wanted at this stage was a problem with the Palace. He nodded to his men and they taped Tuat's mouth before zipping him up in the plastic body bags the American army used. They then picked him up bodily and carried him out. Hai returned to his office. His men knew the drill.

Sitting in his office alone, with a white porcelain dish in which lay his mother's steel needle and green frog hat pin in front of him, he reviewed the situation. It had been five years since President Diem had been assassinated, and the military situation had deteriorated. As soon as American combat troops had shouldered the ARVN aside and taken over the bulk of the fighting, the Soviets had tripled their supply of light and heavy weaponry, while the Chinese had quintupled their supply of ammunition, the lifeblood of war. The PAVN and the VC firepower had grown exponentially. The less territory the ARVN controlled, the smaller the RVN intelligence net was. In some of the northern provinces, CIB agents flew in by day to co-ordinate arrests and interrogation and flew out at 1700 hrs. In America, vociferous demonstrations against the Vietnam war had reached 100,000 strong and were growing in size and number.

Disturbing information had been received concerning his friend Jonathan. He had been introduced to a beautiful Vietnamese girl at a social function at the *Cercle Sportif*, an exclusive sports club formerly reserved for the French and Vietnamese elite, but which now had a large American membership. They had gone swimming together, and she had introduced him to her father, a business tycoon. Her name was Lan Lan, and the CIB knew her as a communist courier. A leftist university student, she had been used to make contact with rich and powerful sympathizers in places like the *Cercle Sportif*, where communist cadres would be out of place. Her lover either was or had been no other than Tuan, who was now in Sai Gon on a suicide mission. Provincial CIB agents had picked up Tuan's trail since he graduated the year before from a special COSVN training course at Phoumi Dak Dam, Cambodia.

More reports were coming in from the moles in the northern provinces. The new dates for the lunar New Year were of importance. For millenaries, all of Asia had used the 8th time zone to compile their lunar calendars and thus designate the auspicious day for the start of a new year. In 1967, to show his independence from China, Chairman Ho had approved a lunar calendar specifically designed for the 7th time zone, which covers all of Viet Nam. Sai Gon kept to the old calendar, based on the 8th time zone. Thus the Ha Noi *Tet* now fell one day earlier than the Sai Gon's. One field report read "If a rat moves in Ha Noi on a Monday, a mouse will move in Sai Gon on Tuesday at the same hour".

Later that week, Hai requested an official meeting with Jonathan Winthrop, Jr. to discuss a problem that was poisoning relations between the new President of Viet Nam and the US Embassy. General Nguyen Thieu, the Chief of State, a ceremonious title, had outmaneuvered General Ky, the Premier, in rigged elections in September 1967, and had replaced him by November. Having been enrolled by the CIA as one of the anti-Diem coup makers, Thieu knew how things worked in the asymmetrical American-Vietnamese tandem and his sense of paranoia grew with time. Fully aware of the high-level American plants within the CIO and CIB, he called their commanding officers in for the kind of maneuvering that he excelled in. He had decided to test them, to counter-attack. Reserved and inscrutable by nature, he could make himself exude warmth and bonhomie when he wanted to. Over tea and biscuits, pipe in hand, he told them confidentially that the US Embassy might have been tasked by Washington with making contact with the National Liberation Front, the Viet Cong. Ostensibly, they were to discuss the American prisoners of war issue. But, his sources had told him, they were meeting to discuss the possible future participation of the NLF in a coalition government that would allow a face-saving American withdrawal. As the foremost intelligence agencies in the country, he was asking them to use their contacts to verify these rumors and report to him within the week. He looked at them in turn, the round eyes in his bland face a picture of sincerity.

When they met, Hai told Jonathan about what the President had discussed with them. Jonathan's face went blank.

"I don't know anything about it," he said.

"But you don't know everything that's going on," Hai insisted. He already knew the answer to the President's question.

"True. You know how things are on our side. Let me find out. Why are you interested?"

"I think that if I can confirm his suspicions, he'll feel better about the CIB. President Diem couldn't abide us, Premier Ky had his own

Chief of National Police, so it's time we got one President's ear. If it's true, he won't like it, but having had it confirmed by us, he may trust us enough to work with us. If it isn't true, he won't believe us, and we'll be back to where we are."

"So you hope it's true?"

"Who are we kidding? I know it's true. You know it's true. It's your Sharkey group, using released VC prisoners of war to make contact with ranking NLF cadres. What Sharkey doesn't seem to know is that before a VC can take a piss he has to obtain authorization from COSVN in Cambo, and they have to clear it with the Politburo in Ha Noi first."

"So you know it's true?"

"Not one hundred percent. I've intercepted couriers between COSVN and Ha Noi, and I know what the NLF is asking, but I haven't seen any answers from Ha Noi yet."

"Is the CIA working with the CIO on this?"

"No. They are afraid of leaks," Hai answered, laughing. They both laughed.

"Oh, by the way," he said casually, "Does Lan Lan ring a bell?"

"Lan Lan? What's she got do with this?" Jonathan had sat up in his chair.

"Let me be blunt. You like me to be blunt, right? Your new girlfriend is a VC courier and her lover is a terrorist. He's been trained to lead a suicide squad into Sai Gon some time this year. Perhaps soon."

Jonathan sat stunned. He believed Hai implicitly. If the Tiger said it, it had to be true. He knew Hai always knew what he was talking about. He looked into his friend's eyes. He had only recently met Lan Lan. She was rich, well educated, stunning. Why would such a girl have anything to do with the VC?

"Continue frequenting her, Jonathan. Sleep with her if you can. Tell her your family supports all these student protests going on all over America. Maybe she'll warm to you and tell you things about her activities. Don't go anywhere with her outside the beaten path. Please."

Jonathan sat silent. Finally, he asked: "Why?"

"Three possibilities. One, she's a naïve leftist university student who's attracted by your good looks, but her handlers know who you are. You follow her, you get kidnapped. Two, she's been told who you are and ordered to draw you into a trap."

"You said three possibilities."

"Yes, unlikely but possible. You are running an operation, you see in her a conduit to the VC, as our President suspects the CIA is doing." Jonathan laughed.

"Thanks, Tiger. Your imaginative mind certainly has all the options covered. Seriously though, I like her. In fact, I can tell you I like her very much. Do you know this terrorist?"

"Yes, I have a photo and a file on him at the office. On Lan Lan too. I have to do something about them soon," he answered.

He could see that his friend tensed up when he said this. It was known that when the Tiger General did something about someone, it was usually terminal.

CIB operatives had located Linh. He was still in the city after all. Although still a part-time writer for *The Awakening*, he hadn't reported for work in weeks. His columns were sent in to the magazine by courier. Under surveillance, one of them had been spotted meeting with Linh. Two CIB teams now relayed each other round the clock. Hai wrote out a comprehensive report on what he felt was happening and the conclusions he had drawn, and set aside the copy for the CIO to disseminate to ARVN, NPD and CIA after he had met with the President. He hand-carried the original copy to the Palace, having asked for an interview beforehand. The new President had since met with President Johnson, who had told him bluntly that "as long as I am president, America is behind you one hundred percent". President Thieu was at first in a charming mood, perhaps because Hai had confirmed to him that the US Embassy was indeed trying to establish contact with the NLF. They made small talk before he handed his report over. The President fished about for his glasses, put them on, put away the pipe he often smoked when alone, sat back and read attentively. When he finished, he took his glasses off, folded them carefully without looking up, and Hai knew immediately that whatever artificial warmth had existed between them had evaporated.

"General Hai, I am surprised at this report. My Chief of Staff has made no mention of a possible Winter-Spring offensive this year. I had dinner with Ambassador Bunker last night and he never talked about anything like this. Does MAC-V concur with your evaluation?" he finally said, his voice neutral.

"No, sir, they do not. In the ARVN, General Sy concurs with me. In MAC-V, General Weyand believes I am right in my assessment of the situation. At the NPD, General Loan concurs fully with me."

The President's face was inscrutable. He had only vaguely heard of General Weyand, and both Generals Sy and Loan were holdovers from Premier Ky's administration. He already had plans to replace them with men he could trust.

"How do you explain that you are practically the only one who sees a wolf outside the door?"

"What we see depends on the professionalism of the information gatherers. The CIB has consistently read the situation correctly and that has been recognized by the CIA."

"Well, they don't seem to think so this time. I know because the incoming Chief of Station called on me this morning. I also hear from my Palace advisers that Ha Noi wants to propose a truce over the New Year. We are thinking of announcing a three-day truce starting the 28th January. MAC-V seems amenable."

Hai felt the follicles at the back of his neck rise. The Palace adviser the President was referring to was none other than Pham Van Phu, his special assistant for military affairs, on whom the CIB had a thick dossier. The man was a deep penetration agent yet the President had appointed him the number two at the CIO. Incredible. Number one is Binh, a CIA asset, number two is Phu, a Viet Minh asset, and you have to report to them. Lucky you only report what you want to. This can happen only in Viet Nam. Hai was wondering what to say next when the President stood up, signaling the session was over.

"General Hai, thank you for coming in today. It is good to be alert at all times, but too much paranoia can weaken the system. I don't think Ha Noi or the National Liberation Front have it in them to launch a nationwide offensive on the scale you are predicting. The DMZ, the far north, yes. The American Air Force will take care of that," he said, nodding with conviction. "In the south, we are quite capable of crushing any VC ground attack. An office like yours cannot afford to be alarmist."

Hai saluted the President and walked out. He felt tired. As soon as he reached his office, he shredded the CIO copy of his report. The CIB would limit its report to the CIA, and even then only to the office of his control officer, Jonathan Winthrop.

53

Spies and Agents

At nine thirty, Hai excused himself from the US Embassy dinner, pleading a heavy workload. He dreaded these Embassy dinners and had groomed his deputy, General Tich, to replace him on the social circuit, but Jonathan had prevailed on him to attend personally this time. His host, His Excellency Elsworth Bunker, the new US Ambassador to the Republic of South Viet Nam, knew of his reputation and tried to persuade him to stay on for cigars and brandy. He wanted to talk to him in front of the incoming Chief of Station, Bob Kilmer, soon to be nicknamed "Shotgun" Bob for his fiery internal memos, but then realized that the Tiger General neither smoked nor drank. Hai didn't want to talk to either of them that night because he had many problems awaiting him at the office. His bodyguards were in the lobby, and he rode with them back to the National Police Headquarters. Traffic was heavy, and the official car inched along. His eyes swept over the sidewalks, which were packed with people preparing for the New Year. In the middle of a war thousands of innocent people were going about their business, caught up in their own problems, ignorant of what was about to happen. He briefly wondered if they were this carefree in the North.

The National Police Directorate headquarters sat in a huge compound that took up one whole city block on Vo Tanh street. It was a formidable landmark, known to all, feared by many. Large and ugly, with high walls thickly ringed with barbed wire and heavily sandbagged entrances, it stood like a huge rock, bristling with guns, in the middle of the city. The driver went past the main building, the NPD building, an imposing old French colonial mansion to which wings had been added to create more offices. At the end of the huge compound a large, gray, two-story building stood alone. Square, windowless, with a flat concrete roof, it was neither tasteful nor imposing. The top of the building served as a helicopter pad. It had four basement floors under the ground floor. Secret exit tunnels led from these basement floors to openings well outside the NPD. This was the Counter Intelligence Bureau, the CIB of the CIO, where Hai spent most of his nights. He rode the elevator down to the fourth basement and walked down a long, claustrophobic, air-conditioned hallway to his office, the last door on the right. Armed police officers assigned outside each door stood up and saluted. Inside his office, the door, walls and ceiling had been painted an off-white color, not unlike a hospital ward. On the floor, off-white linoleum tiles had been laid. It was known the Tiger General liked light colors. Next door was his American advisor's office. It was empty, as Colonel Locke believed in working normal hours. He had another four months to go before his tour of duty ended and he had begun to hit the MAC-V cocktail circuit that always crowned the end of a duty tour of a high-ranking officer.

Hai took off his jacket and tie, unbuttoned his short-sleeved shirt, climbed out of his shoes and socks, slipped his trousers off and sat down at his large mahogany desk in his open shirt and underpants. This was his favorite attire when working at night, and his startled aides had long become used to this unusual sight. A large pot of jasmine tea was brought in, and a platter of fresh fruits. The dossiers that needed his attention were already neatly stacked on his desk. Everything on the desk had been laid out with precision and an eye for perfect alignment. It was known the Tiger General liked his desk to be neat. The pencils had been sharpened, the erasers washed clean, the desk clock set by Greenwich Mean Time, the desk lamps angled just right. The night aide-de-camp had adjusted the air conditioning unit to exactly twenty-six degrees Celsius and was sitting just outside the office, in the hallway. It was known that the Tiger General would sit at his desk till dawn.

At 0530 hrs, sometimes even earlier, his personal assistant and protégé, Colonel Dao, would enter the office and leave with a slim folder containing unsigned written orders that he and his closest operations officers would review carefully in the conference room next door. Notes would be taken by the attending officers and the written orders burned in a small electric stove specifically set up for that purpose. The Tiger General did not believe in filing away written orders. By nine o'clock the officers would split up, return to their respective units and begin to implement the instruction that had been laid out in the written orders. In the meantime, the Tiger slept on his cot inside his office until lunchtime, having unplugged the three white phone lines from the wall. Only the red phone, a hotline to the Office of the President, remained operational. In recent months, given the deteriorating relations between the Palace and the CIB, the red phone had remained silent.

CIB moles had first reported in early April 1967 that the PAVN was planning a massive Winter-Spring Offensive within the year. It could deploy 20,000 regular troops just above the DMZ to seize the five northernmost provinces, American troops would rush up north, leaving the ARVN to protect the southern delta. The CIA analysts on the sixth floor of the US Embassy had tentatively guessed that, in the South, any VC general attack could count on 100,000 fighters. MAC-V had estimated 10,000 for the PAVN and 25,000 for the VC. These vastly different figures prompted a team of high-ranking officials from Washington to rush to Sai Gon in August to look into the discrepancy. After much arm-twisting by MAC-V, a compromise was arrived at and the figure for the PAVN was raised to 15,000 while the NLF forces would be lowered to 20,000. It was important to all concerned that President Johnson continue to believe that the insurgency in the South was being conducted by a small group manipulated by the Viet Minh in the north and that the southern population as a whole solidly supported President Thieu. It was important for everyone to see that general Westmoreland was winning the war, in spite of the fact that McNamara, testifying before a Senate sub-committee in August, had confirmed that the bombing of North Viet Nam was proving ineffective and that the VCs had increased their control over the Mekong Delta, South Viet Nam's rice bowl.

At a CIA meeting in late October, after the team sent by the White House had left, the CIB confirmed its April figures for the PAVN and supported the CIA figures of 100,000 VC fighters. Hai had set an approximate window for the attack, between the 5th and the 20th of January 1968. Ambassador Bunker, MAC-V chief General Westmoreland and the CIA's O'Leary were present. Next to O'Leary sat Jonathan Winthrop, Jr., now O'Leary's deputy for liaison with the

RVN government. On the Vietnamese side were General Liem, head of ARVN MIS, General Chanh of the CIO, Hai of the CIB and his executive assistant, Colonel Dao.

"It's just more of the usual B.S.," O'Leary concluded bluntly, after the CIO, CIB, ARVN MIS, CIA and MAC-V MIS had respectively briefed the US ambassador. He was referring to the large-scale, coordinated attacks that the communists staged every two or three years. In November, a third CIB report underlined the clear possibility of a major offensive coinciding with the Lunar New Year, which would come in late January 1968. That was in two months' time. This report had been shot down in flames after MAC-V and ARVN MIS figures again showed little or no activity on the part of PAVN or VC field forces that would indicate preparation for a large-scale offensive.

In mid-January, two PAVN divisions surrounded 6,000 US Marines in Khe Sanh just south of the DMZ, inflicting heavy casualties. PAVN armored units appeared for the first time. Incredibly, neither President Thieu nor General Westmoreland saw the urgency of the situation, and no changes were made in the December 1967 decision to observe a unilateral four-day truce for the Lunar New Year, which this year would fall on Tuesday the 30th of January of 1968 of the solar calendar.

Jonathan was in Hai's office when the Khe Sanh reports were coming in over the radio. They looked at each other in consternation. Ever since that first meeting in April, Jonathan had worked overtime to convince Station Chief O'Leary that the Tiger General knew what he was talking about. But, as he said, O'Leary wasn't buying that. Jonathan then gave Hai a blow-by-blow account of what had been said between them, and why.

"That Tiger's got you eating out of his hand, John. No one can always be right, and in this case I have to go along with MAC-V. Hell, even the ARVN agree with our interpretation of events," O'Leary had concluded, after hearing Jonathan out. He looked exasperated.

"I hate to say this, Ozzie," replied Jonathan, his hackles rising, "but MAC-V and ARVN have been spectacularly wrong on almost all the major occasions since Diem's assassination, and that was five full years ago. Do you want a list of the crap those military yo-yos have reported lately?" Jonathan was beginning to have his doubts about Oswald O'Leary ability to judge things independently.

"I agree with you the soldier boys have not always been able to see what was coming, but in this case things are different. The CIB gets its information from captured agents, prisoners of war, planted assets, people who see one tiny sliver of the action at a time. They combine these slivers and make one whole slice of the pie, but it is still only one slice," said O'Leary.

"Yeah, the problem is the military's only focusing on the DMZ, which is what the PAVN wants them to do, while the VC build up and move into position," countered Jonathan. O'Leary was considerably older than Jonathan, but, as Jonathan said to Hai, "I can read him like a book."

After graduation from Langley, O'Leary had joined the Directorate of Operations, had done fieldwork in Europe during the Cold War and in South America thereafter. He had survived the bitter in-fighting at CIA headquarters after Kennedy's assassination and, finally, been reassigned to the Directorate of Intelligence, which did analyses of information sent in by the DO. This was his last post, and he was tired. He didn't have the get-up-and-go he had had in Germany and in Nicaragua, or even in Langley, Virginia, and it irritated him that Jonathan did. Like a number of older men at the Embassy, the more O'Leary thought about the Viet Nam war, the less winnable it appeared to be. But to express such sentiments was tantamount to committing career suicide, and he was not prepared to do that just yet. He wanted the war to come to an end, to retire with glory, receive a fat pension and return to South America where a man with a dollar could live like a king, surrounded by beautiful women, good music and wine. That's the problem with these rich snotty-nosed kids they're sending out today. DI's trying to act like DO's. They simply didn't understand that America isn't any good at these piss-ant wars, and anyway what does it matter? Russia matters. China matters. Viet Nam…who gives a fuck about Viet Nam? We can lose ten Vietnams and it still doesn't make one iota of difference. He decided to attack.

"The problem with your goddamn Tiger General is that he thinks he knows everything. You see how he briefs us? Any question and he just answers it without even thinking. I don't know but it seems he knows in advance what's going to happen. Hell, John the last thing we need is a psychic to show us the way. You know what people say about him? Some say he's a queer, he's never had a woman in his life. Others say he's a cold-blooded stone-killer. That man has done more wet jobs than any of us and that's how he got this Grey Tiger nickname. They say he's on drugs, too. Everybody is playing a game of his own in this goddamn war, and he's obviously willing to fight to the last American. I can't figure out why so you're so stuck on him, John," O'Leary said exasperatedly.

"Ozzie, I've worked closely with General Hai for over ten years and I can tell you he's no queer and no drug addict. He's also incorruptible and has no private agenda. He simply does his work the only way he knows how, which is with professional competence. And as to fighting to the last American, Hai would be glad to see all US troops leave Viet Nam tomorrow. In fact, he told me, when I first met him back in 1955, that it would be a catastrophic mistake for American troops to come here and kill Vietnamese, of whatever stripe. I'll never forget he said that a long time before we ever thought about sending combat troops in. If Viet Nam had a dozen generals like the Tiger heading the key agencies and ministries, this government would be winning the war and we wouldn't have to be here. I don't know about his psychopathic tendencies, but our business is hardly a clean one, so it's a case of the pot calling the kettle black. I've often wondered myself about his seemingly psychic approach to things, but he's never missed hitting the nail square on the head every time. I believe his interpretation of the facts this time to be correct, because I know he has contacts in the North. I don't know what they say to each other, or why, but he has consistently been able to get things right. You know, like I know, our intelligence problems since World War I have all been caused by our increasing reliance on machines instead of people. We are good at code-breaking and spy satellites but not good at recruiting spies in the enemy's camp, so when I have a man who's doing just that I support him all I can, and I would like you to support me with Ambassador Bunker on this one. Standing down American troops for a *Tet* truce, especially American troops deployed in Sai Gon, is going to result in us getting caught with our pants down. Won't be the first time, I know."

O'Leary looked at Jonathan. He shook his head, slowly. Jonathan tried one last shot.

"What about Weyand? He's screaming blue murder about the *Tet* truce. What about Sy? He's no dummy. You saw what he did at the battle of Ap Bac. What about General Loan? We may not like the guy, but he's one of the few Vietnamese who's not afraid to take the VCs head on."

"Weyand's problem is that he picked Cu Chi to settle in, and now we know the NLF tunnels are all over the place, right under his camp. He sees VCs everywhere, and I don't blame him. Sy's good, I'll grant you that, but he's on his way out, so who cares what he says. Loan is a snake in the grass where I'm concerned. I couldn't stand Ky, so what Loan says doesn't count in my books. That weirdo hates everybody."

They had looked at each other for a long time. The dislike that floated in the air was palpable but civilities had to be maintained. Jonathan decided to give up on trying to persuade O'Leary. He knew Ozzie was on his way out anyway, and he'd reserve his persuasive powers for the new Chief of Station.

54

Viet Minh/Viet Cong

As his mind wandered all over the place, Hai doodled on a scratch pad and his knees twitched under the table. He looked and saw he had unconsciously scribbled the words "weak leadership", "corruption" and "ambivalence". He knew why he had penned them, even without thinking. They had been on his mind for months. They symbolized the three major problems the CIB was having under the Thieu regime. An intensely secretive man, the President had publicly thrown his support behind Westmoreland's doctrine of massive firepower, whatever he privately thought about the consequences. He already knew what happened to people who opposed the American vision of war. Therefore, the more American combat troops, fire bases and bombing sorties the better. He counted on American weaponry and tactics to keep the reds at bay while strategically hoarding his ARVN in the background, having purged this body of officers who were not personally loyal to him.

Added to this was the cronyism and corruption created by the presidential entourage. With American aid money pouring in, handpicked civil servants and generals were quietly encouraged to divert a percentage of the greenbacks towards the Palace. Captains of shady industries were protected in return for massive contributions, armchair generals and their fat wives were allowed to engage in lucrative drug smuggling operations in the Golden Triangle, using ARVN helicopters and DC3s. These untouchables, conscious of the fact that they had been anointed, broke every law of the land with impunity in their efforts to make more money and win ever greater presidential approval.

As if this mess wasn't enough, American ambivalence contributed to the general feeling of insecurity among the Vietnamese leadership. In public, Washington hawks stood for containment of communism in Southeast Asia, eradication of communism in South Viet Nam and the degradation of communism in North Viet Nam. Yet, behind the scenes, Washington doves were using one faction of the CIA in Sai Gon to make contact with the National Liberation Front to explore the possibility of some sort of power sharing arrangement with the South Vietnamese government. At the White House, policy vacillated daily between the two opposites, either for strategic or tactical reasons, resulting in a green light for the USAF bombing of North Vietnamese dikes one day and for the US Embassy in Sai Gon secretly negotiating with the NLF the next. With an ally that waved both the stick and the carrot at the same time, the President of the Republic of Vietnam didn't know what foot to dance on, and it was not surprising that the levels of paranoia at the Palace grew as the war dragged on.

Sighing, Hai turned his attention to the four dossiers and the folder immediately in front of him. It was December 7, 1967, the *Tet* truce was only three weeks away and he had made up his mind. The President and the US Ambassador, the MAC-V and ARVN military commanders, the CIA and even the CIO could play their little games, cook the books and organize as many truces as they liked. The CIB was going to fulfill its mandate, come hell or high water. At your level and within your jurisdiction, the CIB must do everything it can, whatever the consequences. Bend every rule in the book to its extreme limit and see what happens. He had already been leaning in this direction over the last few months, but the public announcement of the *Tet* truce triggered his final reaction. The national team had begun its slide down the slippery slope, but he didn't want to be dragged along without a fight.

The first dossier was entitled "Mai Thi Lan Lan, VC, courier" and inside was a large 20x30 centimeter photograph of a girl's face. She had a high forehead, oval features and large, slightly slanted eyes. That was the Chinese blood in her, from her mother, he noted. A small Asian nose, with flared nostrils, and a tiny, pouting, fish-like mouth, well-shaped ears and chin, and a fair skin. She wore her thick, jet-black hair in a bang across her forehead and the rest pulled up into a knot on top of her head. She was tall for a Vietnamese, well-built, and had represented the University in free-style swimming. Lan Lan had become involved with leftist student groups and had participated in many demonstrations against the government. At University, she had fallen under the influence of an older student, Linh. A man of high intellect and suave looks, Linh was a charismatic speaker, and had come under CIB surveillance almost as soon as he joined the staff of Sai Gon University. Linh had weaned Lan Lan away from the sundry socialist causes she had espoused until then, and explained to her the wonders of applied Marxism. To think about changing things was not enough, and would never be enough, he told her. One had to act. He suggested she accompany him to a resistance training camp outside the city. Lan Lan had gone, and had become a believer. She started out as low-level courier, carrying messages from one dead drop to another, without ever meeting an agent. After a few months, she was judged reliable and called back for more training. It so happened Tuan was visiting the camp that week. They met, and it was love at first sight. Hai looked at the dossier on Lan Lan's father, Mai Huu Hoang. He knew that his real father, Lord Bach, had been Hoang's principal business partner long before Dien Bien Phu. Since his father's death in 1964, Hoang had carried on alone. A dollar millionaire, he headed the TVB group of companies, a giant conglomerate that was into shipping, construction, real estate, mining, manufacturing and import-export. TVB stood for *Tout Va Bien*, or "all goes well" in French, and the company had been aptly named. It had been in the forefront of the South Vietnamese economy since the turn of the century, when the South was still known as Cochin-China and the *Banque de L'Indo-Chine* was the repository of its fortune. TVB had doubled in size by 1963, after President Diem's assassination and Lord Bach's death. Hoang had entered the construction business as a sub-contractor for a giant US conglomerate, Raymond Morrison Knudsen-Brown Root & Jones. RMK-BRJ was well connected at White House level and regularly won most of the DOD contracts to build, operate and maintain US bases in South Viet Nam. TVB's income had doubled again after Hoang had formed a joint venture with an American-run German company in Hamburg. Needless to say, he was very close to the Palace. He had supported President Diem and his coterie, Premier Ky and his clique and now supported President Thieu and his mafia. He operated like a typical overseas Chinese tycoon, supporting whatever regime was in power in return for special licenses and contracts that brought in even more money. Lan Lan, his only child, was the result of his marriage to Mey Li Li, a beautiful Cantonese singer he had met in Hong Kong. Li Li had left when Lan Lan was only five years old, but the girl had lacked for nothing. The best French education at the *Couvent des Oiseaux* in

Da Lat, a cool hill station favored by the rich in summer, then private tutors at home in Can Tho, a major town in the delta, and now Sai Gon University's Department of Political Science. She hoped to teach at the University. Last year, when she was twenty, she had had her first serious relationship with a boy. Not just any boy, but a ranking communist cadre, Tuan.

He placed Lan Lan's dossier to his left, picked up the second folder, marked "Nguyen Van Tuan, VM, sapper". Inside, a large photograph showed a tough looking young man, with a square, angular face. His wore his hair long, like a civilian, but it wasn't difficult to imagine him with the typical Viet Cong guerrilla haircut. Short back and sides, long on top, with a thatch of hair that bobbed down all around the head, not unlike the overhanging eaves of a bamboo hut. A very northern Vietnamese face, with high cheekbones, the eyes only slightly slanted, the nostrils flared, the mouth large and well shaped. What made him look tough was the fire in his eyes and a large jaw. He had long earlobes, a sign of longevity. His father had been a peasant named Thao, who had joined the Viet Minh in the early thirties, when communism had just begun to appear in Viet Nam. Thao had been a porter for some ten years until the battle of Dien Bien Phu, when he was drafted into digging the trenches that the Viet Minh needed to choke off the heavily defended French outposts one by one. His son Tuan had been trained as a guerrilla after joining the militia, and had been sent across the Demilitarized Zone in 1965. Tuan had first distinguished himself in an ambush of US and ARVN Special Forces in Quang Tri province, and then again in a ground attack against Camp Holloway, an American logistics base in Cam Ranh peninsula. In between he had proven himself as a reliable and able field commander on a number of occasions. He had received a battlefield promotion to the rank of junior lieutenant and was later decorated for initiative and bravery. Retrained in the tunnels of Cu Chi for infiltration work in the capital, he had met Lan Lan in one of the Viet Cong training camps north of the capital, and, against orders and common sense, they had fallen in love. Once in the capital, they had become lovers. In the communist underground context, this was a most unusual story because in the communist system each cadre has a minder. The slightest deviation from the Party line or operational orders had to be reported. And yet Tuan had managed to conduct a year-long affair with Lan Lan. Given the nature of the communist system, he was either lucky beyond belief or cunning as a fox. Hai suspected it was the latter.

The third folder contained a full-face photograph of an intelligent looking man in his thirties with a sardonic expression on his face, and was marked "Tran Dinh Linh, VM, terrorist". Long wavy hair falling across a high forehead and curling around his shoulders, an aquiline nose, a firm mouth, slightly squinted eyes. Obviously not a foot soldier. He gave the impression of being strong of character, and arrogant. This was the son of Tran Dinh Nam, the French-educated Minister of Public Work and Highways, a protégé of the late President Diem, a Catholic and a long time advocate of realigning Viet Nam with France. Father and son had broken up long ago, with Linh slowly drifting further and further to the Left. Like Tuan, Linh had received his training at Phoumi Dak Dam, a NLF camp just across the Cambodian border. His cover was that of a stringer for a Seventh Day Adventist magazine, *The Awakening*, whose publisher, the Reverend Donald McChristie, was a member of the 'in' group that revolved around the Lyndon B. Johnson Presidential ranch in Texas. Vietnamese police attempts to curtail the activities of the magazine had received immediate although discreet criticism from the US Embassy. This reaction had been channeled through no less than the Presidential Palace. The American establishment in South Viet Nam, in its ignorance and naïvete, was protecting a known terrorist. Not for the first time, certainly not for the last, either. But there was someone else of importance also interested in protecting Linh. Hai had received discreet feelers from Hanoi, not once but twice, that suggested that the communists were willing to do a trade should Linh ever be caught. He was told the terms of the trade could be very favorable for the CIB. It was not unusual for the two sworn enemies to make secret deals to protect valuable agents from being executed after questioning. These feelers had come from a source that Hai trusted implicitly. No reason was given, of course. It was too early for that. Would Linh know who his protector was? Would his father know? Or perhaps his mother? He leaned back in his chair again, and looked at the ceiling once more, his legs twitching incessantly.

55

Lan Lan

Hai picked up the fourth dossier, marked "Pham Van Phu, VM, spy". The photograph showed a nondescript, middle-aged man who could have been a small time salesman. The plant, a full ARVN colonel, had been appointed special adviser on military affairs to the President. It seemed they had met during the years the President had spent in the Viet Minh resistance movement, in the late '30s, before leaving it, joining the French Army and converting to Catholicism. The link had been kept alive and Phu was now in the Palace, another untouchable as far as the CIB was concerned. A northerner with a long history of anti-French, anti-Diem and now anti-American activities behind him, he was a born plotter, a man who had lived many lives, all of them in the shadows.

On December 1, CIB agents had intercepted a Viet Cong agent named Huan on his way to meet US Embassy officials. Hai glanced at the photograph, which showed an older man, with graying hair, a cunning face and calculating eyes. This was no university student. This was a high-level agent and the CIB didn't report his arrest to the CIO at first. At CIB headquarters, Huan admitted that he had been sent to meet with CIA officials operating out of the US Embassy. The subject of the meeting was peace talks with the NLF. Jonathan had sworn that he and his team knew nothing about this operation, and Hai believed him. Twelve years after the Americans had become involved in Viet Nam, the situation at the US Embassy had hardly changed. Factional infighting permeated all the divisions, but especially the intelligence community. There was the O'Leary faction, older men who had run foreign agents in the Middle East and South America, which basically focused on Viet Nam, to include the North. There was the Sharkey faction, headed by O'Leary's deputy for operations, Robert Sharkey, which focused mainly on Cambodia, where the NLF headquarters were located. Then there was the Winthrop faction, which focused on analytical work, whether Vietnamese, Laotian or Cambodian. Each faction head had a strong personality, was professionally competent but had a problem with teamwork. Each man had solid political and bureaucratic support at headquarters in Virginia. Jonathan, because of his father, also had solid backing at Department of State level. Each faction beavered away independently of one another, reporting separately to the new Chief of Station, "Shotgun" Bob Kilmer, who seemed to like compartmentalization. Ironically, the most hawkish of the three was Jonathan, who was supposed to be a back-room boy, analyzing documents and pushing papers. Hai reviewed briefly the saga of hawks becoming doves and wondered about Jonathan's future. McNamara, a hawk who had turned into a dove at the wrong time, had been booted sideways to head up the World Bank. Clifford, always a dove but now a hawk had been named the new secretary of defense. Wonder when he'll turn back into a dove again.

On December 6, after five days of intense speculation in the American media, the US State Department broke its silence to concede that a NLF representative had indeed been stopped by a RVN security agency on his way to meet with US officials in Sai Gon. Lost in thought, Hai looked at the transcript before him. If the Americans are secretly talking to the VC and you are not, where does that leave you when America decides to stop fighting the Vietnam war? The signs are already there. If only the White House can find an honorable way out. If we stop them talking to each other here, they can talk to each other in Paris. They are probably doing that already. The French have a direct line to Ho, they're always ready to arrange for such discreet meetings. Étienne has already been at it for some time. Must check with him on this. Sharing power with the VC is like sharing power with the VM. There's no difference between the two. We're where we are because the ARVN has the manpower, the Americans the firepower, but the communists have the willpower. We're carpet bombing our territory, mining our rice fields, defoliating our forests, decimating our population. This wholesale destruction has undermined our morale, our determination is beginning to waver. The Americans are ambivalent because they say the ARVN is militarily incompetent, but if so they have only themselves to blame. They arbitrarily decided to take over all major ground operations; now that they are not winning any more than the French were in the fifties, they're blaming us while turning moist eyes towards the enemy. Talk about *déjà vu.*

He looked at the clock on the wall. It was two o'clock in the morning. He stood up, walked around the office, then stood on the carpet, knees slightly flexed, shoulders relaxed, pelvis thrust forward, and began his breath control exercises, learned in the days when he had joined the communist resistance in the Viet Bac. After a while, he began moving his arms rhythmically as he breathed in and out through the nose. He moved and turned about in almost dream-like slowness, his body becoming light and transparent. These slow, controlled *chi gong* movements helped guide *chi*, the cosmic energy, through the channels that acupuncturists use. Every cell in the body is rejuvenated through *chi gong* and lost energy is replenished in a matter of twenty minutes. Having done his morning exercises, he sat down and drank a cup of tea, then ate a mango. That was breakfast. He then brushed his teeth and urinated, then sat down at his desk. Orders had to be prepared for Colonel Dao. The operational plan was to be divided into four phases.

Phase one concerned the extraction of the CIB moles from the North once they had confirmed the alternative attack scenarios prepared by PAVN military planners for the Military Committee of the Politburo to choose from. The extraction mechanism had been in place for some time and could be activated at a moment's notice.

The second phase was the finalization of preparations for the CIB pre-emptive strikes. In each province, special CIB teams had selected specific targets to be attacked and taken out once the code word came through. Heavily armed undercover agents, equipped with the latest Motorola communications equipment, would fan out on foot, in unmarked cars and buses, head for the communist safe houses and shoot to kill. Communist agents marked for questioning would have to be debriefed on site, to keep the momentum of the counter attacks flowing. Each team carried a portable generator for this purpose.

The third phase was the location and destruction of the Tran Dinh Linh cells already in the Sai Gon suburbs. Linh himself moved around every other day and had avoided arrest so far. But CIB informants had pinpointed three safe houses he would use at the start of the New Year. One was a doctor's residence, near the Presidential Palace. Another was at a go-down at the docks in Cho Lon, the Chinatown adjacent to the city. A third one was the house where Lan Lan's father lived. He was in Hong Kong for the week, and Lan Lan had the house to herself and an army of servants. CIB informants had sighted Tuan leaving the same house at dawn on two occasions. Hai was waiting for last minute information on Linh's movement. Strict orders had been given that Linh was not be killed. If Ha Noi valued Linh he would trade, but he would squeeze him first, then embed a time bomb in his mind before he sent him back. He had other plans for Linh.

The fourth phase of the plan concerned the kidnapping of Colonel Pham Van Phu, the mole at the Presidential Palace. He had been sent an invitation to attend a US-Viet Nam cocktail at the American Ambassador's residence on the 29th of January, on the eve of *Tet*. He would be asked to make a speech after the Ambassador had toasted the President Thieu. What Phu did not suspect was that it was Hai who had engineered the invitation, through Jonathan Winthrop. His name had not been on the original list presented to the Ambassador by the Embassy's social secretary. Upon leaving the reception, Phu's car would be boxed in on his way home and he would be snatched by the CIB. Hai had plans for Colonel Phu. He would make him disappear from the face of the earth.

He re-read his instructions carefully, making a correction here and there. Finally, he was satisfied that the pre-emptive measures he wanted to take had been covered, and he placed his unsigned instructions in a plastic folder marked "Dao: for action". This was a code for Colonel Dao to clean up the copy destined to his American advisor and to destroy the originals by 0900 hrs. The copy for Jonathan, also unsigned, was to be unedited. He knew that Jonathan would pass on only what he thought he should. They had both made up their minds they would work in unison, at their respective levels, and that they would level with each other as much as possible but would observe discretion with their superiors, especially the ones who didn't see things their way.

There was one more thing to do. Long ago, having learned the technique from the Viet Minh in the post-*Citadelle* days, Hai had taken care to set up his own disposal unit. Discreet sites had been selected in the countryside where aluminum cylinders, welded at both ends, could be buried vertically. Holes two meters deep had been dug and then covered up with topsoil. A disposal team had been handpicked and trained secretly. Heavily armed, using swift vans, they quickly dispersed into the countryside at nightfall, lowering the cylinders into the holes, tamping the earth down hard, covering it with bushes and returning by dawn to CIB headquarters. The Viet Minh had wrapped the bodies in old blankets or reed mats. The aluminum cylinders had been Hai's own contribution to this simple and effective way of removing people from the face of the earth. He wrote out the names of the people to be disposed of. At the head of the list was Colonel Phu. Then he put the instructions in a plastic folder marked: "My: for action". Lieutenant My had been in charge of the COB disposal system for the last three years and hadn't put one foot wrong all this time. He had come up from the ranks and was due for promotion by year's end. Hai got up and walked to the military cot. He had done his work for the night. He lay back and fell into a sound and dreamless sleep.

56

Surprise Attack

At noon of Monday, January 29th, Hai received a phone call from the CIB station chief in Hue, the old Imperial capital and the northernmost major city in the Republic of Vietnam.

"New calendar for the rat, old calendar for the mouse," said Colonel Bich, whose mother-in-law's brother was a PAVN officer in charge of logistics. He didn't want his sister and her family to get caught in the surprise attack. In the new lunar calendar, the eve of *Tet* in the years 1968, 1969 and 1985 would fall on the 29th of January, while in the old calendar, it fell on the 30th. The PAVN forces already infiltrated below the DMZ would launch their attacks in central Viet Nam and the coastal provinces in the early hours of January 30th, while the VC would attack throughout the South in the early hours of January 31st. Hai breathed out a long sigh of relief. At last, the long wait was over. The capital had another twenty-four hours. He now knew when the mouse was going to move and he was prepared to crush it into a pulp. He began to make series of coded phone calls, all about rats and mice. At the other end, hand-picked, seasoned officers listened in silence. After putting down the phone, they began to put the finishing touches to plans they had worked out months before and refined every two weeks until that day.

Hai met with Jonathan and rapidly briefed him.

"In Ha Noi, they're one day ahead of us. Today is their first day of the New Year. Tonight, after midnight, PAVN will launch coordinated attacks on our northern provinces, which they call their 5th Military Region. They are banking on us confusing the new attacks with the on-going battles at the DMZ and continuing to honor the truce.

Tomorrow, on our first day of *Tet*, they will attack the southern provinces after midnight. Sai Gon will come under ground attack after midnight tomorrow, early Wednesday morning. The bulk of US and ARVN troops have been on leave since yesterday, and won't be able to react until Thursday at the earliest. The exceptions are Generals Weyand and Sy, who have been in full agreement with me since November and have elected to remain on full alert. They're way outside of the capital, but can mobilize about 10 battalions to counter-attack by mid-day Wednesday. General Loan has some 300 NPD Field Force men deployed inside the city and can call on another 200 troops from ARVN Special Forces. CIB, using *Phoi Hop* PFF I flew in from Quang Ngai yesterday, can field 500. That makes 1,000 on our side available right away."

He paused and looked at his American friend. He saw a very worried man. One emotion chased the other around his face. Hai couldn't help laughing inwardly. Westerners are so poker-faced when they talk about anything, while we Asians contort our faces to show pleasure, pain, hope, and end up looking obsequious. Yet in times of stress we become inscrutable, while their faces open up to reflect every emotion that is passing through their mind.

"In addition to these troops, we have MAC-V's 716th MP Battalion and ARVN's MP Battalion inside the city limits. With three-quarters of their men on leave, they can field about 300 men each. That's about 1,600 armed men who can move about the city. We'll have to take care of about five VC battalions, between 2,000 to 2,500 heavily armed sappers, some of whom have already begun infiltrating the capital. We have five major targets the VC could be interested in, while you have 130 American installations in the greater Sai Gon area."

Jonathan blanched at the figures. He didn't have any doubt about the veracity of the information. Hai had always been precise as well as correct in his assessment of a situation. The *Tet* truce now really appeared in all its ghastly stupidity. Westmoreland's downgrading of the NLF threat had come home to roost.

"Have you told anybody about this?" he asked, finally. His voice sounded hollow.

"What do you mean, anybody? For six months now I've been telling my President, your Ambassador, our Chief-of-Staff, your Commanding General, the CIA, the CIO and the NPD about this coming offensive. No one paid any attention to my reports, except for Weyand, Sy and Loan," Hai answered with exasperation.

"I'm sorry I asked. I know what you've been doing, and I know how pig-headed my people can be. It seems to be the same on your side. What I meant was have you told anybody today?"

"Not yet. What's the use?"

"Jesus, it's that bad is it? What should I do?"

"Get out of your civvies, put on a uniform and get things moving. We have been appointed four-star generals by the will of God! Play general with what you have. I'll do the same on my side. As soon as you hear incoming rockets, retreat with the Ambassador to MAC-V. Alert all US troops in I, II, III and IV Corps. Stay in the basements. The VC will be using B-40 rockets launchers as well as RPG-9, and they can punch holes through walls. Carry a .45, and have a machine gun handy. Put a few hand grenades in your pocket. Stay on the radio so I can update you."

"From one general to another, what are you going to do?"

"Move out and around, watch the VC teams and co-ordinate with you and my people. I've been planning for this day for a long time. For the last three weeks, our CIB teams and Loan's boys have been arresting hundreds of VC agents on the outskirts of the capital. They pulled out three months ago for re-training and instructions and have been returning in bunches. Most of these returnees have been neutralized and I believe that will decrease the impact of the initial attack. In the next twenty-four hours, I am going to smash the ones that stayed behind in Sai Gon all this time. The incoming guerrilla forces need these snakeheads to guide them to their ammo caches in the suburbs and shantytowns, and then to lead them to their targets around the city. By the time it starts tomorrow, there may be 100 snakeheads in the city. After I neutralize them, the sappers who get into the city will have a hard time finding their way around, and once they have shot off the ammo they carry, they won't be able to re-supply. We can blunt their attacks on government targets this way, but I can do nothing about frustrated armed guerrillas running about, shooting at whatever they see. We just don't have the necessary personnel."

"And Lan Lan?"

"Small fry. As long as she doesn't get caught up in the crossfire, she'll be OK. I'll deal with her later. In fact, *we*'ll deal with her later," Hai said, stressing the "we".

As usual every year, for the Lunar New Year Festival, the different social communities in Sai Gon had melded into a massive party that would last three days and three nights, starting on the eve of *Tet*. This year there would be the additional bonus of a three-day truce. In the residential districts, where the rich lived, champagne parties blasted away into the night while well-dressed Vietnamese families and their foreign guests ate delicious *canapés,* drank expensive Scotch and puffed on Cuban cigars. Dozens of servants milled around. The women wore their best jewelry, and diamond rings flashed under the bright lights of crystal chandeliers as they waved their hands around, talking excitedly. The young be-bopped to the latest American dance tunes, stopping now and again to drink Cokes laced with whiskey, a habit they had picked up from American GI's. In the gardens, the German shepherd guard dogs had been chained up. Excited at the noise and the coming and goings of people, they barked without let up, adding to the unbearable noise level.

In the streets, in the shadows, beggars pushed and shoved each other to get at the garbage cans, which were overflowing with tidbits that had come from the main houses. They tipped up the beer cans, wine and whiskey bottles and sucked out the last drops, then helped themselves to the leftovers that piled up as the party went on. In rags and for the most part toothless, they danced around, singing in hoarse voices. It was *Tet,* the war had temporarily stopped, and it was time to have fun. It was time to remember the days when they had been young, when they had had families, jobs, money, and didn't know what begging was.

In the central shopping districts, on the first day of the Lunar New Year, the national party had already lasted one full day. Rich and poor, Vietnamese and American, everyone was determined to have fun. Never truly representative of Vietnamese society, Sai Gon had always represented the best and the worst of a dynamic port society. Part Chinese, part French, part Vietnamese, part American, it had always been wholly sybaritic. Known as 'the Paris of the East' in French days, it had become the Wild Wild East with the advent of the Americans. Thousands of cars, motorbikes, *cyclo-pousses* and bicycles jostled with hundreds of thousands of pedestrians, each fighting for vital space along the main arteries of the capital. The noise level was indescribable. Car horns blared continuously, trying to clear a path for themselves. Everyone was shouting and laughing at the top of his voice. Hundreds of GI bars, open night and day, poured out torrents of pop music at full blast, through open doors and windows. Outside the bars stood bevies of very young bargirls, skimpily dressed, with full makeup on. In the side streets, furtive fixers sold a variety of drugs at very competitive prices and child prostitutes gave blowjobs to clients standing up against the dirty walls, a look of pure bliss on their faces. American GI's were everywhere, drunk to varying degrees. Some rock-and-rolled with their girls, others drank from bottles they held in their hands. Vietnamese families, composed of twelve or more persons, held hands tightly as they walked along, desperately afraid of misplacing a toothless old grandfather or a myopic auntie. The baby of the family, bewildered by all this humanity and frightened by all this noise, screamed at the top of his shrill voice, tears flowing out of his eyes and snot from his nostrils. Everyone was out on the streets, dressed in their best clothes, drinking, smoking, yelling, dancing around. No one seemed to be going anywhere in a hurry. Occasionally, a National Police jeep, filled with armed policemen, siren blaring and roof lights flashing, churned through the dense crowd, followed closely by an American MP jeep with a swivel-mounted machine gun, with long ammunition belts clanking against the dashboard. Their radio units crackled and hissed as the officers spoke to other units nearby. They were heading for a bar fight that had gotten out of hand, or an accident, or maybe a killing. For them, this was a working night. But around them no one cared, and no one made an effort to let them through. From the top of tall buildings, strings of firecrackers that reached the ground blasted away without letup. For every twenty-five small firecrackers, one jumbo exploded with a thunderous sound, making everyone jump with crazy laughter. Just after midnight, it seemed as if the tempo of the festivities was increasing. Huge explosions were heard every now and again, coming from the suburbs, and it seemed that the number of giant jumbo firecrackers was increasing. Tracers began to light the sky, and many of the revelers thought the fireworks show was beginning.

It took some time before people began to realize that the sharp, flat tat-tat-tats were not firecrackers but AK-47s, a sound that everyone was well acquainted with. And the explosions were not giant firecrackers but explosives, not unlike bombs, with which the population was also very well acquainted. In central Sai Gon, the crowd became less noisy. People began looking at each other, their survival antennas tasting the air. Somewhere, someone switched a radio on. The National Broadcasting Station announcer was in hysterics. "We're under attack! We're under attack! We're under attack!" he kept on shouting, like a broken record played at maximum volume. The crowds around the radio fell silent. Many of the men were dazed and drunk, but the women weren't. Hysterical screams tore the air as they picked up their children or pulled their men away. The crowds began to break up, picking up speed as people realized, through a haze of alcohol and adrenaline, that something was wrong. Panic set in and the crowds began running in every direction, trampling over the very old and the very young. The streets of the capital cleared, as if by magic. The lights of the shopping district remained full on, highlighting the shoes, bags, debris and detritus that now littered the empty boulevards and deserted streets. Abandoned cars, doors wide open, stood grotesquely all over the boulevard, some halfway up on the pavements, where their owners had left them. In the suburbs, the rich had TVs, and one look at the anchor woman screaming that the VC were in the NBS building was enough to convince everyone to stop partying. Telephone lines burned through the city as everyone called everybody else to say that the VCs were in the capital, and houses snapped shut tight, all the lights being switched off as if by magic. The family dogs were pulled inside and tied up. No one wanted his dog to bark at the VC death squads as they came by. In the streets outside the mansions, the beggars scurried into holes in the wall and cardboard boxes. The VCs were unlikely to want anything from them, but they didn't want to get caught in the crossfire. Not one military, Vietnamese or American, could be seen anywhere. The National Police had also disappeared. The nightmare people had lived with for so long had become a reality. It was one o'clock in the morning of January 31, 1968, and the attack on Sai Gon had begun.

By 0230 hrs, in various parts of the battened down city, hesitantly at first, heads appeared from the darkness, from behind low walls and hedges, like hyenas sniffing the air. Squads and then platoons of men, all dressed in black peasant pajamas, with white, yellow or red armbands, appeared from the shadows. They grouped in small bunches, whistles blew and they loped off silently towards specific targets throughout the burning city. All wore the Ho Chi Minh sandals, made out of tire material, and over their shoulders hung bandoleers of ammunition and AK-47 assault rifles. The group leaders wore a yellow headband and ran on ahead of their men. The flat, slap-slap-slapping sounds of their rubber-tire sandals beating in perfect unison on the asphalt could be heard distinctly in the houses they ran by, like packs of wolves. Inside, the inhabitants' greatest fear was to hear the slapping sounds stop. This meant a search, and everyone had heard horror stories from provincial capitals that been temporarily taken over by the VCs. The death squads had lists of enemies of the people and collaborators, and they winkled them out one by one, leading them out into the street, making them kneel down, shooting them point blank through the head, blowing it apart like a ripe water melon.

In the central district, recently the scene of bacchanalian revelries, a group of guerrillas appeared, silhouetted against a department store. They moved swiftly but silently to the main street, Tu Do, Freedom Street, known by generations of French settlers as Rue Catinat in kinder times when Sai Gon had been the Paris of the East. More men appeared, hand signals could be seen, then a shrill whistle pierced the air. Immediately a large group of armed men formed up. They were for the most part small in size, even boyish-looking. An older guerrilla read something out as they stood in disciplined silence, their eyes on him. Immediately above their heads hung a huge red neon sign that read "The Pink Pussy Bar". Below the name, the Vietnamese and American flags crossed, in colored neon, and the words "American GI number one!" flashed on and off, garishly lighting up the boys' faces. Another whistle rang out, and the men split up into two groups. One headed for the American Bachelor Officers Quarters near the City hall, the other for the Post Office near the Cathedral. For the inhabitants of the capital, the whistle said it all. The Viet Minh during the French war, and now the Viet Cong during the American war all used whistles and trumpets to coordinate their troops. By 0300 hrs of the 31st, VC guerrillas had penetrated into the heart of the capital of the Republic of Viet Nam. The PAVN's Winter-Spring Offensive, the so-called *Tet* Offensive, dismissed with casual arrogance by American and ARVN generals and talked down by the President and the US Ambassador, had materialized in full force. Within hours, the international media was flashing a blow-by-blow account of the mind-boggling development around the capitals of the world. Washington was stunned and the White House phone line to the US Ambassador in the republic of Viet Nam burned all through the night.

The previous afternoon, well before the guerrilla forces had surfaced inside the capital, CIB teams had fanned out in civilian clothes and unmarked cars. They had rehearsed these dragnet operations many times before. Absolute radio silence was to be observed. The communist cells had sophisticated Russian communications equipment inside their safe houses and could eavesdrop on police and military channels. By 1800hrs, the CIB hit teams were in position. Some struck at once, others waited till 1900hrs. They kicked down flimsy doors, smashed their way through barred windows, shot their targets at point-blank range. Those they needed to keep alive for questioning were gagged and tied up to a chair. The aim was to find out if there had been any last minute change of plans, and where specific arms caches were. The arresting officers knew that when the Tiger General said at once, he meant immediately, and they had perfected shock interrogation techniques. Each group had a portable generator. It was rare that a prisoner did not give up everything he had on his mind within the first two minutes of interrogation. By 2200hrs, over sixty members of the NLFI had been neutralized, with the remaining number being actively hunted down, street by street. Radio reports kept the Tiger General informed as the list was whittled down, one by one. By 2330hrs, all except for eight had been accounted for.

At 2100hrs, when the capital was in full swing, Hai boarded an unmarked car and headed to the Chinatown go-downs. At the *arroyo Chinois,* near the docks, by the evil-smelling river, his bodyguards and he got out and began walking towards the dockside warehouses. It was dark, and they followed their guide, an informer Hai had used before. After a while, in the dark, they climbed in between filthy bales of goods to be loaded, stacks of moldy old ropes and the odds and ends that litter a go-down. The fetid effluvia of the thick brown sludge that passed for river water hung like a curtain in the air. Large, mangy rats clambered about, totally unimpressed by human beings. The guide pointed to a figure sitting on a box, almost ten meters away, casually smoking a cigarette and looking at the turgid river. Hai nodded, and one of his men raised a crossbow he had brought along for silent neutralization. He fitted a steel-tipped arrow and took aim. After an eternity, he pulled the trigger. A loud twang was heard, followed immediately by a thunk, and the man toppled forward into the water. They didn't even hear the dull, muted sound he made when he hit the thick, muddy waters. The noise of New Year's eve dominated the star-filled night sky, with firecrackers and car horns drowning out the drunken revelers. Every now and then, a megawatt blast tore through the town, dulling the ears. They resumed moving forward, silently. The guide pointed again.

Another man was standing further along the quay, partly hidden by a broken wall against which he was urinating. Twelve meters away. Up came the crossbow, out came another arrow. There was another long wait. The man was shaking his penis, and about to return it to its normal place. Twang, thunk. He slid onto his knees, clutching at the wall. It hadn't been a clean shot. One of the CIB men silently ran up to him, clapped one hand over his mouth and slipped a blade into the man's kidney with the other. The guide signaled the road was now clear, and they walked past the dead man towards what looked like a small shed, but was actually the entrance to a large room in which seven men were sitting around a table. Kerosene pressure lamps hissed and burned in front of them, filling the room with the smell of burnt fuel. There were ashtrays on the table, filled to the rim with cigarette butts. Teacups and teapots were everywhere. A military radio post was on the table, crackling away, its static clearly audible. Four telephones sat on the table, all of them in front of the man called Linh. He was talking to someone on the phone, looking down at the table. He had both elbows on the table, his chin resting against one fist while the phone was cradled to his ear.

Hai slipped through the door into the room like a cat. In his hand he held a Walther PPK fitted with a silencer. The first man to see him froze, unable to believe that anyone could have reached the hut without being cut down by the guards outside. Then he jerked involuntarily and reached for his gun, which was on the table in front of him. At the last moment his hand froze, his eyes locked onto Hai's large, protruding cat's eyes. The others looked up, their jaws dropping. This slim man with the large eyes had appeared like a ghost. They all knew about him but it was the first time they had seen him in the flesh. It was an unnerving sight. Hai was already at the table, his gun covering all of them. He thrust the gun towards Linh.

"You want to die now?" he asked softly.

Linh looked up into his shiny, rather wet eyes, flecked with yellow, which were swiveling slowly from left to right. Imperceptibly, he shook his head.

Hai made a small jerking motion with his gun and they all put their hands up. Behind him, the bodyguards, two of them with sub-machine guns in their hands, moved to handcuff the seven high-ranking cadres. Their eyes and mouths were taped. With another flick of his gun, Hai sent Linh and two others out. He then stepped behind the other four and shot each man in the back of the head. They fell against the table, smashing the teapots and scattering the ashtrays. Cigarette butts flew everywhere. Another huge jumbo cracker tore the night sky outside, and a chorus of drunken yells and shouts accompanied it. He joined his men outside, and they all walked back to the van that was waiting for them. He looked inside at the three men and nodded. He then climbed into his car.

"Tuan's next," he said to the driver.

57

A Long Night

Hai looked at his watch. It was almost 2300hr. Perfect. Their unmarked car turned into an alley and he got out. The alley was full of people talking, laughing and horsing around. No one paid any attention to the CIB team. They moved ahead, again with a guide. The houses were all made of bricks and were nicely painted. At no. 43, a one-story house with small garden, the team paused. Two men ran to the back, while one affixed a small cake of explosive to the lock of the front door. It blew the door inward and they rushed in, with Hai in the lead. He wanted Tuan, and he wanted him badly. A woman screamed, a baby wailed. The other two men had come in through the back windows. They all stood around, looking at each other. Tuan was not there. They searched the house from top to bottom. They asked the woman where Tuan was, describing him. She said she knew him as Minh, not Tuan, and that a taxi had come for him at eight o'clock. That bastard must have been warned. By whom? Within minutes, an all-points bulletin was flashed to all NPD checkpoints. With a sinking feeling in his stomach, Hai looked at his watch. It was time to return to headquarters. The attack would start in another hour or so, and Tuan had slipped the net. What was his target? Outside, a crowd had gathered. Silence hung in the air as the CIB team walked out with the woman and her baby and bundled them into an unmarked van.

Once inside his office, he had barely sat down when Colonel Dao rang to say that Operation PVP was complete. Hai got up at once and walked to the interrogation room at the end of the corridor. Guards saluted smartly as he passed. The interrogation room was large, air-conditioned, all tiled in white. Glass cupboards lined the walls, and inside were all types of drugs and syringes and swabs. Between the cupboards stood state-of-the-art machines and equipment used to interrogate a prisoner and to determine the veracity of what he said. Wall cameras, overhead cameras, microphones and tape recorders were everywhere. All sessions were taped, and CIB experts, trained in the US and assisted by Vietnamese-speaking American advisors, would review them again and again to make sure nothing had been missed. During interrogation time, and especially when force was being used, most of the senior American advisors would withdraw to the next room, from which they could still hear what was going on over the intercom. A few hard-core US advisers would stay on with the Vietnamese interrogators, who would apply interrogation techniques authorized in the US Army's MIS manuals as well as a few techniques of their own that were not in the US manuals.

The interrogation team, composed of Vietnamese CIB and Special Branch officers and their American advisors, had withdrawn to the adjoining room to give the Tiger General a free hand. A high, narrow gurney, the kind used by paramedics at accident scenes, stood in the middle of the room, and a naked man was strapped down on it. Hai approached and looked at Colonel Pham Van Phu, the target of Operation PVP. Their eyes locked. Hai's, protruding and yellow-flecked, were expressionless. Phu's, flat, black and hard, were full of hatred and defiance. He spat at Hai, but was too weak to shoot the spittle out and it dribbled down his chin. A brave man, not afraid to die. Deserves to die standing up, and he will. He fought the good fight but he lost, and in our games losers always die. If *papa* was right, Phu's death will contribute to the progress of mankind. Like me when my turn comes. If it comes. He raised his hand and Colonel Dao handed him the interrogation transcript. He glanced at it, speed reading through the four pages, nodding to himself. You were right all along; this man is really high ranking. He's exactly what you thought he would be.

"Dispose of him," he said to Colonel Dao. He saluted, and Hai left the room. He now had to worry about Tuan and his suicide commandos. Assuming the US Embassy is still their target, where are they all now?

Back in his office, piles of reports had begun to come in from the field by fax, telex and radio. He sat down and read through them steadily. In the northern provinces, CIB hunter-killer teams had moved six hours before the deadline imposed by the 7th time zone and had decimated the NLFI in the provincial capitals and larger district towns before evacuating according to plan. By midnight of January 29th, they had gathered up their moles and flown them by helicopter to Da Nang, where large US bases offered relative safety. A total of 465 high-ranking cadres and some 300 low-ranking VC had been killed, 100 more than had been targeted. No prisoners had been taken. ARVN and American forces had been notified of the CIB operations after the CIB evacuation had begun. Hai smiled to himself. Move quietly. Hit hard. Your boys are good, very good. All that training and discipline have paid off. They always do. You learned that in your resistance days. Also on that night under the bridge. Hélène with an iron bar in her hand; the crumpled skull. Hai returned to his reports.

Further south, which had kept to the 8th time zone, a similar picture appeared. 600 cadres had been killed, 150 more than had been targeted. No prisoners had been taken. CIB agents had regrouped in Cam Ranh, a deep-water port the USN now used as a logistical supply point. In the south and southwest, only 340 communist cadres had been killed out of 640 targeted. 300 had slipped out into the countryside before the CIB raids, indicating a leak in the system. Hai felt his jaw tighten and his eyes narrowed to pinpoints. That leak has to be plugged. The bastard must regret he had ever been born. He then let go of this negative thought and returned his mind to analyzing the results so far obtained by the CIB boys. He drank some tea. In the North and the Center, one hundred percent success. In the Mekong Delta, only fifty percent. That will have to be remedied, after the offensive. The phone rang at 0300 hrs. He picked it up. It was Jonathan. He sounded excited and was yelling into the mouthpiece.

"The Palace, the US Embassy, the NBS, the ARVN and Naval HQS and Tan Son Nhut Airport are all under attack as I speak. Various US BOQs are also under attack. The VC are using hand-held rocket launchers and rifle-propelled grenades. What's your report?"

Hai gave him an overview of the situation, as seen from the CIB viewpoint, and asked him where he was.

"We're all at MAC-V HQS," Jonathan said, calmer now. "They can shell us all they want, but they can't break in. We've got all the firepower we need. Westy's using the 716th MP battalion and the USAF 377th Security Police Squadron as mobile forces to relieve American installations under attack, but the VCs were waiting for them to leave their compound and ambushed them. Reports coming in say the provincial capitals have been hit pretty hard. There's no getting away from it, we've been caught with our pants down. You were right all along."

"Thanks. A bit late now. What's happening at the Embassy?"

"MPs and Embassy Marine Security report that one Citroen sedan, one Peugeot truck and one taxicab unloaded nineteen sappers outside the Embassy at about 0245 hrs. They used B-40 rocket launchers to blow their way into the Embassy building. Four American and one Vietnamese security guards dead so far. Westy's ordered the 716th to retake the Embassy but the unit they sent got pinned down in an alley not far from here."

"Any word from the 25th Infantry in Cu Chi?"

"Yes, Weyand is gearing up to move, but he can't get his act together until dawn tomorrow. As you predicted, he is teaming up with Sy. They're having a hard time mobilizing enough helicopters to ferry the troops in, and it looks as if by the time they arrive the airport will have been taken by the VC, so they'll have to fight for the airport first. There are three heavily armed VC battalions attacking it from three sides right now. Do you have any plans?"

"Yes. I have to make sure CIB Headquarters is not overrun. I'm keeping 100 men and two heavy machineguns here. I was ordered by the Joint Chiefs of Staff to send 200 men to the Palace. I have 200 men roaming around the city. Five are at the NBS right now and I'm sending twenty to the US Embassy."

"The Embassy? What's your interest there?"

"There's one guerrilla I want, and he's the one leading the suicide commandos. You might be interested in him too. He's Lan Lan's lover."

"Oh, shit. Where's Lan Lan? I talked to her this morning. Sorry, yesterday morning. She said she was staying home because her dad was in Hong Kong. I invited her to an Embassy bash but she said no."

"I'm not surprised. Tuan was with her all day yesterday. They had an argument, he decided to commit suicide with his squad, to atone for breaking orders and because he felt there's no hope for them. She's rich, he's poor, that sort of thing. He was only supposed to guide the squad to the Embassy, not stay with them."

"Holy mother of God! How do you know all this shit? Were you under the bed when they were screwing?" shouted Jonathan.

"No. It's simpler than that. I have a maid inside the Hoang mansion working for us. Tuan left a letter that devastated Lan Lan. She's been crying ever since. I've got the letter here."

"That explains it. Over the phone, I could hear that she was very upset about something. I told her "It's *Tet*! It's time to party!" and she said something like 'It's OK for you Americans to party any time, but we Vietnamese have many sorrows'. I didn't know what she was talking about. Should I make contact with her?"

"No. Leave things alone till we retake Sai Gon. We'll both talk to her then. I have to talk to her father very seriously. But right now we've got to concentrate on the important things. It's going to be a long night."

He settled down to his command and control responsibilities as intelligence data continued to pour in by phone and by telex. His aides had come in and were all around him, cutting and pasting the relevant snippets of information and presenting them to him as he talked to field agents on the phone. The office was like a madhouse but there was a method to the madness. The hours ticked away, minute by minute. Reports showed that the VC guerrillas were interested in six main targets. Tan Son Nhut Airport, the Presidential Palace, the American Embassy, the National Broadcasting Station and the Vietnamese JCS and Naval HQS. The airport was on the edge of the city proper, and could be reached directly from the countryside. No guidance was needed. Three VC battalions were attacking it. The other five main targets were well inside the city, because the city had grown around them over the years, and VC forces from the countryside needed guidance to find them and approach them from the right side. Surprisingly few VCs were used to attack them, and once they ran out of ammunition, a stalemate ensued. The defenders couldn't break out, the attackers couldn't break in. The infiltrators had entered the city in small groups and, without guides, were having problems regrouping. Much needed reserve ammunition was also not coming through the pipeline. Obviously, there had been a lack of guides and back-up support. Hai felt his heart smile. Chopping off the snakeheads was like cutting them off at the knees.

While talking on the phone, he leafed through the updated reports, which now showed a pattern.

At 0130 hrs, the Presidential Palace was attacked with mortars, B-40 rockets and a truck laden with explosives; the President had left by helicopter for an undisclosed ARVN base. Stalemate.

At 0200 hrs, sappers attacked the ARVN JCS HQS, near the airport; they were repulsed and regrouped for a second attack. Inconclusive results.

At 0246 hrs, VC commandos blasted their way into the US Embassy compound and main building, using B-40 rockets; they penetrated the lower floors of the building but ran out of rockets; fighting continued with rifles and pistols. Stalemate.

At 0255 hrs, 12 sappers blew a hole in the Vietnamese Naval HQS on Bach Dang quay and entered the main building; 10 VC were killed instantly, 2 were captured. VC defeat.

At 0255 hrs, the NBS was attacked by VC guerrillas dressed as Vietnamese riot police; they killed a platoon of ARVN paratroopers with machinegun fire and occupied the broadcasting station. VC victory.

At 0400 hrs, US Marines and MPs were dispatched to the Vietnamese National Police to escort them to the US Embassy to assist; they refused to leave their station. Having sent most of their men to help defend the Palace, they were undermanned and feared a ground attack on their HQS. The Vietnamese MPs, when contacted for the same purpose, had only 25 men available out of the 300 supposedly on guard duty. *Tet* truce stupidity.

At 0408 hrs, 716th MP Battalion alert force and MP Unit C9A, sent to relieve a BOQ under attack, were ambushed in a narrow alley by VC armed with B-40 and heavy machine gun; subsequent reinforcements also pinned down. VC victory.

At 0600 hrs, advance American and ARVN troops blasted away the 269th, 267th and 213th VC battalions at the airport and entered Saigon. They rushed to MAC-V and ARVN JCS HQS to relieve the defenders there. Weyand and Sy had moved much more quickly than anticipated. VC defeat.

At 0855 hrs, the 14 VC still alive in the surrounded National Broadcasting Station blew themselves up, damaging most of the equipment; within three hours, ARVN electronics experts had restored communications facilities. Government announcers then warned the people a total, citywide curfew has been imposed by General Sy. Anyone seen on the streets would be shot on sight. VC defeat.

Throughout the night and well into the next morning, groups of heavily armed VC guerrillas were sighted running aimlessly around the city. Every now and then, they knocked down a door to ask the terrified homeowners for directions. They were looking for various US and Government installations and it was obvious they hadn't a clue as to where they were. Some of the residents were forced to lead the guerrillas to their assigned targets, where they were shot out of hand.

In the suburbs, where Government civil servants lived, small groups of VC elimination squads went from house to house, with lists of names and addresses in their hands. The door was forced open, and officials whose names were on the list were dragged out and shot on the spot. The targets were civil servants, police officers and collaborators, a term that covered anyone who worked for the Americans.

Undercover CIB and NPD agents deployed by General Loan roamed the suburbs and shantytowns of Sai Gon and Cho Lon, blending into the street population, on the lookout for secret supporters and sympathizers who surfaced now that the attack had begun. Disguised as pedicab drivers, peasants on their way to the morning market, street hawkers, beggars and common criminals, they identified targets and reported by pocket radio. At CIB HQS, Hai's aides assiduously noted names and locations for future action. Hai looked through these notes with satisfaction. Unless these secret sympathizers withdraw with the VC guerrillas when the time comes, they're dead meat. They've come out into the open, the bastards, and they're going to get chopped in the neck.

By 0915 hrs the US Embassy was declared secure. Four Vietnamese guards and five American MPs had been killed. Seventeen VC sappers were killed, one captured, one was missing. CIB agents, camped outside the Embassy grounds since the attack began, had been following the sporadic firefights inside the seventeen-story building for seven hours. No one could have slipped through them during the night. They now examined the dead commandos. Tuan was not among them. They identified the captured sapper, who was dying. It was not Tuan.

Hai at once ordered that all hospitals and clinics in the area be searched. By 1000 hrs Tuan was found, with a bandaged head wound, in a 7th Day Adventist clinic nearby. American Marines retaking the Embassy had mistaken him for one of the Vietnamese security guards and had brought him to hospital. He was dazed, but could speak. Within minutes he was taken to CIB HQS and strapped down to a cot inside a small soundproof cell. A hard rubber bite-block was placed in his mouth, to stop him from committing suicide by biting off his tongue. In another cell nearby was Linh, also with a bite-block in his mouth.

All day long, a far away high-pitched humming noise could be heard in the sky, interspersed with rocket and machinegun fire. Hundreds of helicopters hovered above the airport, waiting for their turn to land and disgorge ARVN troops. Truckload after truckload of soldiers then roared into the city to relieve the US and Government installations still under attack. Some had been fighting for ten hours straight.

Throughout the rest of the day, sporadic fighting continued here and there, with platoons of guerrillas attacking different targets at random, breaking off as soon as ARVN troops approached, to regroup further away and continue attacking targets of opportunity. The communist attack was losing steam now that the advance ARVN and American forces had returned in force to the capital, but independent guerrilla elements, coordinating with whistles and trumpets, continued to rampage throughout the huge city. They shot at obvious signs of the American presence, such as Coca Cola and Marlboro ads, the US Cultural Center and American cars parked on the streets.

At 1630 hrs, the VC troops holed up inside the Presidential Palace were finally crushed. 32 were killed, 2 were captured. The siege had lasted 15 hours.

At 2000 hrs, the 716th MP unit pinned down by the VC in an alley were rescued. 16 MPs had died and 21 were wounded. The fight had lasted 16 hours.

Above the deserted metropolis, American helicopter gunships darted and hovered like angry wasps in support of ARVN troops busy flushing out suicidal groups of guerrillas. Their searchlights probed in between houses for hidden guerrillas. On the ground, ARVN military trucks and jeeps careened around city, dropping off troops that ran down side-streets and alleys, ready to shoot at anything that moved. The city bristled with heavily armed troops. On the radio and TV, in between bursts of martial music, government announcers asked the population to stay indoors and to remain calm. Fires burned out of control among the shanties on the city's edge. Dense smoke enveloped the capital. Gunfire could be heard in different parts of the city, with an occasional rocket shell exploding.

58

Settling of Accounts

At dawn of February 2nd, a Thursday, ARVN Marines and Airborne troopers, assisted by the National Police, entered the capital in force. The President had returned to the Palace, which looked a little worse for wear, and had appeared on TV. He ordered the military to secure the capital. The sweeping operations began, with small, tough ARVN troops systematically cleaning out the remaining guerrillas, street by street. Hundreds of wounded or lost guerrillas were captured, mostly turned in by the population, which had found its courage again now that the national army had returned in force. By evening of February 2nd, the capital was declared secure and the curfew was lifted. The ARVN now turned its attention to Cho Lon, Sai Gon's sister city and the home of the ethnic Chinese population. This had been the VC's fallback plan and they methodically pulled back from the wide boulevards, parks and tree-lined avenues of the capital proper towards Chinatown, with its dense population and rabbit-like maze of alleys.

Ha Noi's propaganda machine had predicted that the Saigonese would rise as one man to support the *Tet* Offensive, but in fact the population of the capital was actively helping the government troops in their block-by-block search-and-destroy operations. Even though the attack had taken place during a truce, and the element of surprise had been achieved, the resistance put up by the few Americans and Vietnamese troops on duty at key installations had been ferocious, temporarily slowing down the flow of the attack. Perhaps more important, the snake heads had not shown up at the designated meeting points in the suburbs as expected, the caches of ammunition hidden in the many safe houses had not been found and most of the commando units, running short of ammunition, had soon found themselves lost in a huge city that had turned hostile. Things had gone radically wrong for the communist forces, but, typically, they did not lose heart. Ready to die for the cause, they regrouped, reorganized and prepared for one last stand. Discipline was tightened, new orders were given. It was now time to punish the American imperialists, their puppet ARVN troops and cowardly supporters by inviting a rain of bombs onto the crowded urban centers of Chinatown and dying a glorious death in the process.

When curfew was lifted, Hai rang the house of Mai Huu Hoang, Lan Lan's father. It was eight in the evening. A relative answered the phone, then passed it to Lan Lan. Her father had just phoned to say he would return from Hong Kong by tomorrow noon. Was it urgent? Yes, she would tell her father to expect a visit from General Hai at three in the afternoon. Yes, she would make herself available for that meeting. What was it all about? Oh, business talk. Hai phoned Jonathan and asked him to attend the meeting the next day, at Hoang's residence. Jonathan sounded nervous and wanted to know more, but Hai cut him short, saying that he had other things to attend to.

He then sent his car for Tran Dinh Nam, the Minister of Public Works and Highway. They met in his office at around midnight. Nam had originally been a civil servant under the French in the North, before 1954, and had been reintegrated into the successive Diem and Thieu administrations, as had Hai. A technocrat by nature, he had learnt to survive by bending with the wind. A staunch Catholic, morally upright, he nevertheless continued to head the PW&H Ministry, which was recognized as the most corrupt ministry in the Government by far. It received limitless funds from American aid for projects that were never completed.

"Mr Nam, you've been in Government service a long time, you know what the CIB does, right?" Hai said quietly. Nam nodded. He looked tired, nervous, on the edge of a breakdown. Being a high-ranking civil servant, he hadn't slept for two nights, for fear of being visited by VC elimination squads.

"Do you know where your son Linh is?"

"No, I don't," answered Nam at once, his face clearing. He now understood what all this was about. He always knew Linh had had leftist tendencies while at University, and the CIB was an organization that was interested in leftists. "I haven't seen him for over two years. He never writes or phones. He doesn't even attend our family's death anniversaries."

"Mr Nam, your son is a high-ranking communist cadre who coordinates a number of cells in the capital. We arrested him last night. He has confessed to everything."

Hai paused for effect. Nam became very agitated. His voice rose.

"What's all that got to do with me? I haven't seen him for years. We never even speak to each other!"

"People don't know the relationship between your son and you. They only know that you are his father. Like father, like son, or vice versa. If I make public your son's confession, the President will fire you, and the CIB will have to investigate you as a potential communist sympathizer."

"Are you blackmailing me? You should know better than anyone that I have nothing to do with the communists! I'm a Catholic!" Nam's voice rose and sweat broke out on his forehead.

"So was your son, I believe. At least, he was baptized in a Catholic church in Ha Noi. Yes, I want to blackmail you, but not in the way you think. I will keep the problem of your son a secret if you will help me."

"Me, help you? How can I do that?" Incomprehension was written on his face.

"Mr Nam, I want you to think very carefully. Apart from Linh, is there anyone in your family, on your father's side, or your mother's, or your wife's, who is or has been a communist?"

Hai got up and fetched a glass of water and a tissue. Nam drank the water in one single gulp and wiped his brows. The tissue disintegrated. Hai got up and brought him back another.

"I hope I can trust your word. I don't want to lose my position, at least not until my daughter has graduated from University. I can think of only one person. When I was a boy, I knew that my father and his brother didn't get along. My father converted to Catholicism and worked in the French administration, my uncle left the family and we never heard from him again. He may have joined the resistance. This was in the 'thirties, when many young men left home to join the resistance."

That's true. The railway bridge, your first talk with Phong, the motivation talks at training camp. Back then, if you were young, the resistance was the only road.

"I know," Hai said. "Describe him to me."

"Medium height, slim, large forehead like my father. Long fingers. Very powerful voice."

"Any particular sign or characteristic that stands out?"

"Let me think...It's been such a long time. Yes...perhaps a scar on his forehead above his eyebrow. The right one, I think."

"How old would he be now?"

"Oh, I don't know. Let me see. He was younger than my father, so he could be in his seventies. I don't know. Why do you want to know? I have nothing to do with him," said Nam, perplexed.

"CIB business, Mr Nam. I thank you for your help, and I shall not make public what we know about Linh. That will be our secret. My car will take you home now, sir."

At three in the morning, Hai visited Tuan in his cell. In his hand, he had the interrogation report. Behind him stood his closest assistant, Colonel Dao. Tuan was awake. His face was closed, he refused to look at his jailers. The bite-block had been taken from his mouth. This was an indication that the interrogation had been successful. He could now do what he wanted with his life, including biting his tongue off and bleeding to death.

"Tuan, I understand why you hate us, why you did all this. I understand why you joined your suicide squad against orders. If I had been you, I would have done the same, and I wouldn't be afraid to die, as I know you are not," Hai said gently, in a fatherly tone. This approach intrigued Tuan, who turned his head towards them after a while.

"You're right. I'm not afraid to die," he affirmed. His voice was firm, clear.

"That's right. I know that and I admire you for it. But I'm not here to discuss your cause or my cause. We're both right in our own way, and it's a pity we are pitted against each other. Maybe in the next life we shall be on the same side."

"Maybe," he said, a small sneer lurking around the corner of his mouth.

Hai looked at him. Very symmetrical features, bold eyes, well-defined lips, a sense of humor. He could see what Lan Lan saw in him. He smiled at him.

"You have already talked," he said, holding up the report. "Don't feel ashamed. No one can resist the interrogation techniques we use today, especially when we have plenty of time. Many of the chemicals we use were developed in the Soviet Union, by the way."

He paused. Tuan looked at him, his eyes hard, his face set.

"But there're three things more I'd like to know. First, why did you move out from your safe house so early in the evening? Second, where were your cellmates? Third, who thought of going to the Embassy by taxi?"

Silence. Defiance. The sneer had gone. The jaw muscles clenched.

"I'll make a deal with you. If you answer me, I'll tell Lan Lan you are dead, so she can forget you and rebuild her life. I'll then send you to Con Son Island and Lan Lan to a Buddhist nunnery for a time. Your life is already ruined, whether you answer me or not. But if you don't answer, I'll tell her you are still alive and I'll then arrest her as a communist agent. I know everything that happened between the two of you. She's not a senior cadre like you, just a university student who fell in love. By disobeying Party orders and loving her, you have ruined her life. I am giving you a chance to save her now."

Tuan looked at them, then glanced at the floor. Old hands at interrogation, they relaxed. When they look down it means they've been hit dead center. They'll stop denying and start thinking. There's hope for negotiations.

Hai took the letter Tuan had written Lan Lan out of his briefcase, very slowly, read through it and showed it to him. His eyes never left Hai's face.

"I know *everything*," he said, stressing the last word.

Tuan sat there, frozen.

"Do you want to ruin her life as well as yours?" Hai said, preparing to stand up.

"Wait!"

The Tiger General's argument had hit home, and Tuan had made up his mind.

"After she read my letter she came by taxi to talk to me," he said rapidly. "She didn't want me to carry out my mission. She came to the safe house in a taxi, and sent the driver in to call me. We drove around and talked, and I promised her I wouldn't join the commandos, because she said she would commit suicide if I did. By the time I left her, she was calmed down. I had sent my cellmate ahead to our other safe house because I had half-expected Lan Lan to come for me. She knew all three of our safe houses. To rejoin my team, I rode in a taxi, and I saw how easy it was to move around. No police checks. At the safe house, I broke radio silence and called Linh to ask for three taxis but no one answered. I called another handler and he sent a taxi, a car and a truck, all loaded with guns and ammo. That's all. I trust you will keep your word and not tell Lan Lan I'm alive, or that I died in the Embassy. Whether I live or die, I don't want her to know that I lied to her in our last moments together."

Amazing. A romantic communist cadre, a suicide commando at that. It must have been a real love affair, not like with Thanh and you…

"You can trust my word. I'll tell her you were shot the following day on your way out of the city."

He returned to his office and worked the rest of the night, surrounded by his staff. Reports continued to come in from all over the country. PAVN troop concentrations just below the DMZ were being pounded into smithereens by a combination of B-52 bombers, USAF fighter-bombers, heavy artillery and naval guns firing in from the Tonkin Gulf. The northern provincial capitals that had fallen under the onslaught the night before were being retaken by ARVN troops backed by US helicopter gun-ships and artillery. Those under attack had been relieved by the ARVN Airborne. Further south, the picture was the same. The VC forces had suffered staggering losses and were still being hammered into submission by American and Vietnamese forces that, for the first time in many years, could actually see the enemy. CIB forces, assisted by National Police, had devastated the VC ranks in the towns and cities, killing thousands of cadres and capturing dozens of well-equipped arms caches. It was payback time, and open season. All those who had risen in support of the *Tet* Offensive were put to the sword. Vengeful families who had lost relatives during the offensive gleefully pointed out communist agents, real or suspected, to the military and the police, who simply shot them on the spot. Three battlefields now remained where the communist forces intended to make their last stands, the cities of Quang Ngai, Hue and Cho Lon. In the capital, the CIB had regrouped to launch a new round of operations against secondary communist sympathizers and supporters identified during the first twelve hours of the offensive. 300 had already been brought in. The

CIB had borrowed holding space from the three National Jails in anticipation of many more. The VCs had made their play, and it had been magnificent while it lasted. It had failed, however, and they would now have to pay the ultimate price for that failure. The game they were playing had one simple rule: winner takes all.

The following day, Hai picked up Jonathan on his way to see Hoang and his daughter, Lan Lan. In the car, he brought Jonathan up to date. When he finished, it was Jonathan's turn.

"I don't know how to put this. You know what people say about the dead turning in their graves, right? Well, Ambassador Bunker, General Westmoreland and the former Chief of Station O'Leary are like that, turning in their graves right now, except that they're still alive!" Jonathan couldn't help laughing. He was enjoying being right all along, and he remembered O'Leary's face at about three o'clock that morning, when news about the Embassy compound being penetrated had come in. Leary had looked at Bunker, and his hard, once-handsome face had melted into a pitiful mess. The first B-40 rocket fired at the US Embassy had also blown away his career, his pension and his dreams of South American wine, women and songs.

"Bunker sat in a corner and said nothing all night long, but the aristocratic old man kept a steady gaze on Westy and Ozzie as they made hundreds of calls, shouting out urgent orders. He never said anything to them, but these two knew that their time was up, no matter how they played it. Johnson was on the phone to Bunker all night long, and Westy had to give hourly briefs to Taylor in Washington. No one really cared about the northern provinces and the highlands and the Mekong Delta. What really hurt was that the US Embassy, MAC-V and the US BOQs had been attacked in strength, right here in the heart of Sai Gon, where we've been masters of everything we could see for the last fourteen years! It didn't matter what these two yo-yos said, it just sat there, right in our faces. You should have seen the look on Bunker's face as he watched them desperately locking the gate after the cows had gone!"

At Hoang's magnificent residence, they were received by Lan Lan, who allowed Jonathan to kiss her on the cheeks twice on each side, Parisian style, before shaking hands with Hai. She looked perfectly composed, and smelt of some marvelous perfume that brought back memories of *Madame* Louise Saintenoix. They sat down in the living room, and servants brought in tea, coffee and cakes. Jonathan and Lan Lan were busy talking about the offensive when her father came bouncing in, the picture of a successful tycoon. He looked fresh, he smelt of talcum powder, he was wearing a suit and tie. A gold Rolex watch peeped from under one cuff, and a thick gold bracelet from under the other. Hai bet to himself that Hoang would also be wearing a heavy gold neck chain. He didn't really know Hoang, except for what his father and the CIB had told him about the man. He had agreed with his father that they would keep their relationship secret and, although Hai had visited him and Lady Nhan twice or three times a year, he always made sure that their friends or business partners were not around during these family get-togethers. The CIB's interest in Hoang concerned his relationship with his American business partners in Germany. Introductions were made, polite conversation followed until the time came for more serious matters.

"Mr Hoang, you've worked with the Government for many years. I'm sure you know what the CIB does," he said. It was his usual opening statement—factual but ominous.

"Yes I do, General," Hoang answered pleasantly, very much at ease. "What does the CIB want with me?" He looked from Hai to Jonathan and then back to Hai.

"Mr Hoang, what I am going to say is not pleasant. We know that TVB operates a number of bonded warehouses in Cho Lon and that in those warehouses are American ammunition, medical supplies and dual-use goods. Your joint venture with Surplus Sales GmbH. in Germany has been supplying the black market here with millions of dollars of American goods stolen by US officers and NCOs from American PXs in Germany and Italy."

Hoang turned white and they thought he was going to faint. Lan Lan clutched her father's arm to prop him up. Jonathan and Hai looked on in silence. After a while, the millionaire regained his composure and spoke. His voice was hoarse.

"That could be true. I run a large business, and I employ three deputy managers whom I trust but whom I cannot always control. One of them, a Eurasian, runs imports from Europe. His name is

Michel Gilles. It is possible his American partners are lying to us about the origin of the goods they supply us. I'll put a stop to it right away. We cannot have the reputation of TVB dragged in the mud like this! This is intolerable!"

Hoang was sputtering indignantly, working himself up into a righteous rage. Hai looked at him steadily, saying nothing. His large, cat-like eyes grew larger and larger in his thin face. He knew that his bulging eyes with their yellow flecks always had an unsettling effect on people, especially those who knew him as the Tiger General. Tigers have yellow eyes. Tigers eat people. The bubble Hoang had worked himself up to slowly deflated. He sank into his chair.

"Mr Hoang, we are not the police, and we don't really care about your black market activities. But if ammo stolen from US stocks in Europe is found in your warehouses, you will have serious problems with the American Criminal Investigation Division. And if it has found its way into VC hands, you will face an ARVN firing squad." He paused to let the message sink in. "I want to make a deal with you," he then said.

"Yes, yes! By all means. We are civilized men, we understand what war can do to a man. I am ready to pay for my deputy's mistake."

He had recovered the moment he heard the word 'deal'. For him, wheeling and dealing was what life was all about and Hai's last statement immediately put him at ease. He was now in his element. Hai allowed himself to smile. Thinking they had come to an agreement, Hoang smiled too.

59

Connecting the Dots

"Mr Hoang, your daughter here began working as a VC courier soon after she attended university. She's been under CIB surveillance for over one year and is on the CIB arrest list, category C. This means she's a confirmed enemy agent but a low-level one, to be watched but not arrested."

Hoang turned to look at his daughter. She gulped in a mouthful of air and burst into tears, covering up her face with her hands. Her father jumped up and hugged her to his chest.

"It's all my fault," he blurted out, his face red with emotion, "it's all my fault. Her mother left us when she was young and I was always working and traveling. I never had any time to spend with her. She grew up alone, without any guidance. All those stupid university students are leftists anyway! It's all my fault, it's all my fault!"

Both father and daughter were crying. Jonathan looked like a tiger about to leap. He wanted to reach over and hug Lan Lan, to comfort her, to protect her. After a while, Hai motioned with his hand.

"Please compose yourselves," he said evenly, "so we can continue."

Hoang whipped out a clean handkerchief, recently bought in Paris, and handed it to Lan Lan. It had the red Lanvin logo on it. He used the napkin on the table for himself. They had a sip of tea, cleared their throats, and sat back, chests heaving still, prepared for the worse.

"Here's the deal. Lan Lan will retire to a Buddhist convent in Can Tho for one year. I will introduce her to the senior nun. Her role has been a minor one, and I have other people to consider in the matter," he said, glancing at Jonathan. "For the next few months we can expect some serious settling of accounts. The VCs have burnt down many homes and they have killed a lot of innocent people. But they showed their faces on that first day, people now know who they are and will take revenge on them. Anyone suspected of having helped them during the *Tet* Offensive will get short shrift over the next few months. This way we take her out of the picture until things calm down."

He looked at Lan Lan and her father. Lan Lan bent her head in a sign of respect and acquiescence. Hoang nodded slowly a few times. That was settled.

"TVB will immediately dissolve the joint-venture with Surplus Sales GmbH. Your Mr Gilles will report to my friend here at the US Embassy at nine o'clock tomorrow morning to give him all the details on this PX mafia and we'll let the American authorities clean up their own house. Gilles will then report to me, at noon tomorrow, at the CIB. I want to know who his buyers here are. Some of them have been reselling war *materiel* to the enemy, and that's punishable by death. If Gilles tells us all he knows, I shall not arrest him. I suggest you then fire him, and we'll deport him."

Hai looked at Hoang again. The latter nodded again, slowly, many times.

"I will send a CIB expert accountant to TVB to audit your books. I want to know how much profit you made from your PX venture. Whatever it is, TVB will publicly donate the totality to a list of charities I will provide you with. In this way, children who have been blinded, orphaned or crippled by war can get some extra rice. After this amount has been exhausted, TVB will continue to contribute voluntarily to these charities a set percentage of its profits every year until the war ends. These donations will make TVB famous nationwide, and you will be seen as a philanthropist. This will wipe out the debt you owe your country."

This time Hoang took longer to nod. This was money, and he understood money. He also understood power. Hai could almost read his thoughts. He was thinking that this policeman was doing his work with impartiality on a salary a rat couldn't live on. And yet he held the power of life and death in his hands. This man could have taken all of TVB, and no one could have stopped him. But he probably didn't understand how the system worked. TVB made money because it was allowed by the Palace to make money, for everyone close to the top to dip his hand into the TVB kitty when he needed untraceable cash. He, Mai Van Hoang, worked hard, from morning to night, to feed the President and his top government ministers first, and only then his family and himself. But to reveal all this would simply make him more enemies than he already had.

Finally, he nodded again, slowly. A deal had been made.

"I will let your daughter tell you what she wants to tell you about her activities. I suggest, Miss Lan Lan, that you tell your father everything. I'm sure he will forgive you, whatever you tell him. From this moment on, you must not entertain any contact with leftists, sympathizers, supporters and communists of any sort. There can be no more links between you and the communists."

Hai looked at her. She kept her head down, her face a mask, hiding Tuan deep in the recesses of her young mind. Febrile on the surface, she was calm inside. As long as this policeman didn't know anything about him, she was safe. They were safe. The war could go on, or end tomorrow, she didn't care any more. He had promised her he would not join the Embassy attack and she had something to live for. After she had served her sentence in a Buddhist nunnery, she would find him. Rich or poor, capitalist or communist, love would always triumph in the end. The main thing was to remain steady, not to break, not to reveal.

Lan Lan looked up. Her eyes were puffy, but she had regained her composure. All things considered, she was getting off lightly.

"Miss Lan Lan, I have to inform you that your lover Tuan was shot a few hours ago as he attempted to break through the military cordon around Cho Lon. We've had him under surveillance for two years. I identified the body myself and ordered the cremation at once, before he could be thrown into a mass grave."

For an eternity, everyone sat there, frozen into stone. The cakes sat there, appetizing but uneaten. The tea and coffee sat there, untouched, going cold. Then Lan Lan stood up, a shriek of primal pain came out of her mouth and she ran out of the room. Her father looked at Hai uncomprehendingly. Jonathan looked at him accusingly.

Hai poured himself some lukewarm tea, drank a little. He picked up a cake and bit into it. What needs to be done has been done. It's better to cut and to cut clean so the work of rebuilding can get started. These rich and powerful people wouldn't have given your mother or you the time of the day had you met them then. Now they're in your hands, you can squash them like insects if you want to. But they're non-combatants, so you choose to treat them with compassion. Is your mother guiding your hand the Buddhist way, or is it because of your friendship for your brother Jonathan?

"Lan Lan has been a very bad girl," he said in between chewing his cake. "If it weren't for me, she would be undergoing interrogation right now, and you know what they do to women prisoners. There's a massive witch-hunt on for agents who helped the communists, so it is important we get her out of the city. But it is more important that she knows her link to the communists has been severed. Forever. Otherwise she might entertain thoughts of looking for her boyfriend after her one year in exile. You talk to her, Mr Hoang. Tell her she made a mistake, perhaps because you neglected her, and that's it's all over now. A clean slate. A new life. She's young, she'll soon forget, especially if you show her a father's love."

Hoang reached over and took Hai's free hand in both of his.

"General, I don't know how to thank you. I shall do my best to talk my daughter back into a normal life again. You're right, she's still young, she'll get over it," he said in a voice where gratitude mixed with shock. The existence of Tuan had hit him like a bolt from the blue. He was beginning to realize what might have happened if the Tiger General hadn't called upon him this day. He now understood why it was imperative for his daughter to make a clean break with the past.

"I hope you'll succeed," Hai said. "I would like to introduce you to my very good friend, Jonathan Winthrop, an American at the Embassy. He has met your daughter, and you have met him once already, but you didn't know then that he was my very good friend. With your permission, of course, Jonathan would like to develop his friendship with Lan Lan. With time, who knows? Perhaps Lan Lan will look upon Jonathan as more than a friend. Between the two of you, you should eventually get Lan Lan back on the right track again."

As they rode back to the Embassy in the CIB car, he glanced at Jonathan. "You think I was too hard on Lan Lan. But in a few months' time, when you visit her at the nunnery, you'll see I was right. It is very necessary for her to believe Tuan is dead. Otherwise that boy will always stand between her and her father, between her and you, between her and a normal life on our side of the barrier. She has fallen, now you have help her get back on her feet. Time should help. I wish you luck."

"You mean he's not dead?" Jonathan asked, eyes wide.

"No. Wounded in the Embassy attack, arrested by the CIB, interrogated, but still alive."

"What are you going to do with him?"

"I have plans for him. You know all those US senators and congressmen who fly out here to see what the war is all about, or to see what the enemy looks like? I have put together a bunch of hard-core guerrillas who look good, can express themselves and have no fear of death. I'm going to fly your politicians to the tiger cages on Con Son Island for lunch, give them interpreters and let them see the real face of the enemy. After they have talked with these dedicated communists, they'll understand what we're up against. All that mealy-mouthed, pious human rights bullshit Washington is constantly throwing at us is picked up by the American media, and it's like fighting with one hand tied behind your back. The people we are fighting are like the Japanese in World War Two. They're single-minded, they believe in their cause, and they're not afraid to die. Why do you think Truman dropped the atomic bomb on them? Because, when it comes down to the nitty-gritty, your human rights are more important than the enemy's, and that's how it should be here until the war's over."

"So what should we do?"

"Well, since we can't use the nuclear bomb against them, we have to look beyond force."

"What does that mean? Surrender? Pull out?"

"No, of course not. We want to win but we, or rather you, have to push the right buttons, offer the right deal, negotiate with the Soviets to cut out its support for Ha Noi, then carpet bomb the north for as long as it takes, then offer peace. Chairman Ho'll take it because he's not stupid. He doesn't mind dying for Viet Nam, but he'll never die for communism. Without Russian ammo, Ha Noi's offensive will die out within the year. Without American ammo, we would fold in six months. You and I both know this. The question is: why do the two superpowers keep supplying ammo?"

"Hai, you're preaching to the choir," said Jonathan, laying a hand on his arm. "You're a genius, my friend. You should run for President. But maybe you can do even better than that."

"And what might that be, young Jonathan?" Hai asked, laughing.

"Become an adviser to the State Department. Move the movers and shakers who influence the Western world. I know you. You like to work in the shadows, to be the brain behind the brain. Me too. That's why I stayed an analyst all these years. I could have taken over as

Chief of Station had I wanted. O'Leary was tired and has been making mistakes, they sounded me out, I declined and that's why "Shotgun" Bob is here."

Hai looked at his old friend. He suddenly realized how many years they had worked together, in the shadows. They were like two peas in a pod, doing the right thing but not getting anywhere. One more *Tet* offensive and they would both be out. It was time to rethink all this.

"Congratulations, my friend! Congratulations! I think you took the right decision. When are you leaving?" he asked.

"When I see that it is useless to continue down this path. America cannot lose the war against communism, meaning the Soviet Union, so the present fight will go on until either democracy or communism folds. This war here is a sideshow. Win or lose, it will not affect America. But Ha Noi, even if it wins this war, is going to have to make some hard choices. Communism is not the answer for the North, or for anybody. I want to work behind the scenes to offer this country an alternative, but I want to do it right this time. Anyway, State is where I'm going when I get out of here," said Jonathan, dead serious. "And I swear to you that I'll do whatever it takes to bring you over there. I want to prepare my country for Round Three. And I want you to work with me as I do this."

"Round Three?"

"Yes. The French lost Round One, Round Two is touch-and-go and we have to win Round Three in a convincing manner. It's the last round."

Before Hai could say anything, they had arrived at the US Embassy and Jonathan got out.

Bemused, Hai returned to CIB HQS and caught up on the incoming reports. The battle for Chinatown was shaping up into an ugly fight that was rapidly destroying the old city. Helicopter gun-ships fired hails of rockets into district after district, coordinating with ARVN killer-hunter teams that conducted house-to-house searches, blowing up ammunition caches every now and again. The head of the NPD, a three-star general who was nominally Hai's boss, a southerner with a vitriolic hate of communists, whom he saw as foreigners from the North, cold-bloodedly shot a captured VC point-blank in the head as they passed each other in an alleyway. The terrorist's terrified face contorted in a deathly grimace as he saw the gun pointed at his head. A spit second later, his head blew open, and he dropped like a stone to the ground. An AP war photographer using a still camera and an NBC TV cameraman with his portable unit captured the whole scene, from start to finish, and the gory incident was flashed on TV around the world that same evening. What the TV reports did not say was that General Loan, wearing a bullet-proof vest and hunting down VC terrorists with his men, had learnt an instant earlier that his closest friend, also an officer, had been killed by VC snipers. The general had been fighting from street to street for three straight days and was critically wounded later the same day. For the American public, however, what counted was that a high-ranking South Vietnamese police officer had shot a handcuffed prisoner in cold blood. He hadn't read him his rights. On TV, the whole Viet Nam war issue was reduced to that.

For Hai, it was time to take care of the last unfinished piece of business. With Colonel Dao in tow, he visited Linh in his cell. It was almost midnight. The bite block was removed by Dao. He massaged Linh's jaws for a while, and Linh swallowed once or twice. His face wore an expression of contempt.

"Mr Linh," Hai said, "you know who I am, right?" There was no answer.

"I'm General Hai, head of the CIB. I've read the interrogation reports on you and everything in them conforms to what I know about you. We've been watching you for a long time."

There was a short silence before Linh spoke.

"Everyone knows the Grey Tiger. You've murdered enough nationalists and innocent people to be infamous for ten generations. But if, as you say, you know everything already, then what are we meeting for?" he said in a cold and precise voice.

"Your father is Tran Dinh Nam, and his brother, your paternal uncle, was Tran Dinh Nhung. Once I had a description of him and his rough age, I was able to trace him from the time he joined up until 1956, when he was elected to the Politburo, in spite of his bourgeois background. Do you know anything about your uncle?"

Linh remained silent. Hai looked at him pleasantly.

"Linh, you already know we can make you talk. You cannot resist the drugs we use today. Colonel Dao didn't ask you this particular question then because we didn't know about your uncle until I talked to your father yesterday. If you don't wish to converse with me, you'll go back to the interrogation room for a couple of injections followed by an electric therapy session. Is that what you want? You want me to degrade your mind and leach this information out of you?"

There was a long silence. The expression of contempt left Linh's face and was replaced by one of intense concentration. He nodded once.

"Good. You're a man of intellect, not a muscle man. The Party values your brain, not your brawn. I also value your brain, and I have no desire to harm you. I need you to make a deal with your uncle. His name is now Le Bac, and he oversees political training in the PAVN. He writes the doctrine for all the thousands of PAVN commissars to follow. It is a very powerful position. About three months ago, through contacts I maintain with Ha Noi, I was told that should one Tran Dinh Linh ever be captured, I should treat him well and keep him for prisoner exchanges. I was told that Ha Noi would be willing to give me a good deal in return. I didn't answer, since I didn't have you in custody then. But it now appears they are willing to trade ten American flyers for you and two others. Ten for three. A good deal indeed, don't you think?"

"Are you sending me back to Ha Noi?" asked Linh, alert all of a sudden.

"Yes. I asked for twelve downed American pilots, including two majors and a colonel. They agreed. But that's not what I want to talk to you about. How well do you know your uncle?"

"We've never met. He learned that I was recruited in 1958. He recognized that I was his nephew, because I hadn't changed my name. We talked by courier for years without ever meeting face to face. I respect him for what he is, and he seems to support what I do. Why?"

"When you return, I want to you to sound out your uncle. Do it gradually. Use your intelligence."

"Sound him out on what? You're not thinking of turning him into an agent for this miserable country, are you?" He burst out laughing.

Hai looked at Linh in silence, for a long time, his yellow eyeballs orbiting their sockets slowly, unblinking, their weight heavy in the air. Linh's contemptuous laugh died away. The silence between them grew thick as seconds turned into minutes.

Finally, Hai spoke. "First of all, although this country is indeed in a miserable condition, it is our country. Yours, mine, your uncle's. Secondly, this war is just another step this miserable country is taking towards a bright future. I'm a lot older than you are, and I've seen it all.

Feudalism, colonialism, fascism, now capitalism and communism. It is not finished yet. Other 'isms' will come and go before this miserable country, as you so aptly call it, can become normal again. You and I have a role to play in this transformation. What I want to do with your uncle is to open a channel I can use to discuss things as they develop. He must obtain permission, of course. I wouldn't want to talk to him otherwise. It will be very useful for him, for your Party, and for us. You can be the go-between. You're intelligent, you're young, you can see what's happening around you. Adding contacts in South Viet Nam or America to your Russian and Chinese contacts cannot hurt. You'll not be a traitor, but an unofficial representative of your regime. We can talk unofficially about things we cannot discuss openly. Do you understand what I'm saying?"

"If it can be worked out at all, my uncle will speak for the Politburo. Who will you speak for?"

"An excellent question but the answer is more complicated than that. Your uncle will be speaking for a Soviet-backed Politburo and I'll be speaking for an American-backed South Viet Nam, but that is not what I want. I want him to speak for the common Vietnamese, for all the millions out there who don't really understand what you and I stand for, who only want peace and security so they can live without fear and raise their families without hunger. I'll do the same on my side."

"I see where you are heading. What you say could be of interest and I'll discuss it with my uncle when I am returned to the North. I don't know what he will say. If we think we are winning, why talk at all? If we think we are losing, talking might be a good idea. Right now, I would say we are winning."

He grinned. He had regained his confidence and felt at ease now.

Hai shook his head slowly, a look of tired exasperation spreading over his face. He asked Colonel Dao to leave them. As soon as he had left, Hai took out his Walther PPK pistol and cocked it. Linh sat up, every nerve in his body tingling. Hai's abrupt change in attitude had unsettled him.

"Linh, I want you to listen to me with the utmost attention you are capable of. If I see your eyes look away from mine at any point, I shall shoot you in the face and throw your body in mass grave. You will never return to Ha Noi. Do you understand what I am saying?"

His eyes fixed on Hai, his face drawn and blank, he nodded imperceptibly. This was the Grey Tiger talking.

"You are still young. Please try to see beyond today. So far, America and the Soviet Union are playing a chess game in our country, using our people as pawns, supplying the heavy weaponry. Whichever side wins, eventually, it will not be the Vietnamese people and certainly not their leaders, communists or otherwise. Whoever wins, we, North and South, have to keep on talking until we can thank our respective Big Brothers, invite them to leave so we can settle down to build Vietnam-ism. We have always benefited from foreigners we come into contact with, no doubt about that, but at a certain time the lessons must end, the teacher must go home and the student must stand up. We took the best from China and from the Mongols, crushed the Khmers and the Chams and defeated France. Yes, I recognize Uncle Ho's victory. Everybody does. But now we have to choose the best from the Russian and American systems. I stress the word *from*, because if we choose *between* them, we become dogmatic and are condemned to live in their shadow. Neither system is totally good for us, but each has something that will work for us. As a people, we are not mature enough for American-style capitalism but we want the democracy that it brings. That is a stage we hope to reach one day, because everybody wants freedom more than anything else. Even Chairman Ho has said so, many times. Feudalism we've already had, so we are too mature for Stalin-style communism, which is nothing but feudalism turned upside down, like a triangle standing on its head. Instead of a small, cultured elite running the country, you have a large, semi-literate dictatorship running things. On the other hand, a certain degree of social discipline will be needed in the transitory stage and communism has perfected this skill. We now need to sit down and work out what to keep, what to reject. This can only be done by intelligent but moderate people who have the country's interest at heart, people with an open mind. On both sides we have fanatical ideologues, with closed minds and a thirst for power. It is possible we need such people to make or break a revolution, but once they have succeeded, they must be replaced by moderate and intelligent men who can return things to normal and move the country forward. The pot cannot be kept boiling after the rice has been cooked. A country cannot remain in a perpetual state of effervescence, which is what happens if you don't change the leaders after they have fulfilled their destiny."

Hai carefully un-cocked his gun and returned it to its holster. A long silence ensued. Many years later, in Paris, when they had become friends, Linh was to tell him that on that day he had surpassed himself with this analysis of the situation. He said that it was like a veil had been lifted from his eyes and he could see the future clearly for the first time since his university days. But at that moment, Linh was lost in deep thought. Hai couldn't blame him for having difficulty looking beyond the immediate present. He was in a bad situation, lucky to be still alive. He had never thought he'd be discussing the intellectual approach to war and his main concern now was how to get out of this cell. Anything else had to be secondary.

He sat looking at the floor. His agile brain raced along, weighing all the options and alternatives, touching on everything but settling on nothing. He must have concluded that Hai was right, that there was no harm in establishing discreet contacts, and that it might benefit the country as a whole some day. And he would be asked to play a role in it. Much later, in Paris and then in Washington, he told Hai that once he had returned to Ha Noi, he had begun to see the enormous harm the war had done to the civilian population in the North, the very people he was supposedly fighting for and even then, in 1968, he concluded that there would not be any real winners in the end. The bombing raids on the North unleashed by President Johnson each time the Politburo rebuffed one of his overtures didn't kill many northerners each time but seriously degraded a subsistence economy. Unlike in the South, where there was no shortage of food, his own relatives told him they had never had a full meal since independence in 1954, and he knew that the vast majority of the population went to bed hungry every night. Although the cause was just and the Party above reproach, there might just be some validity in Hai's argument that there had to be a better way of settling disputes, he thought. We are just slaughtering our own people. As he watched Hai, conflicting thoughts ran through his mind. It is amazing that this bloodthirsty pig is able to talk the way he does. Is he just trying to make you say things he can use against you later? Are we being taped? The best is simply to go along with whatever he says and maybe be sent back to Ha Noi. We can see then whether setting up a back channel makes sense or not.

"General, there's already a back channel, as you must know."

"Yes, I know all about the secret contacts in Paris," Hai said, allowing himself a small smile. "Although it looks like it is between Washington and Ha Noi, it is in fact between Washington and Moscow. Your representative is merely an observer. The two superpowers' main concern is not how to end this war, but how to keep it going without letting it get out of control. As long as American troops are here,

Moscow will not allow Ha Noi to invade Sai Gon, and Washington will not help Sai Gon attack Ha Noi. When they finally decide to end it, whatever they agree on cannot be the best solution for us, North or South. Those two powers negotiate over us with an eye cocked on China. Any agreement these three come to will be to their benefit, not ours. I am talking about a back channel between North and South Vietnamese, with no foreigners involved. Our concern would be the kind of country we want to have once the war ends, whichever side wins. I repeat, capitalism is too advanced for us and communism too backward. There are in-between steps we have to climb before we can get to true democracy, which is what we must have. We need to borrow the best from all these systems, and we can only do so if we start dialoguing once the foreign powers stop interfering in our growth process."

Another silence followed. Finally, Linh looked up.

"General Hai, let me shake your hand. Your intellect astounds me. Your arguments are also very persuasive, and you are not afraid to say what many think but dare not say. I promise nothing, but if my uncle listens to me at all, I'll work towards Vietnam-ism, as you call it," he said.

Hai put his hand out and they shook hands solemnly.

60

The Aftermath

By early March 1968, Hue had been retaken by the ARVN Marines after one month of savage house-to-house fighting. By mid-April the nightmare called Khe Sanh finally ended after a 77-day siege during which the PAVN and VC forces lost 10,000 men to round-the-clock USAF bombing. Throughout the South, the VCs had been mangled beyond repairs and the *Tet* Offensive had come to an end. In the central and southern provinces, ARVN troops had rallied and turned the table on the VCs. 80,000 well-armed guerrillas had been hurled in frontal attacks on military bases and some 40,000 had been mowed down by US and ARVN firepower. The rest had been savaged in subsequent ARVN search and destroy operations. Military and civilian jails had standing room only, and large open air camps, ringed with barbed wire and Claymore mines had to be set up in the countryside to accommodate the surplus.

In Washington, the offensive drove home the fact that MAC-V and the US Embassy had seriously underestimated the enemy's capability all along. Westy had been spectacularly wrong. Only a small number of CIA analysts had called the shots right but they been shunted aside by MAC-V's 'team players'. The American intelligence apparatus, a million-dollar-a-day monster, had failed spectacularly. By March, President Johnson announced he would not accept his party's nomination for the upcoming election and, by June, General Abrams had replaced General Westmoreland. To save the administration's face, Westy was kicked upstairs like his principal supporter McNamara.

Both in the US and in Viet Nam, no one was officially and publicly blamed for the *Tet* Offensive debacle, although both the American and the Vietnamese security services continued to point the finger at each other in private until the end of the war.

In Ha Noi, the DRVN leadership was bemused. The bold and brilliantly executed Winter-Spring Offensive, which was never intended to take over the South but simply to show America that the North wasn't buckling under the USAF onslaught, had failed militarily but had succeeded politically. The message had been heard loud and clear in Washington and, politically, the offensive could be chalked up as a major strategic success. On the other hand, the National Liberation Front forces, the VC, which had taken twelve years to build up, had suffered terminal damage both militarily and politically, and supporters and sympathizers were deserting the cause like rats leaving a sinking ship. Certain members of the Politburo, however, saw in the eclipse of the VC a heaven-sent gift: the removal of a possible rival once the South Vietnamese Government had surrendered. The PAVN was ordered to prepare for the massive infiltration of regular VM divisions into the South to replace the shattered NLF forces.

Because of USAF's mastery of the skies, crossing the DMZ was far too costly. The dozens of trails that ran along the jungles and mountains along the borders separating Viet Nam from Laos and Cambodia were the only viable routes. An impenetrable jungle canopy hid the trails from American bombers circling overhead. Under the supervision of PAVN military engineers, the civilian population of entire districts living along the border was mobilized to enlarge and strengthen the existing trails while entire hamlets were ordered to hack out new ones. Soviet and Chinese trucks carrying ammunition and anti-aircraft guns began to pour into the South while USAF B-52 bombers from Guam flew round-the-clock interdiction flights. In a desperate effort to stem the tide of communist men and equipment flowing down the so-called Ho Chi Minh trails, MAC-V and ARVN began cross border operations into Laos and Cambodia. Ha Noi responded by creating the Pathet Lao and the Khmers Rouges. USAF and VNAF planes began conducting secret bombing runs into these two countries. The final phase of the 'American' war in Viet Nam had begun. To Hai, it looked like a replay of the French war, when the secret services had opened new fronts in Laos and Cambodia for exactly the same reasons.

In Washington, the shockwaves of the audacious *Tet* Offensive had ushered in President Nixon. The old guard, holdovers from the Kennedy administration and newcomers during the LBJ days, all disappeared from public view. They had tried, and they had failed. The field was now open to Henry Kissinger, a man Hai saw in his mind as the European version of Chou En-lai. Outwardly, Chou was silky while Kissinger was gruff, but inwardly both had mastered the essence of the philosophy expounded by Nicolo Machievelli in his Renaissance masterpiece, *The Prince*. With Kissinger behind him, Nixon, a small-town American with no particularly distinguishing characteristics except a well-developed instinct for survival, played *real politik* with the verve of an 18th-century European politician. Nixon and Kissinger, so different in every way, came together like peas in a pod to show the world a classical exercise in how to exercise naked power under the pretense of upholding ideals. Bombing of the North was resumed, but no more American troops were sent to Viet Nam. General Creighton Abrams, a pragmatic soldier, couldn't see Westy's light at the end of the tunnel, and he didn't want to go looking for it either. He immediately reduced the use of American combat troops in the field, focusing on giving the ARVN massive air and artillery support and kick-starting the policy of Vietnamization, which had existed on paper since the Kennedy days. Essentially, this meant that all combat operations would be undertaken by the ARVN, with or without American advisors. Hai thought back to the days when France, realizing the game was up, drew up the same plan, calling it *le jaunissement des forces armées*, the yellowing of the armed force.

The Paris peace talks were expanded to include a reluctant South Vietnamese government. A French cartoonist in *Le Monde* said it all with a picture showing a little boy being dragged kicking and screaming to a party by his mother, who was determined her son would enjoy the party. The defiant little boy was a Thieu look alike, his mother had a ski-jump nose not unlike Nixon's, and the welcoming party at the door was composed of the portly Kissinger with a VC pith helmet on his head and the smile of a second-hand car salesman on his face. He was standing in the middle of a bunch of skinny Asian-looking boys and girls, all dressed up, with balloons in one hand and an AK47s in the other.

For the National Police Directorate and the CIO, Vietnamization didn't change anything. Vietnamese police officers and men, whether working for the RVN or for the many American agencies involved in intelligence gathering and interpretation, had always been in the front lines anyway, if only for language reasons. The CIB's US advisors continued to advise but Hai could see that their hearts were no longer in it. Career-wise, Viet Nam after the *Tet* Offensive was no longer an attractive posting and updating bio-data sheets became popular. As his latest American advisor said, "VCs are out, CVs are in!"

For Hai, Vietnamization went the other way. The *Phoi Hop* program he had started was taken over by the CIA because Jonathan had tried to find a sponsor and had failed. Inevitably, word had gotten out that there was a successful program working on a small scale in the provinces and, after bouncing around CORDS and APP, it found a home in the CIA, where it was renamed the Phoenix Program. As Hai had predicted that fateful day in Jonathan's office, it rapidly turned into one more American circus and in the US the media pilloried it mercilessly. The doves in Washington saw in this initially sound program the epitome of everything the hawks had done wrong in Viet Nam. To placate the doves, the Phoenix Program was broken up and parceled out to different organizations, and it soon degenerated in to a patchwork quilt of intelligence operations run by different American interests under a common flag. Within one year of its inception, no American with career prospects wanted to touch the Phoenix Program with a barge pole.

61

CODEX—Made in USA

One day Hai received a call from Étienne Saintenoix, who invited him to Paris. After Dien Bien Phu, Hai had stayed well away from Étienne for five years, gradually renewing their relationship only when they were sure that CODEX had evaporated from the French political spectrum. Just before the *Tet* Offensive they had started talking seriously to each other again because Hai was interested in the Washington–Ha Noi talks being set up in Paris. Étienne, who had maintained contact with the top echelons in the Politburo, including Chairman Ho, was being used in the American version of a CODEX operation initiated by the new US Secretary of State.

"Give me a reason," Hai said.

"*Plus ça change, plus c'est la même chose,*" he answered in French. That was their code. "Help!"

"I'll be there next week," he answered.

The more things change, the more they stay the same. How true that was. In fact, the 'American war' for South Vietnam had turned into a carbon copy of the 'French war' for Indochina. Some of the more discerning dailies in the US were already calling it the 'second Indochina war'. The hawks and the doves in the White House fought each other as bitterly as those at *l'Elysée* had done. Before the *Tet* Offensive, American generals had courted the media like film stars, as the French ones had done, determined to leave their imprints on history. American ambassadors to Viet Nam and French Governors General to Indochina were alike in that they behaved like Roman pro-consuls in a conquered country. The French SDECE had taken over the opium trade to finance the military's secret wars in Laos and

Cambodia, using ethnic tribesmen to cut Viet Minh supply lines and harass its jungle camps. The CIA, using Special Forces troops and its private airline, Air America, were now doing exactly the same, in many cases using the same French-trained *montagnards* fighters and buying their opium harvests from exactly the same hill villages. In fact, many Special Forces NCOs and officers communicated in French with their newfound recruits, commonly referred to as the 'Yards'. The *Deuxième Bureau,* frustrated by the stubbornness of captured agents, had institutionalized brutal, medieval interrogation techniques. The CIA and the Phoenix Program, born of a *Phoi Hop* program gone sour, had become notorious for exactly the same reasons. France had sought to develop an exit strategy at the height of the war by secretly meeting with the sworn enemy and had lost the war ignominiously. America was now doing the same. Paris had operated CODEX, in vain, and Washington was now setting up the American version of the same project.

Once in Paris, Étienne brought him up to date on what was happening. Secret meetings in France with the Politburo's Xuan Thuy had been arranged through Étienne by Kissinger. Nothing had come of them so far because of the Politburo's intransigent stand. They knew the *Tet* offensive was perceived in Washington as a strategic victory for the North and they were determined to milk every drop of success from this unexpected political windfall.

"You remember how frustrating it was in our days?" Étienne asked over dinner.

"Yes, I do." Hai shook his head thoughtfully. "I have to tell you that the sense of *déjà vu* is so strong at times I forget where I am."

Étienne laughed with delight and clapped his hands.

"Bravo, *mon ami*! I couldn't have put it better myself. I agree, we seem to be making all the same mistakes all over again. Such a tiny, miserable country, making us both look stupid and helpless."

The dinner conversation moved on. CODEX was recalled, they spoke about Touquet, Herment, Blanchot and Dien Bien Phu. They had been through so much, each fighting his own battles on other side of the world, linked to each other by respect and admiration that had grown into friendship and affection. But Hai knew this was not the reason why he had been invited to Paris.

"Why am I here, Étienne?" he asked during a break in the easy conversation.

"Well, two heads are better than one, or the more heads the better. I don't sit in on these meetings that we organize but I have been designated by our President's office to co-ordinate the agendas, the translators, the recording of the sessions and the Americans often ask me afterwards for my views on what the Vietnamese said. As a result of this involvement, I know pretty much what was said inside. But my ability to read Ha Noi's real intentions is limited. I haven't dealt with them for ah... what... fifteen, sixteen years now and I'm not sure I really understand what they are saying. I know you, I trust you and I need you to interpret the meaning behind the words."

"I am not an accredited party to the official Paris Peace talks so how I can I attend the secret Kissinger talks?"

"You don't have to. I'll brief you in detail without anyone knowing. I shall need you to analyze and interpret specifics so I can better advise my American client."

"Who are you working for, France or America?"

"Both. We also have plans in case America leaves Viet Nam and Ha Noi takes over."

"How long do I have to stay here? People might start suspecting things if I'm away from the CIB too long."

"You can go home in a few days and come back every three, four months. These talks are going to take years. Remember ours? Everything we send you will come through the French Embassy in Sai Gon, in code. You can work out the reasons why you need to make contact with French diplomats every week. It'll be like the Touquet setup but this time you'll be dealing with a civilian."

"*Le plus ça change...*" Hai started saying..., "*le plus c'est la même chose!*" Étienne exclaimed, and they both laughed heartily. A few heads turned towards them.

"No problem about the French embassy. Tell me, how do you see all this ending?" They were having desserts. Étienne stared at his plate for a long time, fiddling with his spoon. Then he looked up, his face serious.

"Like France in '54, America is tired of fighting this war. America will leave the battlefield, tail between its legs, like we did. It will cut its military support to Sai Gon, while the Soviets will continue to help Ha Noi. The RVN will not be able to fight on by itself; Ha Noi will win, the country will become communist."

"Why would the US withdraw its military support?"

"For the same reason we pulled out when Diem told us to do so.

Battle fatigue. Loss of the will to continue fighting. Dien Bien Phu gutted us; the *Tet* Offensive is gutting America. We both thought we could do this war on the cheap, but we were both wrong. It has cost the Americans much more than ours cost us, not only financially and militarily, but psychologically. European powers are used to winning some, losing some, but the Americans cannot accept defeat. The taxpayers won't stand for continued aid if Washington is composing with Ha Noi. It'll have to cut and cut clean, I'm afraid."

"When do you think they'll do this?"

"In a couple more years. Nixon is standing on a three-legged chair juggling sixteen balls of different sizes in the air, with Kissinger running in the crowd encouraging them to cheer. But they are running out of tricks; it will all come tumbling down soon. What President Thieu wants has nothing to do with it. The US decision to fight or fold in Viet Nam will depend strictly on internal politics and relations with the Soviets."

"What's the state of these relations?"

"Well, we have to look at it in the framework of the Cold War. It's been up and down since '45. Eastern Europe was a defeat, a total disaster; Korea was a half-victory; Cuba was a victory, of sorts, even if Kennedy agreed to remove his missile sites out of Turkey. Now it seems that Washington is coming around to the conclusion that South Viet Nam was the wrong place to challenge the Soviets, and it is going to move the arm-wrestling contest to a different place, perhaps to a different level."

"So the US will accept defeat by the Soviets in Viet Nam?"

"Not in so many words, but yes, that's what they'll do. But they'll make up for it by coming down hard on Soviet pressure points in Europe. Brezhnev is trying hard to pick up the pieces after Kruschev broke the Stalinist mold, but there are plenty of places for the Americans to exert pressure on. The capitalist–communist war will continue, but it's focus will simply shift elsewhere."

They looked at each other. Hai nodded. He had been thinking the same for some time. Once again, mountains of work for nothing. *Papa* used to say lose yourself in your work, love your work, do it with all your heart, don't think about success or failure, just think about doing your very best. "You're not alone in this world," he would say, "to win or to lose a football match depends on eleven players but to score a goal depends on only one player, the one who shoots the ball. Practice shooting, enjoy shooting, make sure you score. Win or lose, be philosophical about it." Intellectually, he could accept it, but it hurt nonetheless. Disappointment hurts, failure hurts. Especially a second time.

They sat there wrapped in their own world of silence, the desserts were cleared away, coffee and a bottle of *Armagnac* appeared. Étienne clinked his balloon glass against Hai's, his face lighting up suddenly.

"I almost forgot! I have a surprise for you, my friend. Prepare for a shock!"

Thinking his good friend was simply trying to cheer him up, Hai looked up with a smile, as if he were really interested.

"And what might that be?"

Étienne, being French, couldn't express himself without moving his hands or shrugging his shoulders or pursing his lips or wagging his eyebrows as he nodded his head with deep self-satisfaction. This time he was doing all of this, and Hai knew something big was coming up.

"Madame Hélène," Étienne said, jiggling around, spreading his arms out and chuckling in a smug manner.

At first, Hai hadn't a clue as to what he was talking about. His mind was wrapped around Dien Bien Phu and he was trying to visualize what an American version of this historic battle would look like, or could look like. Jonathan and he had watched many war movies at MAAG and MAC-V and he could see a million bombs per day raining down on the South. Will there be time to disengage, or will you all be running with your tails between your legs, as Étienne puts it? Where will your mother and you go?

"I beg your pardon?"

"Hélène, you remember her, don't you?"

"The only Hélène I know was a girl who lived with me under a bridge in Ha Noi thirty, no, forty years ago or something like that. I was in love with her but she had a French boyfriend, a soldier. After Captain Escudier left for France, I never saw her again."

"That's the very one, my friend. But she is now Madame Hélène, she's a French citizen and a very rich one. We all refer to her place as Madame H. She remembers you very well. In fact, she's told me a lot about you that I didn't know."

"How did you meet up with her? What's she doing now?"

"Well, it all happened by chance. After the war, I'm talking about the Indochina war, of course, France gradually became richer and richer and the quality of the entertainment houses for gentlemen rose. I think we have some twenty very high-class brothels in Paris alone now. But none can equal the girls at Madame H. They are all young, well educated, refined, and they have been trained to fornicate like college girls. Dainty, pulpy, the mind of a girl in the body of a woman. Our services use Madame H to entertain foreign diplomats, and you would be surprised to know how many world leaders have visited her establishment. Hélène has very good contacts in high places. The DST sometimes uses Madame H as a safe-house to debrief foreign VIPs, mixing business with pleasure. It's very expensive, and you can only get in if you are sponsored by cabinet ministers or above."

He paused, drank some cognac and looked at Hai triumphantly.

"Surprised, *mon cher?*"

"I am holding on tight to the table, otherwise I would fall off my chair," Hai said, laughing. His heart was singing. Is this the Hélène you know? Has she finally realized her dream? Does she even remember you?

"When can we meet her?"

"Tonight, after dinner. I shall leave you two alone but we can meet tomorrow for lunch. I may have some Americans with me. They want to see what you look like. Don't be surprised if you recognize some of them. You've seen them on TV."

Hai looked at his old friend, his mind miles away. His heart was beating fast and he felt waves of happiness roiling inside his chest. You're going to see Hélène again, after so many years. What will she think of you when she sees you? You're still a peasant while she's become a sophisticated society woman.

"Thank you, Étienne, thank you. I don't know what else to say."

"Don't say anything, but please allow me to call you Minh the Nut Kicker!" Étienne said, laughing wickedly at the discomfiture that showed on Hai's face when he heard his old nickname. "You see? We talked a lot about you!"

62

Madame H

Hai hardly recognized her at first. He saw a Parisian beauty with a slightly Asiatic touch in the upward slant of her eyes. The harelip was completely gone. Her figure would have done a thirty year old proud. Tall, with her auburn hair piled high on her head, she exuded charm and sophistication. As she moved gracefully around, a faint smell of perfume lingered in the air after her. One alabaster white hand tipped with blood red nails held a long silver cigarette holder at which she puffed every now and again. Her French diction was perfect and she was air kissing a guest on the cheeks French style, once, twice, thrice as he was taking his leave. She glanced at Étienne and smiled brightly at him, taking Hai in at the same time but not recognizing him. Étienne hadn't warned her that he was in town. Now Étienne stepped forward, took Hai's hand and joined it with hers, saying "Hélène, this is the Nut Kicker." On his smooth, well-fed face, a smile of unadulterated joy stretched from ear to ear and he looked like a cat that had swallowed a flock of canaries.

She turned to look at him, hard. Her crimson mouth opened, a shriek followed and she jumped on him, hugging him and kissing his cheeks and mouth, smearing her lipstick all over his face. He took the opportunity to hug her back and managed to kiss her full on the lips, something he had always wanted to do since the *Citadelle* days. They stood there, locked in embrace, staring wide-eyed at each other, bubbling with laughter, each wanting to say something but incapable of getting it out. All around them her assistants and staff looked goggle-eyed at their employer, usually the epitome of queenly reserve. Some of the departing guests looked at each other, eyebrows raised, questions racing across their minds. Her lover? Her father? A Japanese prime minister? H'mm, you never knew with these Asiatics.

After Étienne left them, they went to her office. Everything in it was tasteful, just the right tone and color, imbued with a faint but fresh fragrance that immediately put him at ease. As the French say, it was all *bon ton bon gout.*

"You first," he said in Vietnamese, as soon as they sat down. She was so refined, and every move she made was so gracious she reminded him of *Madame* Saintenoix. He was transfixed; he couldn't take his eyes off her. They were sitting on a plush sofa whose ornate, hand-carved frame was decorated with turtles, doves and royal emblems beautifully painted in gold and silver and for a split second he saw Ha Ngoc village again. He had seen dozens of these being built by the local craftsmen for the French back then.

They sat side by side, turned towards each other. Her knee was against his thigh, burning a hole in it. He wanted to reach forward and take her into his arms, but he hesitated, and didn't, taking her hand instead. It was strong and fleshy but soft and she squeezed his hand every now and again as she spoke. Every time she did this, a thrill ran through him like an electric current. How strange it was sitting in this elegant boudoir, as in a dream, listening to a beautiful Parisian woman talking in Vietnamese. She was addressing him as older brother and referring to herself as younger sister. Under the bridge that night they first met he had addressed her as older sister and called himself younger brother. Somehow, the roles had now been changed.

"Well, it's a long story, as you can imagine, but I'll make it short because I'm dying to hear your story," she gushed. "Wait, let me catch my breath first," she said, waving a hand at him and having a sip from her champagne glass. He also drank from his although he disliked the acidic taste of champagne and had often wondered what was so special about it. She began speaking in a slow, measured tone.

"Pierre Carchereux and I went to France as planned when he was discharged and we lived for a while on his parents' farm in the south. They were peasants, but they had plenty to eat, not like our peasants. We never got married after all because his mother didn't like me. His father did, though, and I had to hide from him when no one was at home, the randy old man! Anyway, after a year or so I left Pierre and went to Paris. I worked as a barmaid in bistros until I met a nice Algerian named Ben Boula. He ran a dance hall in the Marcadet Poissonier district, and above it he had a short-time hotel. I danced downstairs and did upstairs what I had been doing for years in Viet Nam but now I was being paid for it, and well paid. I got my face fixed, even though it cost a fortune! Seeing that I was smarter than the other girls, Ben taught me how to keep the books and I would fill in for him when he had to go out. Our clientele was for the most part working-class French, with some Arabs and a tourist now and then. One regular was a Dane, Mortensen, and he negotiated with Ben to take me out of there. I moved into a small studio, cooked and cleaned for him and when he died he left me his car and twenty thousand francs. He was a really nice person, with a family and all in Denmark, but he drank like a fish. I went back to Ben Boula and bought half of his business, becoming his partner. I didn't have to work anymore, but managed the dance hall as well as the brothel. After ten years Ben went back to Algeria, to his family, and I bought him out. I cleaned the place up, made it look less Arab, hired a combo and concentrated on the tourist trade because I had learnt my lesson. One Mortensen was worth ten Frenchmen and twenty Arabs! I made a lot of money over the years, and went to adult classes to learn to read and write. I also took a course in accounting, so no one could cheat me out the money I was earning. Later, I sold my business and bought into a two-star restaurant in the *7ième arrondissement* because I wanted to become a respectable businesswoman. I enrolled into cooking and hotel management classes and supervised the restaurant, working eighteen hours a day and saving every penny I could. I commuted by bus from my studio, the one Mortensen had given me. I had only one good dress, a little black one, really simple, but seven pairs of expensive shoes. Customers, especially women, always look at your shoes to see what kind of person you are. I enrolled in a charm school, to learn how to dress and behave like the ladies who ate at my restaurant. I wanted to go up in the world, to become somebody. I wanted to become a lady."

She stopped talking, to see what he would say. He squeezed her hand and she squeezed back. Her grip was strong but her hand incredibly soft. Everything she had said was so like the Hélène he had known, he would not have expected anything else. Honest, down to earth, no pretensions. She always knew what she wanted and she wasn't afraid to do what was necessary to get it. As he listened to her, his admiration for her courage and determination grew. This was a woman he could love forever. This was a person like him, unsinkable however rough the seas of life were. He had been in love with her all these years but simply hadn't had the time to think about it.

"Continue, my darling. Everything you say sounds like music to my ears," he said, melting in his chair. She laughed, sipped her drink and gave him a quick kiss. He could taste both the lipstick and the champagne on her lips.

"About ten years ago, I met an English customer at my restaurant, a very British gentleman. He worked for the British Embassy in Paris, while his family lived in England. Christopher Drape-Webber was his name. He wasn't young but he had a strong personality and we became lovers, like in the movies. You know what I mean? He treated me like a real person, a lady. For the first time since I arrived from Viet Nam, I told someone the truth about me. Everything. You see how we trusted each other? He was that kind of man. He returned the compliment by telling me everything about himself and I had to laugh. It turned out he was from a working class family that could hardly feed itself, but he was ambitious and taught himself how to talk and behave after he joined the intelligence service. He adopted an educated upper-class accent and added Webber to his name to make it look aristocratic. He was delighted to hear how I had started out in life. He said we were two of a kind, successful frauds, and we should be proud of it. He suggested I put up an establishment that catered to gentlemen with money to burn. He said they had this sort of high-class brothels in London but the British public was against them. If I opened up one in Paris, he would introduce it to many rich English clients. After a year or so, he and his friends put up the money and I opened Madame H in the *16ième arrondissement.* That's the classiest district in Paris. After two years, I was able to repay my loan. When Chris died last year, he was buried in Cambridge, where he had been born. I attended the funeral and everybody kept staring at me! England is so drab and I felt like a peacock surrounded by hens!" She laughed delightfully and pressed a button near her. A woman appeared and she ordered *canapés* and a new bottle of champagne.

"And now it's your turn, Minh. Sorry, I meant Hai of course. It's just that I can't forget I first knew you as the Nut Kicker!" she laughed again, falling forward into his arms, her head on his chest. He held her tight and they kissed, lip to lip, open mouthed, European style. They had kissed before, at the *Citadelle,* but it always had been Vietnamese style, pressing the nose against the cheek and inhaling. In those days, she still had a harelip and he didn't know how he would have responded to a lip-to-lip kiss. Having lived through two wars during which he was engaged in police work, he had never had the time to practice much kissing, European or otherwise, but, like a miracle, it all came together in an effortless way that night. It was as if they had always been destined to love each other, and in that first real kiss he knew that she had always been his first true love.

He told Hélène about his life after he had left the *Citadelle*, including his years in the resistance, about *papa* Escudier, the Japanese occupation, Étienne, Dien Bien Phu and his Americanization during the Diem regime. He then told her about his mother's death and reincarnation, of how he had saved his father from execution by the Viet Minh. He told her about Thanh. He told her he had never forgotten her through all these ups and downs and that he had nearly had a heart attack at dinner that night when Étienne spoke about her. She laughed and laughed and asked him how long he was staying in Paris.

"A couple of days, but I have a few meetings to attend. I'm not on a holiday," he answered.

She stood up and pulled him to his feet.

"You are on holiday until nine o'clock tomorrow and you belong to me until then," she said. "Étienne can have you until tomorrow night, and I'll return you to him the next morning. We have a lot of catching up to do, my darling. We've got to get that serious look off your face. This is Paris, the capital of love. There is no Viet Nam war here!"

The next two days flashed by in a blur and to this day he cannot remember exactly what happened, who said what to whom during those two heavenly nights. From nine at night to nine in the morning, once he had arrived at her luxurious apartment, he floated on an air cushion of love, soft whispered confessions, exchanges of innermost secrets and declarations of undying love. They bathed in the Jacuzzi inside her bedroom, they ate the most deliciously prepared French and Vietnamese dishes, they talked and made love and then talked and made love again. As soon as he had finished saying whatever he had to say, she took over until she ran out of breath and it was his turn again. Four decades, forty long and tortured years unraveled tranche by tranche as they talked, laughed, kissed, hugged and commiserated with each other. They knew, as they poured their hearts out, that from that moment on their lives had entered a golden age where they could not be hurt anymore because they were no longer alone and lonely. The smell of her body, her breath, her bed stayed with him all day long, a heady blend of lush and sexy floral scents in which there was linden blossom, honeysuckle, jasmine, lily of the valley, musk, vetiver and sensual woods.

63

The Circle Closes

Extract taken from a taped interview with the Tiger General in 1994.
The author, *Paris, autumn*

Hélène and I met again many times in Paris, London and Washington over the next few years but never in Viet Nam, which had no attraction for her. We holidayed often in the Caribbean and once tried skiing in Switzerland. We tried living together in France and in the US for six months at a time, but she couldn't stand the American way of life.

"They have no sensitivity," she would say. "Their life's all about money, isn't it?" and we would laugh because she recognized that she had also been after money, money, money all her life. "True, very true, but in France we do it with style, with finesse, with charm," she would add.

I also couldn't really get away from my work with the Tiger Team for such long periods, so we worked out a compromise whereby she would continue to live in Paris and I would continue to work in Washington and we would meet in Italy, or Greece or simply Paris for one blissful month three times a year. We decided not to get married, because, as she said, we had already been married for over forty years in our minds. I phone her every other day and we speak for an hour at a time. It seems we always have something to talk about, even if after I hang up I can't remember what exactly took so long on the phone. With my mother resting in peace, Liem Trinh shining bright above me and Hélène a phone call away, my life has finally stabilized and I have been able to devote my full attention to my work with Jonathan and his team.

As much as possible, I stay in the background, aware that the American system of government encourages the clash of competing interests and a regular change of faces at the top, a system that is often conducive to throwing the baby out with the bath. By standing discreetly in Jonathan's shadow and intervening only at the propitious moment, I have been able to nudge things along in the right direction or, when necessary, prevent us from shooting ourselves in the foot.

Inch by inch, report by report, I have been able to make sure that our Viet Nam—Round Three project turns out the way I want it to. After nineteen long years, colonization, feudalism and communism have all moved on and serious progress has been made towards developing a socialist system with Vietnamese characteristics, what I called Vietnam-ism when I prepared to shoot Linh in the face if he didn't pay attention to what I was saying. For the time being, that is the best that we can hope for. Real democracy, again with Vietnamese characteristics, will come in time, after the masses can eat three meals a day, have a roof over their heads and real schools to send their children to. With patience, perseverance and incredible luck, the sinkhole that we thought at first was unbridgeable turned out to be bridgeable after all. The so-called liberation of the South in 1975 was followed within a decade by a change of mind in Ha Noi, which decided to opt for a market economy. Along with Eastern Europe, Cuba and Afghanistan, the unfortunate combination of misfits that made up the Soviet Union had begun smelling smoke early in the mid-'80s and sure enough the Russian Empire imploded in 1991. There followed talk of an exchange of embassies, and to me this was the second positive step. Now it is time for Viet Nam to rejoin the community of nations. Closer relations with the developed West will open the door to a multi-party system that will set my country on the road to Vietnam-ism, and will allow my mother and me to sit in peace on our chairs in Heaven for eternity. All the sacrifices made by the North and South have not been in vain; the communists won the war, then lost the peace and are now looking for something more acceptable to the people: they are returning to the market economy system that they overthrew in 1975. As papa said many times, after each catastrophe, man-made or nature-made, Man rebuilds something better. Catastrophe is the mother of progress?

As I near the end of my seventh life cycle, Jonathan headed the first high-ranking American delegation to officially visit the Socialist Republic of Viet Nam. We had worked out the details down to the last dot, and I had advised him to take Lan Lan along. On his return I debriefed him and her for the purpose of these memoirs. I also asked Linh and various official SRVN government representatives that I have been dealing with over the years to fill me in on what had happened in Ha Noi on that historic occasion and I have included their impressions in these memoirs, which are almost finished now. Soon, my publishers, will finally get what I promised them almost fifteen years ago.

POSTSCRIPT

The End of the Beginning

The Airbus 320 was about an hour away from Sai Gon when Lan Lan felt butterflies returning to her stomach. The Air France flight had left Hong Kong on time, lunch had been served, and, in the first-class cabin passengers were settling in for a rest before arrival. She turned to her husband, Jonathan Winthrop, Jr., now the US Assistant Secretary of State for Southeast Asian Affairs, who was studying some documents and making annotations every now and again. "Yes, honey, what is it?" he said without looking around at her. Lan Lan felt a surge of warmth spread all over her instantly. Her husband always knew exactly where she was, what she was doing, what she was thinking. A man in a million, and he married me, she thought. Three children, a few extra pounds because of American food, yet he still loves me as he did when we got married.

"Nothing, dear. I was just thinking," she said, trying to sound casual. Jonathan put his documents away. A woman's heart was full of secrets and to understand her he had to listen to what she had to say; and he certainly wanted to understand his wife, his love and the mother of his children. He slipped his ballpoint back into his shirt pocket, took off his glasses. He pinched the top of the bridge of his nose for a moment, then had a sip from the glass of wine that remained from their lunch. He turned to her and smiled. "You're thinking what's going to happen when you meet those guys again, after all these years. You're worried what their attitude towards you will be, and you can't figure out how you'll deal with them if they show hostility. You're wondering if I was right in taking you along on an official trip," he said. She burst out laughing and grabbed his arm, shaking it playfully but carefully, so as not to knock the wine glass over.

"How did you know? But you're exactly right, I am worried about them talking down to me in Vietnamese, showing disrespect. I couldn't take that, not now, and I might call them a few names too, and then it would ruin your whole show," she said in a rush, glad that it was now out. It was uncanny, but Jonathan always knew what was on her mind. Even in the early days of their marriage, when she was so busy learning to become an American, he always knew when her mind wandered back to those terrible days that had followed the *Tet* Offensive. He had always been so gentle with her. Every time she had felt the pull of Viet Nam and had weakened in her resolve to build a new life for herself, he had taken her hand, figuratively, and quietly led towards their new lives, which had turned out to be full of beauty, comfort and warmth.

"Honey, that's not going to happen, and I'll tell you why. When the Tiger General does something, he always does it well. He's like wine, he gets better with the years. Nobody is going to step out of line with you or with me. We have been officially invited, and every word or deed on their side will have been cleared in advance. That's the communist way. We're dealing with the moderates, who want to open the door to the West, and I can guarantee you they'll be on their best behavior, whatever they think of us in private. The hard-liners wouldn't even have invited us in".

She thought it over. It sounded reassuring. Men were always so sure of everything, but he could be saying that because he didn't want her to worry. But why had he brought her along? He didn't have to.

"I feel better already," she smiled. "I know that Uncle Hai can be depended on to deliver, and I trust your judgment but don't you feel a bit nervous? It's been nineteen years, you know." She looked at him, searching his face for a reflection of her fears.

Jonathan leaned back in his seat and took her hand into his. He spoke without looking at anything in particular. This was a habit he had, she knew, when he was threshing things out in his own mind.

"Well, I've got to admit I feel something funny every now and again. This is my first solo flight, so to speak, and I've got to look good. The Secretary has a short temper, there are many Assistant Secretaries hoping I'll fall flat on my face so they can replace me. Seven US Presidents have made a mess of the Viet Nam problem so far, so we can't say we've learned our lesson. But then again, Ha Noi has lost the support it was getting from Moscow, relations with Beijing are cryptic, so they have to mend fences with us. And we also want to mend fences with them. There shouldn't be any problems as long as we stick religiously to the written script. No off-the-cuff remarks, no ad-lib speeches, no letting our guard down."

He paused and turned to her.

"And I'll bet you anything you like they're just as worried about this first meeting as we are, maybe more so. For me, it's only my ass that's on the line. For them, it's their neck," he added, chuckling.

The French air-hostess, a buxom lady of a certain age, elegantly attired in her uniform, perfumed and wearing pearls and earrings, stopped at their seat.

"The captain says the weather is good and we should be landing on time. Can I get you anything, sir, madam?" she inquired pleasantly in English, her French accent coming through.

"I will have another mango juice, please" said Lan Lan, turning to Jonathan. "I don't want to join you in another champagne glass. I might be all red when we land".

"A champagne for me, thank you," said Jonathan. To Lan Lan, he said, "Don't worry about being red, that's their favorite color!" and they both laughed.

The drinks came and Lan Lan, sitting near the window, pulled the shade down. They both settled back in their seats and Jonathan let his mind ramble, returning pleasurably to beaten paths, cornerstones and signposts that had implanted themselves in his subconscious over the years. Some memories were more pleasant than others, of course, but, generally speaking, such trips into the past were always enjoyable. So much had happened, yet he was still alive, happily married to a woman he couldn't have found in America in a million years, on his way to the top, and still full of vim and vigor. The present was good, the future was rosy. In that light, the past didn't look so bad either. In fact, it looked better each time it was revisited! Smiling to himself, he decided to let his mind return to his formative years. Like an octopus, it would slide along the ocean bottom from nook to cranny, making itself small or large depending on the space available, its flexible tentacles touching everything gently, tentatively, ready to seize it or to let it go as the situation required, its brain calm and deliberate, equally ready to clamp down on an unsuspecting crab or to shoot away from a baby shark in a squirt of black ink.

After the *Tet* Offensive had been crushed, he had been promoted to Deputy Chief of Station. He had not been offered the Directorship of the CIO, although in terms of experience and seniority he outranked his boss, the redoubtable "Shotgun" Kilmer. He didn't mind, because he wanted to stay out of the limelight, having made arrangements to return to the State Department to continue working on "Vietnam–Round Three" with the team he was already putting together. This team would have to work out of Washington, and the earlier they started the better they would be able to negotiate their position in the Washington rat race. They had both resigned in 1972 and the Tiger General, now promoted to three-star rank, immigrated to the US where he was promptly hired by the State Department as a special consultant to the new task force, to be called the Tiger Team.

On April 30, a Russian-built T-54 tank, serial number 843, smashed through the gates of the RVN Presidential Palace, bringing the Viet Nam war to an end. The tank had come from the 203rd Armored Brigade, which spearheaded the People's Army of Viet Nam attack on the capital, Sai Gon. The unified republic would be named the Socialist Republic of Viet Nam, the SRVN, instead of original name given in 1954, the Democratic Republic of Viet Nam (DRVN). Purportedly, this was to show the world that Hanoi had achieved socialism after twenty one years of communism. Whatever the name, however, it was to be a communist state, and suffocating regimentation remained the order of the day.

At the working level of the State Department, the Tiger Team had been deeply involved in preparing for Viet Nam–Round Three, assisted by the CIA field inputs, NRO Sigint satellites and a host of 'brains' in Washington. Foremost among these brains was the Tiger General, the former head of the RVN's Counter-Intelligence Bureau. The Tiger was used for direct liaison with Politburo representatives, whom he met with regularly for years on neutral ground, mainly in Paris. The Secretary of State had agreed that having agents on the ground, or "humint" in intelligence parlance, was the only way to return to Asia, and the Tiger's role in the general scheme of things grew in importance as the years went by and something that looked like a light appeared at the end of the tunnel.

Jonathan closed his eyes. He wasn't tired in the least, and he wasn't apprehensive either, having reviewed the situation in his mind a thousand times in the last fortnight. Like a dog gnawing on a large bone, his mind had wrestled with the coming event from every angle, trying to get the right grip on it. He smiled to himself. The Tiger

General, whom Lan Lan always called Uncle Hai, Vietnamese style, had worked eight years on this visit to Hanoi, ever since communist Viet Nam had reluctantly agreed to join the free market. Leaning heavily on his guidance, the State Department, the CIA and the White House had slowly and carefully prepared for an eventuality that was becoming clearer by the year.

For Jonathan, it was important that this mission be a success, especially if the negotiations resulted in an exchange of embassies. An old friend of his father's, a senator close to President Bush, had told him that if the first official contact showed promise, he would be appointed as Ambassador to Ha Noi. Now here he was, flying into Noi Bai airport.

The Tiger General had told him that the Politburo team would be comprised of seven high level officials, ostensibly all from the Foreign Affairs Ministry. In reality, only five were from the Ministry. Two were from the Public Security Ministry's Department for North American Affairs. One man, Major Tam, represented the hard-line faction in the Politburo, and the other, Colonel Binh, the moderate faction. The key man in the team was the colonel, and not the team leader, a Deputy Minister from Foreign Affairs named Quan. The Tiger had also told him that neither Major Tam nor Colonel Binh were using their real names, as was common in the communist system, especially where security officials were concerned.

"You must understand that none of them, including Binh, is allowed to think for himself," the Tiger General had stressed. "All decision-making, and I mean all, is done at Politburo level, so we must be patient with these people. The communists take a long time to make up their minds, but when they do they usually keep their word."

The Tiger General didn't hate communism, although, as the Grey Tiger, he had killed many communists in his time, and he recognized the positive aspects of Lenin's ideology, unlike many American political analysts, who were only able to see things in black and white terms. Jonathan had often wondered what the Tiger General really thought about the US, with its constant chopping and changing of plans, programs and faces.

But whatever his private thoughts, over the years the Tiger General had done a yeoman's job of explaining the lie of the land. He seemed to know where the minefields were, where the swamps lay, where the undergrowth was too thick to attempt to penetrate. Like a University professor, this wonderful gentleman, who had never had a proper education, even by Vietnamese standards, was slowly educating men with MBA's and PhD's, brilliant and ambitious men who were convinced they already knew everything. His simplicity and directness won them over. His insight and experience bowled them over. Like Jonathan, they had soon become fervid supporters of the man they all called our Tiger General.

"You speak Vietnamese well, you sometimes think like a Vietnamese, you understand the importance of face and you have studied communism," the Tiger General had said. "If anyone can do it, you can. I have faith in you, and I have told Colonel Binh that if you fail in this first mission your replacement is a man who has no sympathy for Viet Nam at all. Binh is my key man there, and he said he understood the importance of this first contact being successful. His uncle died a few years ago, but Binh has won the support of the reformist faction, so what he reports will have a strong influence on what they think."

The pitch of the jet engines had changed, as the plane began losing height in its approach to Noi Bai airport, which had only recently opened to international traffic from the West. Soon the Captain's voice came over the intercom system, and the passengers began to sit up, re-buckle their belts, comb their hair and adjust their clothes.

Jonathan shrugged himself awake. The review of the past and of the present had flowed along most pleasantly, but one nagging thought stuck in his mind. The Tiger General had advised him to bring Lan Lan along, but not to tell her too much about the official program. Why?

On the tarmac, the seven SRVN officials stood together, flanked by three Viet Nam Airlines ground hostesses wearing the long, gracious, flowing national costume, the *ao dai*. It was December, and the damp northern weather was miserable. A cold wind was blowing, the sky was gray with low-hanging clouds, a hint of rain was in the air. Not an auspicious day for such an important event, thought the team leader, Deputy Minister Quan of the North American Department at the Foreign Affairs Ministry. Hope it doesn't rain. Maybe we should get the umbrellas out anyway. The Party's watching this like a hawk. One mistake and there's going to be severe criticism. He turned to the hostesses and instructed that the large beach umbrellas with the Viet Nam Airlines logo on them be brought out, just in case. He also asked for the three Mercedes limousines to be brought up nearer, adding, "We don't want them to walk too far". The hostesses scurried off, half-frozen but still elegant, with their colorful *ao dai* floating around them like butterfly wings. It was difficult to imagine that these dainty, ephemeral girls in their near transparent national dress had come from stocky, ugly, coarse peasant families that had spent the last four generations fighting the war. During that time, not one person had ever seen an *ao dai*, let alone worn one. That's Viet Nam. The beautiful and the ugly come at the same time, he mused, watching them run laughing across the tarmac.

The officials had been instructed to wear leather shoes with their Western suits, shirts and ties. It was important that the welcoming team looked Western, because this was a landmark occasion in the history of VN–US relations, which had been glacial since the liberation of the South in 1975. The shoes pinched large, flat peasant feet with splayed toes that were used to open sandals, and the socks caused sweating, even in winter. The suits, all made at the same time by the same government tailor, were of the same color, a dull bluish gray. They had been assured that this was the color favored by English gentlemen, who all had their suits hand-made in Saville Row. The suits didn't fit well and none of the ties had been knotted properly. Lucky my son knows how to knot a tie, thought Quan. I couldn't have done it to save my life. No one felt comfortable, and there was a lot of squirming of the shoulders and stretching of the necks and jaws to escape the encircling confines of tight shirt collars. Look at us, he thought angrily, we haven't started yet but we're already on the wrong foot. We should have dressed the way we normally do. If it's good enough for Russian state guests, why wouldn't it be good enough for Americans? By dressing up like monkeys we're sending them the wrong message right from the beginning. He calmed down after a while, comforted by the thought that this wasn't really his show anyway. In fact, it wasn't the Ministry's show at all. This thought revived his anger and he gritted his teeth. There was another unnecessary monkey trick, he said to himself. If Public Security had to run the show they should be allowed to deal directly with the Americans. Why is it made to look as if it is my show when I've not even been given a copy of the agenda? He shook his head slowly. The Party operated in the greatest secrecy, never explaining the reasons for its decision. If it succeeded the Party reaped glory, if it failed a scapegoat was found and the matter swept under the carpet. There had to be a mountain of scapegoats in the Party's closet. Their number was fast growing and maybe that was why the Party was realigning itself with the West? He decided to abandon this line of thought. He knew the Party had ways of finding out who had thought what and it was always better to stick to the Party line, even in the privacy of one's head.

The Deputy Minister glanced around him. The limousines had crept up to the group, the umbrellas had arrived. He felt the National Radio TV Broadcast technicians, with their TV cameras and klieg lights, were too close to his group and waved them back. His colleagues, uncomfortable and self-conscious, were all twitching and scratching in their new clothes, including Colonel Binh. Tall, lank, self-confident, Binh had streaks of premature gray hair running through his long, jet-black hair. He looked like an aging Japanese film star, thought Quan. Didn't look Vietnamese at all. Questions popped into his mind. Was Binh really related to the Politburo's political affairs committee chairman? Was that why he was here today? But who would know? Everything was a state secret.

Colonel Binh saw Deputy Minister Quan look at him, and he smiled politely. His shoes were killing him, and his jacket was much too tight under the armpits. By the time they arrive I'll be dead of suffocation, he told himself. He tried an old relaxation technique, breathing in deeply, visualizing the cosmic *chi* streaming straight up his nostrils into the brain, energizing the millions of gray cells before flooding down the inside of his spinal column, arm and leg bones, revitalizing the marrow therein. He then breathed out slowly, conscious that this life force, having rejuvenated his brain and marrow, now exited through the millions of pores in his legs, arms and body. As it left him, he consciously told his muscles, sinews and ligaments to let go of their grip, and he felt his whole body, even his brain, relax. The shoes became bearable. He wriggled his toes, then looked around him and smiled encouragingly at everyone, including Major Tam, a man he disliked intensely.

In the far distance, an approaching plane could be heard, and a collective sensation of excitement and apprehension ran through the group. After forty years, the Americans were returning to North Viet Nam, not in sleek fighter-bombers but in a fat Boeing civilian commercial aircraft. The enemy had become a friend. And National TV would record the fact that they, all seven of them, would be the first to meet with the American delegation.

Colonel Binh looked into the far distance, but the clouds were thick, and though the plane could be heard, nothing could be seen.

Not unlike our situation really, he thought. No one can see where we're heading either. We want to make friends but don't know what to ask for. They want to return but don't know what to offer. We're like the traditional tray carriers in the olden days, at wedding ceremonies; long lines of porters holding over their heads large wooden trays covered with bright red lacquered lids with dragons and phoenixes hand-painted on them, walking to the beat of drums and cymbals. Under the lids were special traditional dishes whose ingredients cost a fortune, whose preparation took a whole day. The more tray carriers the more face the groom had. Colonel Binh couldn't help smiling to himself as he visualized the wedding procession. The presentation of a long line of hand-borne trays had become so institutionalized that even poor families who couldn't really afford any gift of expensive food at all nevertheless felt compelled to hire the required number of porters. Underneath the lacquered lids were heavy, cheap rice cakes wrapped in bright colors, in case a carrier tripped and the gift dishes fell out. Ha Noi was the super-power in Southeast Asia; America was the super-power in the world. They wanted to get married and he was a tray carrier, proudly holding high above his head a beautiful hand-carved tray loaded with cheap nothings, hidden under an elegant lacquered lid. If the Americans accepted that this was a tradition and didn't expect real, expensive abalone, lobster, black chicken, bear's paw, cobra's bile, stuffed pigeons, calf's brain, barbecued suckling pigs and other dishes he had heard of but never eaten, he was all right. If they wanted to lift up the lids to see what they were getting, he would have a problem. He hoped that the Tiger General has prepared their minds for what they were going to get.

His mind roamed over the last few years, recalling the many indirect conversations he had had with the Tiger General in Paris, Geneva, Hong Kong and Washington. They had spoken and negotiated at length through intermediates posted outside the Socialist Republic of Viet Nam, and had come to know each other's mind well. On several occasions, they had met face to face in Paris, at the house of Mr. Saintenoix, a shadowy French gentleman who, in his time, had known Chairman Ho and had served as a conduit between the US and Viet Nam in 1972, in the days of Kissinger. The Tiger General, who knew Saintenoix well, had come to Paris, and had taken him out to eat in a number of Vietnamese restaurants there. The food was always delicious, much better cooked and presented than anything he had ever seen in Ha Noi, even at Politburo functions, but it always felt strange to be sitting in front of the old Grey Tiger of yesteryears, sharing food with him. The general had inquired after Tuan, who had returned from the liberation of Sai Gon a hero, received a promotion to full colonel rank and been reassigned to Public Security. Tuan had married a female police officer and had fathered three children. He had remained a hard liner and in the many discussions with Binh in later years they had agreed to disagree. Given a common, shared past, they could disagree and yet remain friends. Binh had asked the Tiger General about Lan Lan and had been told that she had married an American. Binh and the Tiger General, who always referred to him as Linh, had become good friends although, for the sake of protocol, they had at all times to remain formal. It was now possible to photograph people from a great distance, with special lens, and even to reconstruct every word spoken. At home, it wouldn't do at all to be seen as being too friendly with a foreign power, especially America.

Colonel Binh's eyes penetrated the dense clouds, trying to locate the sound of the approaching plane. He moved to the front, to stand near the ground hostesses. He recalled the first time he had met the Tiger General, who was then known to him as the Grey Tiger. There was a gun in his hand, pointing at his forehead. One twitch would have meant a bullet in the face. He had looked at the Grey Tiger's eyes. Like the eyes of an insect, reflecting everything with extreme clarity but no life in them. The second time was in his holding cell, and the Grey Tiger had also had a gun in his hand. The arguments that he had then outlined came back to him over the years, many times. After meeting his Uncle Le Bach he had realized that it was not the right time to bring up the matter of Viet Nam-ism. There was a war to be won. After liberation in 1975, there was no need to bring it up. Victory had been won. Euphoria enveloped the Politburo. Six years later, Russia crumbled into a mess and war with China was shaping up over a dispute in Cambodia. By then his uncle was dying, but Binh had managed to talk to him, and his uncle had introduced him to his closest comrades the Party and Politburo. It had been the right time to bring up the subject. Gorbachev's *perestroika* policy had given birth to Viet Nam's *doi moi*, economic re-structuring was in the air and, after some time, he had been given the green light to get the back channel started.

The plane was now in sight, and it was a matter of minutes before it would land. Colonel Binh thought he had to make a gesture to signal that the past was closed, that on his side they wanted to make a new start, that he was the man in the middle, a man the Tiger General could trust. There was an ambassadorship to America for him if he could start off on the right foot, but how could he say all this to a foreigner, and an American at that? He had never dealt with Americans before. His English has gotten worse since liberation and it might take years to develop the personal chemistry needed for this sort of relationship.

The plane landed on the apron and slowed down, coming to a stop. Then, majestically, it turned around to taxi up to the parking bays where the welcoming committee stood. Finally, it stopped. The unpleasant high-pitched engine noise died down as the powerful jets were shut off. The French captain and his co-pilot could be seen in the cockpit. They knew Ha Noi well, and waved to the welcoming committee. Tense, their minds elsewhere, the grim-looking officials ignored the friendly waves, though the ground hostesses responded with bright smiles. They knew the French pilot always brought them little gifts from the Hong Kong duty-free shops. A self-propelled Viet Nam Airlines ladder trundled up to the side of the plane, and within minutes the plane door opened. A French air hostess appeared, looked closely at the welcoming committee, then stepped aside.

A tall, hefty American appeared, well dressed and suave looking. He had wavy gray hair, clear-cut features, not unlike an American film star, and his suit hung well on his large frame. His eyes lit up with pleasure, real or feigned, and he turned around to give his arm to an Asian woman, who took the proffered arm as they carefully stepped out of the plane onto the platform at the top of the ladder. They smiled at the welcoming committee below and began walking down the steps. Behind them appeared three more Americans, one of whom was a black man. They all looked huge, well-fed, fresh and well-dressed. They exuded money and power. But the welcoming team's eyes, like the eyes of the National Radio TV cameras, were locked onto Jonathan's wife. She was tall for an Asian, even statuesque, very well made up, wearing her hair piled high up on her perfectly oval face. Everyone gaped at this apparition, at first with surprise and then with pleasure. The Asian lady, whose presence was totally unexpected, was wearing a beautiful, peach-colored *ao dai* with a faint green bamboo pattern on it. Her feet were shod in high-heeled vermilion-colored clogs with sequins on them. She seemed a little apprehensive, and was consciously hanging back, so that her husband could arrive on the tarmac first. He, on the other hand, was smiling widely and quietly pushing her into the lead.

Colonel Binh took all this in. For a moment, he felt as if he was going to faint. His mind flashed thirty years back into the past, his heart pumped furiously. He saw the Sai Gon university's water fountain, where he had first met her. Seventeen or eighteen, already into socialism, already anti-establishment. His control officer had told him she was ready to be recruited, and he had moved in. He had lost track of her after she had been assigned to the VC courier service but had met up with her again after he inherited the Tuan group. Their previous control officer had been shot. Through Tuan he had met up with Lan Lan again. He soon realized that they were having an affair. This was impossible, this couldn't be true, he remembered thinking at the time. Both would die if he reported them. He had talked to Lan Lan at length about her work, about the meaning of revolution, of liberation, of unification and, in the process, had felt that she knew little or nothing about what Tuan was supposed to do. It was just what it seemed, a simple love affair. It was unfortunate that these two people were not authorized to have love affairs. The date of the *Tet* Offensive was approaching, and he didn't want to rock the boat at that time. Then he was caught by the Grey Tiger and it was no longer his problem. And now, she was here again!

With tremendous willpower, he controlled himself. As the Asian lady stepped onto Vietnamese soil, he moved forward, took the bouquet of flowers from the hands of a surprised ground hostess, and walked up to the American couple, well ahead of the Deputy Minister and his team. He was conscious that the National Radio TV cameras had started rolling. His eyes lit up, he smiled widely, opened up his arms as if he was about to hug her, but at the last moment presented her with the bouquet, saying "Welcome to Viet Nam, Mrs. Winthrop! Welcome home, Miss Lan Lan!"

Jonathan and Lan Lan stood stock-still, speechless, mouths open. The government officials standing behind Colonel Binh were motionless, hardly breathing. The ground hostesses looked on with wide eyes. Only the TV cameras kept moving.

A few seconds passed by that seemed like an eternity. Lan Lan stared at Binh as if she had seen a ghost. Her face had paled considerably. Then she burst out "Linh! It's you! Oh my God, I never thought I would ever see you again!" and she stepped forward, took the flowers from him and held his hand in hers. In America, she would have hugged him, even kissed him on both cheeks, but this was communist Viet Nam, where public signs of affection were frowned upon. She couldn't control her surprise and joy, however, and was talking ten to the dozen to Colonel Binh who, after being initially overwhelmed, was also talking back excitedly. Everyone could see that Lan Lan's eyes were glistening with tears.

Jonathan thought, well, there goes protocol, and stepped around the two to shake hands with the Deputy Minister, who then introduced him to the members of his team. Jonathan introduced his three State Department officials, and began speaking to the Deputy Minister in Vietnamese. He could see that this went down well with the Vietnamese team. They asked him if he or his wife was tired, and when he said "No" they invited him into the lead limousine, where he sat with the Deputy Minister. Lan Lan climbed into the second car, with the ground hostesses. Colonel Binh and Major Tam, his minder, climbed into the third car, and the rest of the team got into the fourth car. After a very short ride, they arrived at the VIP lounge reserved for government guests, on the second floor of the main building. Inside a large, well-decorated and air-conditioned room stood more ground hostesses. There were flowers everywhere. Russian champagne and beautiful Czechoslovakian glasses stood around a box of Japanese biscuits. Everyone sat down, and lower level officials collected the American team's diplomatic passports to have them processed. The Deputy Minister and Jonathan toasted each other's president, and they then conversed while the National Radio TV cameras rolled.

Seated next to Linh, or Colonel Binh as he was now called, Lan Lan could hardly contain herself. Linh looked a lot older, and he had deeply etched wrinkles on his brow and around his mouth, but otherwise he was essentially the same, all skin and bones, handsome and arrogant in a professorial way. Did he think she was fat? None of the hostesses weighed more than a hundred pounds soaking wet and the men didn't weigh much more either. That's funny, she thought, the Vietnamese hadn't seemed so small and light when she was living there. Maybe she had been around Americans too long.

After they had covered fifteen years in a few minutes, Linh held up a finger and Lan Lan stopped talking. How many times she had seen him using that gesture as he was lecturing them in various hideouts. He looked at her and asked quietly "Did the Tiger General send you so that we could meet again?"

Lan Lan thought back, trying to remember bits and pieces that Uncle Hai and her husband had told her over the last few months, but couldn't find anything conclusive.

"I don't know," she answered, "he never told me anything. You know him, he doesn't always tell you everything he's doing. But I am almost sure now that he did. The more I think about it the more I'm sure that I wouldn't be here if he hadn't recommended it to Jonathan, to my husband".

"That's good," said Linh. "That's excellent. It means that he wants to set up an alternative back-channel made up of us three to make it easier for people like your husband to talk to our officials." Linh nodded towards Jonathan, who was busy exchanging compliments in Vietnamese with Deputy Minister Quan. "I am very glad this has happened, Lan Lan. That was a stroke of genius, bringing you into the picture. Now that we're all working towards the same end, a team of insiders like us can make all the difference between success and failure".

The passports returned, and the party broke up. The Deputy Minister walked the American group down to the cars and they headed for the downtown Metropole Hotel. As her car drove off, Lan Lan caught Linh's eyes. He was smiling, not as a welcoming official, but as a friend. She smiled back. Some things never changed. Maybe it was true that history repeated itself, or maybe it didn't repeat itself but simply returned to haunt us. Yesterday she had been on one side, convinced that she was right. Today she was on the other, also convinced that she was right. But history had seen to it that, right or wrong, she would be playing the same role. The courier of the past had now become the conduit of the future.

TIMELINE

Year	Event	Hai's age
1908	Cinnamon born	
1913	Cinnamon pregnant	
1914	**Meo born**	
1918	Convent	4
1922	Saintenoix	8
1925	Bridge	11
1930	Papa	16
1933	Buffalo Head Gang	18
1934	Resistance	19
	Citadelle	
	Alliance	
1938	Godot	24
1940	Japan Occupation	26
1946	CODEX	32
1950	**End of 36 year curse**	**36**
1950	CODEX	
1954	CODEX/ Lord Bach	40
1954	Dien Bien Phu	
1955	Diem	41
1962		**48**
1968	*Tet* Offensive	54
1972	2nd Offensive / Hai leaves VN	58
1974		**60**
1975	Saigon Falls	61
1980	Biography starts	66
1986	**Doi Moi**	**72**
1995	US Embassy in Hanoi	73
1998	**Hai dies**	**84**

GLOSSARY

Viet Nam is an ancient country, with a unique culture. The Vietnamese think differently and do things differently than in the West. This brief glossary will try to bridge that gap.

Life Cycles and the Lunar Calendar

The Lunar calendar is based on the twelve animals of the Buddhist zodiac. These are: rat, ox, tiger, cat, dragon, snake, horse, goat, monkey, rooster, dog and pig. Hai was born in 1914, became the Tiger General in 1950 (after three life cycles), passed away in the USA in 1998 (after seven life cycles). All these three significant dates are in the Year of the Tiger.

The Importance of a Name in Viet Nam

Traditionally, all Vietnamese names are composed of three monosyllabic words.

A typical name would be: Nguyen Van Minh (male), Nguyen Thi Hien (female).

The first word is the family name, inherited from the father, whose ancestors were from the Nguyen clan. It may have had a meaning in the distant past (like Dr Fred Farmer or Janet Titcombe), when whole communities would take on the name of the provincial warlord or national emperor, but this is no longer important today.

The second word is the 'pillow' word, to phonetically balance the first and third words. It usually indicates the sex of the person, with Van being common for men and Thi for women. Since the advent of communism in Viet Nam, many people have dropped their middle names.

The third word is the given name. The first given name is usually a 'nothing' name. New-born infants have to be protected from the evil spirits that roam the night and are given 'belittling' names to fool the spirits into believing that the child is not important enough to merit the attention of someone as prestigious as an evil spirit. Frog, Pimples, Mud and sometimes worse were common before World War Two, especially in the countryside.

After the first year or so, a meaningful name is chosen by the parents with great care, to embody some virtue or quality the parents hope their child will develop. Girls often carry names of flowers, or precious stones, or names that indicate purity or refinement, while boys will be given names that connote bravery, brilliance or strength. In the above examples, Minh means intelligence, while Hien means gentleness.

In the countryside again, but not only there, nicknames are important. Physical or mental characteristics are soon picked out and an appropriate name given, to be used by close friends or sworn foes alike but never in formal conversation.

The Importance of the Form of Address

The Vietnamese, unlike the Chinese, Japanese and Koreans, address each other formally yet use their given names. Nguyen Van Minh will thus be called Mr Minh. Nguyen Thi Hien will be called Miss Hien until she marries, after which she will be known as Mrs Hien. Only close friends will call them Minh or Hien. In English, this would be like addressing someone as Mr John (Brown).

The Vietnamese, like the Chinese, Japanese and Koreans, live in extended families where most members of a clan are related to each other somehow, either by blood, marriage, adoption or social convention. Age and social position in the family further reinforce the necessity of addressing almost everyone as an older or younger uncle/auntie or brother/sister, even when there is no obvious family tie. In the compound where the clan lives, Mr Minh will be addressed as Uncle Minh by almost everyone younger than him, and Miss Hien as Younger Sister by almost everyone older than her. Different forms of address are used for senior/junior relatives, for paternal/maternal relatives, and it is important to use the right form of address. Unless very young or very close to each other, the Vietnamese form of address is always formal: the appellation immediately sets the social context. The French equivalent, in a much milder form, would be the mindset that uses 'vous'—never 'tu'. The informal and generic English 'you' does not exist.

Tones and accents

Vietnamese, like Chinese and Thai, is a tonal language. There are eight accents used to pronounce eight different inflections. Thus the same word can have two or three (or sometimes more) totally different meanings depending on how it is pronounced. Although the pronunciation of the northern, central and southern dialects differs a little, people from the three regions can understand one another without much difficulty—unlike in China or India, where the 'dialects' are in fact different languages. For foreigners, tonal languages can often mean horrible mistakes, such as *ao dai*, the flowing national dress with one vent in front and another at the back, pronounced with a sinking accent, means 'dress long', but, with a rising accent, means 'dress penis'.

Main Vietnamese Names / Persona in Order of Appearance

Ho Thi **Que**: Cinnamon's full name
Que: Cinnamon, her given name
Trinh Xuan **Giap**: Lord Giap, the Old Mandarin, Lord Bach's father
Trinh Xuan **Bach**: Lord Bach, the Young Master
Venerable Thich Van **Huyen**: Chamberlain to the Old Mandarin
Meo: cat, Hai's name as an infant
Ho Xuan **Hai**: Meo's adult name, given him by his mother before she died
Tran Thi **Tam**: the Chicken Seller Lady
Tran Van **Bich**: the Chicken Seller Lady's son
Sister Anne-Marie Vu Thi **Tuyet**: a young nun at the convent
Sister Eliza Pham Thi **Hue**: older nun at the convent
Robert Ho: Hai's Christian name at the convent
Chi Nguyen Thi **Huyen**: older sister Huyen, the Saintenoix's cook
Minh: Hai's name under the bridge the first time
Hélène Doan Thi My: Hélène, Hai's love
Tam: Hai's name under the bridge the second time
Tran Van **Chau**: nicknamed Dau (head) **Chau** (buffalo), Buffalo Head
Nguyen Van **Chanh**: 'Hammer & Tong', the gangster
Tran Quy **Phong**: the recruiter who led Hai into the resistance
Van: Hai's name in the resistance
Thanh: Hai's first lover
Don: Hai's name at the *Alliance* and at Lamy's cafe

Vu Van **Long:** Don's handler at the *Alliance*
Nam: the *Alliance*'s deputy security chief
Le Van **Loi**: Hai's name as a French police asset
Tran Van **Xuan**: Hai's name as a Japanese intelligence analyst
Phan Boi **Chau**: famous political activist of the early twentieth century
Nguyen Ai **Quoc:** original name of nationalist leader who later became
    known as Ho Chi **Minh**. Strangely enough, he became known as
    Bac ('Uncle') Ho (Chinese style) and not as *Bac* Minh.
Mai Thi **Lan Lan**: student activist and communist courier
Mai Huu **Hoang**: Lord Bach's wealthy business partner, **Lan Lan**'s
    father
Nguyen Van **Tuan**: **Lan Lan**'s lover and communist cadre/infiltrator
Tran Dinh **Nam**: Minister of Public Works; **Linh**'s father
Tran Dinh **Linh**: Viet Minh infiltrator, later Public Security Ministry
    official known as Colonel **Binh**

Places

Thanh Hoa: province in Annam
Phu My village: Meo's birthplace, small village in Thanh Hoa Province
Phu Hoang village: the Chicken Seller Lady's birth place, near Phu My
Sai Gon: capital of Cochinchina
Ha Noi: capital of Tonkin
Quang Ba: suburban district outside Ha Noi
Nghe An: province in Annam
Ha Tinh: province in Annam
Sam Son: beach resort town near Thanh Hoa town
Song Hong: Red River, which runs through Ha Noi
Hai Phong: port east of Ha Noi, on Tonkin Gulf

Things

Liem Trinh: miracle star in Hai's Career House after thirty-six years old
Thien La: Hai's first bad star. Cruel star. Hard life
Co Than: Hai's second bad star. Orphan star. Lonely life
Dia Khong: Hai's third bad star. Blocking star. Delays success
Bach Ho: Cinnamon's star. Subject will remain single
Co Than: Lord Bach's star. Subject will marry many times